THE

PUNK _{THE}

PLAYTHING

WHEN RIVALS PLAY SERIES

B.B. REID

DEDICATION

This book is dedicated to the original Jamie Buchanan, who ruined everything by finding her happily-ever-after, marrying some douchebag named Brian and becoming a Johnson. Cheers.

ALSO BY B.B. REID

PROLOGUE

The Plaything

"WE'RE HERE, MISS."

I could feel Joe, my father's driver, watching me through the rearview mirror as I stared out the back window of the Escalade. What was it about the sun shining brightest on the darkest of days? Was it irony or did the universe have a sick sense of humor?

There was nothing special about today if you didn't count orientation. Traditionally, it was a rite of passage reserved for freshman, but at Brynwood Academy, the seniors also had one. It was no secret the future upper echelon would pass through these doors, so the board wanted to ensure that none of the academy's prestigious diplomas were squandered.

Still, I was unable to silence the doom roiling in my gut since the moment I opened my eyes this morning.

Joe came around to open the backdoor, and the moment my patent nude Pigalles touched the brick, a hush fell over the crowded lawn. If Joe noticed, he didn't remark, but he wouldn't have even if he had. My parents didn't treat him as a member of the family. Their insistence on decorum had long surpassed nauseating, becoming stifling and often condescending.

"Pick you up in a couple of hours?" he inquired. I didn't miss the concern in his gaze, though there was nothing he could do. A tight smile was all I could offer him before facing the school.

Shoulders back.

Chin high.

One foot in front of the other.

I didn't dare take a page from Dorothy's book and click my heels together—home was the last place I wanted to be. The building seemed to stretch further and further away with each step I took, but, eventually, I reached it, and the group crowding the front doors parted like the Red Sea. I didn't acknowledge any of them, and they didn't dare greet me. They weren't my peers. They were my subjects. And they didn't just fear me—they hated me.

"Bitch," someone daring enough whispered as I stepped inside the air-conditioned building.

I didn't even flinch. It wasn't the first time I'd been called such, and as usual, I pretended to be oblivious.

Bitch.

Barbie.

Snake.

It was all true.

Keeping my strides long and my head high, I strutted into the nearest bathroom. The moment the door closed behind me, however, I finally let my shoulders sag. Closing my eyes, I took a deep breath as I rested my head against the door.

It was just one more year.

I couldn't turn back time, but I could look to the future. In ten months, I'd be eighteen. In ten months, I'd be free.

The sound of three short vibrations had my eyes snapping open. I quickly dug through my father's gift for my sixteenth birthday last year. Most kids got a car, which was pretty extravagant. I got a baby Birkin that I'd nearly thrown up in when my father boasted about the price. If you're curious, I'll give you a hint—my father could have bought *three* cars with the money he'd spent on this bag.

Pulling my phone, I read the message.

Ever: Be there in five, dear.

My lips twisted in a wry smile as if I hadn't just been close to tears. At least one of us was enjoying the irony of our relationship. Once upon a time, I thought… maybe…

Shaking my head, I typed my response.

K.

Moving to the mirror, I studied the reflection staring back at me. The seconds stretched into minutes, but still, I waited, hoping for a glimpse of the girl I once cherished.

Nothing but barren blue eyes stared back at me.

I told myself it was for the best as I lifted a tube of lipstick from my purse and applied a fresh coat of dark cherry until my lips appeared fuller. Mother hadn't approved of my choice, preferring I wear a softer shade. One that said I took people's shit with three sugars. *Yeah, no thanks.* Ask anyone, except maybe Ever, and they'd tell you there was nothing *peachy* or coral about me. The lipstick contrasted the paleness of my strawberry locks that was red to some and blonde to others. It made me appear unapproachable. Unattainable.

Thanks to my father, that was no longer true.

Satisfied I wouldn't besmirch the Montgomery name with a single strand of hair out of place, I left the bathroom and followed the brightly colored signs.

Tables filled with informational pamphlets about the ACT/SAT tests and financial aid, as well as swag from various colleges, lined the walls of the hallway. I bypassed them all and headed to the long line marked *M-O*, where a team of administrators and teachers were handing out class schedules from behind tables pushed together. I was there maybe a minute or two before I felt gentle yet strong fingers grip my elbow.

Glancing up, I met eyes that could have been melted pools of gold and fanned by long lashes. They did nothing to soften the harshness of an impossibly hard jawline and pronounced chin dimple, but, man, was he still a pretty sight. His lips were so thick they formed a perpetual pout. I often felt their softness brush my forehead or cheek. Ever McNamara should have been on someone's magazine cover. Unfortunately, he'd never welcome the attention. *Unlike someone I once knew.*

"Been here long?" he inquired.

"No. Just a few minutes before you."

He nodded before groaning when he noticed the slow-moving line. It seemed like everyone had a list of questions to ask and waited until now to do it. "Fuck, this line is long. Why are you even standing back here?"

I frowned. "What do you mean?" Where else was I supposed to wait?

Gripping my elbow tighter, he wordlessly steered me toward the front of the line. Scorned gazes followed us as we blatantly cut the line, but no one dared protest, not even the whispers I was subjected to often.

Ever's wrath was a motherfucker. Just last year, his new stepsister had learned that the hard way. Barely a month after she blew into town, Four Archer had been sent to some reform school in Europe. According to Vaughn, our best friend and Ever's right hand, Ever had *personally* handed his father the pamphlet.

We reached the table just as a guy stepped away with his schedule in hand and another was ready to step forward. With one look from Ever, however, he stepped back in line.

"We need our schedules," Ever told the woman waiting behind stacks of folders. He hadn't even bothered offering our names. I didn't recognize the woman whose name tag read Mrs. Thomas, so I assumed she was new. Still, if she wanted to survive this job, she'd learn ours and quickly.

"Young man—"

"I don't have all day," he said before she could finish reprimanding him.

Nervously, I began to tap my heel against the linoleum tile. I was sure everyone assumed it was with impatience. Most of what people knew or thought about me was based on assumptions, and nothing I did would ever change their accustomed view of me. I'd long ago decided they weren't worth the effort. It's not like any of them had ever bothered to know better.

Mrs. Thomas looked ready to try scolding again when Mr. Stalls, a freshman lit teacher, leaned over and whispered in her ear. After a few seconds, she searched through the stack marked *M* with pursed lips and pulled our schedules.

Ever accepted them without a word of thanks before pulling me behind him down the hall. Eventually, we stopped in front of the boys' bathroom. "I gotta take a leak. Will you wait here? We need to talk," he added at my questioning look.

"S-sure."

My stomach turned and tightened, threatening to fold me in two at the wary smile he flashed me before disappearing inside.

Oh God...had he had enough? Was he ending this?

My mind began to race as I attempted to figure out what I would do. I hadn't prepared for Ever breaking up with me. I knew him. He was loyal, almost to a fault, to those he cared about. And what's more, he never gave me any reason to doubt him—until now.

Feeling like the walls were closing in on me, I looked around for an escape and realized my distress hadn't gone unnoticed. The whispers were back.

Barbie. Bitch. Snake.

It was all true.

All around, people watched me as they gossiped to one another. I never understood the point of talking behind your hands if you were only going to stare. They made no secret that they were whispering about me. They *wanted* me to know.

I was a queen without a crown. A fraud. Alone.

Forgetting Ever's request that I wait, I rushed for the front doors and straight into a thick cloud of smoke that sent me into a coughing fit. My eyes stung for a different reason now as I fought to clear my lungs. I was pretty sure it was from more than just cigarettes, too.

I turned toward the source—a crowd of four or five huddled in the corner enjoying their smokes despite the campus being a nonsmoking zone. I met each of their gazes, allowing them to feel my fury. That rage turned to sheer panic when my gaze connected with the tallest offender.

Suddenly, I couldn't breathe for a different reason entirely. My only solace was that he looked just as shocked, although he recovered much quicker. Nostrils flaring, he took a threatening step forward before stopping short and blinking as if remembering where he was…and that there were witnesses. With curled lips, his gaze swept over me from my heeled feet to my perspiring hairline.

I stood perfectly still, knowing that if I tried to run, he'd chase me. It was all for the best. I wasn't so sure my legs wouldn't give out the moment I tried to get away.

"Well, isn't this the most delicious surprise."

My head confirmed what my eyes were showing me, but my stubborn heart still refused to believe. Jamie was back from Ireland? Why hadn't Ever told me? Neither of those answers seemed to matter as much as *why* Jamie was back.

The short sleeves of the button up he wore were rolled and bunched at the shoulders, displaying the muscles he'd grown since I'd last seen him four years ago. The white cotton only pronounced his tanned skin. He'd left the buttons undone, allowing anyone who laid eyes on him to see his hard chest and defined abs…and the many tattoos that covered them. Most of them were angry and aggressive, almost scary as if he were showing off his demons for anyone to see. Recalling my sweet Jamie from long ago, and what happened the last time I'd seen him, I knew I was responsible for every one of them.

Gone was the gentle boy next door with a full mop of hair,

a lanky body, and an easy smile. This boy standing before me was darker, edgier…more tragic to my lonely, fragile heart. Was that yearning burning in the pit of my stomach or fear of the unknown? Because I didn't know this Jamie, and judging by the wicked gleam in his eyes as he flashed that mocking grin, I didn't want to know.

"What the hell are you doing back here?"

"Is that any way to greet your first love? I got to say"—his gaze slowly traced every dip and curve of my body—"I *love* how well you've grown up, Bette."

"First love?" I scoffed, even though it felt like he'd stolen my breath. "You were hardly that."

"Then what was I?" he challenged, backing me against the opposite wall. "I'm *breathless* to hear more of your lies."

"You were nothing."

He flashed me that sad, beautiful smile I hadn't realized I'd missed so much. I stood perfectly still as his wolfish gaze ate me up. As close as he stood now, he wouldn't miss a single fucking flaw. There were many, but no one dared looked close enough to see. I might as well have been Medusa. As he ran his gaze over me, I took the time to study him as well, noting the silver bar piercing his right brow and the small diamond in his right nostril. I could have sworn I'd even glimpse a flash of metal piercing his nipples. Jamie had taken all that sinful deliciousness he naturally possessed and multiplied it by ten thousand. As if the world didn't already have enough injustices.

"You're so beautiful. Did it hurt?" He kept his gaze on me as he turned his head and blew out smoke.

"Did what hurt?" I could feel the heat from Jamie's cigarette when he defiantly brushed his thumb across my bottom lip. To Jamie's knowledge, I belonged to his cousin now, but he clearly didn't give a damn.

"When you fell from heaven, Satan."

I slapped his hand away while telling myself to get a grip.

Jamie might have surprised me, but he was nothing I couldn't handle. "Get lost, Jameson."

Tapping the end of his cigarette, he sprinkled ash onto my designer blouse. A piece of the flame had fallen, burning through the sheer material, scorching my skin. Before now, I'd never thought Jamie capable of hurting me. The truth was now so blatantly blazed into our history that it could never be unwritten.

Without warning, he pressed closer until I could see nothing but the angry blackness of his eyes. "I'm afraid I'm not going anywhere. By the time I'm done with you, Barbette Montgomery, you'll be crawling back to me... but I doubt I'll want my cousin's sloppy *thirds*."

"I wouldn't hold your breath." I wasted little time pushing him away. Tragically, the moment my hand connected with his warm skin, the electricity threatening to make my broken heart beat again became too obvious to ignore. I tried to run from it, but some inexplicable need to seal our fate had me spinning on my heel to face him again. "Better yet, Jameson, do us both the favor, won't you?"

This time, when I walked away, I didn't dare look back. With every sorrowful step, I could feel him watching me. I didn't dare let my shoulders sag as I kept my chin high. After all, it wouldn't be the first time we turned our backs on one another.

A year no longer seemed like such a short time away, and I had a feeling by the end, my heart will have been broken a thousand times more. Pathetically, there was nothing I cared to do about it. I deserved every bit of the pain Jamie had promised.

CHAPTER ONE

The Punk

Eight Months Later

"YOU WANT ME TO DO *WHAT*?"

I stood in the farmhouse kitchen, biting down on my lip as I gave Lou my best bedroom eyes. Never mind the fact that her boyfriend sat a few feet away with one eye wisely on me and the other on the large breakfast he was wolfing down. Lou couldn't cook for shit, so I had one guess who was responsible. The sweet thing Wren was lucky enough to call grandmother. She'd been staying with them for the past couple of months. Considering Wren and Lou were still in the honeymoon phase of their relationship, no one outside of the three of them knew why. The moment I tasted Winny's cooking for the first time, I stopped caring. Hell, I hoped she never left.

Winny hadn't had any trouble making friends in Blackwood Keep, so it was anyone's guess where she was right now, but my guess was she was with the elderly gentleman up the street who I'd witnessed flirting with Wren's grandmother a few times. I was willing to bet my entire inheritance that Wren knew nothing about it.

"Buchanan," Wren slowly said as he chomped down on a cinnamon roll, "what did I tell you about that flirting shit?"

"Me? Flirting? With Lou? Not sure I'm daring enough to *fuck my best friend*," I teased. "Too slippery a slope for me."

I almost laughed when his eyes did that weird shit changing from a dull gray to a startling blue. I thought any moment now, his eyes would shoot lightning from their depths, and I'd be dust. The jealous fucker looked more pissed about me taking his place as her best friend than the possibility of me getting in her pants.

Of course, it went without saying I'd never cross that line. At least, now I wouldn't. A few months ago, I was close to falling to my knees and begging Lou to make me forget. My sink into depression was interrupted when Lou shoved my shoulder.

"Do you know how much time and dignity it took me to wear him down? Leave him alone."

Since the two of them looked like they'd tag team my ass, I backed off with a shrug. "Are you going to help me or not?" I grilled her.

"No," Wren answered before she could.

Rolling her eyes, Lou whirled on him before planting her hands on her hips. "Excuse me," she snapped, giving me hope. "I have lips and a tongue—not to mention a brain. I can speak for myself." She then faced me again before he could rebut. "Sorry, bestie." Wren growled at her for calling me bestie, but then his lips tipped up in a satisfied smirk when she added, "Wren says I can't."

She rounded the island, and he welcomed her onto his lap before wrapping his arms around her waist as I gave them both a blank stare.

"I thought we'd broken past your 'us against the world' phase. We're one big, happy family now, remember?"

Wren was a former Exiled lieutenant, who came to Blackwood Keep seeking haven for Lou. She'd witnessed his boss murdering an innocent family, which had effectively ended Wren's career as a criminal. In exchange for our protection, he offered to free Ever's mom from Fox's clutches. Ever and Wren both harrowingly held up their end of the bargain, though no one expected us to become attached. Now we have a reformed gangbanger and a still at-large pickpocket added to our merry band of misfits.

Subtly, I patted my dress pants and sighed when I felt my wallet still tucked inside. Lou was as slick as she was brazen.

"Yeah, and you're asking us to help you sow discord in our newfound family," Lou pointed out. "The answer is no."

"You mean Wren's answer is no. Since when did you shy away from causing trouble?"

Lou stumbling her way into my life was like a dream come true. Finally, I had a wingman I could count on to bring the mischief. Everyone else had a stick shoved up their asses. Four had once been a promising prospect, but then she and Ever went and fucked everything up by falling for each other. Sometimes I missed their rivalry. It got pretty boring in this sleepy town. Unfortunately, like Wren, Ever was determined to keep his girl on the straight and narrow.

"Since you got her some time over my knee last week," Wren cut in before Lou could respond.

My eyebrows shot up when I glimpsed the red staining her cheeks before she hid her face in his chest. *Guess he wasn't kidding.*

"Which reminds me," he drawled, "I owe you a black eye."

He started to rise from the stool, but Lou quickly wrapped her arms around his neck, keeping him in place. "Let's just hear him out," she pleaded.

"I did hear his plan," Wren shot back. "It's sneaky, cruel, and not our business."

"But aren't you a little curious what the hell is going on?"

"No."

"Please," she whined. "I'll let you put it in my butt," she tried to whisper but failed.

"*The fuck?*" I yelped before I could catch myself. I felt like the biggest cockblocker when Lou squealed and hid her face again, causing Wren to glare at me over her head.

Not cool, man, his expression read.

I scrubbed a hand down my face, realizing there was no way in hell I was getting them on board now. "Fine. Fuck it." I started to turn, assuming defeat, but then I snapped my fingers. "Almost forgot. Vaughn wanted me to invite you two over tomorrow morning. We're having brunch." Vaughn and Tyra were the first to be crossed off my list. Not only were they Four and Ever's best friends, making them the easiest pawns to capture, but I knew they were just as eager for answers.

"Fucking rich people," Lou muttered.

Wren snickered before sparing me a glance. "We'll be there." He dismissed me by whispering in Lou's ear, probably eager to revisit a certain conversation.

Nodding, I used both fingers to flip them off before starting for their front door. Of course, neither of them noticed. I didn't dare let my grin free until I stepped outside and inhaled the morning's fresh air.

Check-fucking-mate.

Well... almost.

I still had the guests of honor to invite.

The sound of Brynwood's bell signaling the end of the school day startled me out of my impromptu nap. I slowly rose from my lounge against my Jeep's windshield and stretched just as the front doors burst open. Searching the crowd, my gaze connected with Tyra, who rolled her eyes, and then Vaughn, who greeted me with his chin as he forced her toward his ride. I couldn't help but snicker at the odd pair. Vaughn was too damaged for goody-two-shoes Tyra, but she seemed to be handling her own. No one, least of all me, had thought she'd last or hold Vaughn's interest for this long. Before Tyra, it was normal to witness two girls attempt to claim him by ripping each other's throats out, and after they had finished, Vaughn would pretend he'd never met either one of them.

A few minutes after Vaughn peeled out of the parking lot in his white Lamborghini—a bribe from his father—Four appeared. I watched as she searched the parking lot, and my chest tightened at the warm smile she flashed when she spotted me. I already had my arms out by the time she reached me, and she stepped into them.

"It's so weird," she spoke into my chest, her voice muffled, but I heard every word. "I keep looking for you in the hall. How does it feel to be done with school finally?"

"Like I have too much time on my hands."

She lifted her head and met my gaze. "You should stay out of your head."

"Believe me, if I could, I would."

She chewed on her lip before taking a step back and crossing her arms. "So what did you do today?"

"I went to see Wren and Lou…" I hesitated before lying through my teeth, "and then I came here."

"You've been sitting out here all day?"

I shrugged. "It's a beautiful day."

She looked me over as if she had just noticed my appearance before squinting. "You're pretty dolled up for sitting around."

Leaning against the hood of my Jeep, I reached into my pocket and pulled out a fresh pack of smokes. I was going through half a pack a day now. "Want one?" I offered.

"Hell no, and don't change the subject. Why are you dressed up?"

"I'm not—not really."

"You're wearing a tie." She looked down, and then her eyes bugged out of her head. "*Is your shirt tucked in?*"

"Force of habit."

"Nice try, but you never followed the dress code. I'm sure Mrs. Adams is relieved that she doesn't have to write you up every day now," Four retorted, referring to the school counselor.

"Please. She only pretended to care to cover up the fact that she kept staring at my dick."

"Then stop offering to show it to her!" Four shouted. When I simply grinned, she rolled her eyes and folded her arms over her chest. "So how do you explain the dress shoes?"

"*You're* wearing them," I pointed out.

"Not. Willingly."

I took a second to light up as I searched for a way out of this conversation. I didn't want to tell her that I'd been in the city all day or even why. It would only demand more answers that would hurt too many people.

I only truly gave a fuck about hurting one, though. It may not have been my choice to lie to him, but it had been my choice to keep it going.

"Hey, what's up?" Ever greeted. Trapped inside the whirlwind that is my head, I didn't even notice him walking up. "What'd you do now?" He immediately grilled me when he saw the look on Four's face.

Their identical glowers were evidence that Four and my cousin were genuinely becoming one. It took most couples ten years to achieve this level of synchronicity.

"Oh, thank fuck." I sighed, feigning relief, though my stomach had turned even more with Ever standing in front of me. "Keep your woman out of my business."

Ever's gaze shot down to Four, and the look she gave him dared him to try. I rolled my eyes when he shrugged and regarded me once more. I was almost disgusted at how pussy-whipped he'd become *and* in such a short time. By contrast, my respect for Four only grew.

"Why are you dressed up?" he asked, echoing Four.

Rising to my full height, I flicked my unfinished cigarette into the grass and yanked open the driver's door. "We're having brunch at Vaughn's tomorrow morning," I announced, ignoring his question. "Be there, and bring your other woman, too."

I didn't wait for a response or even a sign that they'd show up before speeding out of the parking lot. I made it a mile down the road before my phone beeped with a text. Glancing at the screen, I quickly read the short message.

Lil' Lou Who: I'm in.

Smirking, I threw my phone on the dash. One way or another, I'd get answers. They could all bet their life on that.

CHAPTER
TWO

The Plaything

"EXACTLY WHERE ARE YOU TAKING MY DAUGHTER DRESSED LIKE a hoodlum?"

I cringed at the disgust in my father's tone, all the while wishing I could muzzle him. I knew he wouldn't be addressing my "fiancé" that way if he knew Ever was aware that our family was at his mercy. Elliot Montgomery enjoyed having control almost as much as he enjoyed spending money he didn't have.

"We were invited to brunch," Ever replied, barely concealing an eye roll. "I don't need a tie to eat."

I cringed even harder this time at the defiance in Ever's tone. As if showing up in sweatpants and a T-shirt with his hair still mussed from sleep wasn't bad e-*fucking*-nough.

I sighed, feeling resigned to the inevitable.

Our charade had nearly run its course, and it was only a matter of time before Ever jumped ship.

I expected to feel my heart quake from fear, but instead, I inhaled the fresh air blowing in from the open window of my father's office until it filled my lungs. I didn't have time to wring my hands like some damsel. I'd rather take my fate into them.

"You do if it's my daughter on your arm," my father countered.

"But I won't have your daughter on my arm," Ever slowly replied, and my gaze narrowed at the hidden meaning. "I'll have my fiancée." He finally looked my way, grinned, and winked.

I made a mental note to draw and quarter his balls later.

"Yes, well, I haven't walked her down the aisle yet, which means her best interests are still my responsibility."

I almost snorted, but according to Mother, ladies don't snort, so I settled for a subtle eye roll instead. And just in case my father happened to see, I rapidly blinked as I picked at my eye with a perfectly manicured nail. I'd tell him there was an eyelash stuck in it if he asked, but he didn't. He'd likely already forgotten that I was in the room.

"Brunch will be an intimate affair with a friend of the family. We won't be in the public eye."

"And who is this friend of the family?"

"Vaughn Rees."

My father's thick brows pulled down even further at Ever's answer. "I'm not sure I want my daughter in the company of a Rees."

"Our fathers have been considering business together. It's in *everyone's* best interest that we push aside our personal feelings."

My father's only response was to sit back in his chair, and after a moment of contemplation, he nodded to me. Elliot Montgomery would never pass up the chance for more money. Money that he'd never get his hands on if I had anything to say about it.

I crossed the room on the Mary-Jane Prada pumps my mom insisted I wear. Just as I cleared the door, I heard my father speak. The light feeling that came during the rare times I was free of my father's thumb dissipated at his demand.

"Have her back in two hours, or you won't see her again until your wedding day."

Ever's back was already turned, so my father couldn't see the dark expression that clouded his face, but I did. I also knew there would be serious trouble if I didn't separate them right now.

Grabbing Ever's hand, I pulled him toward the front door. I actually broke a sweat since he was resisting a little. Somehow, I managed to get him out the front door. The moment we stepped outside, I spotted Four leaning against the passenger door of the G-Wagon. She wiggled her fingers in greeting, but when she caught our hands clutched together, her eyebrow rose. I dropped his hand as if it were made of hot coals, which only made her grin harder. Even though touching Ever had been innocent and extremely necessary, I had trouble meeting Four's gaze. The shame sweeping over me made me loathe this arrangement even more. I almost wish she'd done what any woman would have and kept Ever's ring when I'd given it back to her. When I cornered her in the girl's bathroom five months ago, it was the last thing I'd expected.

"It's not like Ever and I could go public, anyway," Four reasoned as she lifted the ring I'd laid on the counter. "Our parents are still dating, and Rosalyn"—Four exhaled as her shoulders sagged—"she wouldn't take the news well. She'll just think I'm trying to ruin her relationship with Thomas. I don't want her to get sick again."

"What are you talking about?" I prodded with a frown. If Rosalyn was her mother, why did she call her by her first name? And why would Four dating Ever make her mother sick?

"It doesn't matter now," Four answered cryptically. And then she handed me the ring. What the hell? "Think of this as you doing me a solid too. Us girls have to stick together, right?"

"I don't think this is what they meant."

A small smile was Four's only response, and despite the fact that I felt weird about it, I gave her a hesitant smile back as I accepted the ring. I had the feeling this wasn't going to end well for anyone.

"Trouble with your future in-laws?" Four jested, jerking me back to the present as we climbed inside Ever's truck.

Ever gave her a look that said, "Not now," and I concurred as I leaned my head back and closed my eyes. Feeling someone watching me, I popped them open seconds later and found Four leaning around her seat in the front.

"Are you okay?" The furrow between her brows made me think her concern was genuine. Since we didn't know each other all that well, I wasn't ready to get my hopes up that we could be friends. I was fake dating her boyfriend while she hid in the shadows as his dirty little secret. How could I ever expect her to get past that?

"I'm fine." It was obvious she wasn't convinced when she continued to stare. "Do you really care?" I asked after a few seconds passed, and I begin to squirm.

Shrugging, she turned to face forward. "I don't have to if you prefer."

I was grateful she was no longer watching me when I felt a smile tugging at my lips. I didn't want to like Four, but I did. I couldn't help myself. Four was everything I wished I could be again, and if I could have met her years ago, I would have gladly traded the guys for her. Regret shoved aside my envy, but before I could apologize, Ever sighed loudly, shutting us both up. The truck was silent for the remainder of the ride.

When we arrived at Vaughn's, I sat up abruptly, seeing the red Jeep parked in the driveway. I looked to Ever and found him already watching me over his shoulder.

"We can leave if you're not comfortable."

Yes! Leave! That was an option. Why hadn't I thought of that?

Some long-forgotten cord in my chest tightened at the thought of seeing Jamie. Each time was like the first—a lot of panic and anticipation. Jamie's moods were as unpredictable as his intentions, so I was always on my toes.

I bet he'd rather you be on your knees.

I felt my fists ball as my chin lifted. I didn't want or need Jamie's mercy. We both knew who still had the upper hand anyway. "It's fine." It would be a cold day in hell before I let Jameson Buchanan run me off. When I ran, it would be *my* choice.

I climbed out of the truck, and they followed. Ever rang the doorbell, and Vaughn answered, looking us over before rubbing his brow. That was his tell when he was agitated, so I knew Jamie must have been in rare form today.

Squaring my shoulders, I was the first to step inside, and while it was probably rude, I didn't wait for Vaughn to show me the way. I needed to do this on my own.

Following the voices, I made my way to the kitchen and paused in the entryway. It was only seconds before my bravado faded. Wren, Lou, Tyra, and Jamie were standing around a huge breakfast spread, and each one of their smiles faded away the moment they saw me. The only one who didn't seem surprised was Jamie.

I shook away the crushing feeling at their reactions and plastered on a gracious smile. My mom once made me practice it for hours in the mirror until I got it right. I should have been used to being unwanted. A guilty pang shot through me because that hadn't always been the case. Against my will, my gaze traveled to Jamie. Those brown eyes of his immediately pulled me in, so I looked away before I could fall too deep.

Jamie's snort drew my gaze back to him. He was sneering now. "Coy doesn't fit you, Barbette. Although, with a body like yours—"

Thankfully, he didn't get to finish his train of thought because Lou had pinched his lips shut. She'd *actually* taken her fingers and forced his lips together. Glancing my way, she winked, and I couldn't help my small smile. I didn't need rescuing, although my present circumstances gave a different impression. Still, it was good to know I had backup. Catty women were the norm, and although they were wary of me, I didn't get that vibe from Four, Lou, or Tyra.

After a few seconds, Wren jealously grabbed Lou's hand and pulled her away from Jamie. I watched, failing to hide my amusement as he wrapped his arms around her waist and used his hips to press hers against the counter when she squirmed to get free.

Ever, Four, and Vaughn slipped past me into the kitchen and took their seats. The large ceramic island had stools all around, and the only place left was in Jamie's direct line of sight. I held his gaze as I sat down, and he threw his elbow over the back of his chair, slouching low as he bit his bottom lip. Eyelashes lowered, he looked like he was enjoying dirty porn rather than sharing a meal with seven other people. When I continued to hold his gaze, he blew me a kiss.

Feeling as if he'd brushed his lips against mine, I pressed trembling fingers to my lips. Meeting his gaze again, I saw the playfulness leave his eyes, and in its place, a promise I shouldn't want him to keep. But so what if I did? It was my little secret.

Finally breaking the connection, he turned to Tyra, who was sitting next to him, spooning eggs onto her plate.

"Tyra, you're black, right?"

I blinked. Where the hell was he going with this? It was completely random and not to mention unnecessary.

Already used to his antics, she didn't miss a beat as she continued to fill her plate. "Ask me if the carpet matches the drapes, and I'll disembowel you right here, Buchanan."

Jamie snorted and scooped a huge helping of eggs into his mouth. "Give me a fucking break," he said with a mouthful. "I answered that question thoroughly years ago. Besides…" He swallowed this time before saying, "I already know you're as bald as a baby's ass."

Everyone looked shocked and a little disturbed while my eyes narrowed on him. He wouldn't meet my gaze, which only confirmed my suspicions. Rather than getting to me, I'd gotten to *him*, and just like a child who didn't get their way, he was acting out.

"How the fuck do you know that?" Vaughn roared, breaking the stunned silence.

Jamie's smile was small as he methodically slathered cream cheese on a bagel, perfectly content to leave us in suspense.

Eventually, he winked, but I still wasn't sure if it was because he was teasing or confirming what we were all thinking. "Saw the reminder for her wax appointment on her phone."

Everyone seemed to release a collective breath—everyone except Tyra.

"You guys actually think I fucked him?" she screamed.

"Jamie can be persuasive," Four muttered guiltily. Tyra rolled her eyes, but it was Ever's scowl that stole the show.

"How persuasive?" he demanded.

I was taken aback at the possession in Ever's tone. I still remembered him as the kid who was a little *too* carefree, never caring about the consequences of his actions or the long term. He'd lived for the now. I'd need my fingers *and* toes to count how many times he'd come close to death—and jail.

We all watched Four woo Ever with a kiss that melted him instantly. Jamie was the only one who wasn't moved at their display of affection. I watched from the corner of my eye as he watched me instead. I knew he was waiting for my reaction, for me to scream, and to play the role of a scorned lover. Instead, I made a show of examining my fresh manicure.

"Only ever you," Four promised Ever.

If I hadn't been sitting so close, I wouldn't have heard her whisper. I couldn't help but wonder if she'd meant it. I hoped she did. Ever had been a shell before Four came to town. Guilt would do that to a person.

I'd know.

"Fucking better be," he whispered back. He smirked, probably thinking it would hide his blush. I almost snorted. *Boys.*

"So, guys," Tyra shouted cheerily to Lou and Wren. She seemed eager to change the subject, and I agreed. "How are you liking living together? It isn't weird?"

"Not at all!" Lou answered with an affectionate smile. "I'm learning so much about my baby. Like how fast the toilet paper goes when he's around."

Wren's lip curled into a mocking sneer. "I'm sorry that I need more than two squares to wipe my ass."

"More like two rolls," Lou corrected before laying a sympathetic hand on his arm. "It gets a bit explosive down there, huh?"

I snickered and then panicked, thinking someone might have heard. My mother would not have been amused. In fact, she would have run from the table. Fortunately, Jamie's loud guffaw drowned out the small sound I'd made while the rest of the table pushed their food away. I quickly became entranced by Wren and Lou's bickering until the grimness in Vaughn's tone when he spoke pulled my attention away.

"Jamie," Vaughn drawled, "it's your lucky day. That stunt you pulled got you chauffeur duty. The girls want you to drive them around when they go dress shopping."

Jamie's nonchalance at the announcement surprised me as he reached for a strip of bacon. I used to think he was like every other boy, unwilling to take orders from a girl until I realized he didn't like orders no matter who was giving them. To say I was relieved would be an understatement. They say most girls fall in love with a man most like their father. I was glad that hadn't been the case for me. Jamie and my father loathed each other beyond redemption.

"Only if I get to help them try some on," he retorted lasciviously.

"You don't," Ever, Vaughn, and even Wren echoed.

"Dresses?" Four questioned, making my heart stop. "For what?"

The trippy organ inside my chest began to beat again but much too fast.

Ever hadn't asked Four to prom.

Even though I knew it was in vain, I closed my eyes, praying that it hadn't been because of me. When I opened them again, I glanced around the island, seeing everyone's bewildered expression.

Lou was the one who finally answered when everyone else just stared. "For prom, silly."

"Okay, how does she know that but not you?" Jamie quipped.

"For one," Lou sassed, "I'm going. And two, maybe she just forgot."

Jamie's gaze narrowed before traveling back and forth and then settling on Ever. "You haven't asked her yet, have you?" At Ever's silence, Jamie's lips spread into a wide smile. "This should be interesting."

"Why would he need to ask her?" Lou argued in a tone suggesting Jamie was dense. "She's obviously his girlfriend." Her sneaky smile and mocking tone made me shift uncomfortably in my chair. I knew where this conversation was headed, and suddenly, I wondered at the real reason I was invited. I was the black sheep here, not Jamie, who was clearly out to stir the pot.

"No, she's his dirty little secret." Jamie stood up from the table with a dry chuckle that I knew all too well.

I wanted to run through the open French doors leading to the back lawn, but I couldn't bring my feet to move. Besides, there was nowhere to go. Even with as uncomfortable as my present circumstances made me, it was still better than being trapped in that gilded cage my father could no longer afford.

"Everyone will be expecting him to show up with *her* on his arm," Jamie said while pointing accusingly at me.

I felt vomit rushing up, and I wanted to grab for my water—or slap the smirk off Jamie's full lips—but my hands shook too badly to dare either. I pressed them into my lap, hoping no one would see.

"But don't let that distract you from the fact that I can't get my dick wet in peace without being asked if I have a date to the prom," Jamie grumbled.

"How is that relevant?" Tyra questioned.

"Most of these chicks care more about prom than they do

graduation, but somehow, the most coveted day of the year escaped our dear Four's notice."

"And? She's got a lot on her mind."

"So wouldn't a night dancing in her lover's arms be the perfect chance to escape her woes?"

No one had a response to that, not even Ever. Silently, I was pleading with him to stand up and claim her for his date, but I knew he wouldn't. Because of me. The amount of relief I felt when Four had given me back Ever's engagement ring made it hard for me to look myself in the mirror afterward. I should have been able to face my demons on my own. I took a deep breath, eager more than ever for the day that I could skip town and never return. There was too much pain here. Pain that I helped to cause.

Four's voice, filled with venom, distracted me from feeling sorry for myself. I would have enough time for that when I was once again alone. "While your concern is touching, Jamie, you don't need to speak for me. I never had any intention of going to prom."

"Oh, you'll go," Ever decreed.

Four's head whipped in his direction, and the glare she pinned him with made me smile. It was nice to know that I'd be leaving my best friend in capable hands. Everson needed someone who could stand up to him.

"On whose command?"

Bracing his hands against the table, Ever leaned forward, looking ready to stand and continue the conversation in private, but then Lou spoke, causing him to sit back and sulk.

"I know this is super taboo and a little insane, and I may be starting something that I can't undo, but... I have to side with Jamie. And you should know," she added before anyone could argue, "that it is not because he's my new best friend." A growl from Wren caused Lou to look his way. "Oh, sweetie," she cooed. "You didn't think you'd have your cake and eat it too, did you?" She kissed his cheek when he continued to glower, and he relaxed—if only a little. "Relax, chief. You get to see me naked."

"Get back to the part where you were agreeing with me," Jamie insisted.

"Don't push it," Lou snapped before zeroing in on Ever. "Unless there's an audience, I've never seen you act like more than a friend to her." She threw her thumb over her shoulder to me, and momentarily forgetting who I was expected to be, I rolled my eyes. Still, I did nothing because a part of me wanted this to happen. Even though it wasn't in my best interest, it was in Ever's, which was enough for me. "And when no one else except us is looking, you dote and fawn and screw Four, rather *loudly* I might add." My eyebrows rose at that, but thankfully, no one noticed. "And in front of your supposed girlfriend."

"Lou, it's not our business," Wren bit out.

Ignoring her boyfriend, who was seriously intimidating, Lou turned to Four. "I know Tyra said she wouldn't judge, but I made no such promise. I respect the hell out of you, Four. I might even look up to you." Lou looked on the verge of shedding a tear when she said, "You're the big sister I'll never have."

"Wait one fucking minute," Ever said with a growl. "This so-called breakfast is a goddamn intervention, isn't it?"

"Yes!" shouted everyone, except Four, Ever, and me.

"Un-fucking-believable," he spat.

Four finally glanced my way as if remembering I was there, and I wasn't sure what she saw, but I had a pretty good guess when her gaze became worried. I gritted my teeth as the girl I used to be raged internally at me for being so weak.

"Something is up," Vaughn said. "And if you don't tell us right now what's going on, that vein in Jamie's forehead is going to burst."

"Let me guess," Ever responded with a lick of his lips. "This was all his idea."

"Of course," Jamie answered proudly.

"We only agreed because it's driving us crazy, too," Tyra rushed to explain.

"Tell us what the hell is going on with you three," Vaughn demanded.

"If it was any of your business"—Ever stood up—"we would have told you." Taking Four's arm, he pulled her from the chair before nodding toward me. All the grace and poise that had been drilled into me since I was thirteen years old was forgotten as I stood on shaking legs and followed. I could feel Jamie's angry glare and knew he'd seek retribution for things not going his way.

And, as always, he'd look to me to pay the price.

The hours after Four and Ever returned me home blurred together. Jamie seemed to be taking his sweet time, knowing that I was anticipating his arrival. I wouldn't be surprised if he were biding his time until I lost my nerve. It was a shame how easily he could get under my skin. Then again… maybe he'd never left, not even after all these years.

Rather than give him what he wanted, I locked my door—even though I was home alone—shoved aside my nightstand, and lifted the floorboard underneath. Once I found what I needed, I grabbed my bag and headed out. Since neither my oxfords nor my five-inch heels were appropriate for the terrain, I dug out the cheap flip-flops my mother had no idea I'd purchased. There was no telling where my parents were or when they'd be back, but it was a risk I was willing to take. The walk through the small forested area surrounding my house was short. A pity, really. Sometimes, I wished these woods were large enough to get lost in.

Reaching a familiar glade, I sat down against my favorite tree and pulled out the one true treasure I had left. Using both hands to hold it to my lips, I blew into and through a few of the ten holes. The tune I played was simple, the only one I'd learned on this old harmonica, but it always managed to make my heart flutter with nostalgia.

I felt a tear slip by the time I reached the end. I dropped the harmonica to my lap, but I didn't bother to wipe it away before pulling out my journal and pen and settling back against the tree once more. Instantly, I was transported back to a different tree six years ago, where my first kiss was so brazenly stolen. Putting pen to paper, I poured what little feelings I still allowed myself onto a clean page.

I should have seen it coming
It was right there in your eyes
The window to your soul
My lips your window to mine
I had no secrets when you kissed me
And, clever boy, you knew it well
But those days are gone now
I've wished your love farewell

An hour and three poems later, I shoved the journal and harmonica inside my bag. I felt like a fool, but I couldn't help thinking that it was better than feeling nothing at all. I've had that journal since I was twelve, and eight months ago was the first time I'd touched it in four years. I didn't allow myself to believe that the timing was anything other than a coincidence. This spark of life I was suddenly feeling could very well be because of my impending freedom.

Inside, I held my breath as I ascended the stairs to the third floor where my bedroom was, mercifully alone. I didn't need to question if Jamie was up there. Luckily, I had the foresight to check the hiding space where we kept the spare key. Needless to say, it was empty.

A part of me delighted in the chance to take him by surprise. Usually, it was *Jamie* who was always two steps ahead of *me*.

Reaching my bedroom, I pushed open the door just as Jamie emerged from my closet. I was sure it'd been ransacked thoroughly. For a few seconds, we stood there, staring at one another before he broke the silence.

"What are you doing here?"

His question had me cocking my head. "Shouldn't that be my line? This *is* my bedroom."

"What's yours is always mine, Barbette. I thought you knew that by now."

"Get out."

"When I'm done here." Arrogantly, he turned toward my dresser and yanked open the top drawer where I kept my panties. "Where were you?" he demanded as he took his time rifling through them.

"If that were your business, I'd have already told you." Walking over to my bed, I deftly slid my bag under my bed before sitting on it. "Looking for something?"

I already knew the answer, and knowing what he was looking for had me kicking my purse further underneath the bed. Turning to me, our gazes connected once more, his burning while mine remained carefully shuttered.

If I let him see…

Even after I'd made him doubt my feelings for him, Jamie was relentless. I could never risk giving him even a glimpse of hope.

"Where is it?"

"I don't know what you're talking about," I lied, averting my gaze.

Slowly, he crossed the room until he towered over me. With strong fingers, he lifted my chin, making my heart beat a little faster. "Yes, you do."

I considered playing coy again, and he must have seen it in

my eyes because his hand drifted down to my neck in warning. "I lost it," I blurted before I could talk myself out of lying again.

"You lost it?"

"Why do you even care so much? You've got a million guitars."

His dark eyebrows pulled together in confusion before he spoke again. "You know what I'm talking about," he pushed through gritted teeth. "Where is it?"

Oh… that.

I thought for sure he was after something else, although the truth didn't make me feel much better. In fact, my stomach twisted just a little more at the thought of him reading what was inside my journal.

"I don't do that anymore."

"Because you're such a cold, unfeeling bitch?"

"You tell me, Jameson. You're the one touching me."

After a brief pause, his hand trailed from my neck, and for a moment, I thought he'd slip the buttons on my blouse free, and— *Don't you dare think about that.*

"So I am." Pulling away, he dug into his pocket and pulled the spare key out before dropping it into my lap. "I always get what I want, Bette. You should know that by now."

Lifting my chin, I met his gaze. "Then why do you look so worried?"

Jamie stared down at me for such a long time that I began to squirm, and I wasn't sure if it was because of my nerves or the warmth pooling between my thighs.

"Where is she?" he demanded.

"Who?"

Jamie's gaze was unflinching as he held my eyes hostage. "You know who."

I looked away because I did know. "She's gone," I whispered. The desolation in my tone echoed through my heart.

"Bullshit," Jamie spat. "I know her better than you do."

When I didn't respond, he took a step back and then another. "Have it your way. I know how to get her back."

I watched, perplexed, as he walked over to the gold, ornate, floor-length mirror that sparkled diamond dust when the light hit it just right. My father had paid seven grand for it.

Confusion quickly turned to amused disbelief when Jamie began chanting Bee, my childhood nickname, three times while staring at his reflection.

"Wait a second…so in that thick skull of yours, I'm the *Bloody Mary*?"

"Of course not." Jamie's flirtatious gaze met mine through the ridiculously over-priced mirror. "You're way hotter."

"I'm not going to thank you for the compliment," I said when he continued to watch me. I could feel a small smile forming and on its heels…hope. Maybe Jamie and I could be friends again?

"No thanks necessary," Jamie drawled as he turned to face me. "I speak the truth unless the truth won't get me laid."

My gaze dropped to my hands in my lap. "Is sex all that matters to you now?"

I heard his scoff, and when I looked up, the white flag we'd waved was gone. I should have known better than to think it would last. Jamie and I were poison with no cure in sight.

"What did you expect?"

I was not about to answer that. I expected nothing. Or at least…I shouldn't have. "Obviously, you want more if you hold yourself back from those other girls. I've heard the rumors, Jamie." Or could it possibly be that his issue was physical rather than emotional?

"When and how I come is none of your business, Barbette." He paused, and then his pierced brow quirked as the flame in his eyes rose higher. "Unless you're offering?"

I felt my cheeks warm, and my nipples pebbled underneath my silk blouse. "What makes you think I'd want your broken dick?"

The withering look he'd given me made me wish I'd kept my mouth shut, *especially* when he crossed my bedroom, pushed me on my back, and climbed on top of me. He was careful not to touch me any more than that, though. No, that would have been catastrophic for both of us.

"Tell me, Barbette," he whispered, lips poised dangerously close, "what's keeping me from pulling my *broken* dick out and fucking you senseless?"

I stared back at him, wanting to swear that I wasn't willing, but we'd both know I would be lying, and he'd see right through. And *that* was even more embarrassing than telling the truth.

"Nothing."

He froze, and I could tell by his startled gaze that he hadn't been expecting the truth. I wasn't sure how long we had laid there gazing at one another before he finally broke the stunned silence.

"Then consider yourself lucky that I'm not interested," he mumbled. Shooting to his feet, he rushed for the door.

"Then why did you come here?" I yelled as I quickly stood as well. "Why do you keep looking at me as if fucking me is all you want to do?"

And *why* the hell was I even arguing with him?

I should be letting Jamie go, not secretly hoping he'd stay.

Ripping open the door, Jamie stated over his shoulder as he walked away, "All's fair in love and war, Barbette."

The moment my bedroom door slammed shut, I sank to the floor, feeling boneless. He'd taken all my strength and common sense with him.

Again.

CHAPTER THREE

The Plaything

Summer… Six Years Ago

"H E'S SO DREAMY." OLIVIA SIGHED AS SHE STARED OUT HER bedroom window. Olivia Portland had been handpicked by my parents as a suitable playmate, and while she was nice enough, we had nothing in common. Olivia was glitter, gloss, and rainbows—while I… didn't shine so bright.

Blonde ringlets framed Olivia's face, but I didn't need to see to know she was blushing. She was lying on her stomach, ankles crossed in the air without regard for the frilly, yellow dress she wore. Her fists were propped under her chin, and I could practically see the sparkle in her doe-brown eyes in the window's reflection.

It was the same reaction we *both* had whenever a certain boy came around.

Against my better judgment, I moved to stand over her perch on the cushioned window bench.

Olivia glanced over her shoulder and flashed me an uncomfortable smile. "They're waiting for you, you know."

I knew.

I'd already changed into my favorite red ball cap with my freshly-curled hair shoved underneath, cargo shorts that Vaughn had long since grown out of, and the Fall Out Boy T-shirt that

Ever had been reluctant to part with. Vaughn ended up having to win it for me in an arm-wrestling match since Ever hadn't been quite so chivalrous.

For some reason, I was stalling. Perhaps I was just waiting for the butterflies to go away so I wouldn't make a fool of myself.

I chose not to respond as I watched Ever wrestle Jason, Olivia's twin brother, on the front lawn. They'd discarded their shirts and were grunting and groaning as they used what they liked to pretend was their considerable strength to best the other.

Ever managed to get Jason in a headlock that, after several seconds, his opponent found it impossible to break and tapped out. I nearly swallowed my tongue when the boys broke apart, and I got a glimpse of Ever's sweaty chest. He was smiling victoriously while Jason wore a scowl and stomped away. I couldn't help rolling my eyes, even as Ever and Vaughn frowned their confusion at Jason's retreating form.

"My brother is such a sore loser," Olivia remarked, voicing my thoughts.

"Shouldn't you be on his side?" I teased. "He's your twin, after all."

She flipped onto her side and grinned. "Not by choice. Besides," she added as she tucked her blonde hair behind her ear and blushed, "Ever is going to kiss me soon. I just know it."

Fearing Olivia would notice the jealousy brewing in my veins, I turned away before she could see my face and hurriedly slipped on my sneakers. My mother would die if she caught me wearing them instead of the pretty ballet flats she'd forced me to wear this morning.

I told myself to get a grip.

So what if Ever kissed her? It was no business of mine.

My very unfortunate and sudden crush was an affliction. Something easily cured—if only I could find the remedy.

"Want to come to the park with us? You can ride on my handlebars," I offered in vain. I already knew she'd say no. She was firm in her belief that boys went to Jupiter to get more stupider while I believed that they were on to something. Girls just wanted to have fun while boys were sure to have it by any means necessary. If I could find another girl in this town like that, hanging out with her instead would be a no-brainer. It would certainly make my mother happy. She didn't think it was appropriate that I was the only girl in a group of rowdy boys. What she didn't know was that I could hang with the best of them.

Not to mention that I'd never quite related to other twelve-year-old girls and their plights. I still didn't get Justin Bieber's appeal nor had I figured out what made *Twilight* such a big hit.

"No, thanks. Jessica's mom is taking us skating today."

I waited, thinking of a way to turn her down if an invitation followed, but none came. I tried not to think of why that hurt my feelings. I didn't even want to go. "Okay, then... see you later."

"Bye!" she yelled with a cheery wave.

My steps were slow, and I still wore a frown by the time I reached the front door. However, my sadness melted away the moment I stepped outside and saw the eager expressions on Vaughn and Ever's faces. Jason, I suppose, was still somewhere sulking. I'd go after him but I'd learned the hard way that it was better to let him stew until he was ready to get over whatever was eating him.

I couldn't quite claim Jason as part of my tribe since I was still feeling him out. He was always so closed off, and when he did open up, it was usually out of anger. Maybe one day I'd find out what Jason's deal was, but right now, I couldn't be bothered. Glancing at Ever, I quickly averted my gaze, hiding my blush when he smiled.

Clearly, I had my own issues to sort out.

"Is your cousin still staying with you this summer?" Vaughn asked Ever as we made glue and glitter bombs with the balloons Vaughn had managed to procure. Summer had just begun, but Tommy Vann, one of our classmates, hadn't wasted time terrorizing everyone on the playground. He'd also been talking crap about me, and I was determined to shut him up once and for all. The guys offered to kick his ass again, but I had a better idea. Everyone had a role in our tight-knit crew. I was the brains, and they were the brawn.

"I'm not sure," Ever grumbled. "He got into trouble again, so my aunt and uncle grounded him for the summer."

"What did he do this time?" Jason questioned through his chortles. His mood had improved considerably since we left his house. Maybe the promise of taking his anger out on someone more deserving had cheered him up. "Moon the cafeteria ladies again?"

I frowned as I wondered why someone would flash their butt to strangers? It wasn't the first time I'd heard about Ever's cousin, and the stories only seemed to get wilder with each telling. I grimaced. Not for the first time that day I felt a warmth spread across my lower stomach accompanied by a dull ache.

"He got caught playing seven minutes in heaven with some eighth-grader's boob."

Vaughn and Jason roared uncontrollably as they high-fived each other. I, on the other hand, didn't find a damn thing funny. Ever's cousin sounded like a real tool, and I was glad he was staying far away this summer. I had enough trouble keeping these three in line. I didn't need some outsider getting them riled and stirring up trouble.

We finished filling the balloons and carefully sorted and loaded them into the empty backpacks we'd brought.

The park was pretty full on a summer afternoon, but I wouldn't let that deter me. Olivia, back from skating with Jessica and the rest of her friends, was across the park near the hopscotch.

They were all huddled together, whispering and giggling about something or someone I couldn't see. I didn't dare look their way and risk making eye contact with one of Olivia's friends. There were only ever two reactions—eagerness to make me one of them or disgust because I wasn't.

I met Ever, Vaughn, and Jason's stares as they dutifully waited for my command and realized they were likely the only friends I'd ever have. Surprisingly, on the heels of that epiphany was acceptance. Why have a ton of "friends" who wanted to change you when you could have three who accepted you as you are?

It certainly saved me cash at Christmastime.

"Tommy will be here any minute. Jason, you stay here and give the signal when you see him coming. Give two short whistles if he's alone and a long one if he's got company." I waited for his nod before turning to Ever and Vaughn. "You two take the glue bombs. One of you take cover over there," I directed, pointing at the tree on the other side of the path. "The other will take cover here."

"What will you do?" Ever asked with his hands tucked in his pockets.

I tossed a glitter bomb in the air and caught it as I grinned. I then pointed at the tree branch hanging over our heads. "I'm going to rain fire from above."

Tommy wouldn't know what hit him. Literally.

Ever grinned back, and with the rope I brought, I hurriedly bent to loop it through the bucket's handle before he could see my blush. It seemed that was all I did lately, but at least I was good at hiding it. He moved to help me carry the bucket once I was finished, but I gave him a curt shake of my head.

With his hands up in surrender, he backed away a few paces, and I felt like I could breathe again. I knew I was acting weird, and Ever, despite his nerve-racking recklessness, was sharp enough to notice. He was also too polite to call me out on it in front of an audience.

Careful to avoid eye contact, I tied the other end of the rope around my waist before climbing the tree. Ever had taught me how to climb, and I used to spend hours in a tree, hiding from my parents, and Ever... he was always there to keep me company. I never minded because he never pried, and I was more grateful for his silence than having a shoulder to cry on. I wrinkled my nose at the thought as I climbed to the second branch overhanging the path and pulled the bucket the rest of the way while the guys took cover. Some of the glitter had spilled, but that was okay. I had plenty.

We were on the backside of the park where Tommy liked to wreak havoc with his own crew. I'm sure he'd even come to think of it as his territory.

Well, it was ours now.

Jason released two sharp whistles, and I was almost disappointed that this would be easier than I thought. His cronies wouldn't be around to witness what I had in store, so I guess the entire playground would have to do.

A second later, I spotted Tommy's mop of brown curls and his cheeks covered in chocolate as he demolished a candy bar he probably stole from one of the smaller kids on his way in. It was funny that he never tried that on someone his own size.

I checked Vaughn and Ever's hiding spots, but I couldn't see either of them. Not until it was too late. Vaughn emerged first, and that wicked arm of his had Tommy's entire right side covered in glue before I could blink. A shocked Tommy released his grip he had on the candy bar when Ever emerged. My best friend took his time as a wicked grin spread his lips slowly. I watched as Tommy's eyes bulged, and his mouth dropped in horror. Big mistake. Ever's first balloon hit Tommy square in the face. Jason, who'd been tiptoeing behind Tommy, joined in. It wasn't long before Tommy was pelted with glue bomb after glue bomb. It wasn't until Ever glanced up at the tree with a look that said "Well?" that I jumped into action. By now, Tommy was covered head to toe in glue. He looked like a big white blob.

"Hey, Tommy?" I called down.

He struggled to lift his head, and I stifled a giggle when all I could make out underneath all that glue was the blue of his eyes.

"Who's the girl now?" Without warning, I tipped over the bucket, and his cry of terror was cut short as a waterfall of sparkly pink glitter rained down on him.

The boys could barely contain themselves and were bent over, clutching their stomachs as I climbed down from the tree. When Tommy started to cry, I actually started to feel bad, but I knew that showing mercy would only prove his point. Instead, I chose to prove mine.

I was running the show now. Balls or no balls.

"Stop crying," I snapped.

His wails instantly dissolved to whimpers. One of my crew snickered when he even hiccuped. I stepped closer until I was standing on the ring of pink glitter around him.

"Jason?" I called, and he stepped forward, waiting for my command. "Search his pockets."

He did as he was told with a crooked grin, which dissolved into disgust when he pulled out a crumpled Lincoln covered in lint and something... sticky. "Gross," Jason griped.

"Find out who that"—I pointed to the Butterfinger lying on the ground covered in glitter—"belonged to and give them the cash."

"But that's the last of my allowance!" Tommy raged.

"Does it look like we give a fuck?" Vaughn coolly replied.

It always amazed me how easily curse words flowed from his lips. He did it naturally and never seemed to care if an adult might hear. Considering who his parents were, I guess he wouldn't. His mother's family not only founded this town but his grandfather was also the mayor. And if that weren't enough, his father... well, no one knew what his father did, but what we did know was his father was bad news. Everyone in Blackwood Keep gave Franklin Rees a wide berth. Including his son.

Jason set off to complete his task. It wouldn't be hard to find the kid because Tommy wouldn't have just settled with taking the candy. Somewhere on the playground was a helpless kid nursing a black eye or a busted lip.

"What do you want to do with him?" Ever inquired, sounding bored already. I knew he was probably eager to be done with Tommy. Ever was a terror, too. However, it was usually just himself that he ended up hurting. Mr. and Mrs. McNamara were having a tough time controlling their son's restlessness. Or perhaps running a multibillion-dollar hotel chain didn't allow much time for parenting. It seemed beneath Ever to act out just to seek attention from his parents. Then again, maybe that was just the crush speaking. Ever was no different than any other kid.

But I was.

I had to be the only kid on the planet who wished their parents would forget they ever existed. Right?

"We're going to let him go," I answered, earning Vaughn and Ever's disappointed frowns and Tommy's hopeful stare.

"Seriously?" Vaughn griped.

I nodded and stepped even closer to Tommy. I wasn't afraid he'd try anything. Not even he was that dumb.

"But you're going to stop picking on the smaller kids, and you're going to stop talking crap, or else you're going to find out what was behind door number two. We clear on that, Vann?"

Tommy nodded eagerly.

"Good. You can go."

He tried to step around me so he could leave out the back way where no one would see him covered in sparkly pink glitter. Did he really think it would be that easy?

"Where do you think you're going?"

He stopped dead in his tracks. "L-leaving."

"Oh, no. We didn't get you all dressed up for nothing, hot stuff. You're going to take the scenic route. Let everyone see what a pretty girl you are."

Vaughn and Ever both snickered.

"But—"

"Walk," I commanded, leaving no room for argument in my tone.

Vaughn closed in on him, forcing Tommy to back up step after step until he was retreating on his own. Ever suggestively whistled as Tommy hurried away as fast he could, covered in all that glue and glitter.

We followed at a slower pace, wanting to witness his humiliation without being dumb enough to be caught red-handed.

Vaughn and Ever were still howling while I allowed myself only a small smile. I didn't like what I had to do, but I knew it had to be done. Still, I never claimed to be an angel, so a teeny-weeny part of me enjoyed it.

As we rounded the corner, their laughter came to an abrupt halt at the rough yet high-pitched trill piercing the air. Strangely, I began to hum 'Aint No Sunshine' by Bill Withers as I drifted toward the sound and the culprit behind it. I didn't see anything out of the ordinary.

At first.

There was this boy—tall, lanky, and dressed in all black. The sun shining through the leaves of the tree he was holding up highlighted the red in his lush brown hair. His eyes were closed as he held his cupped hands to his mouth, oblivious to the stares of everyone around him. I was sure I'd never seen him before yet I couldn't take my eyes away as he played what I could only guess was a harmonica. It wasn't until he reached the end of the number that he slowly opened his eyes and lowered his hands, letting me see the sensual set of his wide mouth. His head suddenly swiveled my way and then he grinned, lazily pushing away from the tree as if the world personally spun to his rhyme. I held my breath as I stood transfixed.

Did I mention he was achingly beautiful?

As I stared at him, the pain in my belly increased until it felt like I was being stabbed from the inside.

Something this good couldn't be true, which meant he had to be bad news.

"What the hell?" Ever exclaimed as he and Vaughn walked right up to him. Suddenly, I felt punched in the gut. It was obvious that they knew each other. "Jamie?"

"Who the hell else could I be?" Trouble shot back.

My lips flattened as I watched the hypnotic roll of Jamie's hips as he met my friends halfway. Someone was mighty sure of himself.

The boys hugged, being careful not to let their embrace linger too long and risk appearing less macho. The newcomer then turned to Vaughn, and to my surprise, they embraced, too. Wide grins covered each of their faces, and I could already see the mischief brewing in their eyes. I shifted uncomfortably because, for whatever reason, I felt left out.

They were happy to see their friend, which was perfectly understandable.

Except my gut wouldn't stop warning me that the tide was changing, and there was nothing I could do to stop it. And when faced with danger, I did what any sane person would do.

I turned and ran the other way.

There were no calls for me to come back as I fled the park, which meant my friends hadn't even noticed I had left. I ran all the way home, and though I was drenched in sweat and out of breath, the tumbles in my tummy hadn't stopped. It felt as if I'd left a piece of myself back there, and I was sure it was my pride. I'd run like a coward, and I didn't even know why. Pressing a hand to my lower stomach, I frowned. The fluttering had finally ceased, but now it felt like my insides where being wrung dry, ebbing every few seconds, and leaving behind a dull ache. My skin was warm, and it had nothing to do with the sun beaming down on me like my own personal spotlight. A few seconds later, I was grateful there was no one around when I doubled over. A small cry even slipped through my lips. And then another cramp hit me before I could straighten.

Now I wasn't one to curse. Mother said it isn't ladylike.

But *what the hell*?

I limped through the gates and slowly made my way up the drive, not stopping until I reached my private bath. Normally, I'd turn up my nose at all the pink walls and decorations my mother insisted on, but there was no time. Suddenly, the baggy cargo shorts were too constricting, so I hurriedly unbuttoned them and shoved them down my trembling legs. When it still felt like my stomach was being squeezed, I realized it was the elastic in my panties. In a moment of desperation, I shoved them off, too, and the sight of blood immediately brought tears to my eyes.

Something was wrong, and I didn't know what to do, so I did what any little girl who was sure she was dying would.

I screamed for my mother.

I stepped outside and breathed in the fresh air. It had been five days since I started my period, and thankfully, the nightmare was finally over. I'd cried fresh tears when my mother informed me that I'd have to endure that *every* month. At least until menopause. I didn't know what that meant, but I couldn't wait more than ever now to grow up.

Hopping on my bike, I pedaled as fast as I could to Ever's house. He didn't live far, but on a bike, it felt like forever. Part of the reason I was so eager was because I hadn't seen my crew in almost a week. I'd been avoiding them out of embarrassment. Thankfully, the only excuse my parents had given my friends when they eventually came looking for me was that I was sick.

I was sweaty and out of breath, not to mention my thighs burned when I reached the humongous house Ever lived in. It had everything—*two* pools, a theater with every movie ever made, and even an elevator, though Ever said it was reserved for the hired hands.

I reached the end of the drive and frowned when I found four bikes already lying by the stairs. I didn't recognize the black one with red wheels.

Ringing the doorbell, I smiled when Mrs. Greene, their housekeeper, answered. "Oh, Barbette! I'm glad to see you're feeling better. Ever said you were sick."

"Yup, but I'm all better now!"

"I can see that." With a smile, she stepped aside.

I ran inside, but the sound of her clearing her throat had me slowing my stride. "Sorry," I said, giggling. "I forgot."

"That's okay. I made chocolate chip cookies. They're just fresh from the oven." Mrs. Greene pinched my cheek as she passed.

As eager as I was to see my friends, I couldn't resist Mrs. Greene's cookies. Once again forgetting her rule about running inside, I charged into the kitchen only to stop short at the sight of a boy I didn't know but recognized. He was alone, standing in front of the counter, shoving a cookie in his trap while clutching five more in his fist. I looked at the platter resting on the island. There were only crumbs left.

By the time my gaze returned to him, I had found him watching me as he chewed slowly. I was completely tongue-tied as I took in his reddish-brown hair and lanky frame underneath the plain white T-shirt and red swimming trunks. My attention was drawn to his wide mouth when he licked a crumb from his pink lips. Those lips doing strange things to my insides started moving, and I realized he was talking.

"You lost, bro?"

Bro? It was the first time anyone had ever called me that. Not even Ever and Vaughn, though they called each other bro plenty. I realized then that Jamie thought I was a boy. It was also the first time I'd become self-conscious about my appearance.

Getting my first period hadn't been the only major thing to go down this week. For some reason, my mother had been more adamant than ever that I stop hanging out so much with the guys. I didn't understand the big deal, and she seemed reluctant to explain it to me other than mumbling something about boys going through puberty, too.

It wasn't the first time she'd tried to steer me toward girls, but for some reason, I'd taken it harder this time than all the others and... cut my hair. Now that I was out of the red fog, I felt silly for doing it. I could still hear my mother's horrified screams when she found me with my hair, covering every inch of the bathroom floor. Gone were my long tresses, and what remained barely extended past my ear. Per usual, I wore my red ball cap hiding what I'd done underneath.

"No," I answered before clearing my throat when my voice came out all squeaky. "I'm looking for Ever," I said as deeply as I could. I don't know why, but I didn't want Ever's cousin to know that I was a girl just yet. I'd grown breasts a couple of years ago, but thankfully, my baggy T-shirt kept them hidden. It also helped that I was taller than most girls—as tall as Ever and Vaughn—so he had no reason to be suspicious.

Jamie's eyes narrowed as if hearing my thoughts.

When he began studying my face, I fought the urge to turn my cap around. I'd worn it backward, giving him full access to my face. I cursed my overly long eyelashes that made my blue eyes seem brighter and rounder and my face softer, more feminine.

"He's out back by the pool," he finally offered.

I guess that explains the swimming trunks.

"Thanks," I mumbled. I started for the family room that led out into the backyard and the massive pool the McNamaras owned when I stopped in the threshold. Spinning around, I found Jamie with his back turned, rifling through the refrigerator with one hand and the last of the cookies in the other. "I'm Bee, by the way."

He didn't bother facing me when he said, "Figured that out while you were staring, man."

My cheeks heated, and I knew my face had turned beet red. I suddenly felt shy. Like I'd been caught red-handed crushing. I didn't even know this kid and wasn't so sure I'd like him once I did. My embarrassment morphed into confusion, however, when I realized Jamie knew who I was but had still mistaken me for a boy. How could that be if Ever had clearly mentioned me?

Kicking the fridge closed, he started toward me with an arm full of waters. I counted at least seven.

"And you're Ever's cousin, Jamie?"

"Maybe," he cheekily replied as he brushed past me.

I followed him out, the voices and sound of water splashing growing louder with each step. The moment the pool came into view, I stopped while Jamie kept going. Horsing around in the pool was Ever, Vaughn, and Jason, but they weren't alone. Olivia and two of her friends were there, as well, and they all seemed to be having the time of their life.

I'm not sure why the scene rubbed me the wrong way, but my unease only heightened when Jamie set his load down on one of the patio tables near the edge of the pool, lifted his T-shirt over his head, and backed away. My brows furrowed, but then seconds later, my confusion cleared when he sprinted full speed for the pool.

The girls squealed and rushed to get out of the way while Ever, Vaughn, and Jason cheered at the huge splash he made when he hit the water. The girls were now giggling and batting their eyelashes, and I fought an eye roll. None of them seemed too concerned with the fact the pool was shallow and that Jamie could have been hurt.

I moved to the top of the steps, but I went unnoticed and forgotten as I stood there, watching the scene unfold. I didn't like what I was seeing as two of Olivia's friends immediately gravitated toward Jamie. They circled him, but with the way he grinned at them, I was positive he was the predator, and they were the prey. They'd fallen right into his trap.

Not liking the feelings stirring from watching him, I forced my gaze away, and it landed on Olivia. Shyly, she peeked at Ever from under her eyelashes, waiting for him to notice her. Completely unaware of her attention, Ever pounced on Vaughn, putting him in a headlock. Ever was faster, but Vaughn was stronger and broke free in no time before tackling Ever and driving him underwater.

My heart thundered in my chest when Ever's head came within an inch of hitting the bottom. Breaking free of the panic seizing my body, I quickly descended the stairs.

I'd seen enough.

Before I could speak and tell them to quit being so stupid, a gentle but authoritative voice beat me to the punch. "What did I tell you boys about roughhousing in the pool?"

I spun around and found Ever's mom standing at the top of the steps with her hands on her hips, wearing a no-nonsense expression. Her dark-brown hair was cut short, curling around her ears and nape and covering her forehead, but unlike mine, there was nothing boyish about it. Paired with her olive skin and brown eyes that almost seemed gold under the sun, Mrs. McNamara could knock the breath out of any man.

"Sorry, Mom." Ever immediately left the pool but stopped short when he spotted me. "Bee?" I balked at the question in his tone. It had only been less than a week. Had he forgotten me already? "What are you doing here?" he asked when I said nothing.

"I'm sorry," I said, feeling out place and betrayed. I guess those hormones my mom tried explaining to me hadn't completely returned to normal. "I didn't realize you were busy. I'll leave," I pushed through my teeth. I wondered if I had a right to be mad, but he was my best friend, wasn't he? If so, then why did it seem like he'd been content without me?

I turned to go, but he caught my shoulders and spun me back around. "Go? I missed you like crazy!" he shouted, pulling me into a hug. "Welcome back."

He pulled away, and I returned the goofy grin he wore as something fluttered in my chest. "Only you missed me?"

"I guess Vaughn and J missed you, too," he admitted, "but I missed you more." He shrugged, daring anyone to challenge his claim, and my heart skipped a beat. Although I'd never welcomed my feelings for Ever before, I did today.

Mrs. McNamara came to stand next to us. "Bee, I'm glad to see you're feeling better," she greeted warmly.

"I am. Thank you."

She started to say something to her son when something caught her eye, drawing our attention as well. "Jamie, I need you to put at least two feet between you and those girls this instant. Don't make me call your mother."

I snickered at the panicked look on Jamie's face as he swam away.

Mrs. McNamara returned inside after giving everyone a final warning. The girls pouted when Jamie lifted his body from the pool, and my smugness fell away when I got a full look at his bare chest. He was still developing, but from the looks of it, he was developing well. I watched transfixed as beads of water ran down his tanned skin, and suddenly, my tongue felt dangerously dry. Turning away, I stomped toward the table where Jamie had left the water and quickly unscrewed the cap on one before downing half the bottle. Feeling evil, I grabbed one of the cookies he obviously intended to hog for himself.

Jamie was at my side before I could take a bite.

"Those are mine," he growled.

"Mrs. Greene made them for everyone. You're supposed to share."

"Give it back," he demanded. Clearly, he hadn't heard a word I'd said.

"No." I started to bite into one when he snatched the cookie from my hand and pushed me down. I grunted in pain when I hit the concrete, but Jamie had little remorse as he slowly licked the cookie without taking his gaze from me. Once finished, he did the same thing to the others.

"Still want one?"

I didn't say anything as rage boiled the blood in my veins. Before I knew it, I was on my feet, enjoying the flash of fear in Jamie's eyes as I charged for him. My hands slammed against his wet chest and sent him sprawling back into the pool. The girls he'd been flirting with were once again scrambling for safety. I watched, feeling triumphant as he struggled to break free of the water. Once he finally did, he sputtered to catch his breath.

The cookies he'd tried to hog floated around him in a soggy mess.

"Hey, Jamie?" I called once he had cleared his lungs. He was still blinking the water from his eyes, but I could see the anger in them when they landed on me. "Still want one?"

"Daaaamn, Bee," Vaughn whispered.

I was startled to find Ever, Vaughn, and Jason standing behind me. I hadn't even noticed Vaughn and Jason had left the pool. I knew they'd been reacting to instinct at seeing me get pushed down. It wasn't the first time a boy tried to punk me, but Ever, Vaughn, and Jason were usually the ones fighting my battles.

Not this time.

Hearing water splash, I turned my attention to the pool in time to see Jamie climbing over the edge. He started for me, and I took a step back at the look in his eyes.

He sent me running with three words.

"You're dead meat."

CHAPTER FOUR

The Punk

I STROLLED INTO THE KITCHEN AND FOUND MY UNCLE SIPPING AT HIS coffee with a newspaper in hand. "Late morning for you, isn't it?"

Even though it was a Sunday, my uncle rarely took a day off. I had the feeling he was trying to correct a mistake he made a long time ago. Sooner or later, he'd realize that he was on a suicide mission. My cousin was a lot of things, with manipulative asshole being at the top of the list, but he was no fool. When the truth came to light, there would be no amount of money that could compensate for the lies he'd been fed since he was a child.

"I thought I'd take the day off… handle some things on the home front."

His answer had me pausing, wondering what and how much he knew. He gave nothing away as he continued to sip at his coffee, but I knew better than to underestimate him.

"Have you seen Four?" he questioned as I poured a cup of coffee. "I need to talk to her about her mother."

I forced a frown, feigning confusion as I took a sip from my mug. "She's not in her room?"

"I knocked on her door but got no answer. I checked all the spares and then everywhere else. The only rooms I haven't checked yet is yours… and my son's."

I choked on my coffee.

When I finally caught my breath, blinking to clear my vision as well, my voice was hoarse when I spoke. "She probably went over to Tyra's." This early in the morning, I doubted it, but what else was there to say? Uncle Thomas had finally handed over the keys to Four's bike when he came home early one day and caught Ever breaking into his safe. The confrontation had been amusing, to say the least, and was most likely the cause of my uncle's current suspicions. A lot of good it did Four since Ever still insisted most days that his woman ride with him.

"I thought that too, except her bike is still in the garage."

Snatching one of Mrs. Green's muffins from the wicker basket, I stuffed it into my mouth as fast as I could. I hated banana nut, but it was better than the shit that might come spewing out.

Amusement crossed Uncle Thomas's face before he sighed and set his mug on the table. "So be it."

I suddenly wished I hadn't left my phone in my room as I watched him stroll from the kitchen. There was no way for me to warn Four and Ever about the coming storm, so I popped a squat and grabbed another muffin, then remembered it was banana nut and tossed it to the side. I started for the fridge when I remembered that just a few miles away, brunch would be taking place, and Ever, to his misfortune, wouldn't make it. It had been a month since the intervention, and not a goddamn thing had changed. Ever was still pretending he was in love with my girl, and Four and Bee were both going along with it. Something was up, and not knowing the answer kept me up at night. I'd long ago ceased considering the possibility that it could be true. Thanks to Four, I'd seen what Ever in love looked like. I'd also seen what Bee in love looked like. I'd felt it, too.

There was no fucking way those two shared it with each other.

Running upstairs, I quickly showered and dressed before grabbing my keys and phone and rushing out the door. My stomach growled all the way to my destination, not allowing me time to consider the consequences. When I was *this* hungry, there was only one girl who could sate me.

I flew through the Montgomery's open gates, and after hopping out of my ride, I rang the doorbell. To my immense surprise and displeasure an annoyed Barbette answered herself. Where the fuck was the help?

I hated whenever Bee caught me off guard because I'd forget that I wasn't in love with her anymore. Since we couldn't turn back time, our only option would be to move forward.

Let's just say it will be a cold day in hell before I give her my heart again.

"What are you doing here?"

Rather than answer, I forced her back as I stepped inside and shut the door behind me. I didn't bother to speak until I ran my eyes over every inch of her. She looked soft and pliable in the daisy-printed sundress, and even though she was made of thorns, I briefly entertained the idea of ripping off that deceitful dress and having my way with the ice queen.

"Where's your father?"

"He's on the patio. What—"

"Show me," I demanded before she could waste more of my time. As far as I was concerned, all her fucking questions were rhetorical. No one was going to stop me from doing whatever the hell I wanted. She should know firsthand by now. Placing my hand at the small of her back when she crossed her arms, refusing to move, I forced her out to the patio where her parents waited.

Her father shot up from his seat the moment he laid eyes on me while her mother gripped the string of pearls wrapped around her lovely neck. Suddenly, I was very fearful of Barbette turning out like her.

Over my dead body.

"Oh, dear." Mrs. Montgomery gasped as if she could read my thoughts.

There was no question that I was up to no good. Coming in peace was simply not my style. Pulling out Bee's chair, I gestured for her to sit, and she sank wide-eyed.

"What the hell is he doing here?" her father raged.

"Elliot," I greeted as I sat in the chair next to Bee. The food looked delicious, so I immediately helped myself. "I hope you don't mind," I said as I poured OJ into the waiting glass set for my cousin, "but I came to deliver a message."

"Which is?" Montgomery barked.

"I'm afraid my cousin won't make it."

"And why should we believe you?"

"The choice is entirely up to you, old man. I figured me telling you would be better than getting stood up." *You should be thanking me, you prick.*

"He couldn't call?" Mrs. Montgomery gently inquired.

"He had his hands full, and now he's tied up." I started stuffing my face with the fluffy golden Belgian waffles they had on silver platters.

"Aren't those the same thing?" Elliot snapped.

I had my mouth full, so I took my time answering as I chewed slowly. "I can't answer that without feeling sorry for your wife, Mr. Montgomery."

I heard Bee's sharp inhale and placed my hand on her bare knee. Instead of feeling comforted, however, she tensed, and suddenly the waffles tasted like ash in my mouth. Losing my appetite, I started to stand and get the fuck out of there when I felt her soft hand quickly grab mine. Slowly, the tension left her body, and I couldn't help meeting her gaze. She still looked nervous, and after a glance at her father, I understood why. I might have been playing a game, but this was anything but to her.

All I could do was brush my thumb across her skin, letting her know that I understood. After a few seconds, she freed my hand. I threw my elbow over the back of my chair before regarding her parents.

"Do you honestly think I'm going to allow your daughter to marry my cousin?" I blurted.

After their shock cleared, Elliot slammed his fist on the table. I stared back at him, amused by his display. "I want you out of my home. *Right now.*"

I cleaned my mouth with the cloth napkin as I rose to my feet. "Gladly." As I looked down at his daughter, my heart leaped when I found her watching me like she didn't want me to go. "Walk me to the door?"

"She'll do no such thing!" Elliot roared.

If you asked me, he was being a little dramatic.

Ignoring his tantrum, I pulled back Bee's chair and took her hand as we headed for the patio doors.

"You know I'm going to be the one dealing with him when you leave," she snapped.

I gripped her hand a little tighter even as I shrugged. "If he gives you any real trouble, call me. You better fucking believe I'm coming right back."

"What exactly do you think you can do?" she scoffed. "He's my father."

When we reached the door, I turned to her, not surprised to find that her parents had been hot on our heels. They wisely stood back and watched us with their mouths shut. "But I'm the one with all the real power." Deciding to fuck with her father, I kept my gaze on Elliot as I bent to kiss her forehead. "You're mine. You've always been. You always will be."

I made sure he'd heard me too.

Barbette inhaled, and I could feel the hope in every breath she took after. "I don't know if that's true."

"Because you're lying to yourself."

I didn't linger after that. I'd already stayed too long. Too much time in her presence and the heart Barbette had crushed a thousand times would begin to wonder.

Not wanting to go home to brood, I found myself at Aunt

Evelyn's rental. The car Unc leased for her was parked outside. He could pretend all he wanted, but he still cared. My aunt was a capable woman, but he still took care of her despite his fury.

I shook my head as I let myself in since the door wasn't fucking locked and came face-to-face with a man I recognized. I was sure I was staring at a fucking ghost.

The only thing that distinguished this tall, bearded man from his son were his gray eyes instead of Ever's gold and the gray peppering his dark-brown hair. I even knew a chin dimple was hidden underneath the short hairs covering his lower face.

"How the fuck… *what* the fuck?"

"You must be Jamie," Sean greeted.

"And you're clearly not as dead as everyone thinks you are."

"Lucky for you," he retorted dismissively. "You and my sons would be dead, otherwise."

I frowned, not knowing which of his claims to focus on or address first. "Sons?" I echoed after choosing.

As in more than one?

I couldn't pretend I didn't know Ever's true paternity, but I truly had no idea there was another kid out there with the same deadbeat for a father. *Lucky him.*

I wondered who the poor bastard could be. There wasn't much I knew about Sean other than he used to be best friends with my uncle and father. His parents, who, after thirty years of no contact, assumed he was dead, still came to family functions. Six months ago, they'd shared Thanksgiving dinner with us. Bart and Claire Kelly were kind people who didn't deserve this piece of shit for a son. Three decades and they still mourned him, for fuck's sake.

Before he could elaborate, Aunt Evelyn drifted into the foyer with a questioning look until she noticed me standing there. Panic replaced her confusion as she quickly closed her robe. Was she fucking kidding?

"Jamie, honey, what are you doing here?"

"What are *you* doing?"

"I was just—I—"

"You should know," I said, cutting her off before she could insult my intelligence, "your son is probably on his way over here as we speak." I made sure to make eye contact with them both when I mentioned Ever. "You need to leave," I told Sean when he continued to stand there.

His only response was to cross his arms over his chest as he stared me down. "Maybe it's time he met me."

"You mean after you've been absent from his life for eighteen fucking years? Sorry, but he's not interested."

Okay, I had no right to speak for Ever, but I couldn't help my need to protect him. Ever was more than just my cousin; he was my best friend, and instinct was screaming at me not to trust his douchebag father. Thirty years ago, Sean Kelly set off a chain of events that led us all here, and now he's back to stir up more trouble.

He grinned as if I'd just told a joke, but his tone was wistful when he spoke. "Goddamn, boy, you remind me of your father. He was a nosy shit, too."

I took a step forward, ready to deliver the ass-kicking of the century, and probably get my ass handed to me too, when Aunt Evelyn intervened.

"Okay, Sean. It's time for you to go." She pushed him toward the door, and he let her.

"We'll continue our discussion later," he warned her when he was over the threshold.

"No the fuck you won't," I snarled before slamming the door in his face. Locking it, I rounded on the tiny woman who had caused so much confusion and pain and waited for her to explain.

"It's not what it looks like."

"I think it is. Did you sleep with him?"

"That's *none* of your business, Jameson!"

She had a fierce look in her eye that warned me not to push.

I'd never seen her this angry before. It was too bad I didn't give a shit.

"You did, didn't you?" I prodded. "You actually slept with him in the house my uncle, your *wedded husband*, is paying for."

"It's complicated, Jamie."

"Nothing is ever that complicated."

Reaching up, I thought she'd slap me, but she cupped my cheek instead. "Then you haven't yet experienced real life, my darling. I'd pray you never do, but I know it would be in vain."

My hands shook as my frustration surged to an all-time high. I wanted to reach for the smokes burning a hole in my pocket, but I refrained. "Why did you leave?" I blurted, causing her hand to fall. "Was it really that bad?"

"I can't discuss that with you, Jamie, but I want you to know that I had the best intentions."

Suddenly, I recalled Lou's cynical view that no one truly knows what's best for you other than yourself. I was starting to agree with her. Look at the havoc we often wreak on one another in the name of love. For some reason, my mind drifted to Bee before I shook my head. I couldn't think about her right now.

"You nearly destroyed them," I announced, refusing to beat around the bush. "I don't know what's keeping Unc together, but if it weren't for Four, Ever would still be a shell. He wasn't the same after you left. He thinks he drove you away."

I didn't miss Evelyn's subtle eye roll at the mention of Four, but her next words kept me from calling her out on it.

"Ever is what's keeping Thomas together."

I nodded, accepting her answer. Blood or no blood, Uncle Thomas loved Ever as if he were his own. "Maybe, but he needs his wife."

Turning her nose up, she headed for the kitchen. "Seems like he's moved on just fine to me."

My gaze narrowed on her retreating back. "Is that what this is… you're jealous?"

She didn't answer me as she filled a tea kettle with water.

"Aunt Evelyn," I said with more bass in my tone than proper etiquette allowed.

"Jamie, you already have so much to worry about. This is between Thomas and me." Meeting my gaze, she forced a smile. "I hear you're heading to Penn this fall."

I flinched at the reminder. It was a well-kept secret that I was attending the Ivy League after graduation. With an expulsion on my record, I didn't even want to know how much my uncle had to donate to make that happen. Even with a prestigious degree in hand, I wasn't convinced I'd have it easy in corporate America. No matter how savvy my brain or how big the boardroom I commanded, all anyone would ever see was some arrogant punk with too many tattoos under the expensive suit. A part of me had hoped they would get me out of my duty, but the only other eligible heir was my seven-year-old siblings.

Regardless, I was resigned to my fate. It wasn't like I had any other options. My future had been mapped out long before I could even begin to have dreams, so whenever Thomas deemed me ready, I would take over as head of the family... and overseer of our billion-dollar fortune. It was the real reason I was shipped back to the States, after all, while my mother and siblings stayed behind in Ireland.

The stipulations put in place when NaMara was founded nearly a century ago required a blood heir to assume the helm. Naturally, anyone would assume Ever, as Thomas's sole heir, would take over the role, but Ever wasn't a McNamara. He was a Kelly.

And soon, the well-kept secret would unravel.

Ironically, I was envious of him. I didn't exactly relish the idea of being responsible for an entire clan, most of whom I'd never even met. Every decision I made henceforth would affect entire generations. Acting in my best interest would be a thing of the past.

Minutes later, I was scarfing down the turkey sandwich Aunt Evelyn made when the front door opened, and Ever stormed inside with a duffel and a look to kill.

"Unc kicked you out, huh?"

Evelyn immediately rushed over to her son, but he stepped away when she tried to touch him. The cold look he gave her made me shake my head. It was hard to believe he was the same person who risked his life to bring her home. Now that she'd finally returned, he wanted nothing to do with her.

"Dad said I have to stay here."

It was the only explanation he gave before charging up the stairs. I didn't need to ask why he'd been kicked out, but I doubt he'd enlighten his mother.

"A word of advice," I said as I stood to leave. "Stop pretending as if everything is back to normal. You left them to fend for themselves. Sooner or later, you're going to have to explain yourself."

The next morning, I was alone in the kitchen, shoveling eggs down my throat when Four stomped in wearing her school uniform. I tried not to admire how great her legs looked in that skirt. I'd only end up picturing Bee's much longer ones wrapped around my neck anyway.

"Why are you looking at me like that?" Her nostrils flared a little, making it clear she was in a foul mood and looking for a fight.

Deciding not to tease her, I shrugged. "Just impressed you're still here and not over at Aunt Evelyn's by now."

"Why would I be over there?"

I sighed. Why the hell couldn't I just keep my fucking mouth closed sometimes? I wasn't in a much better mood than Four, so I wouldn't be getting any of my usual enjoyment from dropping bombs. Setting down my fork full of eggs, I held her troubled gaze. "Because he's living there now." I waited to see how she'd handle the news before I gave her the rest. "Unc kicked him out yesterday."

I went back to eating, hoping she wouldn't demand answers that Ever should give himself. Frankly, if it didn't concern Bee, it didn't concern me. It seemed selfish to think so, but avenging my broken heart kept my hands full, so… what could I do?

Four didn't stick around, and I finished my food before heading up to get dressed. Uncle Thomas was expecting me for yet another damn meet and greet at company headquarters. I didn't understand the demand. It would be years before I took control, but I suppose my uncle was unwilling to leave a single stone unturned.

On my way to the garage an hour later, I typed out a text as I did every morning.

Sleep well?

Pocketing my phone, I didn't wait for a reply I knew would never come. I was pulling out of the garage minutes later when my cell whistled, indicating I had a text. Slamming on the brakes, I snatched it from my pocket and read the message.

Bee: Like a baby.

Before I could respond, a second text came through, and I felt like a kid in a candy store.

Bee: Disappointed?

Never. You were dreaming of me.

Bee: Was that a question?

I think the period makes it clear that it wasn't. Were your panties soaked?

I watched the bubbles move until they stopped. Smirking, I threw my phone in the cup holder, knowing that I'd run her off. I'd just made it through the gates when my phone pinged. Foolishly, I kept going as I glanced at the screen.

Bee: I wasn't wearing any.

I swerved, nearly taking out the fucking mailbox before I

slammed on the brakes and threw the Jeep into park. I stabbed at the screen. Two words were all I could manage.

Show me.

As far as I was concerned, I needed pictures, or it didn't happen. I ran my hand down my face as I watched those fucking bubbles appear and disappear for two minutes straight.

Bee: You're too late. I'm already dressed for school.

She was toying with me. I knew this, but I also couldn't help myself. Before I could rethink it, I was calling her. It rang and rang, and just when voicemail was ready to pick up, I heard her voice, hesitant yet full of humor.

"Jameson."

"Maybe you didn't understand me," I snapped, getting right to it. "Pull down that lacy thong I know you're wearing and *show me*."

"And if I don't?"

"Then I'll do it myself." She was quiet for a while, and my eyes narrowed as my thoughts took a turn down a wild road. "But you'd like that, wouldn't you?"

"Goodbye, Jameson."

The line beeped, indicating she'd hung up, and I chuckled, knowing that my afternoon was looking up. I walked into the tower, which held NaMara's headquarters, with an extra pep in my step and whistled as I made my way to the fortieth floor. My uncle kept the entire floor for himself and a few other executives. Christina, his assistant, was already there to greet me, telling me he was expecting me, and I flirted a bit before knocking on my uncle's office door.

I could hear shuffling on the other side, but it was a few minutes before my uncle's gruff voice called out. Hesitantly, I entered, and when I saw my uncle's tense expression, I stopped short. It wasn't until I noticed the man lounging against the wall behind him that I realized why and wondered what I'd just walked in on.

"Uncle?"

"Come in, boy. Don't just stand there."

Glancing once more at Sean, I shut the door behind me and took a seat. My gaze traveled back and forth between the two men. Something was definitely up.

"You look like you have something on your mind," Sean teased.

Ignoring him, I addressed my uncle. "You knew he was alive?" I'd been practicing all night how I'd break the news that his so-called friend had faked his death. Only to find that he'd known all along.

"It's complicated," he said, making me scoff. Why were adults always using that excuse?

"As complicated as him fucking Aunt Evelyn?" I wasn't entirely sure what I'd walked in on yesterday, either, but they'd been up to *something*. I've had more than my share to know what it looked like.

After glancing at Sean, who offered nothing at all, Thomas met my gaze once more. "Watch your mouth, Jameson. That's your aunt you're talking about."

"Suddenly, you're concerned about her welfare? You've tucked her away and ignored her."

"I'll deal with my wife as I see fit *when* I see fit," he rebutted.

I didn't get the chance to call him an asshole before Sean left his place against the wall and began kneading my uncle's shoulders. I squinted as confusion rippled through me at the display. "Clearly, I'm the reason the boy is challenging you, so I'll go."

I sneered at Sean when he smiled at me and wished he truly was dead. It was clear to me that he had both my aunt *and* uncle under some sort of spell.

"We'll talk more later," was all my uncle said in response.

Sean didn't linger, but my murderous rage did long after he was gone. As someone who was usually up to no good, it was easy to spot another troublemaker.

"I'd say I'm surprised at you," my uncle drawled once the

door closed, "but I'd be lying to myself." When I said nothing, he sighed and grabbed his suit jacket as he stood. "Very well. Let's get started."

After my uncle finally released me for the day, I went straight to Aunt Evelyn's, wondering if I'd find Sean there. If my uncle insisted I get a head start learning how to lead this family, then I didn't see why I couldn't take some initiative.

Fortunately, when I arrived at the rental home, I only found my cousin sitting alone in the dark. Ever was slouched low, head resting against the back of the cushions with his eyes closed, but I could still see the scowl behind that perfectly blank expression.

"Still pouting, huh?"

"What are you doing here?" he asked without opening his eyes.

I took a seat on the extra-wide armchair and shrugged even though he couldn't see me. "Checking on Aunt Evelyn since neither you or Uncle Thomas seem concerned."

Slowly, his eyes opened, and that golden gaze of his glistened. I could tell he wanted to hit me, though he probably wanted to hit his father more.

His attention moved from my face, and I held my breath as he slowly took in my attire. I waited for him to say something—anything. After a few seconds, his eyes drifted shut again, and I swallowed the urge to scream at him. He knew, dammit. He had to know.

Our entire family was on pins and needles, waiting for the day Ever would just call us all on our shit. I think we were all hoping for it because none of us were too eager to sink the knife in his back any farther. He was one of our own, and no DNA test could convince us otherwise. Though Ever was a McNamara legally and in name, it wasn't good enough for Conall, our great-great-grandfather who'd been dead and rotting for almost forty years. I didn't want to disrespect the dead or anything, but seriously, fuck him.

"You can't hide from her forever," I said when the silence began to eat at me.

"I wasn't planning to," he mumbled.

"Then let me be more specific. You won't be able to avoid her much longer without pissing her off."

"I know that," he snapped.

Deciding not to push, I grabbed the duffel at my feet and headed upstairs. After changing in one of the guest rooms, I returned to the living room to find Ever with one foot out the front door. I knew exactly where he was headed, and since he'd read my mind, I decided to catch a ride. Gas was freaking expensive.

Ever didn't say a word when he looked over his shoulder and found me heading toward his matte green G-Wagon. The moment my ass hit the leather seat, I whipped out my phone.

Last chance… for old time's sake.

Biting back a grin, I synced my Bluetooth and played *What If I Was Nothing* by All That Remains. Ten minutes later, we were walking through Brynwood's front doors, and just as we were ready to go our separate ways, my phone chimed in my hand.

As if my dick had consciousness, it woke the fuck up. My hands shook as I stumbled to open the text app.

Disappointment whipped through me like a cold breeze when I saw it was only Four. However, that disappointment turned to concern when I actually read the message.

Four: SOS—girls' bathroom

Frowning, I showed the text to Ever who, after a mere glance, took off down the hall. Leave it to him to know exactly where she'd be. Smirking, I followed after him, and when he attempted to charge into the bathroom, I stopped him.

"Let me," I said when he glared at my hand on his arm. "She must have texted me and not you for a reason."

"Yeah," he agreed, nostrils flaring. "To piss me off."

I barely fought back my grin because he was probably right. Four was a little firecracker, and she'd probably knee me in the balls for saying so.

"Just in case, let me go in first. If we're not out in five minutes—"

"Two," he said, cutting me off.

I was pretty sure the asshole was already counting down in his head, so I didn't waste time arguing. I rushed through the doors and stopped short at the sight of Four and a girl whose name escaped me. She reminded me of a chipmunk because she never seemed to stop talking. And girls like her loved to gossip most of all.

It only took me two seconds to assess the situation Four had found herself in.

"This is the girls' bathroom!" the chipmunk chirped.

"Oh, is it? My mistake." Circling my prey, I eyed her up and down. With tits like hers, she had potential. "It must have been fate, though."

"Why is that?"

"Because you're here," I flirted. A breathless sound escaped her as her eyelashes fluttered. *Gotcha.* I cleared my throat when, from the corner of my eye, I caught Four making a beeline for the door. She glanced at me over her shoulder with her eyebrow raised, and I mouthed, "You owe me," as I felt up my new friend.

Amused, Four gave me a curt nod before rushing out the door with thirty seconds to spare. I turned my attention back to my furry little friend, who was still shivering in my arms.

"So, what's your name?" I asked as I lifted her onto the counter. My thumb swept her knee as I waited.

"Amanda. We had Econ together, remember?"

Fuck no. She was hot, so I'd definitely noticed her, but she was delusional if she thought I was keeping tabs. "Last name?" I asked, ignoring her question.

"Clarke," she supplied with a pout.

"Clarke," I echoed with my most charming grin. I had all the information I needed to move forward. "You're pretty cute, Clarke. Can I make you come?" My hand was already inching up her skirt, rubbing her thigh while her lips parted and closed like a fish out of water. The bathroom door burst open before she could answer, and Vaughn sauntered in with a scowl.

"Jesus, I thought Ever was kidding!" he yelled. He'd literally caught me with my hand in the cookie jar. "The fuck are you doing in here, man?"

Shrugging, I turned my attention back to Amanda and found her staring at Vaughn like she was starstruck. "Just doing what I can for the fam." Reaching satin panties, I slipped them to the side. "So what do you say, pretty girl? Two fingers or one?"

Her gaze traveled back to Vaughn. "Is he—is he going to watch?"

I sank my teeth into my bottom lip to fight my grin. "We won't tell if you don't," I assured her.

The bathroom door opened, and a girl ventured inside. She froze from shock at seeing us there, but before she could demand answers, Vaughn's head shot up from his phone.

"Don't you see us having a private conversation?" he barked. Spinning on her heel, she hurried back out. As if we weren't the ones in violation, Vaughn shook his head and muttered, "So fucking inconsiderate."

He went back to fiddling with his phone while Amanda watched. I snorted because he was so far out of her reach he might as well have been a mythical creature.

"Sorry, kitten. Doesn't seem like Rees is interested, but you know what they say… once you go black, you never go back."

I caught Vaughn's scowl in the mirror and grinned. He didn't seem too pleased by my observation, but what was even more notable was that he didn't deny it. This thing he had for Tyra was deeper than he was willing to admit aloud or to himself. Probably because he knew it was hopeless. They had no future. His father would never allow it simply because of how hard he'd so obviously fallen for Ty-baby.

"Maybe you can change his mind," I cooed as I slipped her panties off. "Spread your legs for me." It took only a second of hesitation before she did just that. It was all I could do not to shake my head. Girls couldn't even be bothered to make it a challenge anymore. "Wider."

She did as instructed until there was nothing left to the imagination.

The next few minutes, I spent with my fingers shoved in her cunt and could only be described as clinical, cold, and awkward. Not that Amanda noticed. In fact, she enjoyed it so much she soaked the bottom of my fucking T-shirt.

Little miss chipmunk was a squirter.

I heard Vaughn sigh as I stood back and admired my handiwork. Amanda was slumped against the mirror, completely boneless and out of breath. "About fucking time," he griped as he came to stand beside me. "I could have finished her in two."

"And you would have lost that hand," I said, reminding him of Tyra.

He ignored me as he stared down Amanda. The invitation in her eyes couldn't be mistaken, but a moment later, there was only absolute fear.

"We hear you like to talk. That's something we have in common," he said before she could answer. "And if you speak on whatever it is you think you know about Four and Ever…" I watched him press play before flipping around his phone. "I'll post this on every porn site I know."

Her eyes widened as I listed them on my fingers. "Pornhub, XNXX, XVIDEOS, xHamster, RedTube."

"Don't forget YouPorn," Vaughn added.

I scoffed. "How the fuck could I? They've got the dirtiest blondes."

"True."

Plucking Amanda's purple thong from the floor, I held them out of reach when she tried to snatch them away. "Ah ah ah... souvenir." I shoved them in my pocket as I watched her look back and forth between Vaughn and me. "I know what you're thinking," I said when she couldn't seem to find the words, "and no, we're not bluffing."

We stepped aside while Amanda climbed down from the counter, and when she scurried for the door, I realized she was smarter than I gave her credit. This was not a situation she could argue her way out of.

As soon as the door closed, Vaughn rolled his eyes and deleted the video. Of course, we never had any intention of posting some shit like that online. A lifelong punishment like that didn't quite fit the crime of sticking your nose where it didn't belong. This was just high school. The shit ends.

"You're not going to save that for your spank bank?" I asked as I washed my hands not once but twice. No matter how hard I scrubbed however, they still felt dirty. This was probably the first time I hadn't enjoyed making a girl come.

Vaughn groaned as his head fell back on his shoulders. "The last fucking thing I need is Tyra finding this shit on my phone."

"Why the hell would you give her your password?"

"Give?" He sneered. "I didn't *give* her shit. Her nosy ass must have watched me punch in the code."

I snickered as I dried my hands. "So change it," I challenged, knowing that he wouldn't.

"Fuck you," he spat back.

We both burst into laughter as I tossed the paper towel in the trash. Heading for the door, I paused when I realized Vaughn was creeping toward one of the stalls. "Where the fuck are you going?"

"I gotta shit," he threw over his shoulder.

It was more than enough explanation for me. I was so busy

digging in my back pocket for my phone as I rushed through the bathroom door that I ended up colliding into something soft. The moment I recognized Bee's strawberry locks, I grabbed her waist to keep her from getting away. "Looking for me?"

I watched her blink those baby blues a few times before frowning in confusion at the bathroom door behind me. "What are you doing here?" she questioned while ignoring mine. "And what were you doing in the girls' bathroom?"

Leaning down, I buried my nose in her hair and inhaled. Her sweet scent was playing chemical warfare with my brain. "Looking for you." Technically, it was only partly true, but she didn't need to know that.

"Let me go, Jamie."

Somehow, I knew she wasn't talking about physically. "I can't do that." My hands dropped to the back of her thighs before slowly making their way up. She'd worn her uniform without stockings today, and I felt like a kid in a very naughty candy store. "Because, unlike you, I keep my promises."

Her eyes rounded at the sound of fabric tearing, and I watched her lips part in shock after I held up her lacy red thong. There was no fucking way she hadn't worn these for me. Red was our favorite color.

"How thoughtful of you," I cooed while she continued to gape at me. Shoving my hand inside my pocket, I tossed the purple satin aside and replaced them with the red lace. I'd rather have Bee's scraps any day.

"You're a pervert," she spat, finally breaking free of her shock.

"You won't get any argument from me."

Her eyes became twin balls of blue flames, and even though she was glaring at me, my heart leaped with joy, seeing her fire that I'd missed so much. "Do you honestly think treating me like I'm some whore turns me on? You repulse me."

"And I believe you. I also know it's why you want me, too."

I pressed my lips against her neck and felt her body shiver as I worked my way up. "Because it feels wrong," I whispered in her ear, "and you always liked getting your hands dirty, didn't you, kitten?"

I didn't wait for a reply and left her standing there.

Outside, I managed to catch up to Four and Ever as they stood by his truck. There was zero space between them as he held her, making no mistake as to what they were up to. I shook my head, knowing anyone could have walked up. I wasn't about to finger-fuck the entire school because they couldn't be bothered to be more careful with their secrets.

Four noticed me first and raised an eyebrow. "What's up, quick draw?"

Snickering, I hopped onto the G-Wagon and shoved a cigarette between my lips. My hands shook as I lit up, and since I couldn't have what I really needed, nicotine would have to do. "She wouldn't shut up long enough for me to get my dick out. I fingered her, though. Did you know she's a squirter?"

"TMI, Buchanan. And it's not gentlemanly to kiss and tell," Four scolded.

"I didn't kiss her."

"And my cousin is no gentleman," Ever added.

"Learned from the best, little cousin."

"I'm a changed man."

I cut my gaze his way. "Until Bee's around." I could practically see Ever imagining ways to murder me as if his thoughts were playing on a high-definition screen. "My bad."

I wasn't the least bit fucking sorry, but he could take it or leave it. It was my ex-girlfriend and best friend he was playing, and for whatever reason, Bee was allowing him to string her along.

I lit my fag as Four whispered something to Ever. Whatever she said, calmed him—not that I gave a shit. However bad Ever wanted a fight, I wanted it ten times more.

"Get in the truck," he ordered. I smirked, remembering a

time when he eagerly followed orders rather than dished them out. "You too," he said to Four.

As Four rounded the hood for the passenger side, she said, "There's your one."

Snorting, I hopped in the back, and then Ever announced that we were going shopping.

"You're sure you took care of that issue?" Ever asked me, referring to Amanda. Four, who I had a feeling wouldn't approve of our problem-solving methods, was in the back, trying on dresses. We were surrounded by them in various colors, lengths, and volumes, though the raised marble platform took up most of the main room. Ever had taken Four to this overly posh boutique in town that had a waiting list six months long. Bechette, the forty-something French woman who owned it was in high demand. Not to mention sexy as fuck. It was too bad my game didn't work on girls who'd graduated high school.

"Do you even have to ask?"

Unbeknownst to Four, the whispers about their true relationship had grown louder for some reason, and until today, we hadn't tracked down the source.

Ever sighed, and I could literally see the weight lift from his shoulders, although the worry still lingered in his eyes. "Thanks, man."

I shrugged. "We're family." And I didn't just mean Ever, but Four too. I'd do anything for them, even though they were both pissing me off. Whatever was going on between Ever and Bee, Four was now a part of it, and none of them held any reservations about lying to me.

As if reading my thoughts, Ever rounded on me. "Whatever you're thinking, get it out of your head. I'm not screwing you over."

"I beg to fucking differ. I'd never let Four keep secrets from you."

The muscle in his jaw ticked as he looked away. As much as he wanted to argue, I knew he couldn't. There wasn't a damn thing about Four that Ever would want to be kept from him. For *any* reason.

I'd done my own digging, but nothing surfaced except some sold-off assets. It wasn't unusual to reallocate your funds. I just needed to track down where the hell the money had gone. I'd long ago dismissed the idea that the Montgomery's were bankrupt, but the thought was always there. If they were broke, then what role did Ever play in all of this? Surely, he didn't actually intend to marry her. While that would fix all the Montgomerys' problems, it would ruin our relationship for good after I fucked his wife on their wedding night.

Before my thoughts could run even wilder, the vision that pushed through the curtains stole my attention. Four looked shy and uncertain as she waited for Ever to notice her. Clearing my throat, I nodded, prompting Ever to spin around. I didn't need to see his face to know he was captivated. What red-blooded male wouldn't be? Four wasn't just beautiful; she was breathtaking.

Her gaze found mine, and I gave her a nod of approval, but her attention had already turned back to Ever. Subtly, I nudged him with my elbow.

Say something, jackass.

"Do you like it?" she asked when he couldn't seem to find the words.

"I want to tear it off you." Ever's voice was thick, husky, but Four still somehow misinterpreted his meaning.

"I guess that's a no," she mumbled, looking ready to run for the safety of the curtain. It was hard to believe that she was no longer a virgin. Perhaps she was reluctant to believe him since she still hid in his shadow while he paraded around town with *my* girl on his arm.

Ever was up and on the platform before Four could flee. "It's a goddamn yes, princess." Lifting her chin, he kissed her lips. "You've never looked more beautiful."

As I rolled my eyes, my gaze landed on a red number. The gold and pearl beading twinkled under the bright spotlight while the low-cut bodice and short skirt promised to put on a show. The sheer, red overlaying skirt was dramatically full and overly long, promising to trail the ground with each step. I knew in that instant that I wouldn't be going to prom solo.

"Well?" Bechette inquired as she stepped into the room. "Will it do or not?"

"Oh, it will do," Ever drawled.

"I'm impressed," I chimed in while Bechette and Four exchanged knowing smiles. "She almost looks like a girl." Ever drew Four to his body protectively when she looked ready to give me a piece of her mind. I dismissed them both and regarded the dressmaker. "Ms. Martin. I'd like to purchase one of your dresses for my date."

"Date?" Four echoed. "You have a date? Who is this girl? I must warn her."

"None of your business."

"I'm sorry," Bechette said before Four could interrogate me further, "but I work by appointment only, and I'm afraid I've been booked for months."

"Then how were you able to see us today?" Four questioned with a frown. "I didn't have an appointment."

"And I'm certain you did."

I wonder if Four knew there were stars in her eyes when she gazed up at Ever. "You made the appointment?" When Ever nodded, she added, "When?"

"Three months ago."

My gaze narrowed, and I had the urge to pummel Ever's face until he looked like a deflated beach ball. The intervention had only been a month ago. He'd known all along that he was taking Four. So where the fuck did that leave Bee?

"But you hadn't asked me to go."

"I didn't know I needed to."

"This is all disgustingly sweet," I cut in while trying not to gag. It was getting to be a chore hanging around the two love birds. "But I'm trying to make a transaction here." I turned to Bechette, who still had her nose in the air. "I don't need an appointment. I need that dress." I pointed to the red gown on display.

"Excuse me?" The dressmaker yelped. "Do you know how much that dress will cost?"

"I didn't ask for the price." It was clear she didn't know who the fuck I was. I could buy her and every gown in this goddamn shop without even nicking my pockets.

"Alterations will need to be made for a proper fit, and as I said, I'm booked."

"I already know her measurements."

"You will have to be absolutely sure, young man, or my beautiful design will be wasted."

"I'm sure."

"How?" Four blurted.

I sighed. I never realized before how goddamn nosy she was. "That's for me to know," I taunted after finally meeting her baffled gaze. My fingers curled around Bechette's elbow, and I pulled her aside, away from Four and Ever's prying ears. I waited while she donned a pair of reading glasses and pulled a notepad and pen from the pocket of her apron before reciting the information she needed.

"5 Round Hill Lane."

She peered at me over her thin frames. "Young man, that is an address. I need her waist, hips, and bust size."

"She's got perky B cups, a tiny waist that fits perfectly in my hands, and hips that are a little too narrow for all the babies she's going to give me one day, but fuck, Ms. Martin, no one's perfect."

Bechette flipped her notebook closed before pinning me with her glare. "As I already explained, young man, I'm booked and have no time to do a fitting."

"How much will it cost for you to make the time?"

"Much more than your mommy and daddy give you in allowance, sweetie."

I didn't say anything as I plucked the pen from her hand and wrote down a number. "You obviously don't know who the fuck I am," I teased when she gaped at the figure. "How soon can you get her fitted?"

CHAPTER FIVE

The Plaything

MY ENCOUNTER WITH JAMIE WAS STILL HEAVY ON MY MIND three days later. I'd spent the rest of the school day bare-assed and tugging on the ends of my skirt thanks to him. A whisper of wind was all it would have taken to make that day infinitely worse.

It was now Sunday morning. Mother's Day, to be exact, and so far, my weekend had been blissful because it was Jamie-free. Usually, he'd find one way or another to establish his presence, often without even being present at all. It was like he never wanted me to forget the promise he made me nearly a year ago. He was back, and I was screwed.

"Barbette, you're slouching," my mother observed, cutting into my private thoughts. It was a wonder I was able to still have them. One day, I'd be just another Melissa Montgomery—a modern-day, real-life Stepford wife. It was an inevitable future, wasn't it? Hearing my mother's veiled command, I straightened and found it impossible. I was so on edge that my spine might as well have been a steel rod. "Is something wrong?"

Her tone was soft. Indulgent. Anyone might think she actually cared. The real concern, however, was that I'd embarrass my father. We were having breakfast with the Portlands at the Blackwood Manor, a private country club where only the haughtiest of rich assholes convened. It wasn't enough to pay the hefty membership fee. You also needed a letter of recommendation from an active member. The Portlands had been my family's sponsor before they fled Blackwood Keep and the scandal their daughter had caused.

Four and a half years ago, Olivia had attempted suicide, and despite the rampant rumors, no one knew why. Olivia had been destined for popularity and beauty, and for her, it had been enough. Until it wasn't. No one noticed the light around her dimming until it was too late. Until she'd turned to her crush in a last-ditch effort and then realized Ever couldn't fill that void.

I hadn't seen my childhood friend in years, and truth be told, I wasn't sure if I could call myself her friend. We'd been different and distant despite our parents pushing us together. Mine hadn't approved of me pretending to be just another one of the boys and had hoped Olivia could unearth my more feminine side. Despite the fact that we shared zero interests, Olivia and I had become trusted allies.

Guilt was an impossible pill to swallow, but I grabbed my glass of water anyway and somehow refrained from gulping it down. I was only allowed the dainty sips my mother deemed appropriate of an up-and-coming socialite.

"No, mother. I'm having a lovely time." I turned to Mr. Portland to avoid my father's glare and offered him a charming smile. "Mr. Portland, will you be allowing my father a chance to win back some of the money you bested him out of last weekend?"

My parents and Mr. and Mrs. Portland chuckled. However, their response was stalled by their son approaching our table. Jason was dressed in the club required jacket and tie with slacks, and I knew instantly by the self-satisfied smirk that he'd heard my question. Most days, Jason couldn't tell his head from his ass, but he wasn't a complete idiot. He knew my family was broke, and even more daunting was that he knew what my father planned to do about it. He reveled in it, hoping for a chance to steal me from Ever and finally have revenge for his sister.

Anyone would think that my request was light-hearted teasing. However, the money my father lost playing golf had really set us back. The men who attended the club were high rollers who didn't gamble in mere tens or hundreds but rather tens *of* thousands. It was the kind of thing bored men with too much money did.

My father was a different story, however. I wouldn't be surprised if he were gambling in a foolish attempt to flip the little money we had left. Elliot Montgomery was sinking fast, and he was determined to bring my mother and me with him. It was anyone's guess how he'd managed to maintain our illusion of wealth this long, but I was sure I didn't want to know. Whatever it was would haunt me for the rest of my days. No matter how far away I got from him.

I could have run years ago when I found out his plans to marry me off and fatten his pockets, but the risk of being dragged back again kept me at bay. No one, not even Ever, knew about my single failed escape attempt. My father had made sure to keep it under wraps and painted an ugly picture of what would happen if I tried it again. I'd barely made it out of Blackwood Keep. It was a wonder how I'd make it all the way to Scotland.

Don't go there.

I realized it was no use as my mind drifted to Jamie anyway. I'd been desperate, not for salvation, but for the love I now know I didn't deserve. Knowing Jamie might have needed me, too, drove me to not care about the consequences if I were caught. I blamed my foolish heart and myself for following it, but never again.

I knew better this time.

"Mr. Montgomery, I'd be happy to play a few rounds with you," Jason offered as he took a seat. "That is if your future son-in-law doesn't mind." Jason made a show of looking at the empty setting next to me before looking around the dining room for Ever. "Is he here?"

The tension could have been cut with a knife, but I would

have much rather used it to slice Jason's balls, which had grown considerably in the years since he had left. He'd never been so bold before. Any sympathy I'd had for him had been washed away by his cruelty.

"I'm afraid not," my father answered before his gray brows furrowed. I knew the question that was coming next and took a deep breath. I'd already rehearsed my answer. "Where is Ever? Did he and his mother not receive our invitation?"

"Yes, Father, but since Mrs. McNamara only just returned to town, she didn't think it appropriate to celebrate the holiday." At least, that was what I imagined she'd say if I'd bothered to invite her. And Ever... God. Pretending to be my fiancé now that he was dating Four was complicated enough. Expecting him to celebrate Mother's Day with the woman who abandoned him for my benefit was too much to ask. The last thing I wanted was to push my best friend too far. He'd already given so much. And more than anything, I wish I'd never let him get involved.

"It's just as well," Mr. Portland said with a sniff. "Honestly, Elliot, I don't see how you can allow your daughter to marry that wretch after what he did to our Olivia."

"It's no wonder Evelyn left," Mrs. Portland chimed in. "Her son is a monster."

As if they'd conjured him up, I blinked stupidly at the tall figure crowding the entrance a moment later. His mother was at his side, and although Evelyn couldn't seem to take her eyes off her son, Ever didn't acknowledge her as he searched the crowded room for an empty table.

Forgetting the lie I'd just told my parents, my lips parted to call out to him. His name quickly became lodged in my throat at the sight of his cousin cockily sauntering past them and into the dining room.

Faintly, I heard my name being called, but I couldn't tear my gaze away from the vision Jamie created in dangerously sagging khaki Bermuda shorts and the black collared shirt hugging his chest. He was dressed no different than any other male member, but somehow, he'd made smart casual look sinfully appetizing. Perhaps it was the buttons he'd left undone, giving me and every housewife and debutante in the vicinity something to dream about later. He hadn't bothered to tuck the ends of his shirt, either, although it wouldn't have helped. Jamie's sex appeal wasn't exactly something you could mute.

He was out of place, making me wonder what the hell they were even doing here. I'd only just convinced myself that it was a coincidence they were here until I realized Jamie was making a beeline for our table, with Ever and his mother following closely behind.

My parents' backs were turned to the room, so they'd yet to see them approaching, but the Portlands had, and the air quickly became charged with seething anger and old hatred.

"Barbette, you seem tense," my mother observed while remaining completely oblivious. "Why don't you visit Klara today?"

Before I could answer her, welcoming the chance to escape, the trio reached our table.

"Well, isn't this a treat?" Jamie greeted.

Startled, my parents turned in their chairs to find Jamie, Ever, and Evelyn standing a couple of feet away. Of course, the only one who seemed to be enjoying this awkward encounter was Jamie.

The Portlands all had matching expressions of anger and distaste while my parents, caught in the middle, floundered for an appropriate reaction.

"Forgive me," my father stammered. "I'm afraid you caught us by surprise. Barbette was just telling us that you wouldn't be able to make it."

Jamie, finally gracing me with his attention, smirked. Looking away, I found both Evelyn and Ever frowning their confusion. Of course, neither had known anything about the invitation.

"Join us, won't you?" my mother graciously offered, which

saved them from responding and me from explaining. The moment the invitation was extended, Mr. Portland angrily slammed his napkin on the table and stormed away. His wife rushed after him, but their son lingered behind. Jason looked ready to retaliate for the intrusion and for much more while Ever and Jamie stared back at him unmoved. Eventually, painstakingly, he walked away.

"I apologize for the intrusion," Mrs. McNamara offered as Ever dutifully pulled a chair out for her. Kissing my cheek, he then took a seat between us while shame burned the skin of my nape. I knew Jamie had seen the affectionate display. There was only one empty seat left, and I held my breath, waiting for Jamie to take his place next to me.

"Nonsense," my mother lied with an awkward smile. "It's good to see you again, Evelyn. Perhaps we can finally discuss the wedding?"

As if I'd just been caught red-handed, my gaze flew to Jamie. He was already watching me, hands shoved in his pockets, smug expression gone. When my lips parted to say something, his eyebrow rose expectantly.

"Yes, I'd like that," Evelyn began before noticing that her nephew was still standing. "Jamie, aren't you going to sit?"

"Actually, I thought I'd play a round of golf."

"Golf? You don't golf," I blurted before I realized where I was and who was listening… and that Jamie wasn't mine. The hush that fell over the table as I became the focus had me squirming in my seat.

I was expecting to see smug satisfaction when I peeked at Jamie through my eyelashes. Instead, there was only lust.

He sank his teeth into his bottom lip and lowered his eyelids until he looked sleepy and hungry all at once. "You don't know me anymore, Bette. There are a lot of things I do now, and I do them stunningly well."

Before anyone could respond to Jamie's blatant innuendo, he spun on his heel and strolled from the room. His presence hadn't gone unnoticed, and neither had his departure. I'd seen more than one wandering eye follow him from the room. Jamie was the kind of thrill every girl sought at least once in her life.

Maybe that was all he'd been for me, too.

Except... thrills weren't supposed to last this long, were they?

Feeling an elbow nudge into my side, I turned my head just as Ever leaned over with a goofy grin. "You're drooling," he teased.

"I am not."

He gave me a knowing look before glancing at our parents, who were discussing venues. We hadn't even set a date yet, though none of them seemed to have noticed.

"What are you even doing here?" I asked.

Scratching his head, he shrugged. "It was either here or Denny's."

"I mean, what are you doing here with your mom?" I clarified. "Does this mean you've forgiven her?" I tried to fight back the hope swelling in my chest, but it was impossible. I remembered how devastated Ever was when his mother left and how he blamed himself. She was back now, and even though I didn't know the *hows* or *whys*, I was hoping they could reconcile.

Blowing out air, he looked away before responding. "My dad said he'd consider letting me move back in for the summer if I spent time with her today, okay?"

I glared at the asshat I called my best friend. The only thing keeping me from punching him in the nose was the fact that he at least appeared contrite.

"You're both idiots," I spat.

Pushing his hair back from his forehead, he sighed. "I know."

"You'll have to talk to her eventually, you know."

"Debatable."

"She loves you, Ever."

He finally looked at me, and the sadness in his eyes made me want to wrap him in a warm blanket. "Then why did she leave?"

I didn't have an answer for him, so I said nothing. Sometimes it was best to let people feel whatever the hell they wanted until they were ready to listen to reason.

"What do you two think of having a September wedding?" my mother questioned.

Ever and I both offered distracted shrugs, earning our parents' displeased frowns. The only one who seemed truly disturbed by our lack of excitement was Evelyn. My parents didn't give a shit about my happiness.

"Is everything okay?" Mrs. McNamara inquired. She placed her palm over my mine, and her warmth spread through me. My own mother was busy clutching the pearls she refused to let my father sell.

"Kids," my father said with a chuckle. "They're probably more eager to plan their summer than their wedding."

"We were hoping we could just elope and get it over with," Ever said with a smirk.

The table suddenly rattling distracted our parents from the pain that twisted Ever's features when I brought my heel down on his shin.

"Get it over with?" his mother echoed slowly. Her concern and confusion couldn't be masked, and who could blame her? She'd blown back into town to find her husband had started a new family, and her son was engaged at eighteen. Her world wasn't simply turned upside down. It was mangled to hell.

"Oh, dear," my mother teased with a wavering smile. "I think he's just eager for the honeymoon." It sounded more like a question.

Ever was still grimacing as he nodded. "Yeah, that's it." He then shot an evil look my way as I primly took a sip of my water.

"I think I'll have that massage," I announced as I stood from the table without asking my father's permission to leave. I didn't miss his frown, but for once, I didn't care. Let him make a scene. I dared him.

I floated from the room, feeling their eyes on me. It wasn't until I was alone in the antechamber leading to the rest of the club that I shed my armor. As if I really had emerged from a long and bloody battle, I placed my hands on my knees and took huge gulping breaths. I wasn't sure how much longer I'd last. My birthday was only six weeks away. I could run now, but as long as I was still a ward of my father, I didn't have a legal leg to stand on. And then there was my other issue. When the cops refused to step in, my father would no doubt send others after me—men who weren't bound by the law. I'd need every advantage I could get. Taking a deep breath, I straightened. I could do this. I had no choice because the only alternative was to become some rich asshole's collector's item. A pretty figurine.

Feeling as if someone was watching me, my head whipped toward the balcony doors I hadn't noticed were open. There Jamie stood, leaning against the balcony railing with his ankles crossed and a lit cigarette resting between his fingers. Despite the chill running down my spine, I felt like a ball of flame had engulfed me. I didn't allow myself to consider why as I turned away.

"I'm not going to chase you," he called out when I started for the door without speaking a word. I had every intention of pretending I hadn't noticed him, even though our gazes had connected and held for what seemed like an eternity.

"Good."

I was two steps from the exit when he spoke again. "You're going to come to me."

Falling right into his trap, I stopped and turned. "And why would I do that?"

"Because I just witnessed you having a panic attack. I imagine your parents would like to be aware of their daughter's distress."

The confused frown I wore cleared when I finally caught his drift. "You're going to *tattle* on me? That's your weapon?"

He didn't respond as he tossed his lit cigarette over the railing. God forbid it landed in a bush and burned the whole club down. I doubt he'd care. Jamie hated all things pretentious, which was ironic since he was probably the wealthiest person here.

"Come here, Barbette."

My pussy tightened at the command. Bossy Jamie turned me on just as much as gentle, carefree Jamie, though I'd *never* tell him so.

"No." Shaking my head, I took a step back.

His smile was gentle, and for a moment, I foolishly thought he'd let me go. Warily, I watched as he hopped onto the ledge, but then my heart dropped to my feet when he lost his balance. Without thinking, I was across the antechamber and rushing out to the balcony. My hands gripped his shirt, and I didn't stop to question how I could have reached him in time. I was just so damn grateful that I did.

"I got you," he cooed as if he weren't the one who'd almost fallen two stories. The moment he winked, I realized he'd tricked and trapped me.

"You're such a *fucking bastard*." I ground out each word, but the insult wasn't enough, so I dug my nails into his chest, making him wince.

Crooking his finger, he lifted my chin, but it was the emotion in his gaze that held me. "I'd never let anything happen to you, either."

I felt boneless as my hand fell to my side. I didn't realize his head was lowering until it was almost too late.

"No!" I yelped, ripping away from his hold. "You can't kiss me."

"Why not? You used to love it." His lids lowered after his gaze zeroed in on my lips. "I bet you still do."

Because I'm engaged. "Because I... I'll want more."

I didn't see his reaction because I'd closed my eyes, praying that I hadn't said those words aloud. As true as they might be, they were a mistake.

When I opened my eyes, the space Jamie had occupied was

empty. Spinning, I gaped at his retreating back. "That's it?" I screamed after him. "You're leaving?"

He faced me and started walking backward. "I told you I'd make you crawl, Bette, but you're not on your knees, are you?"

"Screw you."

His smile was the last thing I saw before he stepped through the antechamber doors, but his words rang loud and clear. "Only if you beg."

I'm not sure how long I stood rooted to the spot before the door leading to the dining room opened, and my parents stepped through. Where were Ever and Evelyn? Had the rest of their meeting gone well? My father wasn't beet red, and my mother wasn't clutching her pearls, so I had to assume everything was okay.

"I thought you were going to see Klara?" my mother questioned. Even though my father was the head of the family, my mother did all the talking when it came to me. God forbid Elliot Montgomery actually have a hand in raising and caring for his child.

"I wasn't feeling well, but it was nothing a little fresh air couldn't cure," I said, explaining my presence on the balcony.

"Well, then... we'd better get you home," my father announced. His sharp, blue eyes were boring a hole through me, and I wondered if mine held the same glacial chill when I stubbornly held his gaze. I no longer cared if he hurt me. I'll never bend for him as my mother had.

The week following the clubhouse catastrophe had come and gone without a hitch. It was now Saturday morning, the beginning of what I hoped was another monotonous weekend. My thrill-seeking days were long over, no matter how much Jamie tried to prove otherwise. After my long but mandatory beauty ritual, I descended the stairs to join my parents for breakfast as I did every morning, but instead, I found my mother standing in the foyer with two other women. One of them looked to be just a few years older than me. She was blonde, nervous, and carried a clipboard. The other was older, around my mother's age, and fashionably dressed in a red A-line skirt, cream blouse, and glasses hanging from a gold and pearl chain around her neck.

"Oh, there you are, sleepyhead!"

I blinked at my mother's warm welcome until I remembered our guests. *Let the show begin.*

"I'm sorry to keep you waiting?" I tried my best not to phrase it as a question, but it was difficult considering I had no idea we were having company. My parents didn't entertain as much as they used to because parties cost money. They also didn't want their friends noticing how our once extravagantly decorated house was beginning to look rather... barren.

"This is Bechette. She's come to fit you for your gown."

My stomach turned as I assumed she meant my wedding dress. If my hand wasn't holding the banister, I would have sunk to the floor. Or perhaps made a mad dash for the door.

"Yes, and what a beautiful belle for the ball," Bechette complimented.

It was all I could do to hide my relief. The gown was for prom.

Bechette gestured at the fretful blonde, waiting dutifully next to her like a puppy. "This is Tiffany," she introduced rather dismissively.

The next hour passed in a blur. I along with Bechette and Tiffany were ushered inside the parlor we used for entertaining. All the hard work I'd spent getting perfect was then unraveled as I was stripped of everything but my heels and forced to stand on a stool.

"I don't normally do house calls," Bechette haughtily informed as she wrapped a pink tape around my chest, "but your benefactor was very generous, ma chérie. You must have made quite the impression." Guiltily, I looked away at the knowing look she gave me. "She's as flat-chested as an adolescent boy," Bechette observed with pursed lips. "Unfortunately, we're going to have to reduce the bust."

Ignoring her rude remarks, I asked the question most prevalent in my chaotic mind. "This benefactor," I whispered, "who was he?"

"I'm afraid he wished to remain anonymous, but among his many demands, he did instruct me to give you this." I was startled when Bechette pressed a folded slip of paper in my hand and curled my fingers over it. "Her torso doesn't seem to end," she went on as if nothing had occurred, "so I suppose we must also lengthen the bodice."

It was clear fitting me into the beautiful creation mocking me just a few feet away was becoming a huge inconvenience to her. Poor Tiffany barely had time to notate all of her pushy boss's many alterations.

Bechette moved on to measure the rest of me. It seemed the only part of me she hadn't found an issue with was my small waist, although I did find some of her remarks puzzling. Apparently, whoever sent the dress had warned the dressmaker about my "too slim" hips.

That was the last straw, pushing me with trembling hands to finally open the note.

When the clock strikes twelve, you're mine, Cinderella.
Don't bother wearing panties.

My heart pounded in my chest, and I wondered if Bechette might hear. Fortunately, she moved away to carefully prepare the gown for me to try on. No chance in hell that was happening. There was no question who'd written the note and unleashed Bechette on me, but then again, who was I really kidding? I'd always known. How stupid was I to expect him to be anything other than arrogant? And daring.

Without regard for my audience, I savagely tore the note to pieces and watched it rain on the floor. Stepping down from the stool in a hurry, I mistakenly kicked the damn thing over, drawing my mother's attention. *For fuck's sake.*

"Barbette Elizabeth Montgomery," my mother scolded, "do not be rude!"

I scoffed. I wondered if Mother would mind if she knew what I knew. Naturally, my parents had assumed the gown was a gift from Ever, my *fiancé*, but what if they didn't? What game was Jamie playing, and when did it end? He'd been back for almost a year now and showed no signs of growing bored with me.

The gown had taken my breath away. It was perfect. Better than I could have ever dreamed. Turning it away would feel like ripping out my own heart—just as he'd known it would.

God!

The most frustrating part of all was not being able to give as good as I got without my parents noticing. The chain around my neck would only shorten until I suffocated. And Jamie would never know how much better I could play his game.

"Is there a problem?" Bechette questioned with a smirk. She'd obviously met Jamie and knew exactly the cause of my anger.

"No, no problem!" My mother rushed to answer before I could. I was sick of people speaking for me when I could do it so much better.

Taking a deep breath, I reminded myself that I only had a month. A month until I turned eighteen. A month until I was free.

I tried not to let in thoughts of everything that could go wrong or what or who I might miss when I left Blackwood Keep forever. The only good memories I had in this town had been distorted by the painful present.

"I apologize for startling you," I said with all the grace and poise of a sixteenth-century lady without rights or a voice of her own. "I felt a little faint."

Playing the role of a concerned mother, she rushed across the room and ushered me onto the sofa. I watched while she poured tea into a porcelain Hermès teacup before shoving it into my hands with a warning glare. I could only stare at the expensive trinket that hadn't been pawned yet. This five-hundred-dollar teacup was only *one* of the many reasons I was being sold off like cattle. And we had twenty more just like it.

Our only saving grace was that our home wasn't mortgaged, but if Dad's company went under, it would be the first to be sold to pay off some of our mounting debt.

Anger pushed aside rationality, and I freed my fingers from the tiny handle one by one until the teacup fell through the air and crashed onto the wooden floor. Drowning out the collective gasps around the room, I waited for the sweet tang of revenge that never came. There was only the bitterness of my reality. Staring at the white shards littered around my feet, I realized I was the expensive yet disposable trinket, and *this* was my future.

"Barbette, what has gotten into you!" my mother screeched, forgetting the decorum she'd almost cruelly drilled into me. She still didn't get it. It wasn't what had gotten into me but rather who was fighting to break free. I thought about the girl I no longer knew. The girl I betrayed out of fear. Would I even recognize her?

I was on autopilot as I stood from the couch and drifted from the room. I drowned out the sound of my mother apologizing profusely to Bechette and Tiffany until I was alone in my bedroom. I didn't need to try on that damn dress. Jamie had sent it as a taunt, knowing that I wouldn't need it.

When prom night came, Four would be the one to grace Ever's arm. I knew my friend well enough to know he'd follow his heart. After all, Four had blown into town nearly two years ago and had stolen what was left of it.

Ever and I had been thick as thieves back in a time when I

believed there was no greater force on earth than friendship. It'd taken some time for me to accept that Four was a threat, and for a while, I'd toyed with the idea of playing the villain. However, my very first encounter with Four in our Women's History class had only left me rooting for the southern invader instead.

"Ever can have his fun, but don't get any ideas. He's not going to be with you."

Four's head lifted from her battered flip phone—I wasn't even aware they still made those things—and for the first time ever, I was grateful for my mother's lessons in poise. The full force of her hardened gaze made my spine tremble, and I'd almost lost my nerve. To think I'd spent the entire night pacing in front of my bedroom mirror, practicing this very moment.

"You don't even love him."

"He's my friend," I answered truthfully. *"I care about him, and he cares about me, which is why I'll be the one to wear his ring, and you'll never be anything more than a thrill."*

My stomach turned, and I fought back the shame threatening to spill from my throat. I could feel Bee, the girl I used to know, pounding on the walls I kept her trapped inside.

Be still, foolish girl. You're safe there.

"Keep your satin panties on, Barbie. I have no desire to become the girl he marries and eventually ignores."

It had taken all of my restraint that day not to grin like an idiot. It was at that moment I understood why Ever had fallen hard so fast—even if he hadn't admitted it to himself yet. Four had been a breath of fresh air—for all of us.

Kicking my heels off, I face-planted on my bed. A second later, I was rolling over and snatching my phone from the nightstand. Before I could talk myself out of it, I stabbed his name and held my breath as the phone rang. I was surprised at my disappointment when the voicemail picked up and told myself that it was for the best. I was even grateful that he hadn't answered because now I understood how bad an idea it was.

I'd no sooner thrown down my phone when it started ringing. Panic speared through my chest as I stared at it. The damage was already done. Unlike me, if I didn't answer, Jamie wouldn't simply shrug it off. He'd show up, whether I was alone or not, to taunt and torment me.

Why, oh why did I have to call? I'd let anger cloud my judgment, and now I was trapped in the fucking Jamie matrix.

Do I take the red pill or the blue pill?

Taking a deep breath, I snatched my phone just before the voicemail could pick up and stabbed the green button.

I stared at the screen, watching a sleepy-eyed Jamie blink. Because, of course, he had to take it a step further and video call. His mahogany hair was mussed, some of it falling over his eyes and the rest sticking out every which way. Somehow, he still made a beautiful sight—wrinkled face, dried drool, and all. Thankfully, he was the first to speak because I couldn't find my voice.

"You rang?" His deep voice was even thicker with sleep.

"Of course not," I lied.

Yawning, he sat up until he was lounging lazily against the wall where a headboard should have been. I could see the bottom of what looked like flags hanging on the wall above him. Even after he was settled, he didn't speak. He simply watched me.

"What do you want, Jameson?"

"You. Come over."

I barked out a laugh. "You can't be serious." Once again, he didn't respond. He just stared at me until I began to squirm. "I'm sorry I woke you," I whispered nervously, thinking that might be why he wasn't his normally chatty self. Jamie wasn't an early bird. In fact, he rarely woke before noon on the weekends.

"I thought you said you didn't call me," he shot back as he stood.

Discreetly, I checked his surroundings while he was distracted, wondering if it was his bed he was rising from and if he'd slept alone.

"Nothing to say?" he asked as he entered another room. I could see him much better once he flicked on a light. I saw a shower in the background and realized too late that he was in the bathroom. Jamie's eyes were closed so he couldn't see my reaction as he relieved himself.

When he was done, he shook himself, flushed the toilet, and propped the phone before washing his hands.

"Are you going to say something?" he asked as he splashed water on his face. He looked hungover, which meant he'd definitely been partying last night. Envy speared through me as I wondered what it would be like to have that freedom.

"Would there be a point?"

"Not if more lies come spilling out of that pretty mouth."

A flush crept up my skin, warming my neck and cheeks, but luckily, Jamie was to occupied drying his face to see. By the time he'd tossed the towel away, I'd returned to normal. Mostly.

His gaze fell on the phone, and he licked his lips before looking away and grabbing something off camera. A few seconds later, I watched him lather his lower face with shaving cream.

"You know, you could save time and just pluck those baby hairs," I teased, forgetting myself and what we'd become.

He paused, and I didn't miss the surprise in Jamie's eyes or the way his lips twitched. "Is that what you did to your mustache this morning? You missed a spot."

My jaw fell before I covered my mouth, glaring at him over my hands. He didn't miss a beat as he lifted the razor and started shaving away the shadow covering his jaw and chin. I was mesmerized more than I should have been watching him go through his morning routine. It felt intimate, and I couldn't help wishing I could be there with him doing the honor.

Suddenly, I was thankful he was preoccupied. I was afraid of what he would see if he looked at me at that moment. It would only take a glance for Jamie to know everything I was feeling.

Of course, he had to go and ruin the moment.

"So spit it out," he demanded when he finished shaving and tossed the razor aside. "Thank me for the dress."

"I didn't call to thank you. I called to tell you that I'll be returning it to you... in *ashes*."

I wanted to punch the screen when he smirked. And then he spoke, choosing each word with care. "No, you won't, Bette."

This should be good. "And why not?"

"Because I'll tell your father that your fiancé is cheating on you with his stepsister."

It was all I could do not to shoot up from the bed. I had to settle for gripping my sheets instead and being grateful that he couldn't see. "He won't believe you."

Perking an eyebrow, he held my gaze. "Even if I have proof?"

I didn't even want to think about what kind of proof he had. Or how he got it in the first place. "Why would you do something like that? Ever would be pissed."

"Ever is in love with Four, and he's just dying for the world to know it." Finally, he looked at his phone screen, and our gazes locked. "I'm curious, though, why *you* aren't upset. I just told you the guy you're going to marry is in love with someone else."

"That's your opinion."

"It's a fact, but I'll play. Even if he isn't in love with her, he's fucking her, and that's not just speculation. *I've heard them.* Caught them in the act a couple of times, too. Of course, they don't know about the second time." He winked before his luscious lips spread, and I almost returned his grin. Realizing I was supposed to play the part of a scorned fiancée, I looked away, feigning anger and denial. "I can tell you what position they did it in if you like."

"That won't be necessary."

"It was doggy style," he blurted anyway because he was Jameson *freaking* Buchanan. He wiped the last of the lather away with a hand towel before gazing down at the screen again. "So, how do you want to do this?"

"Do… what?"

"Get him back for cheating on you. Get even."

"Let me guess… I should sleep with you?" He blinked a few times before shaking his head as if recovering from a blow. "Something wrong?"

"It's déjà-fucking-vu. Why does everyone assume my answer to everything is sex?"

"I don't know," I said while gazing at my nails so that he couldn't see what the truth did to me. "Maybe because you've slept with half the town?"

He didn't blink. "That's on you."

I stared at him in disbelief before finally finding my voice. "You're blaming me? You're *actually* blaming *me* for *you* being a whore?"

"Yeah, and I'll fuck every girl in this goddamn town, including the ugly ones, if it will get your attention."

"Jamie… you can't—that's ridiculous." I was breathless when I should have been anything but flattered. I wasn't… not really, but what was I supposed to say to that?

Jamie shrugged as he poked at a pimple on his chin, and I believed him. He really didn't give a damn.

"Stop that," I snapped, earning his frown.

"No can do, kitten. I've got needs, too."

Rolling my eyes, I said, "I *mean* the pimple. Stop messing with it, or it will scar."

"I'm already scarred, Bee, and the ones you left behind are never going away." He held my gaze as he popped the pimple, and I cringed. I watched as he brushed his teeth, and even after he was done, neither of us spoke. I had a feeling we were both afraid because we always seemed to end up at each other's throats when we talked. The silence wasn't awkward, however. I was content to chew on my bottom lip as I watched him move around his room. Eventually, he picked up a hardwood guitar, sat down at his desk, propped the phone up, and began lazily strumming the guitar. I wondered if Jamie's father ever got the chance to finish teaching him before he died. Jameson definitely knew a thing or two but he was no Jimi Hendrix.

"You still write?" he casually asked after the silence had stretched too long. I felt like I'd been punched in the stomach.

"Write?"

"I didn't take you for a parrot," he said as he shoved a cigarette between his pretty lips. "You know what the fuck I mean."

I rolled my eyes when he started to light up. "Do you really need to do that now?" I hated that he smoked. "You just woke up."

"Usually, I beat my dick, but I was trying to be considerate, virgin."

"You don't know that I'm a virgin," I shot back and immediately realized the epic mistake I made when he scoffed and looked away, nostrils flaring. He stopped playing and set the guitar down. I already missed the sound.

"Right."

"I didn't mean—We haven't—"

"I don't give a fuck who breaks you in as long as I get a turn," he spat.

So many emotions, none of them good, roiled in my gut until I felt physically sick. "I have to go," I rushed to say before I hung up. I barely made it to the bathroom before I hurled up my guts. I was surprised at the force of my reaction. Jamie had been crude before, but he'd never been quite so callous.

Fear that I'd lost him for good had me clutching the toilet as I emptied my stomach. It wasn't logical. I couldn't explain it. I looked at myself in the mirror as I brushed my teeth and didn't recognize the girl I saw staring back at me. Barbie may have been a cold, hard shell, but she was impenetrable. She protected the girl I cherished the most. *This* girl that Jamie had reduced me to was weak. I'd never survive him or my father. Not like this.

Marching back into my room, I snatched my phone from the bedspread, and with an evil smile, I dialed.

CHAPTER SIX

The Punk

B EE HAD ENDED THE CALL, BUT I WAS STILL STARING AT MY PHONE, waiting, debating, long after the screen had turned black. I didn't understand why I wanted to call her back. I sure as fuck wasn't about to apologize. I'd given her sweet, and she'd thrown me away. There was only one way that call could go and deciding she'd had enough for one day, I tossed my phone on my desk and stood from the chair.

I didn't have time for this shit. My head kept telling me to stop chasing her, but my heart and dick wouldn't listen. It was two against three, and with every encounter, I was inclined to see their point of view. Maybe if I fucked her—just once—I could finally get over this obsession. As cold as Bee had become, I doubt I'd want seconds.

Jesus, fuck. You're a real Casanova, Buchanan.

Shoving back into the bathroom, I was thankful I no longer had to share the space as I shed my shorts and boxers. It sucked for my cousin, though. There was no way in hell I'd get lucky enough to score some in-house pussy just to give it up willingly .

Stepping inside the glass enclosure, I took a brutally cold shower. I stayed under the spray until my fingers and toes pruned. Padding back into my room, I was wrapping a towel around my waist when my phone rang. For a moment, I was hopeful that it was Bee crawling back until I glanced at the screen and read my mother's name. Smiling, I picked up immediately. Not answering

98 | B.B. REID

wasn't really an option anyway. She'd only hang up and call back until I did. Dilwen Buchanan was a spitfire, and she'd kept my father's hands full when he was alive.

"Hello, beautiful."

"Jameson John Buchanan, is it true?"

My balls immediately shriveled to the size of a prune at my mother's angry tone. She was seriously pissed, and as far as I knew, I hadn't actually done anything this time. "Is what true?"

"That you're smoking!"

I gulped. "Mom—"

"Yes or no, Jameson?"

Hanging my head, I answered her. "Yes."

The phone cracked in my fist when I heard her sob. Each one was a knife to the gut. I deserved the pain. I welcomed it. "How could you? After what it did to your father, how *could* you?"

"I'm sorry."

"Is that all you have to say?"

"I'll stop," I promised as I sat on the edge of my bed. My legs no longer felt strong enough to hold me up.

"You think it will be that simple? Barbette tells me you're going through almost a pack a day!"

My grip loosened, and I quickly caught my phone before it slipped. "Wait a second… Barbette told you?"

"Yes. I just got off the phone with her." There was a pause, and some of my mother's anger faded when she sensed mine. "Don't you dare be upset with her. She's worried about you."

I couldn't bring myself to tell my mother that the girl she adored, the one we'd both been sure I'd marry one day, had used my dead father as a tool for revenge. My mother lectured me for an hour straight, but I didn't hear a word of it. The entire time I was plotting my revenge. Using my father's illness and making my mother cry just to get back at me was out of the fucking question. It wasn't until my mother finally stopped to let the twins speak to me that the red haze faded. Adan and Adara were only seven and barely remembered our father. I tried my best to fill the void he'd left behind—even with an ocean between us.

"So, what's your boyfriend's name, Dara?"

"I don't have a boyfriend," she answered with the cutest giggle. "Boys are gross!"

"Right fucking answer."

"Muuuuuum!" Adan screamed in the background. "Jamie said 'fucking' again!"

"Thanks, you little shit."

"Muuuuuum!" Dara screamed this time. "Jamie called Adan a 'shit'!"

I should have known those two would gang up on me. It was their twin thing and what helped me sleep at night since I'd practically left them to fend for themselves. Sure, they had my mom, and she was as fierce as any lioness, but I was their big brother. I should be there protecting them, but I was here, preparing to take over the family.

Everyone thought my reason for being sent back to the States was so that Uncle Thomas could straighten me out, but that had only been a small part of a very fucked-up story.

I teased the twins for a few minutes more and spent twice that time trying to stop their crying when it was time to say goodbye. My mom ended up taking the phone from them and then issuing a very clear warning to cease smoking. I didn't doubt she'd fly over three thousand miles to box my ears until I bled if I didn't.

I quickly threw on clothes after hanging up and was out the door to pay Miss Chatty Patty an overdue visit. I'd left her alone this past week, but clearly, that was a mistake. Barbette was feeling neglected and in desperate need of my undivided attention.

I didn't see Elliot's car in the drive or the garage when I peeked through the window and knew the lapdog Barbette called 'Mother'

was likely to be with him. I'd worry about the servants, but it seemed the Montgomerys no longer employed any. The first time I'd broken in here, I assumed Elliot Montgomery had fired them in a fit of rage, but it's been months, and this place was a ghost town. I started for the stairs, intending to catch Bee by surprise when the sound of glass shattering stopped me in my tracks. I rushed toward the kitchen—where the noise had come from—without stopping to think who it might be and that I didn't belong in here.

The moment I reached the kitchen, I stopped short at the sight of Bee sweeping up what looked like a tiny porcelain teacup. She wore a smirk you wouldn't expect to find on someone who'd just broken expensive china. However, it wasn't only her expression that left me reeling but also her appearance. Bee looked completely different from when we video chatted an hour ago. Her hair was pulled high in a messy bun, the makeup was gone, and she wore what might have been described as rags compared to her usual attire, but to normal people, it was simply a T-shirt and shorts. The biggest question mark, however, had to be the apron tied around her waist and the rubber gloves.

Was Barbette doing… chores?

Before I could make sense of things, her head shot up, and her blue eyes widened at seeing me standing there. I'd been as quiet as a mouse and as still as a statue. The moment some of her shock cleared, she dropped the broom as if it were a gun, and I'd just caught her murdering someone.

"What are you doing?" I snapped.

Someone had better give me some answers right fucking now.

Huffing, she stormed across the kitchen until she was standing toe to toe with me. "I'll ask the questions. What are you doing here?"

"I came to choke the life out of you, and instead, I find you doing chores." Crossing my arms, I pinned her with my glare. "Explain."

"Don't be ridiculous, Jameson." She tried to walk away, but I gripped her arm, keeping her in place. "Fine," she spat when she realized I wasn't letting her go until she answered me. "I was having coffee, and I broke a cup."

"So you changed clothes to clean it up?"

"Hey, that rhymed!" She flashed me a goofy grin, and I squeezed her arm in return.

"Nice try. If you were having coffee, why does it smell like lemons and bleach in here?"

"Not everyone is comfortable with the smell of dirty socks and used condoms, Jameson. Now let me go!"

I almost laughed at her assumption, but then she tried to free herself and ended up with her breasts pressed against my chest when I pulled her closer. I leaned down and enjoyed the pure panic flashing in her eyes until I began sniffing her rubber gloves. Poison Ivy actually thought I was stupid enough to kiss her.

"What do you know... lemon. You were cleaning. *Why?*" She looked away, and when I finally let her arm go, she began smoothing out her apron. "Stop stalling and answer me."

Her gaze narrowed to slits at my tone, so I leaned against the wall and got comfortable.

This should be good.

"If I tell you, I'll have to kill you, and then I'll have to get out the bleach again to clean up all the blood."

Sighing, I stood up straight. "Well then, it's a good thing I'm here. Bleach won't hide blood from a forensic expert. Where's the body?"

Not missing a beat, she nodded toward the double doors I'd snuck through so many times. "Buried out back."

"Please tell me it's your dad."

Her smile was contagious, and before long, we were grinning at each other like idiots. It didn't last, but for the first time since returning to Blackwood Keep, I didn't lose hope. Moments like these were happening more and more often. If only I could find a way to make them last.

Frustrated, I shook off those fanciful thoughts. I wasn't

interested in falling for Barbette Montgomery ever again, but if I could make her fall for me… oh, what sweet revenge.

"Sadly, he's still breathing and off somewhere terrorizing the villagers. He'll be back soon, so you should leave."

I started to respond when something she said stopped me. *Sadly?*

Barbette and Elliott had never been poster models for an ideal father-daughter relationship, but to my knowledge, she hadn't hated him. And not nearly enough to actually want him dead. Knowing I wouldn't get any answers today, I filed the thought away for safekeeping.

Barbette had already turned away, so I couldn't see her face when I spoke. "Speaking of dead fathers, I'd like to know why you think it's okay to use mine for revenge."

She spun around, her beautiful face twisted with confusion. "What are you talking about?"

"You made my mother cry, Barbette"—slowly, I placed one foot in front of the other until I was close enough to wrap my hand around her lovely neck—"so I came to make you cry."

"I only told her you were smoking, and your disgusting habit was getting worse. She was angry, but she seemed fine."

"People are not always what they seem, Barbette. You taught me that. You taught me so many things."

Her nostrils flared, but she wisely steered clear of my claim. "What does your smoking have to do with your father's death?"

"He'd been a smoker all his life, Bee. You know that. He died from lung cancer." My hand tightened around her throat, making her eyes bulge. "You want to tell me you didn't know?"

"I didn't," she whimpered.

I scoffed, unsure if I believed her, but knowing it didn't matter. "And you think that excuses you?" A tear slipped from her beautiful, blue eyes, and I swiped it away with my thumb. "Is the fact that you didn't care enough to know how my father died supposed to make me feel better?"

"I cared!"

"Not. Enough."

"I was afraid, Jamie."

I paused. What the hell could Bee have possibly been afraid of? That I'd reject her? *Never.* Not only was I not strong enough, but I could never do what she'd done to me. "So was I. It was *my* father who died, and you didn't even fucking call." I shoved her away and was caught completely off guard when she didn't flee for safety. Her hands were reaching for me, and afraid I'd finally crumble if she touched me, I grabbed her bun in a vicious hold and backed her against the nearest wall. "Stay away from me. Forget I ever existed, and I'll do the same."

Lies. All lies.

Instead of heeding my warning, her trembling hand cupped my cheek. "I didn't mean to hurt you, Jamie."

"You've had five years to think of what to say, and the best you can give me is a fucking cliché?"

"It's true!"

"I don't give a fuck."

Her temples were becoming red due to my harsh grip on her hair, so I let my hand fall. After everything she'd done to me, I still couldn't bring myself to harm her. My frustration boiled until I eventually exploded, driving my fist into the wall next to her head. She didn't even fucking flinch.

Even Bee knew when it came to her, I'd always be weak.

I'd shoved away from her and started for the door when her voice stopped me. "You have to stop smoking, Jameson. Before it kills you."

I came to a screeching halt, and then slowly, I turned, my gaze narrowing on Barbette, still holding up the wall. She didn't shy away and even lifted her chin. My nostrils flared in response as my chest rose higher and faster. What right did she have to make demands on me? If that was how she wanted to play it—as if we still cared for each other—then so be it. I had a few requests of my own.

"You want me to stop?" I taunted, closing the distance between us once more. "Give me something I'll want more."

I already knew what her answer would be but that didn't stop me from dreaming. Although I hated the very air she breathed, it didn't change the facts. I wanted Barbette, which meant I wouldn't be turning down a night with her if by some miracle she offered. I'd even be generous and fuck her good in the morning before sending her worthless ass back to my cousin.

Barbette's brows furrowed until understanding dawned. "You expect me to sleep with you in exchange for saving your own life?"

"And not just once," I clarified, abandoning everything I'd said earlier. Moving on wasn't an option. Barbette was it for me—my slice of heaven and my one-way ticket to hell. I could never trust her with my heart again, but maybe I was kidding myself thinking I could stay away completely. "Whenever, wherever, and *however* I want it. You game?"

"Absolutely not."

"Didn't think so." I started to turn away when I caught her by surprise, trapping her against the wall with my hand around her lovely neck. Before she could react, I had my other hand down those tiny shorts, cupping her bare pussy. She wasn't wearing panties today, not that they would have stopped me.

"Jamie!" she yelped when most of her shock finally cleared.

"Shut the fuck up." She did just that, eyelashes fluttering when my middle finger teased her opening. Her pussy was practically salivating. I could have slid right in. "Not game? That's the third lie you've told me today." Strumming her clit and making her gasp, I yanked my hand free of her shorts the second she reached the edge. Cutting it off instead would have been less painful. "Make it your last. *Ever.*"

Standing back, I waited for her to beg me to finish it—to give us both what we shouldn't want. Her blue eyes slowly drifted open and the desperation in them nearly stole my breath. She'd never looked more beautiful, and I was crumbling all over again.

Panicking, I didn't look back when I walked away this time. If I had, the lust clouding her eyes and judgment right now would have me fucking her up the wall and into the middle of next week.

Not for the first time, I wondered if I was losing the war I started. I'd always been able to separate sex from emotions but with Barbette I wasn't so sure. Most of the time, I couldn't decide if I wanted to fuck her, kill her, or fall to my knees and beg her to take me back.

CHAPTER SEVEN

The Plaything

Summer… Six Years Ago

Y OU'RE DEAD MEAT.
>   *You're dead meat.*
>   *You're dead meat.*

The three words Jamie had uttered seemed to echo inside my mind in time with my pounding heart as I ran, not for the safety of the house but the woods surrounding it.

Stupid! Stupid!

The last thing I'd heard before I disappeared among the trees was Ever, Vaughn, and Jason trying to restrain Jamie after he'd climbed from the pool. I had no idea if they had succeeded. I definitely wasn't sticking around to find out.

I wasn't sure how long or far I'd run before I was out of breath. Slowing up, I chanced a glance behind me to see if I was being followed. Seeing no one, I planted my hands on my knees and breathed a sigh of relief.

So much for fighting your own battles.

I'd never seen so much anger in one person before. Jamie had been explosive, a bomb with a very short fuse. I'd have to tread carefully.

I gritted my teeth at the thought and discarded it as quickly as it had come. This was my town, my crew. Jamie, like it or not, was just going to have to get in line.

Finally catching my breath, I stood up straight, prepared to face the music, and at the same time, I heard what sounded like a twig snapping. The moment my head swung in that direction, I was tackled to the ground.

The force of the impact knocked the breath I'd just caught from my lungs. I felt dazed, but I could still make out the fist hovering in the air, and Jamie's handsome face, wet with pool water, twisted in anger. His hair, which was longer in the front, was now plastered to his forehead and dripping water into brown eyes that seemed darker now. I started to feel bad for pushing him into the pool until I realized his fist was heading straight for my face. I dodged the blow just in time, leaving his fist to crash into the ground. The pain I could imagine radiating up his arm right about now distracted him long enough for me to wiggle from under him. Once free, I saw my red cap lying a few feet away and scrambled to grab it.

Big mistake.

I felt Jamie's hand clamp around my ankle, and then he was dragging me back. I suddenly felt like the stupid heroine in a horror movie who'd just tripped over an invisible rock. The sticks and stones scraping my skin had me gritting my teeth. Despite my struggling, Jamie managed to flip me over and grip my wrists. I was pinned, and fighting to free myself only made this cruel boy tighten his grip until I whimpered from the pain.

Losing my cool, I screamed in his face. "It was just cookies, asshole!"

Jamie didn't respond.

In fact, his anger was gone, replaced by shock as he stared at my chest. My T-shirt had lifted during the struggle, exposing my bright pink training bra underneath. His shock seemed to clear a few seconds later, and then he was stumbling back in horror.

I fixed my shirt with a huff and stood, too. I watched him warily while he tried to process what he'd seen. Despite my bra no longer being visible, he was still staring and blinking stupidly at my chest. My boobs that I resented so much were once more safely hidden by my baggy t-shirt.

"You're a-a-a—you're a girl."

"That's right," I admitted shamelessly. "I am." And then I drew my fist back before sending it flying into his nose. It was the first time I'd punched someone, and boy, did it feel good. I understood now why the guys were always eager for a fight. I fought a smile, suddenly hoping that Jamie didn't hold back.

Instead, he stumbled back while clutching his nose.

I became alarmed by the amount of blood spilling past his hands. I turned toward the sound of running feet. Ever, Vaughn, and Jason had found us, and they looked as bad off as Jamie. Clearly, there had been a fight between them, and clearly, Jamie had won. It made me think twice about hitting him. Three against one were tough odds, and my guys had never been bested.

"Dude, you okay?" Vaughn asked as he tipped toward Jamie.

"I think she broke my nose!"

I rolled my eyes at his dramatics while fighting a smile. It was hard to feel sorry for him since he'd started it. It didn't have to go this far, but obviously, he'd wanted to prove a point. I hugged myself as I admitted a part of me had wanted to prove myself, too. The guys constantly got shit for taking orders from a girl. I was afraid that one day they'd give in to the pressure, and I'd be without friends.

"We should get back," Jason said. "My sister probably already told your mom what happened," he said to Ever, who nodded.

With a final glare, Jamie stormed away with Vaughn on his heels.

"Dude," I heard Jason whisper to Ever. "Your cousin totally got his ass kicked by a girl." I could hear the awe in Jason's voice and Ever's snickering.

With my back turned to them, I smiled while trailing Jamie

and Vaughn. I was sure to keep my distance, though. Every once in a while, Jamie would glare at me over his shoulder, and I'd simply lift a brow.

Ready whenever you are, douchebag.

When we finally reached the house, he turned on me. Blood coated his upper lip, and I had an urge I didn't understand to lick him clean. My mouth even filled with a coppery tang as if I'd already done so. "You're lucky I don't hit girls," he spat.

Slowly, I clapped my hands. "Congratulations. Want a cookie?" I taunted, knowing that choice of words would piss him off the most.

He stormed inside the house without responding, but those dark-brown eyes of his still promised retribution. Jamie may not hit girls but that didn't mean he was willing to let today go unpunished.

I lifted my chin as I watched him go. Maybe I was lucky he didn't hit girls, but either way, I refused to be afraid. Jamie had made a grave mistake underestimating me, and if he forced me to, I'd show him exactly why.

"I don't want you coming home with more scrapes and bruises," my mother had warned. "You know how your father gets." I watched as she removed roller after roller from my hair. They had been hell to sleep with last night, but my mother hadn't heard my pleas. She'd been determined to make me look like a girl despite my shorn hair. "And stay away from those boys. It's not seemly for you to run around with them alone. You really should play with other girls. You'll have more in common with them."

Tomorrow was the Fourth of July, so a carnival had come to Blackwood Keep. The entire town would be out today, which meant I had to look my very best. I wanted to be excited about the rides, food, and fireworks, but I knew it just meant I'd be seeing Jamie again. Thanks to my fight with him in the woods, I'd gone home with bruises that I couldn't explain without being grounded. The scrapes on my hands had been the hardest to hide after my bike fell apart from under me. I'd been on my way home when it happened and discovered the front wheel had been loosened. I didn't need to question who'd done it. The pranks hadn't stopped there. I got a jar of spiders dumped down my shirt the next day and found a poisonous snake in my sneaker on the third. I hadn't realized the snake was fake until after I'd come dangerously close to a heart attack. Yesterday had been unexpectedly peaceful. I'd been on pins and needles waiting for Jamie to try something, and he'd spent the entire day pretending I didn't exist.

As hard as I'd tried to blend in, to be just another one of the guys, I was beginning to feel like an outsider. I could already feel Ever, Vaughn, and Jason gravitating more and more toward Jamie. I'd become accustomed to calling the shots. Anything I'd wanted to do, they used to want to do it, too. Unfortunately, Jamie had made a habit of challenging me at every turn, and now the guys were beginning to look to him for leadership.

And then there was still the question that needed answering.

Why hadn't Ever told Jamie I was a girl?

Before Jamie came to town, I believed I was one of them. That they had accepted me for who I was and who I could never be.

Not wanting to face the betrayal, I still hadn't confronted my best friend. Instead, I let the hurt eat away at my heart while trying to figure out how to deal with one Jameson John Buchanan.

The warmth that spread through me the moment I thought of him was nothing new, although I still hadn't become accustomed to it.

"Barbette, are you listening?"

I met my mother's gaze in the mirror and prayed that her

beauty was all I'd inherited from her. Melissa Montgomery had shrewd brown eyes, and, thanks to her frequent salon visits, lustrous hair that was a true red, unlike mine.

My eyes, however, were unmistakably blue—a trait I inherited from my father. I wondered if mine were as cold. He certainly had the icy demeanor to match.

"Yeah, Ma."

She paused. The only movement was her hand tightening painfully around my hair. "Excuse me?"

I stilled, too, forgetting myself. Or rather… who I was supposed to be. "Mother. Yes, Mother."

She promptly removed the last roller from my hair, although her scathing glare remained. "Young ladies with a future as promising as yours do not talk as if they've crawled from the gutter."

"Yes, Mother," I answered gracefully.

Because *that* was my future, saying yes and being gracious all the time to any demand. My parents believed that a proper upbringing for a daughter meant being a well-worn doormat.

My mother finished fluffing the bouncy curls adorning my hair and stood back to admire her handiwork. I gritted my teeth as I stared at my reflection. I looked like Annie after she'd gone to live with Daddy Warbucks.

"May I be excused?" I asked when she was done inspecting me for imperfections. For the most part, my parents accepted that I was a kid just like any other. The only exception was when there was someone to impress. I wasn't allowed even a hair out of place then. To be fair, it was normal to want your kid to look nice for special occasions, but I couldn't help but wonder if my parents cared a little too much.

A few months ago, we'd dined with a business associate of my father who also had a son my age. Parker had been bragging the entire night about his brand-new treehouse until I couldn't resist seeing it for myself. I remembered my father's rage after I'd torn my tights climbing the large tree in the Jeffersons' backyard, and I could still feel the bite of his belt striking across my back after we'd returned home. I shuddered.

"Be home in time to wash for dinner."

It was all I could do not to sprint from the house as fast as I could with the wind whipping through the hair she'd just spent an hour styling. Not to mention the risk of scuffing the black patent leather Mary Janes. I inwardly groaned and tried not to pick at the itchy white tights covering my legs. The frilly pink dress my mother picked out for me was bad enough.

I knew I'd be getting shit from the guys the moment they laid eyes on me. I'd be the butt of their jokes for the rest of the day.

Hopping on my bike, I pedaled to a field a couple of miles from Brynwood, the prestigious academy we'd all be attending in a couple of years. The fair was being held there, and we'd all agreed to meet up by the ticket booths. There must have been hundreds of cars covering the neighboring field designated for parking. After locking up my bike on one of the racks, I crossed the gridlocked road. After waiting five minutes of waiting in line, I paid the ten bucks, accepted the stamp on my hand, and let one of the stone-faced guards scan me with a wand for weapons. I hadn't bothered bringing a bag, so I got through security quickly.

I immediately began scanning the crowd for my crew and saw them standing near the lost and found. Ever was clutching an orange Gatorade, listening to whatever Vaughn and Jason were discussing so animatedly while Jamie sat atop the hood of a white pickup that didn't belong to him. He looked far too alluring in his black muscle shirt. It was so big on his lanky frame that I could see his dusky nipples peeking at me through the sides of his shirt. I tried to tear my gaze away but found it impossible. I wasn't even sure where the urge was coming from. I had never despised anything or anyone more than Jameson John Buchanan. Not even my father.

As if sensing my thoughts, his gaze drifted to me. Neither of the others had noticed me yet. Only him. I waited for his signature smirk or for him to instantly dismiss me as usual, but he didn't. He watched me watch him, and I wasn't sure how much time passed with us just staring at each other before we were forced to break the connection.

"Holy shit, Bee!" Vaughn's eyes nearly doubled in size as he looked me up and down. "You look like a girl!"

For a second, I thought I saw a spark of interest in his eyes before I dismissed the thought. *No way.* This wasn't the first time he'd seen me like this, so why now?

"She looks so pink," Jason chimed in with a snicker. "I mean pretty," he said when he caught my look.

My gaze traveled to Ever, who only shrugged with a crooked smile. Feeling like the worst hadn't been so bad after all, I started to relax when Jamie began whistling. It only took me a few seconds to recognize *Tomorrow.*

Even though I'd had the same thoughts about my resemblance to Annie, the obvious taunt still made my cheeks flush.

"Holy shit." Vaughn gasped. It seemed to be his new catchphrase. "Are you blushing?"

"What? No!"

Ignoring me, Vaughn grinned at Jason. "I think she likes you, bro."

Out of the corner of my eye, I noticed Jamie's lips flatten. My stomach tightened, and I lost my breath. I didn't know which way was up as my world spun out of control. How was such a powerful reaction to such a simple gesture possible?

Once again, I dismissed the thought of a boy liking me—of Jamie actually being jealous—as quickly as it had come. Since arriving, Jamie had done nothing else but make me feel unwelcome in my own town, my own *crew.*

Not wanting to hurt Jason's feelings, I said nothing, which only seemed to piss Jamie off more. Did he think I liked Jason?

Shrugging, I told myself I didn't care. It was weird that he'd be mad, anyway, since we hated each other.

Ever's bored sigh drew my attention. Keeping him enter-tained was getting to be a full-time job. When Ever got bored, Ever got reckless, and his mother... his mother seemed to be at her wit's end. His parents had just kept him from being sent to juvie last month when he went joyriding in our math teacher's car and all because Mrs. Lynch had given him detention for get-ting gum in Becky Marsh's hair. He hadn't done it on purpose. The boys had a stupid contest to see who could spit their gum the furthest. Unfortunately, I'd been in social studies at the time, or I might have prevented it from happening.

"What do you guys want to do first?" Ever asked.

"Bumper cars."

"Turkey legs."

"Ferris wheel," Jamie and I said at the same time. He looked at me, and I wondered if my expression matched his—curious but wary.

"Why don't we just split up?" Vaughn suggested. "I'm starved, and I don't want to ride some fucking wheel. Since the bumper car line is long as shit, Ever and Jason can hold our spots while Jamie and Bee do whatever they want."

Whatever we want, my mind echoed.

What did I want? The answer should have been 'nothing,' but my heart felt like it was doing cartwheels at the opportunity.

I started to argue when I realized it was actually a good plan and one I would have thought of if I hadn't been making eyes with the enemy. *Keep your friends close and your enemies closer.* I'd heard it in a movie once, and until Jameson Buchanan, I hadn't understood. I used to think of Tommy as my archnemesis, but he had nothing on Jamie. Tommy didn't keep me up at night or make me toss and turn whenever I did find sleep, and his presence didn't do weird things to my insides. He didn't make me want to run and hide.

And then hope he found me.

"Sounds good to me," Jason said before he and Ever took off.

I gritted my teeth because the last thing I wanted to do was be left alone with Jamie. Vaughn hadn't stuck around, either, to make sure I was okay with his plan, and was already halfway to one the many turkey leg stands.

Don't be a chickenshit, Bee. You can do this.

One glance at Jamie and his cocky smirk, and I nearly choked on those words. I didn't say a word to him before storming away. I didn't have to look over my shoulder to know he was following me. I could feel his gaze burning hot on my back as he effortlessly kept up with my lengthy strides. My long legs allowed me to stand shoulder to shoulder with my crew. I knew one day they'd tower over me, but it wouldn't matter. By then, their respect for me would outweigh the laws of biology. I'd make sure of it.

"You can run, but you can't hide, pretty girl."

I nearly bumped into Jamie when I whipped around. "What did you say?"

He stared back at me with a bland expression. "I didn't say anything."

"Yes, you did," I bit out. "You were being a creep."

"I don't have time for this. Get your ears checked," he spat before moving around me.

Refusing to follow him, I matched his lazy strides until we arrived at the Ferris wheel. There were only a couple of people in line, so in no time, we reached the operator. I slapped my forehead when the pudgy man held out his hand, and I realized he was waiting for our tickets. I'd completely forgotten to purchase some. The sign on the stand read two per rider. Swiveling my head, I looked for the nearest ticket booth and spotted one maybe twenty feet away. Before I could head in that direction, however, I nearly swallowed my tongue when Jamie handed the man four tickets.

"If you just wait for a second, I can get my own." I still had a twenty left over from my allowance burning a hole in my dress pocket.

"I'd rather not," was all Jamie said before grabbing my hand and tugging me through the gate the operator held open. He didn't let my hand go, either, until we took our seats. As I gripped the metal safety bar, my hand was shaking and completely covered in sweat. His or mine?

I glanced at him as he slouched down, appearing completely relaxed as he made a point to stare straight ahead.

Definitely mine.

I might as well have not even been there. "Thank you for the tickets."

The only response I got was his head turning slightly away, shielding his eyes from me. Sighing, I sat back. It was obvious he wasn't interested in being friends. After the hell he put me through this week, no way should I have been considering it.

At least one of us was still thinking clearly.

The lights on the Ferris wheel lighting up was our only warning before the wheel began to slowly ascend backward. When we reached the top, I looked around excitedly. I couldn't believe how high we'd gotten when we reached the top. It was my first time on a Ferris wheel, and when I met Jamie's excited gaze, I knew instantly that it was his first time, too.

If I asked him, he'd probably deny it, so I reluctantly tore my gaze away to watch all the people who looked like dots now. I could see everything, including the empty field not far away where they were setting up for the fireworks tonight. It wasn't until midnight, so I knew I'd miss them.

I began to panic, however, when I realized I was sliding closer and closer to Jamie as the wheel picked up speed and the bench began to rock. No matter how hard I resisted, gripping the safety bar to keep me in place, gravity seemed to be pushing me toward Jamie. Before long, our thighs were touching, and he stiffened in his seat.

"I'm sorry. I didn't mean to—"

"Whatever," he mumbled, cutting me off.

I pulled away only to slide right back into him. I tried again but was stopped when he locked his arm around my waist.

"Give it a rest," he whispered, his lips so close they brushed my forehead. "You aren't going anywhere."

I huffed as I tried to settle against him and ended up squirming out of nervousness instead. I just wanted off this damn wheel.

"So what's your deal?" he asked the moment I relaxed.

I glanced up, but he wasn't paying me any mind as he watched everyone enjoy themselves below.

"My deal? What makes you think I have one?"

"You've been a bitch to me since I got here."

The wheel suddenly stopped, leaving us at the top, so I sat up and moved away. "Excuse me? You threw the first punch." So to speak. Technically, I'd thrown the first punch, but I wouldn't have if he hadn't hogged all of Mrs. Greene's cookies for himself and pushed me down when I confronted him.

"You didn't like me before then."

"How do you know?" I shot back.

He finally gave me his gaze. "I just know."

"Well, that's not good enough for me."

"Clearly, *I'm* not either," he mumbled.

"You're trouble," I whispered defensively. Which meant the smart thing to do was to stay far away from him…right?

I swallowed hard when his gaze narrowed. "You don't even know me."

"I've heard all about you."

"Those are stories. Stories get lost in translation," he said, sounding wiser than he should have.

"How old are you?" I blurted out. Not only was his voice deeper, I'd glimpsed the hair growing under his pits earlier and on his arms and legs. Ever, Vaughn, and Jason, however, were still smooth.

"I'm twelve. How old are you?"

"Twelve. My birthday was two weeks ago."

His gaze flickered, and he sounded almost grim when he said, "I'll be thirteen in three weeks."

I did the math and sucked in a breath. Jamie was nearly an entire year older than me. He was also older than Ever, but only by a couple of months, whereas eleven months separated Jamie and me. If I'd been intimidated before, it was nothing compared to the butterflies fluttering wildly in my tummy.

"So... you're an eighth-grader?" It was the only thing I could think of to say. All my other thoughts were too embarrassing. I almost wished Jamie would turn away again so he couldn't see the way my cheeks flushed.

"I will be when school starts."

"Are you excited?" I asked as I toyed with the hem of my dress. I'd forgotten I was even wearing the monstrous thing. It no longer mattered. Nothing could ever make me feel more feminine than Jamie.

"About eighth grade?"

"Yes," I answered breathlessly.

His eyes dipped, and I had the feeling he was staring at my lips. "I'm excited about a lot of things right now. School isn't one of them."

The ride chose that moment to start again, pulling me back into Jamie until our lips were dangerously close. I was breathing much harder now. So hard, I didn't think I'd ever catch my breath.

"Are you okay?" he asked, brows furrowing.

"I-I-I can't breathe. I need to get off."

The Ferris wheel came to a stop shortly after, and Jamie was yanking the bar up before I could even get a good grip. I shoved past the crowd moving too slowly, trying to get away from Jamie. Unfortunately, it didn't seem as if he was ready to let me out of his sight. I was bent over, gasping for my next breath when I felt him stand next to me.

"Are you afraid of heights or something?"

It wasn't being high up that scared me. It had been the sudden feeling that I was falling. Even now, I still felt like I was tumbling down a never ending rabbit hole. Standing up straight, I met Jamie's concerned gaze, and the feeling intensified.

He reached for me, and I stepped away.

"We should go find the guys." I didn't give him a chance to respond before heading in the direction I'd spotted the bumper cars.

Bumper cars had been the perfect stress reliever—and distraction. Ever and Jason had paired up and Jamie with Vaughn while I'd been like the golden snitch as they all chased me and my blessed lonesome around the track. The guys had pushed and shoved and shouted and cursed each other all the while I laughed until I cried as I dodged them.

By the time we were done, I could barely walk as the world tilted and spun. It was Jamie and Vaughn who eventually caught me, and Jamie had looked the most triumphant. I ignored the fluttering in my tummy as I made my way to the exit with them hot on my tail. Jamie had once again paid my admission when I'd once again forgotten to purchase tickets. It was beginning to feel like we were on a date, but I knew it couldn't be further from the truth. I also refused to be one of those clueless, hopeless girls that Jamie seemed to like so much. In less than a week, he'd already seemed to rack up quite a few admirers. I'd even caught a few of them watching me with daggers in their eyes. Being the envy of other girls was a foreign experience, one I didn't know how to deal with.

We played a few of the games to try to win prizes, and it was sidesplitting to watch the guys try and fail at the rope ladder. I lost count of how much cash they spent and how many times they toppled over before finally accepting that they weren't exactly graceful enough to keep their balance on the angled ladder. Each one of them had tried the same strategy: racing to the top before the rope could tip them over.

I was bent over, holding my sides at the sight of Vaughn landing face-first into the bouncy rubber cushion for the third or fourth time. Ever and Jason were already waiting in line for another try while Jamie was noticeably silent as he stood much too close to me.

"Why don't you give it a try? Show us how it's done," Jamie goaded with a grin. He then waved a few of his tickets, hoping to entice me, but something else had caught my eye. A few feet away, three girls stood next to a cotton candy stand, eyeing Jamie as if he was their favorite flavor. They all wore skin-tight shorts, tiny tops, and makeup. Too much makeup. I had the feeling they were a little older than me and maybe even Jamie, but I wondered if it was because of the face paint or the way they devoured him with their eyes.

Had Jamie noticed, or was he completely oblivious to the attention?

I started to tell him, hoping to tease him and make him blush as he'd unknowingly done to me so many times already, but then a streak of something hot speared my chest, and all I saw was green. I didn't know what it meant, but it was enough for me to keep my mouth shut about his admirers.

"No, thanks," I mumbled as I toyed with the hem of my dress. My mom would have a stroke if I fell and flashed the entire town my bum. Maybe that was why she'd forced me to wear a dress to a carnival. It had been her way of making sure I didn't have too much fun. This dress felt heavier than a pair of iron shackles clamped around my wrists. I no longer blended with my crew and, instead, stuck out like a frilly pink thumb.

"It's just a dress," Jamie said, sensing the reason for my hesitation. "You're still you underneath."

"But you don't even like me. Why would you care?"

"Summer isn't over yet," he replied, unmoved by my suspicious gaze. "There's still time for you to change my mind."

"Yeah, I'll get right on that."

How could he assume I'd give a crap if he liked me or not?

His only response was to press the tickets into my palm. I stared at the ladder, watching Ever and then Jason topple over for the fifth time. *It's just a dress*, I thought, repeating Jamie's claim in my head. *I'm still me underneath.* Vaughn was next in line, preparing to hand over his tickets when I cut him off at the front of line. The operator looked from me to Vaughn with wide eyes, waiting for him to blow up, but Vaughn only stood back and crossed his arms with a grin.

"It's about time you got in the game, princess." In a terrible Jamaican accent, Vaughn said, "I hope you're feeling lucky, mon."

They'd all been trying to win the five-foot banana with the dreadlocks, colorful beanie, and a creepy smile. I shuddered at the thought of waking up in the middle of the night and seeing that thing grinning at me through the dark.

After handing off the tickets, I moved to the bottom of the ladder and filled my lungs with as much air as I could before slowly exhaling. I had the urge to look over my shoulder. To see if Jamie was watching me.

I already knew he was.

Gripping the fifth rung, I started my climb, ignoring the boys' strategy of going fast, and took it slow. But just like the boys, it wasn't long before I topped over and landed on my back on the bouncy mat. Sitting up, I could see Vaughn, Ever, and Jason holding their sides while Jamie watched me with what could only be pride in his eyes. Determined, I rose up, making sure my dress stayed in place and got back in line after snatching the tickets Jamie held out for me. The second time, I made it a little farther, keeping my hands and feet on the outer edge and using the rope. I was only three or four rungs from the top when I landed face-first in the mat.

This time, when I rose to my feet, the boys weren't laughing. They looked a little surprised and more than a little eager. I started for Jamie, ready to use every single one of his tickets if I had to, but Ever cut me off, offering up the last of his tickets. His golden gaze stirred the butterflies in my belly, and I was suddenly reminded of my crush and all the weeks I'd spent secretly pining over him. I still wasn't sure when it began, but I knew then that it hadn't ended. I'd just been so distracted by hating Jamie that Ever had faded into the background. I'd forgotten how handsome, boyish, and kind Ever was. He'd certainly never pushed me down, chased me through the woods, or made me feel unwanted. I slowly accepted his tickets, trying my hardest not to blush, and when I turned for the ladder, my gaze somehow found Jamie's.

His brown gaze, not as bright as Ever's but somehow more magnetizing, never wavered. I knew then that he'd been watching me this entire time. His tantalizingly wide mouth had flattened with anger, making me think he'd read every single one of my thoughts, maybe even glimpsed my feelings for his cousin.

A moment later, I dismissed the thought.

How could he know when Ever himself hadn't noticed?

Shaking off Jamie, my parents, and anything else that made me want to crawl into a ball, I got back in line. I didn't dare turn to see if Jamie was still watching me. I waited five minutes before my turn came, and this time, when I gripped the ladder, I told myself nothing else mattered but ringing that damn bell.

I took my time just like my first try, kept to the edge as I had on my second, but this time, I made sure to alternate, keeping the opposite foot planted whenever my right or left hand reached for the rung above me. I blinked at my right hand in surprise when it actually gripped the top rung, but then the ladder suddenly wobbled even more aggressively than before, desperate to throw me off. As quick as I could, I lunged for the rope and rang the bell a mere second before I was tossed onto my ass. Lying on my back,

I smiled up at the clear blue sky and the bright sun that seemed to return my smile.

I'd done it.

I lay there for a few seconds longer than necessary, listening to the round of applause and cheers, my friends' being the loudest of them all.

"Hey, are you okay?" the pimply-faced operator asked as he came to stand over me.

My friends' goofy grinning faces appeared above me next. Ever was the first to lean down, helping me stand. My gaze traveled the circle, searching for Jamie's cocky handsome face, but he wasn't there.

"Holy shit!" Vaughn shouted before grabbing me up in a bear hug. Trapped in his arms, he spun me around, and I gasped when my gaze landed on the shadowed seclusion behind the cotton candy stand. I'd only had a glimpse, but it had been more than enough. When Vaughn finally set me on my feet, my world spun for more reasons than one. "Shit, sorry," he said, mistaking my distress. I felt like I'd been hit with a Mack truck, and I was sure I looked liked it, too.

"Congratulations," the operator offered. "You're our first winner today. Do you know which prize you'd like?"

Slowly, my gaze traveled back to the two bodies pressed close together behind the cotton candy stand, and I realized my prize had already been stolen.

CHAPTER EIGHT

The Punk

Present

"THAT'LL BE $103.98."

After paying for my purchases, I charged onto the busy New York street with my nicotine patches and chewing gum in tow. It had been six days since I quit smoking, and I was already on my second attempt. I thought I could quit cold turkey, but last night, I'd given in to one addiction to keep from indulging in another. Six whole days since my encounter with Bee, and I couldn't close my fucking eyes without feeling her press against my fingers or hearing her soft, sweet moans. She'd been close, but I'd been cruel.

When I reached the high-rise that housed NaMara's headquarters, I rode the elevator to the thirty-ninth floor and made a beeline for the men's room. Once inside, I locked the door, removed my tie, vest, and dress shirt before cleaning the only spot, except my damn ankles, that wasn't covered by hair or a tattoo. The tiny space between my left collarbone and my arm was just big enough to fit the patch, so after drying it off, I carefully applied it.

I have no fucking clue why I'm even doing this.

Or who I was doing it for.

I didn't give a fuck enough to do it for myself. My mom was in Ireland, still grieving my father while taking care of my grandparents and raising two hellions by her damn self. Although she cared, her hands were too full to take on my shit, too.

That only left one person, and I hadn't decided yet if she was worth it.

I told myself it didn't matter because I'd probably be smoking again by morning. I've never been very disciplined, and before now, the flaw had only served me well.

After redressing, I popped one of the gums in my mouth because I'd been feening all damn day and made my way to my cubicle. There were at least three empty offices on the floor above, but my uncle made me work down here with the grunts because he couldn't help but be an asshole. He said I needed to learn some humility after he caught me propositioning the young receptionist. Whatever that meant.

It wasn't like Lauren would sue the company for sexual harassment. I only approached her because I'd caught her staring at my dick one too many times. The leggy receptionist was mid-twenties, busty, and glossed her lips seventeen times a day. With a wallet full of rubbers, and that was pretty much all I needed to know about her. So even though I didn't have an office with a view, Lauren gave me something just as great to look at whenever I was bored enough.

I didn't care too much about where I sat, either way. It wasn't like I had any responsibilities anyway. Now that I was done with school and waiting for graduation, I had the feeling my uncle was using this "internship" as a way to keep me out of trouble. My workdays were filled with shaking hands, data entry, filing papers, and making countless coffee runs.

I snorted, drawing Lauren's brown-eyed gaze. She had an unobstructed view of me, and she took advantage of it every chance she got, blushing all the time and shit. I started to wave her over, knowing it wouldn't be hard to talk her into the storage closet where they kept the office supplies. As soon as the thought entered my mind, it was shoved aside by the memory of me pushing

Bee against the kitchen wall, slipping my hand down her shorts, and giving her greedy clit a fit. With an irritated growl, I ducked my head, ignoring the invitation in Lauren's smile.

After wasting a few hours watching YouTube and trolling my friends online, my uncle finally stopped being a dick and told me he was releasing me for the day. It was a pleasant surprise since he usually made me stay until five, whether he had something for me to do or not, which was hardly fucking ever. It was a Friday, and the rest of the office had been gone for at least an hour now. After calling down to the valet, I left without hesitation or a single question asked. It wasn't until I reached the lobby and the elevator doors opened that I realized my mistake.

The coldest gray eyes stared back at me, and when he recognized me, he smiled. I didn't smile back. "It's good seeing you again, Jameson."

"Wish I could say the same," I shot back. I made no move to leave the elevator even when Sean stepped inside and pressed the button for the fortieth floor. I gritted my teeth as I watched the doors slowly close and felt the elevator begin to rise. Neither of us said a word for the first ten or fifteen floors, but I was the first to break the silence. "I know you're Ever's father."

Sean didn't react, which only raised more questions. Ever's true paternity had been treated like some sordid secret for so long that I'd expected more. *Something.*

Instead, Sean continued to stare at the steel doors.

"What did you mean when you said that your sons and I would be dead if weren't for you? Who is the other?" *And where the hell was he?*

This time, Sean turned to me, but he seemed amused rather than angry. "Isn't it obvious?"

"If it were, I wouldn't be asking."

Once again, he seemed unbothered as he leaned against the back wall of the elevator, but his gray eyes slowly shifting to blue told me otherwise. The subtle reaction to my line of questioning tugged at my memory for some reason. The elevator began to slow, and a glance at the lit panel told me we were almost on the fortieth floor.

"All you need to know is that the next time you go chasing after monsters in the night, there might not be a ghost in the trees to save your ungrateful ass."

The doors opened, and without a backward glance or a goodbye, Sean slipped through them. I turned his words over and over in my head as I watched him make his way to my uncle's office. The lights had been shut off, but I knew my uncle was still inside, and Sean must have known it, too, because without knocking or hesitation, he slipped inside.

As if the hour drive during rush hour traffic from the city back to Blackwood Keep wasn't grueling enough, I couldn't stop Sean's last words from echoing in my head. By the time I pulled up to the navy-blue two-story with white trim and charcoal roof, I was ready to turn that fucking leaf back over and smoke about fifty fags.

The driveway was already packed with Ever's G-wagon and Vaughn's white Aventador, so I parked behind Four's yellow and black Café Racer. For a moment, I allowed myself to sit back and picture Bee straddling a bike like that with absolutely nothing on. When I felt myself getting hard, I cursed and hopped out of my Jeep. I didn't bother knocking before letting myself in, knowing it would piss Wren off. Lou was always forgetting to lock the damn door.

After what had gone down with Wren's former boss and mentor, they had to keep their guard up. Fox was still out there somewhere, and once he was done licking his wounds, we'd be ready for him. You fucked with one of us, you fucked with us all, and that was the way it would always be.

Turning the lock, I followed the sound of laughter until I found my friends gathered in the kitchen. The second Wren looked up from chopping onions and saw me standing there, he scowled down at Lou.

"I forgot," she whined as she stirred something in a large bowl.

Shaking his head, he went back to chopping while I grabbed the only empty seat left next to Vaughn.

"Dude, please tell me you brought beer?" he whispered for some reason.

"Negative." I frowned as I checked my phone. I had a few texts from a couple of hookups, but none from my friends. *And none from Bee.* "Was I supposed to?"

"They don't have any," he said.

"And neither should you," Winny, Wren's grandmother, fussed as she rounded the corner into the kitchen. "The only person old enough to drink in this house is me. If you're thirsty, have some water."

Vaughn gave me a look that said: "What the fuck?"

All I could do was grin because Winny reminded me of my mother. She didn't take anyone's shit, either.

"Dice those onions smaller," she instructed Wren. "Unless, of course, that's all you want your friends tasting when they eat your food." Plucking her purse from the cluttered island, she headed for the door.

"Wait, you're not staying for dinner?" I called after her.

"I've got plans," she said before rushing out the front door.

I snickered because I knew exactly who with. When I glanced over at Wren, I noticed his nostrils flaring. I guess he knew, too. "I see you finally figured it out, huh?"

"Bite me," he growled.

"Don't be so selfish. It's a beautiful day in the neighborhood, and Grams and Mr. Rogers aren't getting any younger," I teased. "No one should die alone."

I ducked, barely missing the large onion Lou had hurled with expert precision at my head.

Wren smirked as he leaned down and kissed her. "Why are you so fucking sexy?" he asked with a groan against her lips.

Shrugging, Lou went back to stirring. "I ask myself that every day."

Looking around the kitchen, I realized we were missing some people. "Where are Four and Ever?" Their rides were definitely parked outside.

Not one of them met my gaze when Vaughn mumbled, "Upstairs in one of the spares."

I sighed, wondering how long before Four found herself knocked up. They never seemed to stop fucking, and now that they no longer lived underneath the same roof, no place was off-limits.

And I had the feeling they weren't the only ones sneaking around right now.

Rising from my stool, I stood behind Vaughn and placed my hands on his shoulders. The moment his muscles tensed, I began kneading. It only took about two seconds for him to lose his shit.

"What the—what the fuck are you doing, Buchanan?"

I continued massaging his shoulders just as Sean had done my uncle the first time I caught him in his office. "Relax. I'm just trying something out."

"Well, fucking quit it! When's the last time you got laid, man?"

My grip on his shoulders tightened as I thought about last night's rendezvous with my right hand. I'd pretended it was Bee's soft hand gripping me, and in my dreams, she'd been so patient. So tender. Shuddering, I looked down at my crotch and snickered. An inch closer and Vaughn would have felt my erection tickling his spine. "A week ago," I said. I'd hooked up with some random at a party whose name I couldn't even recall.

"Then why the fuck are you hitting on me?" he spat.

"So that was weird for you?"

"Massaging my shoulders? A tad, you fuck."

"You mean you couldn't tell by his squealing?" Four mused as she moseyed into the kitchen with Ever swaggering in behind her. I didn't miss the lazy look in either of their eyes or the satisfied smirk on Ever's lips. "Even we heard him from upstairs."

Vaughn looked ready to tell Four off, but an eyebrow from Ever had him backing down with a roll of his eyes. "Pussy-whipped simp," he muttered.

Somebody was on the bitter train.

It was his own damn fault for letting his father dictate who he could fall in love with.

As if I'd conjured her up, the doorbell rang. I stood to answer it since Wren and Lou were busy trying not to burn the food.

"Hey, sorry," Tyra said as she rushed in. "My relief had car trouble and was late for her shift."

"I've told you before, and I'll say it again, quit that job and these people, and just run away with me," I flirted.

Giggling, she pushed me away. "In your dreams."

"Weren't you listening?" I quipped as I followed her into the kitchen. "Where do you think I got the idea? When I dream, I dream *big*."

Ignoring me, Tyra greeted everyone before kissing Vaughn and stealing my seat. He was too busy scowling at me to kiss her back, though. "Sooooo… what did I miss?" she said as her gaze traveled back and forth between us.

"I gave your boyfriend a massage, and he acted like I groped his dick."

"You may as well have, you fucking prick."

Tyra frowned as she regarded Vaughn. "So what? That doesn't mean anything. You're telling me you'd only get a massage from a female masseuse?"

"He's not a fucking masseuse!" Vaughn barked.

"Oh, God." Tyra groaned as she clutched her forehead. "Please don't tell me you're homophobic. That's a deal-breaker, times ten, Rees."

He sucked his teeth while I chose to ignore her comment about me being gay. I definitely wasn't but getting the answers I needed while avoiding a million questions was worth a little side-eye.

"Of-fucking-course-not," he said, breaking the awkward silence. "I still want to know his deal, though."

Everyone's eyes traveled to me. Even Wren and Lou had broken free of their bubble to regard me. I definitely needed to talk to those two. *Alone.*

"I don't know," I pretended to muse as I hopped onto the island. "I was thinking of trying dick for a while. Pussy is getting to be a little monotonous, you know?"

"No," Vaughn said with a sarcastic twist of his lips. "I don't know."

"But you never know how great it can be from both sides until you give it a try, though, right?" When I winked at him, he rolled his eyes. He wasn't falling for my shit, but at least he wasn't asking questions I couldn't answer just yet.

An hour later, we were packed inside their tiny living room, ready to devour the pizza and wings we ordered after Wren disappeared to take a call, and Lou somehow burned our dinner to a crisp. I watched from the corner of my eye as she checked her phone for the umpteenth time and pursed her lips.

"Expecting someone?" Leaning over, I whispered, "A single friend, perhaps?"

Reaching up, Lou pinched my cheek. "Whatever happens, just remember," she whispered back, "I'm only looking out for my bestie."

"I'm your damn best friend," Wren barked as he returned from the kitchen with a stack of plates. After handing them to Lou, she counted them, and we both frowned when she said she needed eight. There were only seven of us.

Before Wren could grill her, however, the doorbell rang.

CHAPTER NINE

The Plaything

"WE'RE HERE, MISS."

I stared at the beautiful, blue house and the familiar vehicles parked outside of it and wondered what the hell I was doing. Lou had invited me over when we weren't even friends, and I accepted despite knowing who would be there.

Or maybe the promise of who'd be here had been my reason for accepting.

Willingly sharing the same space with Jameson was a bad idea on all counts, but it would only be for one night. A few hours free of my cage. A few hours spent being a normal teen hanging out. Lou had said as much when she called to extend the invitation. I'd hesitated to accept—a million reasons why I shouldn't, waiting to spill from my lips.

"You shouldn't take life so seriously. We can't control when we go or even how we go, but we can control the way we live… So lighten the fuck up."

I couldn't help smiling at her "advice" as I watched the figures moving around inside the house. Lou had said dinner was at eight, and it was now six minutes after. Would they wait for me to start or just assume I'd stood them up?

A moment later, my door opened, seemingly taking the decision from me. As Joe stood there, waiting for me to get out, I took a deep breath and grabbed onto my last bit of courage with both hands.

It's going to be fine.

I had the feeling my monsters wouldn't find me here.

Grabbing the gift I'd brought for my hosts, I stepped from the SUV and offered Joe a shaky smile. I then told him to come back for me in a couple of hours. I had four hours until my curfew, but I was planning ahead just in case this turned into a nightmare. There were rare times my father let me out—usually when I told him I would be making some sort of public appearance with Ever—so when he did, my curfew was at midnight. It was a Friday night, and while most of my peers didn't have one or wouldn't bother heeding it if they did, I knew, for me, it wasn't an option.

It had been a few years since he'd done so, but I could still feel the lash of my father's belt whenever I broke his rules or wouldn't comply.

Walking up the paved path, I tried and failed to push away a certain memory from my mind. The night I stood underneath the stone archway up ahead and sang for two strangers while Jamie played his father's guitar. It had been a cold, winter's night, but I flushed hot with the memory—especially the reminder of Jamie sneaking into my bedroom and stealing me from my bed. He'd risked it all for his friends, and it only reminded me why I'd fallen for him in the first place.

When I reached the black-painted door with a window cut into the shape of a snowflake, the butterflies I hadn't felt in a long time took flight. Slipping my hand in my pocket, I wrapped my hand around the harmonica hidden there and squeezed. *Have courage.*

Freeing my hand, I rang the doorbell.

Well, fuck. There was no going back now.

I could hear voices speaking all at once on the other side, and it sounded like they were arguing. A few seconds later, the front door was ripped open. Wren, who was seriously fucking mouth-watering with his dark-brown hair and stormy blue eyes, stood on the threshold, scowling.

"Hey," he said, a note of surprise in his voice. "Barbette, right?"

Even though his tone was polite, I couldn't help but fidget when he hesitated to let me inside. Hadn't he known I was coming?

"Just Bee is fine."

Before he could respond, Lou appeared, ducking under his arm, and I released a sigh of relief.

"For a second, I thought you stood me up," she greeted with a grin.

"Not at all." Returning her grin, I lifted the case of beer that hadn't been easy convincing Joe to purchase for me. I was pretty sure he only caved out of misplaced guilt. The NDA he signed made him privy to my family's private affairs without worry that he would ever speak a word. "I just couldn't come empty-handed."

Wren's blue-gray eyes widened appreciatively, and then he was stepping aside and pulling Lou with him. I didn't meet their gazes as I stepped inside their home. I didn't want either of them to see just how nervous I was.

Even though I'd been here that night, I hadn't seen the inside. Jamie had taken me home the minute I'd belted the last note and left as if nothing had ever happened. I was curious if the two strangers had found their fairy-tale ending, but stubbornly, I hadn't wanted to give Jamie the satisfaction of leaving me in suspense. He clearly didn't like asking me for help, which was probably why he never bothered and kidnapped me instead.

Looking around, I noticed how little Wren and Lou had, and yet I still felt the warmth of a home. My parents had filled our house with countless trinkets and antiques, but it had never felt like home.

Wren and Lou had kept their furnishings simple and cozy, and I knew that by the end of the night, I wouldn't want to leave.

"This way," Lou directed. "Everyone's in here."

Wren took the case of beer from me, and I couldn't tell if he was being a gentleman or was just that eager for a buzz. It was only a few steps to the living where Ever, Four, Tyra, Vaughn, and… Jamie were all seated on the floor around the long, wooden coffee table. Just like Wren, they all looked more than a little surprised to see me, and I realized then that the only one who'd known I was coming was Lou.

And of course, the only one who actually seemed pissed by my presence was Jamie.

He shot up from his comfortable lounge on the floor, and I tried but failed not to ogle him in his dark gray slacks, matching vest, and white dress shirt adorned by a black and white tie. I had no idea what prompted this change in his style, but my watering mouth told me I hoped it stayed this way. That was, of course, until he opened *his* mouth.

"What the hell are you getting at, Lou?"

"Sit down, Jamie. The pizza's getting cold."

Wren only shook his head as he flopped down on the recliner and got comfortable. He didn't seem the least bit surprised by his girlfriend's antics. To make matters worse, she pointed to the only empty spot left—next to Jamie—and told me to have a seat too.

As everyone waited for an explanation, she piled five or six slices of pizza on a plate before sauntering over to Wren and curling up on his lap. He kissed her lips and whispered something that no one could hear before stealing a slice from her plate.

Feeling awkward enough, I slowly sank onto the floor, leaving Jamie standing alone. He could do what he wanted. It had been nearly a week since I'd seen or talked to him. Given how we left things, his reaction to my being here wasn't a total surprise, but I couldn't help wishing he would take a break from being such a dick. I needed this.

As I felt him seething next to me, I suddenly realized his problem.

Jamie preferred to be the one doing the preying and pouncing. I'd caught him off guard, and now he felt like he didn't have the upper hand. Settling in, I grabbed a slice of pizza and decided I'd do my damned hardest to keep it that way. I thought about how much harder he pushed whenever I pushed back and shivered.

Scanning the room, I noticed Ever had his lips tucked as if he was trying not to laugh while Four rolled her eyes at Jamie before winking at me. Her reaction made me secretly like her that much more.

I forced myself to relax a little since neither Four or Ever seemed bothered by my being here. Eventually, Jamie returned to his spot on the floor but not before throwing me a nasty glare. I chose to ignore him as I savored my pizza. I couldn't remember the last time I'd had any.

"So, what's the occasion for all of this anyway?" Tyra asked after everyone had filled their plates. Ever was the only one to opt for wings only since he steered clear of cheese. "Seems kind of random."

"What's life if not a series of random moments?" Lou answered without actually answering at all.

"Is that why you invited Medusa?" Jamie quipped. I knew immediately he was talking about me. "Because you felt like being *random?*"

"If I were Medusa, I guess you'd be stone since you can't seem to take your eyes off me."

"What?" he snarled.

Finishing off my first slice, I reached for another. *So good.* "It's not like you've looked anywhere else since I've sat down."

"Maybe because I'm still wondering why you're here."

"I was invited."

Looking into his handsome, scowling face, I began to

wonder the same thing. Why had I come? I'd been stupid to believe that Jamie might be eager to see me, too. Six days, and I couldn't get our encounter inside my parents' kitchen out of my mind. I'd even go so far as to say that he owed me an orgasm, though I would never be so bold or desperate to demand he pay up.

I bet he'd like that too.

"Lou only invited you to piss me off. She doesn't even like you," he said, using his words like a whip. Unfortunately, I knew what that truly felt like, yet somehow, Jamie's words stung more.

"Actually, that's not true at all," Lou said. "I don't know Barbette, which is why she's here."

"I've told you all about her," Jamie snapped.

"And now I'd like to get to know her for myself."

I felt a warmth spread through my veins at the sincerity in her voice. Just as quickly, I tossed the kernel of hope away. In less than a month, I would be leaving Blackwood Keep. Getting close to anyone was out of the question. It would only make running that much harder—and give my father a chance to find me. I had no idea how far he'd be willing to go to get me back, but I knew I couldn't risk anyone getting hurt because of me.

"Good luck with that," Jamie said, snorting. "Elliot definitely wouldn't approve of his precious daughter mingling below her station." Suddenly our gazes met, blue against brown. "Does your father know where you are? I wonder what you told him so he'd let you out to play." Turning his head, he regarded his cousin. "That you were on a date with your fiancé, perhaps?" Snickering, his cruel gaze traveled to Four, sitting close by Ever's side. "You three definitely give new meaning to 'double date.'"

With a look to kill, Ever started to stand, but Vaughn beat him to his feet. "Did I hear someone mention beer?" he asked.

"Oh... yeah," Wren said, tilting his chin toward me. "Bee—" we grinned at each other at his use of my nickname—"brought a case. I put it in the fridge to chill."

"Beer's beer," Vaughn replied as he stepped over legs and feet until he reached Jamie. "Come and help me in the kitchen."

"For what?" Jamie said with a twist of his lips. Vaughn's only response was to kick his foot hard as hell. With a growl, Jamie shot to his feet and followed Vaughn into the kitchen.

"Sorry about that," Tyra apologized with a gentle smile.

I shrugged, knowing they all saw through my indifference. Everyone seemed to think I was the one in need of rescuing, but I wasn't the princess in this fairy tale. I'm not even the villain. I'm nothing while Jameson is everything.

As much as I wanted to hate him, I knew if Jamie had callously ripped out my heart as I had done to him, there was nothing I wouldn't do to make him feel that pain tenfold.

So I'd take his lashes and bear the pain with the hope that it lessened his own.

"Music anyone?" Four offered as she stood. "Luckily, I commandeered Jamie's iPod before school this morning." Disappearing upstairs, she came back a few minutes later with an iPod and a handheld speaker shaped like a pill. "Any volunteers for deejay?"

"As long as it's not some old country western, I don't give a fuck what you play," Tyra replied. "I'm depressed enough."

Flipping her off, Four scrolled through Jamie's iPod. "Just because I'm from the south doesn't mean I listen to country."

"It doesn't mean you don't, either."

Sauntering back into the living room as if nothing had happened, Jamie butted in. "Good music is whatever sets your soul on fire. Don't ever let anyone tell you that you have bad taste because you stayed true to yourself."

"Unless it's Justin Bieber!" Vaughn shouted from the kitchen.

"Oh, yeah," Jamie agreed with a vigorous nod of his head. "Fuck that guy."

I noticed he only had two beers in his hand just before he handed me one. Was I mistaken or was this a peace offering?

Hesitantly, I accepted it. When I felt his finger caress mine at the very last second, I wondered if he should be tested for mania. He could be so cold one moment and setting me on fucking fire the next.

When he sat down this time, he was close enough for me to smell his body wash or maybe his shampoo? Whichever it was, it made me lean into him.

Hmm… maybe I need to be checked, too.

It was beginning to feel as if we were trapped on an emotional roller coaster—one that wasn't planning to stop any time soon.

"Did you know that Rihanna is Jamie's favorite singer?" I announced with a bat of my eyelashes. My mind needed a distraction before my body did something crazy. "Not someone notable like Elvis or even Michael Jackson. *Rihanna.*"

Jamie frowned as he took a sip of his beer. I found myself mirroring him and took a sip of mine, too. "Show me someone else who can be *that* savage and still sexy. Go ahead. I'll wait."

"Holy shit!" Four interjected, her southern twang ringing loud and clear. Her eyes were wide as she clapped her hands over her mouth. "That explains everything! There were *far* too many of her songs on your iPod."

"You mean the one you keep stealing?" he shot back.

Four didn't bother defending herself and bit her bottom lip with a grin. Standing, Lou suggested we watch a movie instead, and while she looked for one, Jamie finished his beer. Setting the empty bottle on its side on the coffee table, he grinned. "You guys want to play spin the bottle? I'll even up the ante. Instead of seven minutes in heaven, we'll go for fifteen."

"Because that's all the time you need?" Tyra teased as she came back into the living room.

When the hell had she left? Vaughn appeared only seconds later, and I realized he hadn't brought back the beers.

"Sure," Jamie said, and I knew by the wicked gleam in his eye that he was about to call them both out. "I guess you can relate. Did you at least take a hoe bath?"

Tyra's lips parted. "A what?"

"You know, one of those baths where you wash your ass and pits in the sink."

"It's called a birdbath, Jamie."

"Nah… it's a hoe bath. I've watched plenty of girls do that shit after a hookup."

Planting her hands on her hips, she faced off with Jamie. All five feet of her. "Are you calling me a hoe?"

"Are you telling me you didn't just sneak away for a quickie?"

"I'm telling you it's none of your business." She sat down next to Vaughn and rolled her eyes at Jamie when he blew her a kiss.

"You know, I once took a hoe bath." The room was silent, though Jamie didn't exactly wait around for permission to continue. "This chick I met in a pub didn't bother telling me she was a virgin before I bent her over. She bled all over me, and since I couldn't shower right away, I had to scrub my dick in the sink." When Jamie looked at me and winked, I wondered if that story had been told for my benefit. I didn't doubt that it was true.

"I hope you wore a condom," Lou replied, wrinkling her nose.

Stealing my unfinished beer, he saluted the room before taking a sip. "Always."

Blushing for some reason, I fixed my gaze on the TV in time to see Lou scrolling past *The Conjuring*. My love for horror movies took over, and I sat up, but the request on my lips quickly died when I remembered that I was an outsider.

My disappointment was short-lived when I felt the cold press of Jamie's lips on my ear and smelled the beer on his breath. "You know this timid act of yours isn't going to make my dick hard if that's your goal."

"It's not."

"Mmm." It was all the response he gave before sitting up. "Put something scary on," he told Lou.

"Like what?"

Jamie looked down at me and perked a brow. I guess he wasn't going to do the dirty work for me, after all.

"How about *The Conjuring*?" I asked.

Shrugging, Lou did just that before hitting the lights and returning to Wren's lap. He hadn't said much all night. I had the feeling he wasn't much of a talker.

Jamie stayed close while the movie played, and I tried not to laugh whenever he jumped at something scary. I had the feeling Jamie would have rather sat through a romantic comedy than a horror. We'd just gotten to the part where the Warrens were attempting an exorcism when my phone buzzed in my hand. Peeking down, I saw that it was a text from Joe.

Outside, miss.

The hollow feeling that I hadn't realized was gone now returned with swift vengeance. *Time to return to reality.*

As I started to stand and say my goodbyes, long fingers curled around my phone, stealing it from my hand. I watched Jamie read the text, and then my lips parted when he started typing with his thumb. Once done, he wordlessly dumped the phone in my lap. Picking it up, I read his reply to Joe.

Take the rest of the night off. She has a ride home.

My heart pounded in my chest for two reasons. One, Jamie hadn't even bothered disguising that it wasn't me texting back, and two, I'd get to stay in this fantasy just a little bit longer.

Before I could say anything to Jamie, there was a knock at the front door. Wren started to lift a sleeping Lou so that he could answer the door, but Jamie beat him to the punch. I watched mesmerized as he swaggered lazily from the room.

I could hear him speaking to someone, and the moment I heard Joe's voice rising angrily, I shot to my feet and rushed from the living room. Joe seemed visibly relieved the moment he saw me enter the foyer while Jamie reluctantly stood back, allowing him to see me fully.

"Hey, Joe! Sorry. *I* should have texted you," I said with a pointed look at Jamie. "I decided to stay a little longer than I planned, so Jamie is going to give me a ride instead."

"That's fine, miss." The frown Joe wore now was troubled. "I'll just have to let your father know."

My heart sank to my stomach. I knew my father would demand I come home if he found out that I was with anyone other than Ever.

"Or don't," Jamie snapped with a scowl.

Without thinking, I placed both hands on Jamie's chest, hoping it would silence him. It did, but I could tell he didn't like it. Joe hadn't missed the exchange, and I knew we were no closer to convincing him to risk his job by lying to his employer. He'd already bought me the beer. Maybe I was asking too much. Remembering the wife and daughter he had to consider, I dropped my head. I couldn't allow Joe to lose his job because of me.

"I'll just be a sec." Spinning on my heel, I hurried back into the living room. The movie had been paused, and everyone was staring at me when I entered.

"You have to go?" Lou asked as she stood and yawned.

Wordlessly, I crossed the room and pulled her into a hug. "Thank you," I whispered so only she could hear. She'd probably never know how much tonight had meant to me. Sometimes, the smallest gestures made the biggest impact.

"Anytime," she whispered back.

Letting her go, I waved goodbye to everyone else, and that was when I realized Ever was missing. When I stepped out into the hall, I noticed two things: rain was falling, and neither Ever nor Joe seemed to notice as they spoke in low whispers at the end of the drive. The expression on Jamie's face as he looked on was so intense that I had the feeling he was trying, or at least hoping, to read their lips.

I attempted to slip past him, hoping to escape without making this harder, but of course, Jamie grabbed my hand, and I knew there was no such thing as easy when it came to us. Reluctantly, I met his gaze, and those brown eyes of his seemed to plead with me.

Don't go.

It felt like tearing off my own limb when I slowly pulled my hand away.

I have to.

CHAPTER
TEN

The Punk

I STOOD IN THE RAIN, WATCHING THE TAILLIGHTS OF THE SUV UNTIL they disappeared. Ever had already run back inside without even an explanation on what the hell he'd said to Joe or why he was suddenly so tense.

I wanted to go after Bee.

To steal her away from whatever the hell had caused that haunted look in her eyes. I wasn't blind. I knew she wanted to stay, so why the hell hadn't she? Her father was a prick who hated my guts, but did it really matter how she got home as long as she made curfew?

It was just more questions that needed fucking answering.

Shouting from inside had me realizing that I was still standing in the fucking rain like a complete jackass. I stepped through the front door, and I gritted my teeth because I couldn't stop replaying Bee walking through it.

"I need money!" Lou shouted when I returned to the living room. "How else am I supposed to get it?"

"I give you money," Wren snapped.

With one hand on her hip, Lou gave him a withering look. "I'm a modern woman, Harlan. Mama's gotta bake her own bread." She waved what looked like Vaughn's wallet in the air as if picking pockets was her idea of a job. Vaughn snatched it from her hand, but Lou simply shrugged. I was pretty sure she'd pilfered his cash already.

"Who the hell invites someone to their home and then steals from them? Isn't it supposed to be the other way around?"

I started to laugh at the perplexed look on Vaughn's face, but then I pictured the solemn expression on Bee's face right before she pulled away, and my laughter died. My friends had all returned to their normal lives while I still felt like I'd had a hole punched through my chest. Right where my stolen and then broken heart *wasn't* supposed to be.

CHAPTER ELEVEN

The Plaything

I STARED INDIFFERENTLY AT MY REFLECTION IN THE GOLD-FRAMED vanity mirror while my mom wrapped sections of my hair around a curling wand. When I was younger, she'd pull most of it back and secure it with a white ribbon so that my face could be seen. It was the same hairstyle she had forced me to wear every day. *"You're a beautiful girl,"* she would say. *"You shouldn't hide behind your hair."*

My mom didn't get that it was *because* I was pretty that I hid. Girls who looked like me were rarely taken seriously. No one ever expects pretty girls to get their hands dirty or chip a nail... I *liked* doing all of those things.

"You do know you can talk to me, don't you, dear?"

No, I didn't know that. In fact, I knew better. It had been five days since I had dinner at Lou and Wren's, and somehow, I'd become more hollow than I was before. Deep down, I knew it was because I'd had a glimpse of what could have been.

"Is something the matter?" I hedged. We both knew this wasn't about me, anyway. My parents were only concerned about themselves.

"Your father and I were wondering if everything is okay between you and Ever?"

"Of course," I lied. "Why do you ask?" It was all I could do to hide the truth. I *was* worried. While my engagement to Ever was a farce, I wasn't so sure our friendship would survive. I never asked for any of this, but like a coward, I'd accepted too much from him, and not for the first time, I questioned if I should have let him get involved at all. Faking a relationship had been his idea, but it was my choice to go along with it. I should have run when I had the chance, but I'd been afraid. Terrified that I'd never see Jamie again. There was no way I could ever return to Blackwood Keep if I left.

Once I left.

"He seems... distracted."

Translation: my parents were afraid that Ever was losing interest in me.

I was eager for the day they'd realize we'd been playing them all along, even though I knew I wouldn't be around to see it. Or would I? I could feel Ever pulling away and feared that soon, I'd be on my own.

"Barbette, you're slouching."

This was one time I didn't mind my mother criticizing my form. Squaring my shoulders, I lifted my chin. I guess I was okay with being alone, after all. Ever had Four, and Vaughn had Tyra, and though it didn't bode well for me, I couldn't help but feel lighter knowing that I'd be leaving them in good hands. It was everything a girl could hope for her best friends.

And Jamie... well, he'd never had trouble finding someone to comfort him.

"I'm sure he's just nervous about starting school in the fall."

Ever had chosen to attend Cornell. They had one of the best architecture programs in the country, but Ever didn't seem all that excited. Something told me it had to do with the four-hour distance it would put between him and Four.

From what I had heard, since Ever could never seem to talk about anything other than Four, she planned to race professionally, which would have her on the road often.

"He'll also be marrying you," my mother naively reminded. "Your wedding should be his priority, as well."

"It is."

"He hasn't helped with the planning."

"Did Dad help plan your wedding?"

"Don't talk back, young lady."

I could barely keep from rolling my eyes. "I'm not. I'm just wondering, I guess."

After a brief pause, my mother let out one of those dainty chuckles that were totally fake. "No, I suppose not." She resumed curling my hair, but I knew the inquisition was far from over. "I thought you'd be more excited about marrying the man of your dreams."

My eyes shot up to meet my mom's in the mirror. Was she serious? I wasn't in love with Ever, and she knew it even if my father didn't. My mother had been the one to advise me that love was an illusion, and if I were smart, I'd find someone I at least liked before my father chose a husband for me.

I turned around in my chair, and my mother stepped back with her hand clutching her neck at the look in my eyes. "We both know he's not the man of my dreams, Mother, but he's rich. Rich enough to dig us out of the hole Father dug us into. You should be thanking me rather than complaining. Pretty soon, you'll both be at my mercy, which means I can speak to you however I like."

Her palm cracked across my face, and the pain was almost blinding.

Touching my cheek, I felt shock ripple through me as I met my mother's sorrowful gaze. I could tell she was torn between begging my forgiveness and standing firm. This was the first time she'd ever hit me, leaving the dirty work to my father.

"Don't feel bad," I coolly implored as my hand fell to my lap. "It's the first feeling I've had in years."

She looked ready to apologize anyway before her lips flattened. "This is nonsense," she scolded. "The reporter will be here any minute. Meet us on the patio and try not to be late."

She fled my room, probably from shame, and it only took a

few minutes for me to build the courage to follow. Even then, I could still feel the unease curling in my stomach. I had the feeling something was about to go horribly wrong.

Downstairs, my father introduced me to Grace Harrell, the reporter for the *Blackwood Tribune*. Somehow, my father had convinced them my engagement to Ever was important enough to grace their front page. In my opinion, it spoke volumes about our sleepy town and what passed for newsworthy around here. Sure, the McNamaras were loaded, but wealth was the leading demographic in our town. Two trust-fund babies getting hitched wasn't news. It was strategic.

"So your father was telling me that your fiancé is a childhood friend of yours," Grace said, speaking loud and clear for the recorder. "When did you know that he'd be the one to steal your heart?"

My lips parted, and the reporter, along with my parents, waited for me to pour my heart out. To captivate them with the story of how I'd fallen for the very first time. "It happened on a Ferris wheel," I began, tasting the bittersweet remnants of a half-truth.

I hadn't known then that Jamie had stolen my heart.

Not until he'd already broken it.

He'd been the one to teach me love and, tragically, the first to show me pain.

Half an hour later, I was done with the interview. I'd told them all about our two summers together, all the while feeling guilt creeping up my skin. Any moment now, Ever would arrive, and I wasn't sure how I could face him in the wake of all the lies I'd just told. I thought the hard part would be over now, but for some reason, the bad feeling remained. Pulling out my phone, I sent Ever a text.

Where are you?

I didn't get a response, but a couple of minutes later, I exhaled when Ever stepped onto the terrace. Although he looked like he was being led to the slaughter, I was relieved to see him. He hadn't shown last time, and I found out it was because his father kicked him out for sleeping with Four. Of course, I hadn't told my father that.

Father was the first to greet Ever, shaking his hand. "So glad you deigned to join us."

Seeing the need to intervene, I stood from my chair and reached for the pitcher of lemonade. "Father, have some lemonade." I poured him a glass before shoving it in his hand.

"Thank you." His tone was still cold, but remembering our other guest, my father finally offered Ever a seat. It wasn't wise to air our dirty laundry with a reporter present. "Ever, I want you to meet Grace Harrell. She's a reporter at the *Blackwood Tribune*."

My hands shook underneath the table as I watched Ever struggle to maintain his composure. That mask he always wore now had a crack in it, and it was only about to get bigger.

"Grace, this is Ever McNamara. My daughter's betrothed."

I wanted to laugh because my dad sounded like he'd time-traveled from a different century. I knew firsthand that the way he spoke was in line with his beliefs. Otherwise, he wouldn't be trying to marry me off for personal gain.

"I think it's so romantic how the two of you played together as kids, and now you're getting married."

"It's just marvelous!" my mother chimed in. Ever and I said nothing. "And although it was my dream to see my daughter have a June wedding, with prom in a few days and her birthday and graduation soon after, I think a September wedding once all the leaves turn would be just as beautiful."

As much as I hated to agree with my mother on anything, a summer wedding was a dream I'd once shared with her.

"It sounds like the perfect ending to a fairy tale," Grace gushed. "I think our readers will want to hear every detail from start to finish." She started flipping through her notes, and I noticed Ever's frown as he stared at the already filled pages. "I think I have everything I need except for the photo." I wanted to crawl under the table when she pulled out a camera. My parents hadn't said anything about a photo. They'd expect to capture a loving couple, not two people who were in love with two others. "You two not only have an interesting story but you also make a beautiful couple." The excitement in her voice only fueled my dread. "Do you have a background in mind?"

Always the gracious host, my mother immediately answered. "Oh, yes! Follow me!"

She escorted us inside the parlor, and I noticed that some paintings and expensive trinkets had been added to the décor, making the room look less barren than it had before. I rolled my eyes. If my parents had cared less what other people thought, we wouldn't be in this mess.

The look in Ever's eyes when he pulled me close for the first pose said that I'd betrayed him. I didn't know about the photoshoot, and I was desperate to tell him so.

But would it really have changed anything if you had known? You're selfish and a coward.

"Beautiful!" Grace said after two hours of snapping our photo. "Now, I'd like to get a shot of you kissing your beautiful bride-to-be."

It was then that it occurred to me that we had never kissed. Not even once. In fact, we'd been careful not to touch each other too intimately. Even now, Ever's hand was positioned several inches *above* my lower back.

"Don't you think you have enough?" Ever snapped. His composure was slowly unraveling. I could see little beads of sweat pooling near his hairline.

"I know this can be a little tiring, but I think it will be eye-catching on our front page."

There was a pause, a moment of utter silence that weighed heavily over the room as my parents and Grace waited, expectantly, for us to kiss. It was what fiancés do, after all, and shouldn't have been a problem for two people in love.

"It's okay, son. Lay it on her," my father encouraged. He was smiling, but I could tell he was nervous and more than a little suspicious of our hesitation. He wasn't the only one I realized when I caught Grace watching us skeptically over her camera.

I felt the first of my tears fall when Ever's hand slid from the middle of my back to my waist. I couldn't let him do this. Four would never understand, and why should she?

Which meant... I was screwed.

I pleaded to my best friend with my eyes to stop, go, run now, but instead, he gripped me tighter, pulling me into him. I knew I wouldn't stop him because I was weak and afraid. My father had used his fists and belt and feet to make sure of that many times. Sometimes, he'd even refuse me food for a few days to show me what starving would feel like when the money ran out.

Ever's eyes drifted closed as he prepared to kiss me. Captivated by the turmoil twisting his features, my own remained open. I knew he'd probably convinced himself that the kiss would be meaningless, and maybe to us, it would have been, but not to Four... and not to Jamie. My hands lifted, prepared to push him away when he startled me by stumbling back all on his own.

My eyes widened, and relief flooded through me as I watched him take a step back and then another.

"I'm sorry," was all he said before he fled.

I wasn't.

It had been three days since I'd seen or talked to Ever, three days since he practically ran away from me, my parents, and this screwed-up arrangement. I knew it was over.

Ever had broken off our fake engagement.

Relief and doom blended together. I didn't know what to

feel. My parents had been alarmed by his abrupt departure—my mother, most of all. My father had only stared me down with his cold, blue eyes before ordering me to fix it. Whatever the hell that meant. I wouldn't be fixing shit. Four and Ever were meant to be, and I refused to get in the way of that anymore.

My hand shook as I applied black liquid eyeliner, so it took me three attempts before I drew a line straight enough to pass inspection. I'd caked on more makeup than usual, hoping it would bring me confidence to face the day—or at the very least a sturdy shield.

My foundation and concealer were blended perfectly. My features contoured and highlighted to the gods. I'd even spent extra time on my eyebrows, which I hated doing. When I was done, I signed the look with a matte black lipstick that made me look cold and cruel. Mother wouldn't approve, but I couldn't bring myself to care. She wasn't the one being led into a den of wolves today.

After making sure my hair and makeup were perfect, I sighed, no longer able to stall. I put on my uniform and grabbed my school bag before tiptoeing downstairs. I wasn't allowed to leave home without presenting myself to my parents first, but since their wrath wouldn't be the worst thing I'd face today, I slipped from the house undetected and quickly hopped inside the waiting Escalade.

"Morning, Joe."

"Good morning, miss." He didn't waste time driving away, and even though my heart was beating pretty hard for what was to come, I exhaled as I settled against the seat. On autopilot, I pulled my phone from my bag, and my racing heart skipped a beat seeing the message waiting me. The daily texts that started a mere week after our fates collided once more had become a ritual, and even though I never responded, I looked forward to them each morning. Today, despite all that could go wrong was no different.

Jamie: What do Jameson Buchanan and Barbette Montgomery have in common?

I frowned as not for the first time my fingers had itched to respond. Having learned my lesson the last time, I decided to toy with him, I tossed my phone in my bag and forced Jamie out of my mind. I didn't have time for riddles.

It was possible that I was being paranoid. Maybe nothing at all would happen today. And maybe my entire world would come crashing down.

The ride to Brynwood was short, and as I made my way to my locker, I tried to ignore the fact that everyone was reading the newspaper. The *front page*, to be exact. I gritted my teeth. Despite how wrong that interview had gone, Grace held no reservations about publishing the story anyway.

A few girls had even stopped me with hearts and stars in their eyes to tell me how lucky I was and that I should never let my Prince Charming go.

Too late.

Maybe I was a damn fool, but I wasn't about to spend the rest of my life hoping to turn back time. Jamie wasn't the same anymore, and neither was I. We might have been right for each other then, but now we were poisonous to mix.

After getting what I needed from my locker, I kept my gaze straight ahead and ignored the ones following me. Seriously, what was the big deal? It wasn't as if Ever and I were celebrities. People married every day. My irritation mounted, reaching its peak when I reached a crowd forming near the entrance.

"Extra! Extra! Read all about it!"

Someone shifted just in time for me to see the douchebag, who was yelling and handing out newspapers, shove one in Tyra's hands.

Suddenly, I was choking on a huge ball of regret.

If Four read that paper, I knew what she would think, but I didn't know how she would react. The picture was bad enough, but the story I'd spun behind it would only make it worse. She'd think we'd deceived her. That there was more to us than we'd let on. I started forward, wanting to get to her, to explain, but I stopped short seeing a tall, familiar figure push through the crowd. The anguish on Ever's face as he tried to reach her nearly sent me collapsing to the floor. What had I done?

The second Ever reached Four, he snatched the paper from her hand and brought her to his chest. Jaws dropped, and the gasps and whispers drowned out what he said to her. It didn't matter. I'd seen enough, and so had everyone else. I inched closer, wanting to help but knowing that my presence would only make things worse.

Four shoved Ever away before turning to say something to Tyra, who nodded and started for the door. Whatever the truth, Four wasn't sticking around to hear it. Ever grabbed her hand when she started after Tyra.

"Four, please listen. It's not what—"

"No!" The look she gave him, full of disdain and not the love I'd seen pass between them before, confirmed it. I'd ruined everything. "I'm done listening."

Shock made Ever release Four's hand, and she bolted out the door, leaving him behind. If he noticed the whispers and the stares, he didn't care. He watched her go for a few seconds before turning. The moment his red-rimmed eyes fell on me, he stopped—his jaw clenching.

"I'm sorry." And I was. I didn't mean for any of this to happen, but it didn't mean shit because it *did* happen.

Ever's nostrils flared as he looked away. I held my breath, waiting for him to rip me a new one, but he didn't. He stormed away, and even though I wanted to follow, like Ever, I was forced to watch him go.

The hall was silent, and for a moment, I thought I was alone until someone began clapping slow. Spinning around, I found the crowd watching me, some with sympathetic gazes and others with mocking sneers. I hated them both. Searching the sea of faces, I found Jamie at the edge, leaning against the trophy case. Clapping.

"Congratulations," he said the moment our gazes met. "That's two more people you ruined." He stood up to his full height before swaggering over. I felt about an inch high by the time he reached me. "Nothing to say?"

I hung my head even as my fists balled. I was at war with myself. *All my fault.* Slowly, my fingers uncurled. I had no right to be angry.

I felt Jamie's lips at my ear in an instant. "You see love, you break love. That's what you do."

My head felt heavy when I finally lifted it, but I pushed past my sorrow. "We weren't in love, Jamie. It was summer, and you were fun. Get over yourself."

I tried to walk around him, but he pulled me back with a hand on my arm.

Tilting my chin, he held my gaze. "I still am," he whispered. "A hell of a lot more than when we were kids."

The hand holding my chin slid down my side slowly. As if I hadn't been humiliated enough, the asshole began groping me in front of the entire school.

"We both love unrequited," he continued while caressing my ass, "that's the answer to the riddle. My cousin clearly just made his choice. Have some fun with me."

"If I'm ever in the market for an STD, I'll let you know." Jamie didn't stop me this time when I pushed him away, but I should have known he'd never let me leave with my head held high.

"Let's give it up for Four, everyone. The better bachelorette got the rose." Jamie started clapping again, but this time, he wasn't alone. Slowly, the crowd that had remained to witness the Jamie Freak Show joined him, and they didn't stop there. I could still hear them chanting Four's name when I rushed through the door and out onto the front lawn. I wanted to run, but I realized as I looked around that there was nowhere to go. Ever was the last person I could turn to, and I'd pushed him too far.

I see love, I break love. That's what I do.

I'd gone to bed last night happy to finally put the disastrous day behind me until I realized my nightmare was only beginning. Tonight was prom night, and my parents were fully expecting me to attend on my *fiancé's* arm.

I started the morning pretending to be sick, but by the end of the day, it hadn't mattered to my parents. I was going to prom. They saw tonight as an opportunity for me to warm Ever's cold feet.

Just wait until they heard the rumors.

I could tell them myself, but I had a better idea. I could run.

Who needed a high school diploma, anyway? I'd taken my final exam on Monday and knew that I'd passed. Without a social life, the only thing I had to occupy my time was my studies. I'd studied hard and made straight A's, knowing that college would never be an option. I never got the chance to dream, anyway. I didn't know if I wanted to be a doctor or an astronaut or a reality TV star. *It's not too late to find out.*

"Now, Barbette, tonight is very important," my mother said, chasing away the hope warming my chest. She handed me a pair of gold heels that were cruel to my poor, helpless feet. They hadn't asked for any of this. As I slipped the heels on, I winced thinking about the night ahead that I had in them. "Whatever is going on with Ever, I trust you'll help him see things your way."

"Should I sleep with him, Mother?"

"That's enough, Barbette! This is serious!"

"Regardless, proper ladies never raise their voice," I chastised as she had done me so many times before.

She paused before patting her bun and smoothing the wrinkles from her dress. "We need you to understand what's at risk. Without the McNamara's money, your father and I will be ruined."

"What about me? Do you even care what happens to me?"

"Ever will be good to you."

"And if he doesn't marry me? Would you really let Father marry me to some geezer with a limp penis and a handful of Viagra? Don't you care what people will say then?"

"Don't be dramatic, Barbette. He won't be old."

"But he might be cruel."

"Your father has many friends with young, handsome sons who can give you the life you deserve."

"I deserve to be unhappy?"

"You deserve to have all the finer things in life."

As I looked away, my gaze landed on the pair of scissors resting on my vanity. Like I had when I was twelve-years-old, I longed to cut away my tresses until there was nothing left. Now I knew it would never be enough. Rather than urge me to nourish the good I held inside, my parents carved it out until I was left with nothing to offer except my skin—the beauty they valued above all else.

I was hollow, empty, and now that Ever had finally chosen the only girl who should matter, I was on my own. The reality of my situation sinking in felt like the key sliding into a lock and turning. The door opened, and I waited on its threshold for despair and panic to take hold and devour me.

Something else entirely emerged.

"Would you still believe that if I were no longer beautiful?" Picking up the scissors, I held the sharp end to my face near my temple. The sad, lonely wind swirling inside my shell ceased the moment Ever walked away from me yesterday. I assumed I'd finally broken. I didn't know until this moment that it had only been the quiet before the storm. The tempest I'd fought so hard to protect was no longer content to wait in her tower. She wanted out, and she was done asking permission. "Tell me, Mother. Would you?"

Seeing the wrath brewing in my eyes, she took a step back but her horror when I dug the scissors into my skin kept her from taking another. I kept pressing, relieved that I could still feel pain, and then I dragged them down…

I didn't get far before my mother broke free of her shock and wrangled the scissors from my hand. I watched her toss them across the room.

"Look what you've done!" Rushing into the en suite, she returned seconds later with a first aid kit. I stared at myself in the mirror, unfazed by the blood running down my perfectly made-up face. "You better hope your father doesn't find out what you've done."

I scoffed because my father had given me wounds far worse than this. Besides, Elliot Montgomery barely noticed anything when it came to me. I'd been a daughter when he wanted a son, so he had no interest in me, and before realizing my beauty could garner him millions, he had no use for me, either.

After cleaning and bandaging my cut that was barely more than a scratch, she fixed my makeup before rearranging my hair so that the wound wouldn't show.

Once done, she stood back, searching for imperfections. Finding none, she scooped the scissors from the floor. "You won't be getting these back."

I was silent as I watched her go. The moment the door closed, I stood and crossed the room until I reached my night-stand. For the millionth time today, I picked up my phone, but after a few minutes of staring at the blank screen, I set it back down. Maybe there was nothing I could say to make things right. I was probably the last person Four wanted to hear from, anyway.

Tossing my phone into the small gold clutch that my mother loaned me, I headed downstairs. *Time to face the music.*

There would be no Prince Charming ringing my doorbell tonight and no carriage ride to the ball. I joined my parents in the parlor room, where they waited for Ever to arrive.

My mother glided over to me, a graceful smile spreading her painted lips as if nothing had happened. "Doesn't she look beautiful, Elliot?"

My father barely glanced at me before nodding. "She'll suffice."

I almost longed for the days when there was someone around to impress. It was the only time my father treated me like a human being. Elliot Montgomery couldn't have his friends and business partners thinking he was mentally and emotionally abusive toward his daughter.

At least he doesn't beat me anymore.

During those early days spent turning me into this shell, I'd been the most resistant. It wasn't until my father learned how easily I bruised on the outside that he stopped. They hadn't cared about the scars they'd left behind on the inside.

My mother rejoined my father at his side, and I took a seat on the sofa across from them, getting comfortable before pulling my phone from my clutch.

I was so close to finally beating level ninety-seven of *Candy Crush*. And let's face it, I had all night.

"What time did Ever say he'd be picking you up?" my father questioned. "It's after nine."

"He didn't say," I answered without looking away from my game. Sensing my father's anger, I smiled only to curse under my breath when I ran out of moves.

"Barbette, you'll show your father respect," my mother chastised.

"Why? I have as much respect for him as he does for me." My father angrily shoved to his feet, so I finally gave him my full attention. "Are you going to beat me?" I mocked. "Send me to prom all broken and bruised? What will people think?"

"Oh, don't you worry, daughter. I'll make sure they won't see a damn thing under that dress."

He took a threatening step forward, and although my breath had gotten caught in my throat, I stood, too, inching toward the lamp on the side table. I was no longer the thirteen-year-old girl who'd been too terrified of her father to fight back.

Just as he raised his hand to slap me down, and I dove for the lamp, the doorbell rang. My father and I froze with less than two feet separating us.

"Oh, dear, that must be Ever," my mother announced.

Knowing that it couldn't be, I clutched the lamp tighter, preparing to strike if my father so much as blinked at me wrong.

"Barbette, please put that down," my mother urged. "Someone might see."

"Tell your husband to back off."

To my surprise, he did just that, though the threat in his eyes was still there. "We'll revisit this conversation later."

"Looking forward to it." I had no idea what had gotten into me. I just knew I refused to be their whipped dog any longer.

The doorbell rang again, and my mother rushed to answer the door. I kept my gaze on my father even after he was seated again and sipping his brandy with his legs crossed as if nothing had happened. Of course, he wouldn't want Ever to know that he'd just been preparing to beat his fiancé.

"Barbette." My mother's soft voice carried from the foyer. Tossing the lamp on the sofa, I charged from the room. A man I didn't recognize stood inside the foyer with his cap in his hand.

"Madam. I'm Oliver, your driver for the night."

"Well, where is Ever?" my mother asked. "Shouldn't he be here to escort you?"

"He's probably still embarrassed over the interview." Laying a comforting hand on her arm, I thanked God for not giving me sensibilities as delicate as my mother's. "Give him some time." Turning to the driver, I narrowed my gaze on him. "Ever did send you, right?"

Oliver simply smiled, although nervously, before extending

his hand toward the open front door. I moved until I could see out the door and stared at the white stretch limo parked in the drive. The windows were too dark for me to see who waited inside.

Why had Ever come? He should have been on his knees, begging Four's forgiveness. Hell, I should have been right beside him.

Angry with my best friend for being such a fucking, self-sacrificing idiot, I marched past the driver and out the front door without saying goodbye to my mother.

Oliver somehow managed to beat me to the limo, and I offered him a weak smile when he opened the door for me. The moment it closed behind me, I knew I'd been led into a trap. I saw the shadow of a hand reaching up before there was a click. Light now bathed the other end of the limo and the passenger sitting underneath the soft glow.

The moment Jamie flashed his teeth in a wolfish smile, I reached for the door. Surprisingly, Jamie didn't try to stop me. A second later, I learned why when the door wouldn't budge.

"Child locks," he announced. "Man's greatest invention."

Huffing, I slammed my clutch on the leather bench. "Don't you ever get enough?"

Jamie didn't respond as he leaned over, lifted a bottle chilling on ice and two glass flutes, and began pouring. "You'll be pleased to know that I'm insatiable."

"Why would I care?"

"Because at the end of the night, I'm going to fuck you. Champagne?" He offered me the flute, and after the week I had, I was tempted to take it, but considering his claim and his confidence behind it, I figured it was best to keep my guard up. There was no part of me that believed Jamie would take advantage, but I wasn't so sure I wouldn't.

"No, thank you. How did you even get that?"

"I have my ways."

"You stole it," I said, reading between the lines.

"I have my ways," he repeated. Leaning back, he sipped at

his champagne as he admired me from head to toe. I plucked at the material of my gown and tried not to wonder what he thought since he'd chosen it for me. After yesterday, I shouldn't care. "Come here."

My lips parted for "No" to slip past them until I realized that one way or another, Jamie would have his way. Sliding over to make room for him, I lifted a brow and waited.

Grinning, he came to me, sitting close enough for our thighs to touch.

"Jamie, this bench is at least six feet long. Do you have to sit so close?"

"Six feet?" He turned his head back and forth as if measuring himself. "I'm six-four. It'll be tight, but I'm sure we can make it work." Resting his arm above my head, he leaned down to kiss me, and I pressed my fingers against his lips stopping him.

"You are *not* six-four."

Jamie's eyes sparkled as he grinned down at me. "All right, you got me. I'm six-two." I pursed my lips while he held my gaze, trailing his fingers down my bare arm and leaving goose bumps in their wake. "I like seeing you like this."

"Like what?"

"Vulnerable."

I curled my lip. "You mean *weak*."

"Yes," he replied unapologetically. "I know how strong you are, Bee. I've seen it for myself, but knowing you're as powerless against me as I am for you gets my dick hard, too."

"And who says I want you hard?"

His crooked smile was barely visible in the dark. "Neither of us has much choice in that aspect, I'm afraid."

I didn't have anything to say that wouldn't damn us both, so I let my head fall back against the seat and said nothing. I felt safe in the cocoon Jamie provided.

"We're bad for each other," I reminded him.

His lids lowered as he bit his bottom lip. He looked ready to eat me alive, and I felt ready to let him. "That's what makes it so exciting."

"And when the excitement wears off?"

He didn't respond as he slowly lowered his head. My breaths came hard and fast when he pressed his lips to the top of my breasts spilling out of my gown. How did we get here? Yesterday, we were enemies.

You still are.

My pussy didn't seem to care, and if it weren't for the thick volume of the ball gown, proof would have soaked the leather seats by now. Each of his soft kisses burned hotter than the last.

Jamie started making his way up my neck, and it felt as if he was leaving no part of me untouched. "It's been five years," he reminded between kisses. "Are you feeling less enthused about us yet?"

"Lust and love are not the same thing."

"Thank God," he agreed with a groan. "The human race would never survive."

"Do you really think we can make love without trust?"

He stiffened before lifting his head to meet my gaze. "Make love?" he echoed incredulously before shoving his fingers through his hair and ruining the gel he'd used to style it. "Jesus fuck, you really are a virgin."

"That's your opinion." I looked away to stare out the window.

Gripping my chin, he turned my face toward him. "Then tell me who was stupid enough to touch what's mine, because it sure as fuck wasn't my cousin."

"Does it matter?"

"You were a virgin when I left you," he said, gripping my chin harder. "You should have stayed that way."

"Did you?" I asked, knowing very well he hadn't. He'd flaunted his escapades in my face since he'd come back nearly a year ago. And there were the rumors…

"I wasn't waiting around for someone who preferred my cousin."

"And now you know that's not true."

"I don't know shit," he spat, nostrils flaring. "All I know is that my cousin no longer wants *you*."

Once again reminded of my dismal future, I pushed him away, and he didn't fight me. A moment later, a newspaper appeared in his hand bearing yesterday's date. I stared at the front page with disdain. How could I let them do that to Four and Ever? This time, it wasn't my parents who'd been the villain. They truly believed Ever and I were engaged. No, this one was all on me.

I should have called off the interview, made some excuse. It should have never gone that far.

"'A Fairy Tale to Remember,'" Jamie mused. "I wonder who came up with that."

Unconsciously, I tightened my grip on the dress he'd hand-picked just for me. I'd even followed his bold instructions not to wear anything underneath. I was sure the full skirt of the ball gown would keep my secret. *He'd never have to know.*

At the moment, his full attention was on the newspaper strangled in his tattooed fist. Anyone would think that the announcement of my engagement to his cousin was news to him, but I knew exactly the cause of his displeasure.

"Believe me," I said, ignoring the heavy feeling in my chest, "it wasn't me."

He snorted because his arrogance wouldn't allow him to believe anything else. "Do the people at the *Blackwood Tribune* know that you plagiarized the story you gave them?"

"I didn't plagiarize anything."

"Yeah?" he challenged, teeth bared. "Well, that story sure as fuck wasn't about you and Ever, so what would you call it?"

"It was about me, actually."

"And *me*."

I gave up the battle to appear unbothered and turned my gaze away. I watched the town pass by through the limousine window, but I didn't see any of it. "Get lost, Jameson."

"I am lost, Bette." His voice held a desperate note, pleading for me to understand, to let him make it right. No way did my heart just skip a beat. Foolish thing. "You promised to light the way."

"We were *kids*. Don't romanticize."

"Romanticize?" he spat incredulously. Turning my chin, he left me no choice but to look into his eyes… and try not to fall all over again. "I had only one heart, Bee, and I gave it to you. It was right there in your palm, and you fucking broke it."

My dress was suddenly too confining as I struggled to breathe. I wanted Jamie to act on the pain and lust building in his eyes and rip the dress away. To free me once and for all. "What do you want from me?" I pleaded instead.

Now I was the one sounding desperate.

Pulling me closer, he teasingly began lifting the skirt of my gown. "A kiss," he finally said when the dress was bunched around my thighs. Any higher and he'd know my secret. "You owe me that much."

My glower didn't move him. In fact, he grinned down at me, and I hated how stunning it was—like the moon pulling at an already turbulent sea. That is what his smile did to my heart. It was a tide that brought me back to life only to drown me once more.

Of course, I'd never tell him so. Instead, I snapped, "I don't owe you a damn thing."

"No," he said, his smile falling, "maybe not. But you're going to kiss me, anyway."

"And why is that? Because you'll force me?" I could feel his every breath warming my skin as I was sure he could feel mine. The anticipation had made us both breathless.

"Because you want to… and we both know Barbette Montgomery takes what she wants. Doesn't she?"

"I do not."

As if I hadn't spoken, Jamie's gaze dropped to my lips. "I'm going to fuck up that pretty lipstick you wore for me."

"I'd like to see you try."

Inhaling sharply, I wished I hadn't opened my mouth. Not only did I fail to deny that I'd worn the lipstick for him but I'd also just admitted to wanting him to kiss me.

The lids of his beautiful brown eyes lowered until he looked like he was drunk off me. "Would you now?"

"Yes."

This time, I didn't second guess my answer. There was no regret or fear. Only need. The surprise in Jamie's eyes was fleeting. I couldn't remember anything beyond his hand gripping my nape and pulling me in. It didn't escape my notice that he'd gone slow, giving me time to back out.

I didn't. I couldn't. It would be like cutting out my own heart.

His soft lips brushed back and forth against mine before pecking them. I lost count of how many times before my lips finally parted, and his tongue swept inside.

He tasted like sugar and smoke. So damn sinfully good.

I made a desperate sound, begging him for more, and he answered with a hungry groan. I'd wanted his kiss from the first. The very moment I'd stumbled back into his life and he'd charged back into mine.

Jamie had been right. The years apart hadn't dulled my desire for him. It had only intensified.

When he pulled away, his eyes slowly opened much like the first time we kissed—as if he were reluctant to let go of the fantasy. The fantasy that we were right for each other, that we could be together.

"I really hate you, do you know that?" His eyes had never looked quite so bright before as he stared down at me. "So fucking much."

My stomach twisted tight, hearing those words. I knew what he really wanted to say and knew he'd never trust me with the truth ever again.

A tear slipped from my eye. "I never promised you anything, Jamie."

I truly wanted to believe that I hadn't betrayed him. It was hard enough looking at myself in the mirror or closing my eyes without seeing his face, especially the moments after he discovered Ever and I together. Jamie had haunted my thoughts and dreams every day since.

"No?"

Coming to my senses, I hurriedly lowered my gown as he reached inside his tuxedo pocket. My traitorous heart thundered the moment he pulled out a folded slip of paper. Slowly, he unfolded it until I could see the tape holding the seams together— as if he'd torn it to shreds and then pieced it back together. I already knew what was written on it long before he began to hurl the words at me accusingly. He never once even glanced at the paper as he recited the words. He'd memorized them.

> Longer days and shorter nights,
> I think of summer, and I think of you.
> Butterfly kisses and sunshine smiles,
> Your laugh, my favorite melody.
> The grass is greener when you're here.
> Was the sky always this blue?
> The season has new meaning now.
> I think of summer, and I think of you.
>
> Fated to end, a fling like the wind,
> I watch you sail away.
> With your kiss and your promise,
> I wait for you, solstice.
> Your lighthouse, I'll light the way.

"Gotta be honest," he remarked with a smirk, "it's a little elementary, but at least the meaning was clear. You said you'd always wait for me." As he tucked the tattered poem back inside his tux, I started to speak, but the dark look in his eyes stopped me. "Tread very fucking carefully. If you say we were just kids one more time, you might not make it to prom."

"That wasn't what I was going to say," I snapped even though it was a lie.

"Whatever you say, sweetheart."

A shiver rippled through me. "Don't use that tone with me," I said, gritting my teeth as I crossed my arms under my breasts, pushing them up further. Any other time, his focus would have been drawn to them, but his gaze remained locked with mine, telling me he was *really* pissed.

"What tone?" he asked, playing coy.

"As if *we're* the ones who are getting married."

"According to this article, we are."

"Yeah, well, I embellished a little."

"No, you told it exactly as it happened, and apparently, it was a fairy tale to remember… I certainly do."

"Jamie, don't do this."

"Do what?"

My gaze fell to my lap. "Woo me with memory lane."

"I'm just stating facts… and I have no intention of wooing you. I tried that, remember?"

Frustrated, I pushed away the wisps of hair falling in my face, drawing his gaze to my temple. It was a few seconds before I realized why he was frowning.

"What happened?" he said, referring to the cut I'd made near my temple.

"It's nothing. I'm fine."

"How. Did. It. Happen?"

The longer I hesitated, the more his eyes narrowed to slits. I cursed myself for not thinking of a lie before now. Jamie had the power to distract me completely from the outside world. "I hit my head."

Wordlessly, he peeled a corner of the Band-Aid back to inspect my injury himself. I held my breath the entire time. Jameson was so goddamn gorgeous that sometimes it was hard to believe he wasn't just a figment of my imagination. "She bleeds," he muttered. "I'm relieved."

I blinked. "Why are you relieved, exactly?"

As he slouched in his seat, it was all I could do not to stare at his crotch and the considerable bulge there. "I was beginning to think you weren't human, after all."

"If I weren't human, then what would I be?"

Turning his head, he pinned me with his gaze. "A sorceress who keeps saps like me under her spell."

Before I could respond, our driver broke the silence. "We're here," Oliver announced over the intercom.

I took a deep breath, knowing the night was just starting and would only become a lot more challenging.

"Nervous?" Jamie inquired.

"Petrified."

He leaned over until his finger hovered over the intercom. "Shall I tell the driver to keep going?"

I tried to hide my surprise and failed miserably. "You'd do that?"

His crooked smile made the butterflies in my stomach take flight. "On one condition."

"Let me guess… that I sleep with you?"

He looked away to stare out the window at the couples already heading inside the building. When he turned back, the look in his eyes crumbled what was left of my heart. "You tell me what Ever could give you that I already hadn't—*ten times over.*"

CHAPTER TWELVE

The Punk

B EE LOOKED LIKE A FISH OUT OF WATER AS I WAITED FOR THE answer to the question that plagued me every single second of the last five years.

Why hadn't I been enough?

"Jamie… it's not—"

"What I think? Then what is it? I'm really fucking curious."

Eventually, she could no longer hold my gaze and stared down at her lap. "I was confused."

My lip curled. "Because your feelings for him were so strong," I mocked. I watched a tear slipped from my eye and wished more than anything that it didn't fuck me up as bad as it did. I've broken more hearts than I could count and felt nothing. Had it been the same for Bee when she broke mine?

"You know that's not true."

"I don't know what to believe anymore." Lifting my hand away from the intercom, I opened the door before holding my hand out for her. The moment her small hand slid into mine, the current I tried to ignore grew stronger. Pulling her close, I wrapped my arm around her waist and buried my face in her neck. "Actually, that's not true," I said as I inhaled her sweet perfume. "I know I want you, and I know you still want me. We're going to do something about that, Bee. Real fucking soon."

Lifting my head, I waited for her to tell me no, to push me away, but she didn't.

Oliver was standing nearby, so I turned my attention to him. "Give us a couple of hours," I instructed. I doubted we were staying until the end. Bee could count herself fortunate that I refrained from popping her fucking cherry in the back of the limo.

Bee and Ever might have been over, but she and I still had an old score to settle. I couldn't have her heart, so I'd take her body instead.

It'll never be enough.

I shook the warning off. Sex had to be enough because I had nothing else to give her. Barbette had made sure of that when she chose my cousin over me.

I took her hand and started for the building when I remembered just how badly I was fucking this night up. It hadn't been my intention to make it special, but I was driven by instinct, which meant that sometimes I just couldn't fucking help myself.

Incidentally, it was part of the reason I despised her.

Because no matter what, I just couldn't stop giving in.

"I forgot something." Ignoring her puzzled expression, I left her standing by the giant storybook that read "Once Upon a Time." That was our prom theme.

A fucking fairy tale.

Jogging back to the limo, I approached Oliver. "Did you get what I asked for?"

As he fetched what I needed, I watched Bee looking around nervously. She wasn't lying when she said she was afraid. I didn't think she was as afraid of what people thought of her as she was facing Four and Ever. The urge to kick Ever's ass for not setting her free sooner was beginning to overpower me. Knowing Four and Bee as I did, it didn't make sense why they agreed to share him in the first place. Something was up, and before I dared stick my dick in Bee, I was getting the truth out of her.

"Here it is, Mr. Buchanan."

Accepting the black velvet box from Oliver, I nervously made my way back to Bee, who was hugging herself. "Cold?" It might have been summer, but it was late, and we lived close to the ocean.

"Not really." Her eyes dropped to the box in my hand, and I could see the surprise and wariness in them.

Opening the case, I removed the thin gold bangle. Tradition called for a corsage, but I wanted to give Bee something that would live long past tonight. I didn't say anything as I slipped the band on her arm. It was a perfect fit. 'If found, please return to Jameson Buchanan,' was engraved on the inside, but she didn't need to know that. And in case there was any question...no, I wasn't talking about the bracelet.

Barbette admired it with a sparkle in her eye. "It's beautiful, Jamie."

Lifting her chin, I ignored the stares as I pressed a kiss to her lips. She didn't seem to notice the attention we were attracting. It was as if I spun on her axis, and she spun on mine. I wasn't sure how long we stood there kissing before a throat-clearing pulled us apart.

While the lust clouding my vision took a few seconds to clear, I pulled Bee even closer to my chest... in case she got any ideas about running. Blinking, I grinned at the disapproving scowl Lou wore as she stood a couple of feet away with her arms crossed. Wren, who looked like he'd rather be anywhere else, stood next to her. Lou looked stunning in her strapless royal blue gown, and her dark hair swept up, showing off her bare shoulders. Right now, I doubt she'd appreciate me telling her so, though. Wren looked pretty too, and I was toying with the idea of fucking with him by telling him so when Lou spoke.

"What do you two think you're doing?" she grilled.

"Minding our business." Taking Bee's arm, I started for the entrance with Lou hot on our tails. We gave our tickets at the booth before traveling down the hall. The floor was lined with purple, gold, and white balloons along the wall. A round, fake clock, set to one minute before midnight, waited at the end. We didn't get far before Tyra and Vaughn met us. Vaughn's eyes darted back and forth between us. At the question in his eyes, I shrugged. Already losing interest, he looked away as he took a sip of his drink. Tyra, who wore a yellow floor-length, off-shoulder gown with a high slit and gold, strappy heels wasn't so easy to convince.

"Are you for real, Jamie? Ever just broke up with her yesterday."

Not a fan of repeating myself, I said, "See previous answer," before skating around them both. If this night was going to work—and I was determined that it would—Bee and I needed to ditch my nosy-ass friends ASAP. We traveled through an open set of double doors, and the dance floor was decorated as if we were attending a royal ball rather than prom.

Glancing over my shoulder, I searched Bee's expression for distress. I shouldn't have been surprised when I found none. Instead, she looked amused. "Feel free to jump in and help me anytime."

Smirking, she said, "They're your friends. Besides, why should I when you're so diplomatic?"

I pulled her close and kissed her again. Now that I had, I couldn't seem to stop. "They could be your friends, too, you know."

She snorted. "They don't like me, and you know it."

"Vaughn does."

"Vaughn doesn't know me anymore."

"He knows you, and he misses you." I pinched her side when she looked away. "The real you."

"Too much has happened, Jamie. Even if I could go back, I could never be the same girl you fell for."

"Tell me what happened and let me be the judge of that."

"If I could, I would."

"That's bullshit, and you know it. At least tell me how you could trust Ever more than me?"

"That's not true, and *you* know it. Ever was just in the wrong place at the wrong time, and I swore him to secrecy. Don't blame him for being a friend."

Wrapping both hands around her nape, I pressed my thumbs into her throat. "I don't blame him," I snapped as I pulled her close. "I blame *you* for lying to me all these years. I blame you for ruining us. One way or another, Barbette, I'm going to get to the bottom of what turned you into such a fucking bitch." Releasing her, she stumbled, and it was all I could do not to reach for her again. Not trusting myself with her at the moment, I stormed away.

I needed a fucking drink.

It was a high school prom, so it was safe to say I wouldn't find one, so I settled for the next best thing. I was out on the terrace, staring out at the green lawn, blowing smoke in the air when Lou found me. This was the first fag I'd had in nine days—a record yet—and I intended to enjoy it. I could always quit again tomorrow.

"Four and Ever are here. I guess it's safe to assume they made up since they're all over each other."

"Peachy for them."

"Something tells me you had something to do with that." I didn't bother responding or look her way, but that didn't deter Lou. "I'm curious… was it because you cared, or was it so you could move in on sex-on-a-stick?"

"Both."

"Which one was more?"

"Quit it, Lou."

"Make me."

I looked around for Wren because if anyone could shut her up, he could. Most of the time. "Where's Wren?"

"Keeping your date company, asshole."

"Remind me. Why am I an asshole?"

"Because you dragged her here and left her alone with the vultures."

"I needed air."

"And she needs a date who's not a scumbag."

I looked her up and down. That gown made her look way too innocent. Lou was a fucking menace. "You look beautiful," I offered matter-of-factly.

"Thanks." Her eyes sparkled with mischief as she cocked her head. "Did you bother to tell Bee, as well?"

My gaze averted. No, I hadn't told Bee a goddamn thing except how much I hated her. It was nothing fucking new. She was always beautiful, even when she wore clothes too big for her and was covered from head to toe in dirt and mischief.

I heard a snap followed by a flash of light and was startled when I saw Lou holding up a camera.

"What the hell are you doing?"

"Smile," she instructed before snapping another picture. Pulling the camera away, she winced. "Oh, boy. That is *not* a good shot of you. I'd be a friend and delete it, but I don't like you very much right now. Maybe I'll post it on Instagram," she mused. "Those thirst buckets that follow you need to know the truth. Did someone call for, 'no filter'?"

"For fuck's sake." Realizing she was goading me back to Bee's side, I put out my cigarette and flicked the butt before storming inside in search of my date. I didn't have to look very hard. Even in a crowded room, she stood out. I gritted my teeth, hating that she was so goddamn breathtaking as I made my way to her.

"Done pouting?" she greeted when I reached her.

Wren merely lifted an eyebrow before swaggering away.

"He's nice," Bee remarked. "Doesn't seem to like you very much, though."

"Probably because I tried to sleep with Lou when she first came to town."

I watched as Bee curled her lips in disgust. She'd fixed her lipstick, but all it made me want to do was fuck it up again. "*Of course you did.*"

I shrugged because what was there to say? I was a dog. I see a bone, I sniff a bone. That was all there was to it. "Jealous?"

She took a sip of the punch I hadn't noticed her holding as she scanned the ballroom. "You'd like that, wouldn't you?"

Stealing her punch, I finished it in one gulp before setting it down and pulling her close. "Very much."

Her eyes glistened as she sucked in a breath. "I never stopped thinking of you as mine, Jamie. I just… I realized you never could be again. Not after what I did to you."

She didn't seem so sure. Was that hope in her voice? It was the last thing I wanted to give her. "Dance with me," I said instead. I saw the disappointment in her gaze, but she didn't resist me as I pulled her onto the dance floor. I had no idea what song was playing—some slow, lonely tune with an easy rhythm.

"A live band would have been so much better," Bee remarked. Her body trembled in my arms, and I realized she was grappling for something to distract her from her nerves.

Unconsciously, I began to slowly stroke her back, offering her comfort. "DJs offer more variety," I rebutted. Sighing, she laid her head on my chest, and her trembling slowed until she was so still that I thought she'd fallen asleep. "Bee?"

"Don't stop," she whispered, and I didn't. I couldn't stop touching her if I tried. The song changed to something up-tempo, so I led her off the dance floor and found an empty table. Sitting down, I pulled her onto my lap, shoved my fingers in her hair, and kissed her for everyone to see. I didn't give a damn what any of them thought. I saw Bee when no one else had. She was mine first, and no one and nothing could change that. Least of all me.

"You were right," I said when I pulled away from the kiss.

"Right?" Her eyes slowly opened, and her vision took a few seconds to focus.

"A band would have been better. This DJ fucking sucks."

She laughed, and I'd forgotten how much I enjoyed the sound. So much so that I wanted to punch Ever when he suddenly appeared at our table. The light that had been in her eyes died, too, as sorrow replaced them. I shouldn't have expected her to be over him so soon, but I couldn't help the urge to toss her the hell out of my lap.

She stood, saving me from doing so. "Ever."

My fists balled at the hope in her voice. No way was he taking her back. I swear I'd murder them both before I allowed that to happen. Maybe Four could help me bury the bodies. As if I'd spoken her up, she appeared by his side a moment later.

Confusion chased away some of my anger when Bee said Four's name with the same note of desperation. What the hell was going on?

"Hey," Four greeted with a gentle smile. She was a lot more gracious than I would have been.

"I think we should talk," Ever announced, breaking the awkward silence.

"It's okay," Bee said. "I already know. You don't have to explain. You've both done enough."

I sat up straight at that while Ever shoved his fingers through his hair.

"Believe me, I didn't mean for it to go down like that," Four said. Why did it sound like she was apologizing?

Sure, technically, she'd been the other woman, but Ever made his choice. No one should ever have to apologize for falling in love.

At that moment, I felt like the world's biggest hypocrite. And asshole. I'd given Bee hell for choosing Ever. Except... whatever Bee thought, she wasn't in love with Ever. I knew what Bee in love looked like, and it damn sure wasn't what she'd felt for him.

Not even when I'd promised to help her get my cousin to notice her. Instead, I'd stolen her for myself. Slowly, my fists balled in my lap. Maybe what had happened between us was my own damn fault. I'd given Barbette my word, knowing I had no intention of keeping it.

"Neither of us did," Ever added. He slid his hands in his tuxedo's pockets.

"It was never your fight, Ever. This is between my father and me."

My ears perked at that. What did Elliot have to do with Bee dating Ever?

"Ever has a plan," Four informed her. "I wasn't so sure you'd go along with it but"—her gaze drifted to me when before I'd been pretty much invisible as they talked freely—"now I'm thinking Ever is on to something?"

I lifted a brow at her question. I had no idea what the hell she was talking about, but it was clear this plan of theirs involved me, and they'd seen us kissing.

"I don't understand," Bee said slowly.

That made two of us.

"Look," Ever said as he scratched his brow, "let's just talk about this in the morning and enjoy tonight." The girls didn't look like they were budging, so he looked to me for help. Even though I wanted answers now, I stood to my feet just as the rest of our crew joined us.

"We should bail," Vaughn suggested as he came to stand beside Ever.

Tyra gripped the front of his tux as she stood on the tips of her toes. "And I told you not before I got my dance."

Yanking her even closer, he growled against her neck, "I've got something better we can do."

"You do know we can hear you," Lou said, wrinkling her nose.

Just then, the cha-cha began to play, making Ever groan. "You guys do what you want, but that's my cue to leave."

Taking Four's hand, he headed for the nearest exit. When he glanced over his shoulder seconds later, he smirked when he found everyone following them. He held open the door that led to the hall's back lawn as we all filed through. There was an unlit path with a soft glow up ahead that we followed.

"You guys," Tyra cautioned, "I'm pretty sure we're *not* supposed to go toward the light."

Vaughn quickly scooped her off her feet when she stopped in her tracks. "Don't be a baby," he teased before tossing her over his shoulder.

"Can you blame her?" I said. "We all know the black characters are always the first to go."

"Exactly," Tyra chimed in, shocking everyone, including me. She wasn't exactly my biggest fan, but I was slowly winning her over. I think.

The music had almost faded when we eventually stumbled upon a small gazebo. Vines and rose garlands wrapped around the stone columns while pink gossamer curtains draped the entrance like a canopy. The filigree carving the iron of the domed ceiling allowed the full moon to cast its welcoming glow despite the lanterns. Pink rose petals littered the ground and were crushed under our feet as we reached the end of the path, which sloped up onto the small hill.

It was perfect for a late-night rendezvous, and one glance at Ever, Vaughn, and Wren told me they were thinking the same thing. The girls rushed up the stone steps, leaving us behind and oblivious to our lascivious thoughts.

Before long, we were all silently arguing over who'd get to take advantage of the intimate space.

"Are you kidding me?" Wren hissed when Vaughn and I faced off with our fists lifted over our palms.

Vaughn shrugged as we pounded our fists three times. "Rock-paper-scissors, bro. It's the only way to avoid bloodshed."

"Best two out of three?" I heard Ever ask.

A moment later, they were pounding their fists. Vaughn and Wren both lost, and Ever and I faced off. Before we could even begin the first round, I heard a throat clear. Four stood next to Ever with her arms crossed. Not the least bit sorry, he lustfully stared her down as Bee pinned me with a glare of her own. I slid my arm around her waist, but she swayed into me with a sigh before I could pull her close. As if I'd done it a million times before, I skimmed my lips across her forehead. The feelings stirring in my chest from the action were familiar but long-lost.

Afraid that I might be falling into her trap all over again, I whispered, "It must be killing you to see them together without you in the middle."

She stepped away with her painted lips curled, and I let her go. It was for the best. I couldn't stay away, but I couldn't let her get too close either.

Lou's voice broke through my thoughts, chasing away the turmoil. "You guys weren't seriously playing rock-paper-scissors to decide who gets laid out here, were you?"

Wren scratched the back of his neck as he avoided Lou's gaze.

Four was still glaring at Ever, waiting for a response.

"What?" he asked, feigning innocence. His voice came out high-pitched, making him seem even more guilty. Four's lips pursed, and he grinned before pulling her back inside the gazebo.

Since I wasn't about to let them enjoy it alone if I couldn't, I grabbed Bee's hand and pulled her inside along with the rest of our crew. Vaughn slyly pulled the cord holding the curtains open until we were hidden away inside. For a few seconds, we all stood around awkwardly, resigned to sharing the space. Deciding to set the mood, I pressed a few buttons on my phone before tossing it on the single long bench. "Iris" by the Goo Goo Dolls began to play, and the look in Bee's eyes told me she remembered. It was the first song I'd played for her on my father's guitar. I didn't know then that I'd fall for her. I'd merely acted on instinct when I realized she was the first person I ever cared to know the real me.

If only I'd known it would send her running the other way.

"Jamie…"

I wrapped my arms around her waist and skimmed my lips over her ear. "You remember, don't you?"

"Of course, I do."

I shook my head as I inhaled her scent. "I should have never played that song."

I felt her fingers clutching at my tux. "Please, don't say that."

"You wanted the fantasy, Bee. You didn't want the real me."

She pulled away enough to meet my eyes. "If you believe nothing else, Jamie, believe that you were more than a fantasy. You were a dream come true."

The song ended, and I pulled away. For some reason, I had trouble meeting her gaze. What if I looked into her eyes and saw that she was telling the truth? What would I do then? We'd gone too far to turn back now.

I pulled away, putting some much-needed space between us. It hurt like hell when she let me go.

"One day," I announced, needing to distract myself, "when our kids are old enough, we're going to start our own little league." As if I hadn't just been slow dancing with the only girl I'd ever love, I put my hands together and swung my imaginary bat. Bee was now sitting on the stone bench next to me with her fists clenched tight in her lap and a frustrated look in her eyes.

"How many kids are you guys expecting?" Four questioned. She looked a little nervous to hear the answer. Thank God she couldn't see the devious smirk her boyfriend wore.

"Two," Ever answered, lying through his teeth. I had no doubt they'd make beautiful little devil babies. No way he'd stop at two.

"That's mighty presumptuous of you," Four said after turning to face him.

He rubbed his hand down her naked arm, and even though I was happy to see them beat the odds, I couldn't help glancing at Bee. I wasn't expecting to see relief in her eyes as she watched them. This just kept getting weirder and weirder.

"We both know how lonely it was as an only child," Ever said.

Four rose on the tips of her toes, and Ever eagerly met her halfway.

"Get a room," Lou said, disguising it as a cough into her fist.

I fucking concur.

Watching the two of them struck chords of envy within me while, at the same time, I was happy as fuck for them. They'd clawed and fought their way to this and sometimes with each other. I gazed down at Bee, and a part of me I thought had died wondered if we'd tapped out too soon.

"What about you?" Tyra asked Vaughn, breaking through my perilous thoughts. I almost laughed when I caught the hostile expression on Tyra's angelic face.

Vaughn offered her a gentle yet shy smile. "Two."

While I saw straight through his bullshit, Tyra nodded, obviously pleased and completely missing the devious grin he flashed over her shoulder.

Not one of us was surprised when Lou spoke for Wren and said, "Four. I like things even. Two boys, two girls."

Wren sighed and rubbed his forehead when he should have been rescuing his balls back from her. "Baby, that's not the way it works."

"Well then, we'll keep having kids until it does," she stubbornly replied. The startled look on Wren's face was completely fucking priceless.

"And you, Jamie?" Four asked me when the laughter died. "How many kids do you want?"

I was the one who started the fucking discussion, but the question had me digging in my pocket for my second smoke in less than an hour. Even though I'd technically quit, I kept a handful on me at all times. You know...for emergencies. Like women with their tampons. I chuckled to myself. *Yeah, that sounds about right, Buchanan.*

"Ten," I finally answered while lighting up. I was pretty sure that I'd pulled that number out of my ass just because. "Each spaced a year apart. I want them to be close." It was all I could do not to throw my head back in ecstasy on the first pull. Grinning at my captivated audience, I continued. "Besides, if I give her the chance to snap back, she'll only worry about messing up her figure. We put in the extra effort, get them out back to back, and in ten years, boom, we're done."

Watching my friends struggle for words was almost as enjoyable as the nicotine flooding my system. My gaze slid to Bee, and I smirked at the defiance in her eyes. Married to my cousin or some other chump, there was no question that she'd be the one flooding the world with mini versions of me. And she fucking knew it, too.

"Jamie," Tyra uttered. "It's not like paying off a mortgage."

"Of course not." I couldn't stop my grin when I felt Bee's gaze boring into me. "Making babies is a lot more fun than paying off a mortgage. And in case you haven't realized, Ty-baby, I'm rich as fuck."

Okay, I realized I was beginning to sound like a douchebag, but I couldn't help myself. Put a big red button in my face, and I'm pushing the motherfucker.

Ha...*maybe that's why I'm such a great lay.*

Collectively, their sympathetic gazes traveled to Bee—as if they also knew she'd be the one.

"How do you know the mother of your children will even be skinny?" Lou argued with a tilt of her head. "When you saw a picture of Eliza, you couldn't stop drooling, and she'd never be caught dead wearing a double zero."

I'd been flicking ash on the ground, so my gaze slowly lifted and zeroed in on Bee. Just in case anyone still had their doubts. "Because I know." Although I'd staked my claim, there was still a part of me resisting the urge to give in. "If Eliza is interested, tell her to give me a call," I added while holding Bee's gaze. "A lot of powerful men have outside children."

Unable to take the hurt flickering in her eyes, I hopped the rail, and even though it felt like I was running away, I didn't turn back.

I walked until I found a lone bench surrounded by tall hedges and a thousand fucking rose bushes. I wasn't sure how long I sat there with my head hanging between my shoulders before I heard a voice.

"You sure as shit know how to make an exit," Vaughn drawled.

Lifting my head and seeing how close he stood, I realized he'd snuck up on me. A thick cloud of smoke flowed through my nostrils when I sighed. All I'd wanted was some time alone, but with friends like mine, that was too much to fucking ask. Usually, I was the one doing the meddling. Now I understood just how fucking annoying that must be.

"Are you seriously over here pouting, man?"

"It's called brooding," I argued. "You wouldn't know anything about that. You're not hot enough."

"That's not what your mother said last night." The moment he popped a squat next to me, I pressed the lit end of my cigarette into the back of his hand. "Fuck!" He yelped like a little bitch. After inspecting the burn mark on his hand he glared at me. "What the fuck, dude? Recognize a joke?"

Shrugging, I flicked the butt away and immediately reached for another. "Wrong mom to joke about, bro."

"Jesus, you're such a fucking mama's boy." I didn't respond, so he watched me light up with a frown before saying, "I thought you quit?"

Wordlessly, I unbuttoned my dress shirt enough to rip the damn patch I wore from my chest. I felt like an idiot for even trying. I couldn't quit smoking any more than I could quit *her*.

Fuck it.

"What the hell is going on with you?" Vaughn prodded.

"Why do you care?"

Frankly, I found his nagging ironic since his problems were ten times more fucked up than mine. I guess the quarterback enjoyed throwing stones too.

"I don't fucking know… maybe because I'm your best fucking friend? Is that a good enough reason for you, asshole?"

"A friend would have told me when my cousin started fucking my girlfriend behind my back."

If he was surprised by my statement, it didn't show. It's been five years, but it still felt like it happened five damn days ago. "And that's exactly why I didn't tell you, bro. That was family shit, so I stayed out of it. Besides, I *seriously* doubt they ever fucked."

"Just as I expected… copping out like a pussy."

"Okay. What would you have done?"

"Pray you never have to find out." This pain was one I wouldn't wish on anyone, not even my worst enemy. Ironically, she happened to be the girl who caused it all.

"You have to shake this funk, man. You came back, and you've been given a second chance, but instead of making things right with Bee, you're sulking in some fucking bushes. Yet *I'm* the pussy?"

"I didn't come back for her."

"But she's the reason you stayed."

"I'm not sure I had much choice in that, either. Where the hell would I have gone?"

"That's kind of my point. Up until yesterday, the girl you've been in love with since you were twelve was ready to marry someone else, and I bet it never *once* crossed your mind to leave Blackwood Keep."

No, it hadn't.

Like a chump, I knew I'd rather be in pain every day watching her belong to someone else than never seeing her again. And wasn't that just fucking backward as hell?

They say what doesn't kill you makes you stronger. Well, Bee had wrecked me a thousand times over, and I was still weak as hell for that girl.

My summer love, my ice queen.

She fucking ruined me. It was only fair that I return the favor, so why haven't I?

Bee rounded the corner at that very moment, making me eat those fucking words. She hadn't spotted me yet, so I took advantage, drinking in the sight of her in that red gown with her strawberry locks piled high. I wanted to pull free every single pin just so I could wrap her hair around my fist and kiss her senseless. And maybe, quite literally, take her breath away too.

Feeling my gaze, she turned, and for several long, agonizing seconds, neither of us moved or spoke a word.

Vaughn cleared his throat, breaking the trance as he stood to his feet. "I guess that's my cue. If you two start fucking, I don't want to be caught in the middle. Or do I?" he joked with a waggle of his eyebrows.

I glared at his back as he paused to kiss Bee on her forehead before walking away. Whenever I did finally get Bee in my bed, I sure as hell wouldn't be sharing her with anyone else. The second we were alone, our gazes returned to one another.

"Come here."

Bee didn't hesitate and glided toward me until she was standing between my legs. Bringing her down on my lap, I kissed her lips, making her sigh. "I'm sorry for walking away from you."

Perking a brow, she pursed her lips, and I was tempted to kiss them again.

"Then why did you?"

"Because I'm a needy motherfucker," I answered truthfully. "And what I need is *you*."

Her lips parted, and I waited for her to tell me that I could have her. Once she said the words, I knew I'd let go of the past. I'd stop pining for how things were and start looking to the future and believing in what could be. All she had to do was say the words.

Say the fucking words, baby.

I didn't realize I was frowning until her finger traced the lines on my forehead. I felt my expression soften as she began toying with the barbell piercing my brow. "I…" I held my breath while she struggled for words and tried not to look so eager. A second later, her shoulders slumped. "I had a good time tonight. Thank you."

If I'd been standing, I wasn't sure I would still be. Disappointment coursed through me, making my world spin, so when her eyes closed, so did mine. I didn't realize we'd leaned into one another until our foreheads touched.

"You were never going to prom with him. It was always going to be me."

"I'm glad… even if I don't deserve you."

I held her tighter, wanting to protect her from whatever dark thoughts plagued her. "Deserve me? You're the lyrics to my song, Bette. I don't exist without you."

She shook her head, refusing to accept my claim. "You were right about me, James. I break hearts. I broke you." My eyes flew open at the same time hers did. The growl I didn't expect to release startled her, but there was nothing I could do to wrangle my emotions back in.

Then piece me back together, dammit.

"I survived," I said instead and softened the blow by quirking my lips. She didn't smile back, and I felt like shit when a tear fell.

"I'm sorry," she whispered.

My jaw clenched as something inside of me reached out for her. I promptly shoved it back down as I set her on her feet and stood. Maybe I wasn't as ready to forgive her as I thought.

Not yet.

Shit… maybe never.

Slowly, I ran my finger over the top of her breasts. Her soft skin turned red under my touch. "You looked beautiful tonight." I couldn't believe it took me until the night was damn near over to tell her. "But then you always do."

She grinned despite the storm raging within us both. "Is this the part where you convince me to sleep with you?"

Looking around, I realized we were completely hidden from the rest of the world. I could bend her over the bench and hike up that gown. No one would ever know. *Tragic.*

"When you're ready to be fucked, you won't need much convincing, kitten."

Her gaze narrowed, and I had the feeling she was pissed about being turned down. "But you were so sure it would be tonight."

"Maybe you weren't the only one needing to be seduced."

"So tonight was a test?"

Rather than answer, I slipped my phone from my pocket and checked the time. *Shit.* "It's almost midnight, Cinderella." Glancing down, I tried not to smile at her scowl. My wicked witch could be so fucking adorable at times.

"Stop calling me that."

I paused, and then it was my turn to frown because I couldn't remember when or even why I started calling her that. It was almost like my subconscious was trying to tell me something. I'm not sure how long I stood there searching for the answers in her blue eyes, but never once did she look away. After a few minutes, I had to accept that I wouldn't be getting any answers tonight.

What a surprise.

Although I could tell Bee didn't want to leave, she didn't fight me when I took her hand and led her back to the front. I slowed my stride when I spotted our nosy as shit friends waiting for us by our limo.

"What the hell do you fuckers want now?" I felt Bee squeeze my hand and rolled my eyes before inquiring much more pleasantly, "I meant, is something wrong?"

"We were just waiting to make sure Barbette didn't need

help hiding your body," Wren replied. He then gave her a look as if asking whether she'd still like their help.

I didn't like the way she giggled at his offer, like she wanted to suck his dick or something, so I yanked open the limo door and pushed her inside. "She's fine, you fucking traitors." And then I ducked inside the limo, leaving my friends holding their dicks—so to speak.

The moment my ass touched the seat, I pulled her to me and took her chin in my hand. "Don't laugh at other men's jokes."

"Even if I think they're funny?" she teased.

"*Especially* if you think they're funny."

I could tell that my demand had gone in one ear and out the other. Realizing that I was actually jealous, I pressed my lips against hers, hoping to get rid of the bitter taste of my own medicine.

"Jamie." She gasped when I finally let her up for air.

"Jesus, Bee. Don't say my name like that."

"Or what?" she challenged, but I could tell she was really curious.

"Or I just might fuck you out of that dress." Kissing my way down her neck, I realized she hadn't responded as I inhaled her scent like it was nicotine. "Oh, is that what you want?" More silence. Chuckling, I pulled Bee onto my lap until she was straddling my thighs. "Say the word, and I'll pop your cherry right here and now."

I was already undoing the tiny buttons on her gown when she finally answered. "No..." My fingers paused on the last button, but the look in her eyes had my dick rocking up in my pants. "But I do want you to make me come."

CHAPTER
THIRTEEN

The Plaything

"OH, YOU DO, DO YOU?"

I didn't get the chance to respond to his taunt before he was shoving down the top of my gown. The cool air from the limo brushed my nipples, making them harden even more. I was still wondering when he'd gotten all those buttons undone when his finger slowly traced my spine, setting my bare skin on fire. I wanted him to touch me all over, but in the confines of this limo and with the little time we had until I was home, I knew that wouldn't be possible.

Suddenly, his head lowered, and my lips parted from shock and anticipation as I watched his tongue dart out and then lazily flick my nipple.

When his head lifted, my hands curled around his nape as I guided him toward the other. This time, when his tongue thrashed my nipple, he didn't stop until I was gasping. Only then did his lips finally close around the bud, making my back arch as he suckled.

I had no idea before this moment how sensitive my breasts were and how ruthlessly Jamie would use the knowledge to his advantage.

By the time he finally lifted his head, I was a writhing, sopping mess.

"Jamie," I whimpered. "It's too much." Any moment now, I'd burn, and when he was done with me, there'd be nothing left.

Chuckling, he fingered my nipple as he defiantly met my gaze. "Tell me to stop," he challenged. Even though I was trembling in his lap, we both knew there was no chance of that. "No?" he continued to taunt. "Then tell me how bad you want it."

"Please." I moaned without shame or hesitation.

"Good, but not great," he replied. "Harder, Bee. You can beg better than that."

Slowly, I opened my eyes. I couldn't even remember when I'd closed them. Jamie was watching me, his brown eyes twin pools of flame, and I knew then that he was as desperate for this as I was.

"Suck me, and maybe I'll suck you."

As he caressed my bottom lip with the tip of his finger, his gaze darkened as he pondered my offer. "And just how long have you wanted to get my dick between those lips?"

From the moment I realized I would never be over you.

"Shit or get off the pot, Jameson," was what I said instead.

His pierced brow rising was the only answer I got before his head lowered, and he cruelly sank his teeth into the top of my breast, making me cry out. At the same time, I could feel my clit throbbing almost violently and my toes curling.

This was all before his lips even closed around my nipple.

He worshipped them both, suckling and lashing with his tongue until my eyes nearly rolled to the back of my head. I was vaguely aware of him fumbling to get underneath my gown. I waited with bated breath for the moment his fingers found my neat strip of strawberry curls, and he made an approving sound. I was running out of air as I waited for his fingers to dip lower, to tease my clit, and maybe fuck me with those cruel, talented fingers.

My lips parted, ready to beg like he wanted when I'd been too proud just moments ago, but then he was shoving the hem of my gown up, bunching the heavy material around my waist.

His hands moved away, and I eagerly held my skirt up while he undid his pants before shoving them, along with his boxers, down to his thighs. I couldn't see his dick in the dark, but when he reached out and grabbed my hand, curling it around him, I realized he was a monster in every way. Jamie's cock was thick, warm, and impossibly long. And he was so hard I could feel each of the veins running the length of his dick.

"You have no idea how much I want you to sit on it," he whispered.

Hearing the desperation in his voice, I lifted my hips. Virgin or not, I was ready to throw caution to the wind and stuff my pussy with every inch. Just as I felt his cock parting my lower lips, his hand was suddenly between my legs, cupping me.

"Appreciate the gesture, kitten, but I don't think your little pussy could take it."

I didn't think so either, but I was more than eager to try. As if sensing my determination, his hand started to move away, but at the last moment, I felt his middle finger teasing my clit until my eyes fluttered, and I was leaking all over his hand.

"Jamie," I whimpered. I was so close, and all from just his featherlight touch. It was like he was being careful not to give me too much, fearing he might lose control.

When he pulled away this time, I almost cried, but then his hands were on my waist, guiding me until my warm, wet pussy kissed his rock-hard thigh. Jamie's long legs were spread wide as he slouched low in the seat, giving me the traction I'd need to ride him to climax.

Leaning forward, he drew my nipple between his lips, making me sigh his name as I cradled his head and ran my fingers through his hair. I wasn't sure when my hips began to move, but slowly, I found a rhythm until it felt like I'd climbed impossibly high. The friction fired off every nerve I had until I was gasping and pressing myself harder on his thigh.

"Fuck, Bette. You're riding me like you own me." The guttural groan that followed nearly tipped me over the edge. We both knew I did—just as much as he owned me.

As if needing to prove it, he wrapped a hand around my neck, and seconds later, shock broke through my lustful fog when he lifted the hand still gripping his cock and held my gaze as he crudely spat in my palm.

My lips parted, but no words came.

Slowly, he curled my wet palm back around him, and the only reaction I gave was to press my now throbbing clit down on him harder. Jamie's hand stayed on top of my mine, guiding me, showing me just how he wanted to be touched.

His lids lowered as he bit his lip, and I couldn't help but lean forward to steal a kiss. It was the first kiss I'd initiated, and I glimpsed his surprise just before he lifted, sweeping his tongue between my lips, and deepening the kiss.

"Come on me," he demanded against my lips. "Right fucking now."

Heeding his command, my hand reluctantly left his cock, and I planted both of them on his chest as my hips picked up their pace. The eagerness in his eyes to see me come drove me closer to the edge. Soon, I was bucking and pleading and gasping as I rode his thigh to climax.

I'm not sure exactly what Jamie saw as he watched me come, but whatever it was had him pulling me down and kissing the whimpers from my lips until they faded. The only sound now was me panting as I fought to catch my breath.

"Why didn't you put on the light?" I asked once I did. There was only the gentle rocking of the limo as it drove us home and the pounding of his heartbeat underneath my ear. "Didn't you want to see me?"

"If I saw you, I would have fucked you, Barbette."

And we both knew I would have let him.

Unfortunately, the car rolled to a stop, taking away our chance. Slowly, our heads turned toward the window. Seeing my parents' house looming in the dark was a reminder of all the things that could never be. I was still throbbing and dripping sex all over his thigh when I gazed into his eyes once more. I hated his smugness and even more the adorable dimple appearing in his cheek when he smirked.

"Until next time," he said as he tucked his still-hard dick back into his pants.

I wanted to sink to my knees and return the favor of unraveling him, but he'd been right before. If I sucked him off, we wouldn't stop there. At least one of us had still been thinking clearly. It didn't matter to me where I lost my virginity, but it mattered who I gave it to. My heart and body had chosen long ago, but my reality made it impossible.

Avoiding his gaze, I slowly climbed off his lap before pulling my dress back over my breasts and freeing the skirt from around my waist. "There won't be a next time." I still refused to look at him as I reached for the door. I was afraid he'd see the regret in my eyes or the tears that threatened to spill.

Jamie stopped me from running with a hand around my neck as he pulled me away from the door. "Easier said than done," he whispered against my lips. "Especially when you haven't had my cock inside you yet."

"That will never happen, Jamie."

"Two minutes ago you were begging for it, kitten. Allow me to respectfully disagree."

I bristled at the confidence in his tone, remembering for the first time since he touched me that we were sworn to hate each other until the end of our days. Now that I'd come, mortification began to set in. And not just over what we'd done, but all the things I'd been willing to do in the heat of the moment. All of my inhibitions had melted away, and Jamie hadn't needed to use more than his mouth and hands to make it happen. I'd known he was dangerous before but now… now I was fucking terrified.

"Stay away from me, Jamie."

"Why would I do that?" he arrogantly countered.

The hard set of his jaw and the conquering look in his eyes

made me even more aware of the monumental mistake I'd made. I'd opened myself up to Jamie when there was no future for us, and now …he was falling all over again. I had two choices: I could push him away now or leave Jamie exposed to more heartache.

I heard the words spilling from my lips like acid, and even though I wanted to take them back, I knew I never could. "Because even with Ever out of the picture, you weren't enough then, and you aren't enough now."

I couldn't remember scrambling from the limo or rushing up the stairs to my bedroom. I couldn't remember removing the beautiful gown that moments ago had been in disarray. I couldn't even remember stepping inside the shower. But what I could remember was the utter devastation on Jamie's face—the bleakness in his eyes just before he turned away, letting me go once and for all.

The hot spray of the shower drowned the sob that escaped me, and then the tears I knew weren't for me fell and were washed away.

I see love, I break love. That's what I do.

CHAPTER FOURTEEN

The Plaything

Summer... Six Years Ago

DUSK HAD ALREADY FALLEN, AND ANYONE UNDER THE AGE OF sixteen without an adult had been required to leave. Ever, Vaughn, Jason, Jamie, and I managed to avoid security for about an hour before we were caught.

"I love your accent," Rachel flirted. "Where are you from?"

I was grateful for the huge panda blocking my view of them as security escorted us to the exit. Watching Jamie flirt and enthrall not one, but *all three* of those girls made me realize they hadn't been the ones on the hunt. They'd been prey all along.

I couldn't stop seeing Jamie and Rachel behind that cotton candy stand or how his hand had crept and fumbled underneath her tiny top.

As if that weren't enough, all day I had to force myself to ignore every wink, heated glance, and sexy grin Jamie threw their way while pretending to have a good time with my friends.

"Boston," Jamie answered, though he sounded distracted. I had the urge to peek around my prize and see for myself, but I didn't.

"So what do you guys want to do now?" Vaughn asked once the security guard had left us with an order to go home. I still had an hour or so before curfew, but I was eager to get home and out of this dress. All day, I felt like I'd been wearing someone else's skin. I missed my hat and the baggy shirts that hid the fact that I had boobs. Not to mention this bear was beginning to make my arms tremble. Ever, Vaughn, and Jason had all offered to help, but every single time, I'd felt Jamie's gaze, waiting to see if I'd take them up on their offer.

Stubbornly, I hadn't, and I was more than regretting it now.

Ever murmured something about taking a piss before heading for the row of blue porta-potties down the street. Just then, a screaming kid—maybe four or five—was being carried through the gates by his mother, who struggled to hold onto him. Approaching them, I couldn't help but notice that he was empty-handed. After getting permission from the weary mother, I squatted until I was eye level with her son and offered him the panda. I almost snorted when the waterworks ended *immediately*. Now that he wasn't trying his best to shatter glass, I realized he was pretty freaking cute even with the giant snot bubble hanging from his right nostril.

"What do you say, Alan?"

"Thank you."

Winking, I stood and watched as Alan struggled to carry the panda that was almost twice his size. Returning to my friends, I realized they'd all been watching me.

"Cute kid," Jamie drawled. He looked pretty cozy with Rachel's arm wrapped around his waist. "A little young for you, don't you think?"

"Funny," I retorted, seeing that green haze again. "I was going to say the same to your new girlfriend."

"What do you mean?" Rachel asked, suddenly looking alarmed. When I said nothing, she pulled away from Jamie. He didn't seem to notice as he pinned me with his gaze. "I thought you said that you're fifteen?"

"You're right," he admitted, brown eyes twinkling mischievously. "I did say that."

As Vaughn and Jason snickered, I realized that I'd been right about Rachel and her friends being older. I also realized that Jamie must have lied about his age to hook up with them. I didn't want to be impressed that he succeeded, but I definitely was. Their age difference wasn't exactly something one could shrug off. Jamie seemed too far out of my league, and we were only a year apart.

"So how old are you?"

"Twelve."

"Ugh!" Rachel screeched. "I can't believe you!" She stormed away, forcing her friends to run to catch up. Each of them threw Jamie—and me, for some reason—evil glares over their shoulders. I was a little more than excited to see them finally go.

By the time they were out of sight, the guys were bent over clutching their sides. The only ones not laughing were Jamie and me, though I was sure for different reasons. Spinning on my heel, I carefully made my way across the busy street. Jamie's full attention was becoming too much for me to handle. The moment I reached the bike racks, I felt fingers gripping my arm and tugging me around. I was taller than most girls, so when Jamie towered over me, it was only by an inch or two.

"You owe me a girlfriend."

Scoffing, I pulled away and hid my surprise when he let me. "She wasn't your girlfriend."

"That's not what you said before you made her break up with me."

"I didn't *make* her do anything just like I didn't *make you lie*."

"None of that changes the fact that I'm single now, thanks to you." Suddenly, his gaze narrowed as if he'd come to some revelation. I was sure I wasn't going to like whatever it was. "I think you did it on purpose."

Yup. I was three for three today.

"Well, I didn't," I denied, crossing my arms.

His gaze dipped to my chest, and I realized the gesture had pushed up my breasts. Remembering his hand creeping up Rachel's shirt, I quickly dropped my arms. It didn't matter a second later when he stepped into my space. My breasts brushed against his chest, and we both pretended not to notice.

"Prove it."

"How?" The word slipped through my lips before I could re-think it. His hooded eyes made me think he liked my eagerness.

"Be my girlfriend."

"What?" I cringed when I realized I sounded like a puppy that had just been stepped on.

Jamie's cheeks turned pink when I didn't immediately ac-cept. I had the feeling he wasn't used to the idea of rejection. "You heard me."

"But we've only known each other three days."

Not to mention the mountain of more important reasons why I shouldn't. He was everything that defined trouble. And a liar. If Jamie could easily fool someone two or three years older than him, then what chance did I have?

"That's three days longer than my last girlfriend," he teased.

I suddenly wished I'd never taunted him about Rachel be-cause the warmth in my belly made me want to say yes. *You don't even know him.*

It didn't seem to matter as much as it should have. "I—"

The sound of a long whistle and then a boom drew our star-tled gazes to the sky just before an explosion of color lit up the night sky. Minutes stretched by as we stood shoulder to shoul-der, heads tilted, silently gaping at the fireworks. I could feel the warmth from Jamie's skin when his hand brushed mine, and even though my fingers flexed, eager to tangle with his, I kept my hands to myself.

"Dude, I found them!" Jason yelled. He was covered in sweat and out of breath as he frantically waved to someone in the dis-tance. Vaughn rounded a line of cars seconds later with a frazzled look in his eyes.

Stepping away from Jamie, I met my friends halfway when they rushed toward us. "Everything okay?" As soon as I voiced the question, I realized we were still short one. "Where's Ever?" It was at least twenty minutes since he'd left for the bathroom.

"That's what we came to tell you," Vaughn answered, out of breath. "He just got arrested."

"Shit," Jamie said as soon as Vaughn and Jason finished explaining what Ever had done. Jamie looked nervous as he scratched his temple. It was an expression I'd probably never get used to seeing on him. He was always so cocky and confident with a smile that followed you into your dreams…

I subtly pinched myself to make sure I was awake. I wouldn't be much help to Ever if I melted into a puddle at his cousin's feet.

"I'll call my uncle." Jamie started to walk off, but I grabbed his hand, forcing myself to ignore the current shooting up my arm and exploding in my chest. Like the fireworks Ever had illegally set off.

"No."

Seeing that I had his full attention, I released his hand. Just as quickly, he recaptured mine, drawing Vaughn and Jason's puzzled gazes. Thankfully, after exchanging awkward glances with each other, they said nothing even when Jamie and I continued to hold hands for no good reason.

"You said the security guards have him, not the cops, which means he's just sitting in their office. They probably don't even know who he is yet."

"Your point?" Jamie asked. Not liking his tone, I tried to drop his hand again, but he simply tightened his grip.

"We break him out."

"Are you fucking kidding me?" Jason exploded. "How are we supposed to do that?"

"Easy," Jamie surprised me by saying. "We distract the guards, open the door, and let him out."

"But what if the door is locked? Or he's handcuffed? How are we supposed to get the keys to free him, genius?"

The look Jamie gave Jason made me gulp, and it wasn't even

me pissing him off this time. His hand tightened around mine even more, making me wince. I knew that if he wasn't holding my hand, his hand would be in a fist, probably pummeling Jason's face right about now. Noticing my pain, he eased his grip, and then, a second later, he let my hand go. I tried to ignore the disappointment, but my hand suddenly felt colder than it should have on a summer night.

"A couple of years ago, I got in trouble for hopping a rail that was three feet high," Vaughn said when Jamie only stared Jason down. "Their security office is a mobile trailer that's one loose screw from being condemned. We can get in."

"We'll get in trouble if we're caught," Jason continued to argue.

Realizing the longer we hesitated, the deeper the crap Ever found himself in, I said, "And *our friend* will get in trouble if we don't try." Turning on my heel, I started back for the carnival.

"Do you see anything?"

I was currently crouched on Vaughn's shoulders, forgetting all about the dress I wore, and peering into the dirty window of the trailer Ever was being kept in. Pretty soon, the cops would arrive, and because of all the crap Ever had given them before, they'd have no trouble identifying him. I knew my insolent best friend well enough by now to know that he hadn't told the security guards squat. Not even his name.

Looking around the rectangular room that was empty save for an old desk and several chairs pushed against the wall, I spotted my friend sitting in one of them. Ever's hands were tied with plastic cuffs, and his eyes were closed, appearing perfectly relaxed as he leaned his head against the wall. With parents as rich as his, who foolishly bailed him out of trouble every time, I guess he had no reason to worry.

"I see him!"

"Is he alone?" Jamie questioned a little too casually. Rescuing Ever had been my idea, but now that we were actually doing it, I couldn't keep my heart from racing. I wasn't sure if it was from fear or excitement. Right now, they felt like one and the same.

"No. There's a guard with him, but he looks bored. Distracting him should be a piece of cake."

"Oh, really?" Jamie said. I heard the challenge in his voice long before I gazed down at him. He was standing close while Jason served as the lookout a few feet away. Before I could respond, his hands circled my waist and carefully pulled me from Vaughn's shoulder. "Then work your magic," he whispered as soon as my body was pressed against his.

I couldn't quite catch my breath as I stared into brown eyes that always seemed so full. What was happening to me? I'd been crushing on Ever for *weeks*, but those feelings were nothing compared to what Jamie had done to me in a matter of days.

I heard a throat clear and then, "Uh, guys?"

Vaughn was watching us, and I could tell he was more than suspicious and just a little weirded out. Stepping away from Jamie, I made my way around the trailer, blocking out the sound of them whispering—more like arguing—as soon I was out of sight. When I reached the trailer door, I took a deep breath before knocking. Immediately, I heard chair legs scraping across the floor and then the fall of heavy feet growing louder. Seconds later, the door creaked as it swung open, revealing a bespectacled older man with kind eyes and a white bushy beard. He reminded me a little of Santa Claus except without the huge gut and the flying reindeer, of course.

Immediately, I knew what to say to draw him away from the trailer. "Hi, c-could you help me? I lost my p-parents, and some weird man keeps following me."

"Oh, you poor thing!" he said, rushing down the short steps. "Come inside, where you'll be safe while I check things out." I began to panic when he ushered me inside the trailer and locked the door behind him before shuffling away.

Crap! Crap! Crap!

Now what?

"Bee?" I spun around at the sound of Ever's voice. "What are you doing here?" he asked, sitting up with a frown.

"Well," I huffed, planting my hands on my hips, "I *was* busting you out, but it looks like we'll have to go to plan B."

Despite being in handcuffs and a world of trouble, he flashed me a crooked smile. Seeing it, I waited for my heart to skip a beat as it had done so many times before, but there was nothing. Had I been cured or plagued by something much stronger?

"Which is?"

I have no idea.

Rushing to the window I'd peeked through moments ago, I quickly unlocked it, but when I tried to push it open, it wouldn't budge. My frustration grew, knowing that it wouldn't be long before the guard came back.

"I might be able to help you get that open if you untie me."

Peering through the darkness outside, I saw the guard scanning the area with his flashlight. I just hoped the guys had hidden well enough. I grabbed the pair of scissors I'd spotted on the desk, then rushed over to Ever, who held up his hands. I looked for an opening, somewhere to cut the plastic, but they were so tight it would be impossible to free Ever without hurting him.

"Just do it," he said, sensing the reason for my hesitation. "We don't have a lot of time."

Forcing the sharp end of the scissors between the cuff and his hand, I cringed the moment his skin split and blood oozed from the wound. He hissed from the pain, so I quickly cut away the plastic, though it was tougher than it looked. Once the plastic gave, I did the next one, and in no time, Ever was free. He quickly stood from the chair, but our eyes widened the moment we heard footsteps approaching.

We made a break for the window. "You go first," we both said at the same time.

I was shaking my head before he could argue. "If we're caught, you'll be in a lot more trouble than I will. You could go to juvie."

With the same defiance that got us into this mess, he shrugged. "Then I'll go to juvie. I'm not leaving you."

"You will be if you get *arrested*, and then I'll have to deal with your cousin all summer alone." Ever had been refereeing us all week, and even though I was sure he was sick of it by now, he saw my point.

"Fine, but as soon as I'm through, I'm pulling you out. No exceptions."

"Deal."

Grabbing both sides of the window frame, he pulled himself up and over with ease. I wasn't so sure it would be that easy for me. Even though we were the same height, Ever had way more upper body strength.

None of that mattered a moment later when the trailer door opened, and the guard stepped inside.

"I'm afraid there's no one out there. How about we just give your parent's a call?" The guard looked ready to say more until he noticed the empty chair where Ever had been and the plastic cuffs lying on the floor. "What the—where'd he go?"

Realizing I was the one to set Ever free, his face turned a tomato red. "Why, you little bitch."

I took a step back and then two more when he charged toward me. Seeing the look in his eyes, I realized he wasn't quite as nice as I'd thought. I searched for somewhere to run, but there was nowhere to go, and pretty soon, I was backed into a corner. He reached for me, and my heart squeezed painfully tight. As I wondered if I was having a heart attack, I heard something crack, and then his eyes widened. I'd just managed to jump out of the way when he toppled over.

And standing there, holding a tree branch of all things, was Jamie.

Oh, no no no... What had he done?

"Come on!" he said when I continued to stand there, staring at him through wide eyes. Taking my hand, he dragged me behind him out of the trailer and into the night. Ever, Jason, and Vaughn were all waiting for us outside. None of us stopped running until we reached our bikes, and then we pedaled as fast as we could all the way home.

CHAPTER
FIFTEEN

The Punk

Present

S HORTLY AFTER I CAME DOWN, A SLEEPY-EYED FOUR WANDERED into the kitchen with Jay D at her side. I gave off two short whistles, and her pup immediately rounded the corner before sitting dutifully at my side. Four stopped short, her confused frown traveling from me to Jay D and back again. I smirked, making her prop her hand on her hip.

"What the hell did you do to my dog?"

I slowly took a sip of my coffee. "I taught him a few tricks. Not my fault you didn't bother training him."

Rolling her eyes, she bent low to make eye contact with Jay D. "Come here, baby."

Jay D simply stared back at her. Patting her thighs, she tried again. Like a good boy, he didn't budge.

"Why the hell did you turn my dog against me?"

"Have you thought about who might keep him when you hit the road?"

Her brows furrowed, and she was noticeably quiet, telling me she hadn't thought about it. Four had plans to turn a new leaf and race legally, which meant she'd be on the road a few months out of the year.

Slowly, almost hesitantly, she shook her head. "No."

"My uncle hasn't had much time for his own son these past

few years. He damn sure won't give a fuck about a dog, and since your mom's a basket case…" At her glower, I stopped my train of thought and began running my fingers through Jay D's fur. "I don't think they'll let your bestie keep him in her dorm."

"I could ask Wren and Lou," she said.

I rolled my eyes. "Or you could just ask me."

"Aren't you heading to Penn in the fall?"

"Yeah, but Unc set me up with an apartment near campus. I move in a few days before the semester starts," I announced, which earned Four's frown.

"I thought freshman were required to live on-campus their first year?"

"I have to be assigned to a dorm." I shrugged. "Doesn't mean I have to physically be there."

"But that's such a waste of money!" she fussed.

"I'm worth billions, kitten. I think I'll be okay if I blow ten or fifteen grand."

"There's one person you forgot about," she said.

I snorted, knowing she was referring to my cousin. "You could ask your boyfriend, but don't be surprised if he leaves him on the side of the road and tells you he ran away when you come home."

"Ever wouldn't do that."

"He's not exactly Jax's biggest fan. You sure you trust him with your fur baby?"

"Jax?" she echoed.

"Oh, yeah. I renamed him, too. Jax sounds more intimidating, don't you think?"

I could tell she was fed up with me when she crossed the kitchen and yanked the coffee pot from the holder. "Thanks, but no thanks."

I shrugged as I stood up and placed my bowl in the sink. "Suit yourself. It's no skin off my balls."

She paused from pouring her coffee and squeezed her eyes closed. "It's nose," she said after opening them again.

"What?"

"The saying is 'it's no skin off my *nose*.'"

"But that doesn't make any sense. Who the fuck cares about a nose when balls make babies?"

"Is that why Bee broke yours when you were kids?" she teased. "Because she knew you'd give her beautiful babies one day?" Four's eyes sparkled at me over her cup as she took a sip of her coffee.

"For your information, Barbette didn't break my nose. Ever is such a goddamn liar."

"It wasn't Ever," Four corrected. "Tyra told *me*. Vaughn told *her*."

Jesus fucking Christ. My friends were such dicks. "She didn't break my nose," I repeated needlessly.

"Seems to me she did since you're being a little defensive," Four teased.

"Eat a dick, kitten." Snapping my fingers, I grinned at her glare. "Or is that part of your relationship still one-sided?" I couldn't count how many times I'd caught Ever's head between Four's legs but never the other way around. Ever was clearly a better man than I could ever be.

I didn't miss the heat creeping up Four's neck as she looked away. "That's none of your business."

"There's nothing to be nervous about, kitten. It's really not that complicated. You just suck and swallow."

I expected her to get mad and storm away, but instead, she began chewing on her lip, telling me she was thinking.

Holy shit. I didn't give a fuck how patient Ever was willing to be. I had the feeling he was about to owe me big time. And I'd be damned if I wouldn't make him pay up.

"What if I'm bad at it?"

I raised a brow because I'd only kissed her once, briefly, but it was enough to tell me she wouldn't be bad at it at all. If she blew Ever even half as good as she kissed, they'd have no problems.

"What if you're not?"

"That's not an answer, Jamie."

I sighed as I hopped on the counter and held her gaze. "Look, he's not expecting you to be a pro. In fact, I'm pretty sure that would only piss him off."

"Why would that make him mad?"

"Because if it were me, I'd be wondering how many dicks you had to suck to get that good."

"Jamie, that's ridiculous."

I shrugged. "Maybe. Maybe not." Reaching behind me, I plucked a banana from the basket of fruit and held it out to Four. "Practice makes perfect."

Her phone buzzed, so she checked it, ignoring the banana. Peeling back the skin, I ate half in one bite while she typed. When she was finished, she glanced at me and rolled her eyes.

"You had a problem," I said around a mouthful of banana, "and I'm pretty sure you've just found yourself a solution."

She seemed genuinely confused when she frowned, making it *really* hard to believe she wasn't a virgin. "What do you mean?"

"You need someone to take care of your dog, and Ever needs a blow job from his girlfriend."

"*That's* your advice?"

"Nope. K.L.S.S."

"What does that mean?"

"Keep life simple, stupid."

Her phone buzzed again, and she glanced at it before pocketing it. "Ever will be here any second," she announced. "The three of us need to talk and not about blow jobs."

"Then no can do, princess," I said, calling her by the pet name Ever had given her. "I've got somewhere to be."

"Can't you cancel?"

"Nope," I answered as I hopped down from the counter. I was meeting Jason today for whatever fucking reason. He claimed he had some important information, but I was pretty sure I'd just end up kicking his ass instead. I didn't like him period, I never have, but I especially didn't like the way he was always leering at Bee.

"It's about Barbette," Four announced, and I hated myself for being tempted.

"Then I really don't give a fuck."

"Do you honestly expect me to believe that?" she fussed. When I started for the door without a response, she rushed to block me from leaving. "Let up on her," Four pleaded. "I know you're hurting, but her side of y'all's story is just as valid."

"Yeah?" I taunted around the smoke I'd shoved between my lips. I flicked my lighter, getting even more pissed off when it refused to light. "Well, I don't exactly know her side, do I?"

I wasn't about to sympathize with Bee's imaginary plight. She'd pulled the wool over Four and Ever's eyes just like she'd done me all those years ago.

My triumph when a tiny flame finally appeared was short-lived when Four snatched my lighter and the fag before pocketing them both.

"Give it back," I growled.

She propped a hip against the doorjamb before crossing her arms. "Make me."

Suddenly, I was transported back to the day I met Bee and the moment I fell for the very first time. She'd stolen my cookies because I wouldn't share and dared me to take them back. It was either then or when she pushed me into the goddamn pool.

"I don't have time for this." Spinning on my heel, I headed for the door leading to the family room, but Four somehow beat me there, too.

"If there's a part of you," she continued, "even a teeny tiny microscopic part that still wants to be with her, Jameson, then you have to find a way to forgive her."

I curled my lips at Four's plea. "Just like that, huh?"

"No. But you can start by not treating her like she's the devil."

"Impossible. Even before all of this, she was a goddamn nightmare."

And my wettest dream come true.

"Jamie, please stay. We can figure this out. Ever is on his way to get Bee right now."

"Then he's wasting his time," I said as I lifted Four by her waist and set her aside. "Because there's nothing to figure out." After last night, I wasn't interested in hearing a goddamn thing Barbette had to say. As per usual, she'd opened her mouth and reminded me why I hated her openly and loved her in secret. No one else had the power to cut me as deep.

After escaping the manor as Four called it, I hopped inside my Jeep and floored it all the way to the country club.

Part of my training for one day running the family business included learning how to play golf.

Golf...

Fucking golf.

Not only was it boring as hell, but my dick was too big for these tight-ass chinos. I had to go commando to even get into these pants or risk playing with my boxers shoved up my ass like a thong.

The fucking things I do for unrequited love.

I rotated my neck to release some of the tension there, but my gut was telling me it had nothing to do with this goddamn game. I could still hear Four's voice in my head, telling me to find a way to forgive Bee. Rearing back, I swung my club, hitting the ball and watching it soar through the air before bouncing and rolling straight into the hole.

Never.

"You're getting better," Jason complimented—as if I'd asked for his fucking opinion. He patted my shoulder like we were friends, and it was all I could do not to bend his fucking wrist back and make him scream like the bitch he was.

I handed my shit off to a caddie, and then we made our way down the hill. I could feel my feet dragging with each step. This was so not my fucking scene. I couldn't help but think how better suited Ever would have been for this job.

Down the hill, I politely waited for Jason to sink his ball before getting to the reason, the only fucking reason I'd agreed to meet him. *He'd* reached out to *me*. I wasn't about to pretend to be cordial.

"Tell me what you had to tell me before I beat it out of you with this club."

"Damn, bro, where's the love?"

I blinked at him. "Are you fucking serious?"

"Are *you* serious?" he spat back. "That was *my* fucking sister Ever played, and you all treat me like *I'm* the one who fucked up!"

I scrubbed a hand down my face because I wasn't prepared to deal with this heavy shit. Ever had broken the code, and somehow, we'd all ended up with a target on our back. Those stars in Olivia's eyes had only been for Ever, and it had only been a matter of time before he took notice. "You came back here looking to get even, J. What did you expect?"

"Some fucking compassion!" he screamed with tears in his eyes. "Livvy tried to kill herself. She almost *died*."

"I know, and I'm sorry. I'm so fucking sorry, but you didn't even know she was sick, and you're her goddamn twin. How can you blame Ever for not noticing?"

Angrily, he swiped the tears that fell from his face. "He shouldn't have slept with her in the first place, and you know it, man. Sisters were supposed to be off-limits."

He sniffled, and even though I found myself feeling sorry as hell, I couldn't let it show. Regardless of his reasons, Jason had turned into a fucking snake, and I couldn't forget that. Any sign of weakness would be a grave mistake. Besides, I couldn't make this shit right with Jason. Only Ever could do that. If it hadn't been for his mom leaving and his dad starting a new family, Ever probably would have handled the situation better. Needless to say, my cousin hadn't been very pliable. And now all he wanted to do was protect the ones he cared about from someone who was openly hostile. So no, as much as Jason had lost, he was still partly to blame for how his return to Blackwood Keep had played out.

"If Ever was willing to sit down with you without breaking your jaw, would you be willing to hear him out?"

The muscle in Jason's cheek jumped as he stared down at the ground. Eventually, he sighed. "I don't know, man… maybe."

Clasping his shoulder, I realized the concern in my voice when I spoke was sincere. "I really am sorry about your sister," I said, sounding like a broken record. What else was there to say, though? "How is she?"

Sniffling, he seemed to pull himself together as he squared his shoulders. "Better now."

I frowned because the haunted look in his eyes said otherwise. There was so much I wanted to ask, but I doubted Jason was ready to divulge information about his sister. For the first time since meeting him, I felt like I understood him. If it had been Adara, I would have tucked her away in a tower where no one could ever hurt her again. And knowing my sister, she'd break free and kick my ass for locking her away. At only seven years old, she could easily run circles around all of us. She was going to give me—and quite a few others—hell when she grew up.

"About Barbette," Jason said, pulling me from my thoughts. I was suddenly alert and dangling off a cliff with sharp rocks at the bottom. However this conversation went, it couldn't possibly end well. "Did you know that her father's company has had a high turnover of investors over the last few years? In the last twelve months alone, Elliot lost over a third when MontGlobal began hemorrhaging money. No one can figure out why."

"Does this have anything to do with why he's sold off almost all of his personal assets and half the companies under his umbrella?"

Jason seemed surprised as he studied me for a few seconds too long. Yeah, I've been doing my homework, but nothing ever quite added up. Or perhaps I was just too stubborn to believe the lengths that Bee would go to. Her actions didn't align with the girl I once knew.

So maybe it's time I accept that Bee is gone.

I gritted my teeth, refusing to believe that.

"Seems to me like you already have all the puzzle pieces. You just need to believe what your gut is already telling you," Jason advised.

"The Montgomerys are broke."

"Yes," Jason confirmed without hesitation.

I didn't trust that fucking gleam in his eye, but my gut also told me that he wasn't lying. I wasn't blind. I'd noticed the missing paintings, their lack of servants, and most recently, the sale of their summer home in the Hamptons.

"What the fuck does that have to do with Bee and Ever dating?"

"Elliot is looking for someone with a large enough cash flow to keep his company afloat and pull them out of debt."

My fists balled at my sides. "So you're telling me Bee was after our money?"

All this fucking time, that was what she'd wanted all along?

I wasn't sure if finding out that Bee was a gold digger pissed me off more than thinking she'd been in love with my cousin. I would say the two were running about neck and neck.

"Aw, don't be too hard on her," Jason said while clasping my shoulder again. I shrugged his hand off even while my mind was busy racing. "This lifestyle of ours is hard to give up once you're used to it. Our Bee's a survivor. Always has been."

Hearing that, for some reason, pissed me off. Bee had played me, used my friends, and ripped my fucking heart in two again. When I got through with her, fighter or not, she wouldn't be surviving *me*.

CHAPTER
SIXTEEN

The Plaything

B RYNWOOD'S SENIOR CLASS HAD BEEN PLAGUED WITH A FEVER. IN exactly one week, we'd be accepting our diplomas. While many of them, even the ones attending college in the fall, weren't thinking past their summer plans, I was thinking much farther ahead. In two weeks, I'd be eighteen. I'd also be far away from my father, Jamie, and Blackwood Keep. Forever. Today was just one more step closer.

It was also our senior breakfast day.

The entire senior class had been loaded onto two school buses to prevent the rowdiest of the graduates from skipping breakfast altogether and finding trouble somewhere else. The country club my parents frequented every weekend had graciously given Brynwood access to their ballroom and renowned chefs.

Finding an empty bench on the musty bus, I sat my bag down on the seat next to me. No one would be sitting there, anyway. It was ironic that I'd been crowned queen of the school only to be treated like a pariah. It was only when Ever was around that anyone bothered to bow and scrape, which was fine with me. I'd prefer not at all, but I was no longer interested in changing anyone's opinion of me.

I'd just pulled out my journal filled with poems, keeping it hidden from view, when my bag was lifted from the seat. A body too long for the cramped space took its place, and when I turned my head, I was surprised to find Ever smiling nervously at me.

I hadn't spoken to him in almost a week, not since he sent me a text Sunday morning saying that he was coming over. His only explanation when he never showed up was that something had come up.

"Mind if I sit here?" he asked over his shoulder. His back was half turned to me as he stretched his long legs out in the aisle. "Four snuck onto another bus with Tyra, and Vaughn said it was either his lap or nothing."

Sure enough, I spotted Vaughn two rows ahead, lying on his back with his feet planted in the aisle, forcing people to step over his legs to get by. What an asshole. Of course, no one dared bitch about it to Brynwood's star quarterback. I wanted to ask where Jamie might be lurking since he was technically still a member of the senior class, but when I remembered the last thing I'd said to him, I swallowed the words.

"So here you are," I said instead.

"So here I am."

Shrugging, I refocused on my journal. I wasn't sure how long I stared at the empty page before flipping it shut. No longer alone, I felt too self-conscious to express my most secret thoughts and desires—especially when I could still feel Ever's gaze boring into me. Sighing, I slipped the book back inside my bag where it was safe. His attention, however, was now fixed on my left hand and the pear-shaped diamond ring. I should have taken it off right then, but as meaningless as it had always been, it still had its use.

Knowing Ever wasn't going to ask for it back, I turned away to stare out the window and the trees passing by.

A few seconds passed, and I could still feel him watching me, so finally, I broke the silence. "Don't look at me like that, Ever. I'm fine."

"Yeah, I hear that from you a lot, so here's me being honest—I didn't believe you then, and I don't believe you now."

"What do you expect me to say?"

He didn't respond right away, and when I finally met his

gaze, I could see the apology in his eyes. Ever had nothing to be sorry for.

"I'm sorry that I can't be there for you like I promised. If you hate me, I understand."

Rolling my eyes, I gave him the first real smile I'd offered all week. "I'm not sure that's possible." Ever, just like his cousin, but in different ways, had put a mark on my heart a long time ago, and there was no erasing it. Still, he didn't seem convinced, so I added, "Have I told you lately that I can take care of myself?"

With a frustrated growl, he shoved his fingers through his dark hair with dusty ends. "Jesus, you're as bullheaded as Four. I can't believe I'd forgotten how much."

"I haven't exactly been myself lately."

He shot me a look that was full of disbelief. "You call *five years* lately?" After a rueful shake of his head, he added, "How did everything get so fucking screwed up?"

"I'm not sure," I blandly admitted.

Once again, Ever pinned me with that golden gaze of his. "Maybe it's not too late to fix things."

I frowned at his cryptic statement. "What do you mean?"

"I mean, when you turn eighteen in a couple of weeks, *don't run.*" He took a deep breath and exhaled. "Please, Bee."

After everything Ever had done and all that he'd risked, I would have kept any promise he demanded, but not this. He wasn't the boy I wanted to beg me to stay. And even if Jamie had known, I wouldn't blame him if he didn't.

Before I could respond to Ever's plea, the bus slowed and rolled to a stop. Both of our gazes flew to the window and the country club waiting on the other side of the parking lot.

While a tour of the grounds was being given, those of us whose parents were members took advantage of the amenities since it was much less busy during the week. After the buses emptied, Four and Tyra found us in the crowd and stunned me with their genuine excitement to see me. It wasn't until I couldn't take Ever's watchful pleading gaze any longer that I snuck away to pay Klara a visit.

Lying face down on the massage table, I'd just begun to drift off when there was a knock at the door. Even though there was a sheet covering me from the shoulders down, I was feeling a little self-conscious when Klara opened the door.

"I'm sorry to bother you, Klara, but I could really use your assistance."

"Anja, please tell me you didn't burn someone with the stones again."

The door closed, and I could hear hushed whispering on the other side before Klara returned. "I'm really sorry, madam, but I'm needed in the next room. I'll just be a few minutes."

She was gone before I could even reply.

Deciding that I wasn't all that hungry, I settled in, resigned to miss breakfast. I was sure no one would notice that I was gone, anyway. A few minutes later, I drifted off, and it wasn't until I heard the door open again that I awakened. I wasn't sure how much time had passed, and I decided it didn't matter as I allowed my eyes to shut again slowly. I was barely aware of the sheet slowly being tugged down my back and the faint smell of cigarette smoke. Eyes still shut, I pursed my lips. Clearly, my masseuse had taken the time to do more than just assist a colleague. Instead of being angry, however, I found myself inhaling the tainted air and thinking of a certain boy. The one with a gentle smile and fiery temper. A dirty-talking enigma.

When the sheet reached my lower back, I forced the image away and settled in. A moment later, I tensed when I felt the sheet slip past my waist. I definitely hadn't ticked off my gluteus as a go for a massage. And even if I had, Klara usually started with shoulders...

Unless it wasn't the masseuse at all.

A chill ran down my spine when I felt full soft lips press against my nape. Before I could register that it really happened, I felt another. As soon as I felt the intruder move away, I lifted my head and glanced over my shoulder.

Leaning against the counter where Klara kept her supplies was Jamie in all his delectable glory. I couldn't decide if the pants and the vest he wore were red or brown, but it made a killer combination with his mahogany hair styled to show off his beautiful face. He even wore an expensive-looking watch to complete the look. The white shirt he wore only emphasized his tanned skin and the tattoos he'd mostly hidden underneath his clothes. Unfortunately, his hands and neck would always give him away. I was willing to bet he gave all those girls on Wall Street something dirty to dream about during the day.

Coming to my senses, I stopped ogling him, grabbed the sheet, and covered myself, even though he'd already seen plenty, before sitting up.

"What the hell are you doing here?"

"It's senior breakfast day, and I'm a senior if you recall."

"I meant *in here.*"

"Oh… I got lost."

Closing my eyes, I inhaled before slowly exhaling. Unfortunately, my patience was nowhere to be found. "You got lost?"

Pushing away from the counter, he slowly took the two steps it took to get to me before gripping my chin. I both hated and loved it when he did that. "But don't worry. I found you." He was kissing my lips before I even had a chance to respond.

Or remember that I was naked except for my panties underneath the sheet.

His tongue tasted like mint, and the cologne he wore filled my senses until I was clutching his silk tie, desperate for every inch of him. I'd forgotten the sheet until I felt my bare nipples brushing his chest. The roughness of his vest teased them until they were hard and eager for his attention. As if sensing my thoughts, he pulled away and gently nipped one before tugging it between his lips.

Eyes fluttering, my head fell back as he licked, nipped, and suckled at my breasts. I thought I'd chased him away for good, but it hadn't taken more than a few spoken words to get us right back here. I had the feeling that no matter how deeply Jamie and I cut, we would never stop wanting more.

The little sounds escaping me pitched higher and higher, and when I was dangling over the edge, Jamie stepped away, pulling me back.

"Why did you stop?" *I was so close.*

He didn't respond as he reached for my waist. We played tug-of-war with the sheet before Jamie won, and I was naked. The sheet fell to the floor, and then his hands were in my hair as he ravished my lips. "I want to go down on you," he whispered when he came up for air.

Immediately, I tensed and found it impossible to exhale. If he weren't standing between my thighs, I would have pressed them together. "You can't."

"I can do anything I want," he said, trailing sinful kisses across my jaw. "What are you afraid of? That you'll like it?" I gasped when he nipped my chin. "That you'll want more?"

"Klara will be back any minute," I tried to reason.

"Then she'll get to watch you come," he smoothly replied. "We'll call it a generous tip."

"Jamie... no." Pushing him away, I met his frustrated gaze. "Lock the door," I heard myself say.

The anger faded from his eyes, and then he was across the room, locking the door before I could blink. As he swaggered back to me, he began to loosen his tie. Something about so simple an action made a shiver work its way down my spine. Those talented hands then found my waist and began tugging at my panties. "Lift up."

I did, and in a flash, the scrap of lace was gone.

Stepping between my legs once more, he kissed me until my world was nothing but stars. I hadn't even noticed when his hand slid underneath my knee or when he lifted my leg, planting my foot on the table. He was still kissing me when his hand started on my knee before sliding down, down, down...

I gasped at the first touch of his fingers. The second sent me spiraling out of control. Jamie's nimble fingers strummed my clit as delicately as any of his guitars, and the soft notes I gave him in return was music to his eager ears.

"Can I taste you now?" he inquired when I was so close to falling.

The only response I could give him in return was to push against his fingers, begging for more. "Please."

Kissing me one last time, he knelt, and I almost missed his lips until I felt them on my inner thigh. Glancing down, I found him already watching me through lowered lids. He continued to hold my gaze even when his lips reached my pussy, and he gave it a sensual kiss.

I drew in a breath at the feeling and knew I'd do whatever it took to feel it over and over. "Oh."

This time when he kissed me, he introduced me to his tongue, and my head fell back on my shoulders. I wasn't prepared for how he would take his time, making sure not to leave a single inch of me untouched, unkissed, unloved.

Eventually, Jamie wanted more, so sliding his hand under my other knee, he lifted my leg until it mirrored the other. I was completely open, and he dove right in. Moments later, I was distantly aware of the footsteps outside the door. Neither of us cared as my hand slid through his hair and gripped the back of his head.

Jamie continued to lick me, and over his appreciative moans, I could hear the door handle jiggling.

Finding it locked, Klara knocked. "Miss Montgomery?"

At that moment, Jamie's tongue chose to flick my clit, making me gasp and cry his name. He'd *definitely* done that on purpose.

"Miss Montgomery?" Klara knocked and tried the handle again. "Is everything okay?"

As Jamie continued licking my clit, I felt his finger at my entrance, gently teasing me with the tip. My breathing deepened as his tongue sped up until my hips were lifting off the table, and my shocked cry echoed around the room. I could feel my arousal seeping onto the table and my clit throbbing as fast as my heartbeat. Jamie stood and was kissing me before I could even catch my breath. And when his tongue swept inside my mouth, and I tasted myself, I greedily deepened the kiss.

"I have never wanted anything as much as I want inside you, Bette."

I could feel his erection pressing against my inner thigh and wanted that, too. Reaching for his belt buckle, I decided it was time. I needed my lips, pussy, and hands wrapped around him *now*.

Unfortunately, Jamie's hand stopped me before I could free him.

"Soon. We have to save *something* for our wedding night."

"Huh?" With the force of my orgasm still ringing in my ears, I was sure I was hearing things. Frowning, I opened my eyes slowly, but his gorgeous smile blinded me.

"Nothing."

Jamie helped me redress when my legs wouldn't stop shaking long enough, and when we left the room, he held my hand as we traveled the short, empty hall. We made it to the front unscathed, and I soon realized why when I spotted all three of the club's masseuses, including Klara, huddled behind the receptionist's desk. It left no doubt in my mind that they'd heard everything.

Fear that word would get back to my father suddenly made my hands tremble. Jamie stopped short when he spotted the sign-in sheet, and with one swift movement, he snatched the top page with my name scribbled on it. Leaning over the desk, he scanned the space until he spotted what he was looking for. I realized once he'd snatched it up that it was the client intake form I'd filled out in the beginning.

"Sir, you can't do that!" one of the braver masseuses scolded.

"Oh? Then why did I?" He didn't wait for her response before tugging me toward the door. I wanted to apologize to Klara, but Jamie was moving too fast, so I settled for an apologetic glance thrown over my shoulder. Jamie had led me down one hall and then another before slowing enough to rip and toss the forms in the trash. When we passed a bathroom on the way to the ballroom, I made him stop.

"Hold my bag?"

He took it, kissed me hard, and then patted my rump before letting me go. I was still on cloud nine when I glided into the bathroom. One glance in the mirror, and I knew I'd fallen off the wagon hard. My disheveled hair, wrinkled uniform, and bruised lips told me so. I was beginning to think it was impossible to stay away from Jamie. He was temptation incarnate.

More than anything, I wished I could take back the lie about him not being enough.

Jamie was more than I could ever wish for.

More than I deserved.

Deciding I'd finally tell him so, I hurriedly cleaned the mess we'd made between my legs as best I could with damp paper towels. It looked like I was going commando for the rest of the day since my panties were currently stuffed in Jamie's back pocket. He refused to listen to reason and give them back so I was left praying that the wind didn't decide to play peek-a-boo with my bare ass. Once finished, I tossed the towels and rushed back into the hall.

The *empty* hall.

"Jamie?" My head swiveled back and forth before realizing he was gone. Wondering where he could have gone and with

my bag, I started down the hall. I'd made it all of two steps before I closed my eyes, realizing the mistake I'd made. The first
had been trusting Jamie at all, and the second…

Giving him my bag with my journal full of poems hidden
inside.

He'd been after it for months, and I'd stupidly handed it to
him on a platter. The only place I could think to look for him was
in the ballroom, where the entire senior class was having breakfast.
My heart was pounding so hard that my ears began to throb as I
raced through the country club. I wasn't sure what he planned,
but whatever it was, I had to stop him. By the time I reached the
ballroom, the tears I'd shed prematurely had clouded my vision.

Which was why I came to a screeching halt just inside the
antechamber. My breaths came fast and hard as I began blinking
rapidly at the figure sitting alone on the love seat.

There Jamie sat, my bag at his feet, elbows resting on his
thighs, head bent… and my journal strangled in his fists.

Sniffling as I frantically wiped away my tears, Jamie's head
lifted at the sound, and if I looked even half as devastated as he
did right now… oh, my God.

The second our gazes met, he shot to his feet, and the first
thing I noticed as he ate the distance between us was his eyes
rimmed with red. He didn't stop even after his lips crashed into
mine. He kept going, forcing me through the doors of the antechamber until my back was against the outside wall. This was
nothing like the sweet kisses that made me blush when we were
kids and craved now that we were all grown up. Somehow, though,
my body seemed to want more. I tried pushing him away, but his
hands clamped around my wrists. My journal fell to my feet, but
I no longer cared about it as much as finding out what caused his
anger. As if reading my mind, his grip on my wrists turned punishing, making me cry out from the pain.

He didn't hesitate to let me go, but the devastation in his eyes
kept me in place.

"Oh, did that hurt?" His tone was mocking, so I kept my mouth shut, knowing his question was rhetorical. "You have no idea, Bette." Stepping away, he suddenly looked defeated. "It wouldn't have been even close to what you do to me *every day*, yet I still can't let you endure it."

Somehow, I knew he wasn't talking about my physical pain. He'd wooed me, *tricked* me, and all to steal my journal and expose all of my secrets in front of the entire senior class. And then, for some reason, he hadn't gone through with it.

"Jamie—"

He didn't give me the chance to say more. He shoved away from the wall and from me before storming away.

CHAPTER SEVENTEEN

The Plaything

Summer… Six Years Ago

"MIND IF I SIT HERE?"

I looked up and nearly swallowed my tongue when I found Jamie towering over me. He'd appeared out of thin air like some newly born god who lived only for mischief.

I still couldn't get the image of that guard he'd saved me from collapsing to the ground and Jamie standing there like some storybook hero. I knew he was anything but. In fact, he'd acted like nothing had happened while I'd been a nervous wreck ever since. What if that guard had died? What if we'd *killed* him?

"Oh, um, Ever and the guys are out back."

We were all hanging out at the Portlands' today. A playdate with Olivia had been the only reason my parents let me out today since I'd missed curfew by an hour the night of the fair. Olivia was currently upstairs, painting her nails with two of her actual friends, but, as usual, she was nice enough to let me take cover here.

Jamie said nothing as he popped a squat and rested his back against the tree I'd been sitting under alone.

Closing my journal, I angled my body toward him. He was so close that my knee brushed his thigh. "Don't you want to play catch with the guys?"

He shook his head, and some of his reddish-brown hair fell into his eyes. "Tossing a ball back and forth isn't really my thing."

My eyebrows shot to my hairline. If he didn't like sports, what did he like? "You don't play sports?"

He seemed wary as he looked me up and down. "Is that a problem?"

"No, I just—is it all sports or just football?" My foot always seemed to find its way inside my mouth when Jamie was around. He didn't exactly say all the right things, either, but only one of us was ever apologetic about it.

"The games I like to play aren't considered a sport."

"What kind of games do you like to play?"

His brown eyes twinkled in that way I knew meant trouble. "Have you heard of spin the bottle?"

"Duh," I said, giggling to hide my nervousness.

Cocking a brow, he said, "Ever play?"

My cheeks were suddenly burning, and I had trouble meeting his gaze. "No. Of course not." The thought of my first kiss made my stomach twist and my heart race.

"I can show you how if you want."

As if it would protect me, I clutched my journal a little tighter to my chest. I hadn't expected Jamie to flirt with me again. At the fair, I'd looked like a girl, and I knew without needing to be told that I was a pretty one. But today, I was back to wearing my cargo shorts, and Avengers tee with my favorite red cap turned backward. "No, thanks."

He leaned a little closer, making me want to say yes. "Are you afraid, Barbette?"

I considered lying, but I had the feeling he'd see right through me. "Yes."

Lifting his hand, he tugged on one of my curls. "Then, I can wait."

"Wait? Wait for what?"

"For your first kiss… and for you to get over my cousin."

"Wha—I…" As I struggled for words or a plausible lie, Jamie plucked my journal from my hands. My heart pounded as I made a desperate attempt to steal it back. What if he read what was inside? Everything I felt but was too afraid to say was in that book. Cruelly, he held it out my reach. "Give it back!"

"Admit that you like my cousin."

"No, I don't. Now give me my book!" I shot to my feet, hoping that would give me an advantage, but he stood too, and pretty soon, I was chasing him all over the Portlands' front yard. After a few minutes, I was beginning to tire and ready to give up when he stumbled over a rock. It slowed him down just enough for me to tackle him to the ground. "Jerk!"

I fell on top of him, but somehow, he managed to flip onto his back, sending me to the ground at his side. And that was when I realized he was laughing. Against my will, I began laughing, too. Out of the corner of my eye, I noticed my journal lying in the grass a few feet away. Propping my head in my hand, I made no move to rescue it. I wasn't sure how long we lay on the ground, staring at one another. Eventually, he broke the spell.

"Tell me something about you that no one else knows."

My gaze flew to the grass, hoping it hid my blush. Jamie might as well have asked me to take off my clothes. Remembering all the stories Ever told about him, I wondered… would he stop me if I tried?

Something inside my chest tightened at the thought.

Did I want to try? Isn't that what boys and girls would do when they liked each other? First, they kiss and then they—

Suddenly, my heart was beating fast. Too fast. I no longer knew how to breathe.

I didn't like Jamie. I liked Ever.

Frustration made my fists ball in the grass because it felt like a lie. Ever was the boy who taught me my first secret handshake, the boy I'd learned to climb trees with, and the only one who hadn't run away when I sat with boys instead of girls.

But while I was locked inside these past few days, Ever wasn't the one I couldn't stop thinking about.

"My favorite color is red."

Jamie seemed surprised and excited for some reason. "Mine too."

"Really?" I arched a brow as I looked him over. As usual, Jamie was covered from head to toe in dark clothing. "It's not black?"

"Really?" he mocked back. "It's not pink?" I knew he was making a dig at the getup I wore to the carnival.

"It's red." Suddenly, I felt boneless and lay back in the grass. Jamie and I shared a favorite. I wondered how many more there were.

"Mine too," Jamie echoed, his tone lighter than before. He seemed to be debating something before he spoke again. "He doesn't know that you like him, you know."

Dread filled me until I felt sick. *Oh, no.* Jamie really did know about my crush. "What are you talking about?" I asked, anyway. There was always a chance I was wrong. About a lot of things…

Shifting onto his side, Jamie pinned me with his beautiful brown gaze. "Ever. He just thinks of you as one of the guys. He's never going to see you that way unless you make him."

It only took me a few seconds to realize that Jamie was right. I'd been so busy hiding my crush that I never considered what could be if I only had the courage. "How do I do that?"

I told myself that I only imagined the disappointment I glimpsed in Jamie's eyes, especially when he reached out and fingered one of my curls. "I'll show you."

I didn't even get the chance to ask him how before his lips pressed against mine. His eyes were closed tight while mine were bugged out of my head. Jameson Buchanan had stolen my first kiss.

No, no, no…

My hands found his chest, ready to push him the hell off.

Before I could, his hands circled my wrists, pinning them to the grass. I struggled to free them, but it only made him kiss me harder. One of the guys or not, I realized Jamie was much stronger. And probably always would be.

I should have kneed him in the balls, but slowly, I relaxed in the grass, letting him kiss me instead.

Sensing my surrender, Jamie pulled back a little, softening the kiss, and forgetting that I was unwilling, I chased his lips. I felt his body shake as he chuckled, and then… I felt his tongue. Gently, he teased my lips until they parted, and he slipped inside. It took me a while to notice that his hands were no longer closed around my wrists and that I was free to sock him… so why didn't I? Seconds passed, and my eyes drifted closed. The kiss continued, deepening until our lips were bruised, and we both ran out of breath.

I no longer felt alive when he pulled away. I needed him.

"How many girls—" Still panting, I was unable to complete my sentence. It didn't matter because Jamie already knew what I was asking.

His eyes were still closed, his cheeks pink when he answered. "One."

I swallowed down the emotions bubbling up, but my voice shook even more when I spoke. "Including me?"

Slowly, his eyes drifted open, showing me his cloudy gaze. "Yes."

"I—But you—" I was struggling with the realization that I was Jamie's first kiss, and he was mine.

"I really wanted to kiss you."

"Yeah, well, I didn't want to kiss you!" Shoving him away, I quickly sat up.

He'd *tricked* me. Just like he'd tricked Rachel into feeling her boobs at the fair. Jamie was just as inexperienced as I was. He was just better at hiding it.

My angry gaze met his blank one, but I wasn't prepared for him to kiss me again. And I wasn't expecting to kiss him back.

"Yes, you did," he whispered against my lips. "But I'm not my cousin. I'm not blind. I see you, Bette. I can't *stop* seeing you."

My inhale was sharp, and the ache in my stomach doubled.

"Bette?"

His soft, wide lips found mine again, and just that quick, I was addicted to his kisses. "Something to remind you that you're mine."

I started to tell him there was no need, that I had the feeling I'd never forget, but the only sound that spilled from my lips was a sigh and then his name. "James."

For the rest of the summer, Jamie showed me the way all right.

To his heart. And to mine.

CHAPTER
EIGHTEEN

The Punk

Present

IT HAD BEEN TWO DAYS SINCE I LEFT BEE IN TEARS AT THE COUNTRY club. *Two days*, and somehow, I could still taste her. Getting Barbette to lower her guards hadn't exactly been a chore. I'd learned early on how to best catch flies, but I never thought to use my charm against her.

Now that I knew she was nothing but a gold-digger, all bets were off.

The only good thing that had come out of learning the truth was the clear path I now had to getting what I wanted. Barbette needed a cash cow and I needed...her—in my bed, under my thumb, and eventually crushed beneath my heel. I'd make Elliot an offer, marry Barbette, and fill her with the heirs my family required. Then, when my work was done, I'd sit back and watch my thorny rose wilt for the rest of her days.

My only obstacle was the conviction I seemed to lack. Frustration had caused me to explode that day in the country club. My mission had been simple: expose her secrets and revel in her downfall.

Then why hadn't I gone through with it?

The only time I couldn't seem to give in to her was when she pushed me away. Go fucking figure.

It's not your hate that kills me but the love I see shining through.

You kiss me with your cruel words and caress me with your pain.

I'd glimpsed those words in her journal and just as she predicted, I broke like a dam and swept her away. And just before she could drown in my hate, I pulled her back out again. It seemed I couldn't hate Barbette without loving her twice as hard.

In desperate need of a distraction, I'd driven to the city with Lou riding shotgun, hoping that it would put enough distance between us. The few hours away had kept me from going to Barbette, but it hadn't kept me from thinking about her… or picturing my hand around her lovely neck.

"Bee's right," Lou mumbled when "Kiss it Better" began to play. "You listen to Rihanna way too much, bro."

Grinning, I turned up the volume just as Lou's phone began to ring.

Leaning forward, she snatched it from the dash. "What?" she snapped, drawing my gaze from the road. She was now curled up in a ball as if suddenly feeling the need to protect herself. "Where am I?" Scoffing, she added, "You'd know that if you weren't too busy lying to me." She was silent for a few seconds as she listened to whatever the caller was saying. "Ugh." It was the only warning Lou gave before hanging up.

"Trouble in paradise?"

"I am paradise, and Wren is going to learn that really soon when I leave his ass."

I didn't get the chance to respond to that before my phone rang. Already knowing who was calling, I didn't bother looking at the screen before picking up. "Untwist your panties, Harlan. I got her."

"What the hell are you guys doing?"

Wren was *seething*. I'm talking fire-breathing dragon mad. I could practically hear the steam blowing from his nose and ears, and I snickered.

Of course, I just had to poke the sleeping bear.

"Not much right now. She's just riding me."

"What the fuck did you say?" he shouted, damn near blowing out my eardrums.

"I said *she's riding with me*." Taking a page from Lou's book, I hung up on him. Lou snorted, so I turned my head to meet her gaze. "You know he's going to kick our asses for that, right?"

Sinking lower in her seat, she lifted her legging-clad legs and crossed her sneakered feet on my dash. "Yours, maybe. I've got immunity because I'm adorable, and he loves me too much."

Scoffing, I shook my head. I was beginning to think I'd never figure girls out no matter how many I screwed. "If you believe that, why are you giving him the cold shoulder?"

I glanced over in time to see her lips curl. "Because he's gone most of the day and when he's home, he's in his head and barely sleeps at night. I do not tolerate secrets *or* meeting up with old flames behind my back."

"Kendra?"

"Kendra."

"You don't think that maybe he's just hunting Fox?" I didn't know Wren all that well yet, but I was willing to bet that he wasn't comfortable with the idea of being a sitting duck. No, he was a predator and always would be.

"I know he is."

I waited for her to elaborate, but she was too engrossed in her phone. Wren had been blowing it up with text after text. When I finally pulled into her driveway, I grew frustrated when I didn't see Wren's car. It had been two weeks since their bootleg dinner party, and I was too fucked up then over the way Bee fled that night to get the answers I'd come for. At least now, I had the ones that had plagued me for five years. Shutting off the car, I opened the middle console and dug out the smokes I stashed inside.

"You couldn't wait until I was out of the car?" Lou bitched.

"We need to talk."

"Then, you need to put that out."

"Nope." Taking a drag, I blew the smoke in her face and laughed when she coughed and frantically waved the smoke away. "That night we rescued your not-so-prince-charming, we had help…"

"Yeah? And?" Her tone was defiant, but I noticed she had a hard time meeting my gaze.

"Who was the shooter?"

"Does it matter? You're still breathing, aren't you?" She then gave my cigarette a pointed look. "Maybe not for long," she added, rolling her eyes.

Releasing smoke through my nose, I chose to ignore that. *My body, my business.*

My father died from lung cancer, but so what? He could have just as easily been taken out by a bus. I ignored the pain in my heart at the reminder that my father was gone forever and chose to focus on something I could change.

"Who was the shooter, Lou?"

"A friend."

It was the same answer she'd given that night when she met up with someone. *Twice.*

Ever and I had been reluctant to let her out of our sight, but we'd learned that night just how stubborn Lou could be. And while Wren was being rescued, Ever and I had been ordered to wait at the edge of the woods where it was safe like some chumps. Before leaving us there, however, she'd pressed a memory card into Ever's palm and said we'd know what to do if she didn't come back.

Lou had indeed returned, though, empty-handed. The only explanation she'd given was that Wren was alive and that he was safe.

"Does this friend happen to be Sean Kelly?"

She paused, but then just as quickly recovered. "Who?"

It was all the confirmation I needed. "Tell me how you know him and for how long," I pressed.

"Sean Kelly is dead."

My gaze narrowed at the confidence in her claim when only

seconds ago she'd pretended not to know him. "How the hell do you even know that?"

"His mother told me so at Thanksgiving. I was there, re-member? Nice woman that Claire."

I remember a lot of things. Including Lou's boyfriend press-ing a gun to my kneecaps under the dinner table to protect some-one he barely knew.

"Sean Everson Kelly is dead," Lou repeated. Done playing games, I was ready to kick her ass out my car when she said, "But *Crow* is alive."

"Who the hell is Crow?"

"He's Exiled. Or he used to be. He's also Wren's father."

My head spun as the wheels began to turn faster. If Sean and Crow were one and the same... Just as the last puzzle piece clicked into place, Lou nonchalantly set off the bomb.

"Four seems to think he's Ever's father, too."

I'd only just recovered from the blow Lou had dealt when Wren suddenly materialized in the passenger window. Thanks to the large hood he'd thrown over his head, I couldn't see his eyes, only his rigid jaw and the hard set of his lips.

Lou's back was turned to the door, completely oblivious to his presence. Before I could warn her, the door was ripped open, and she was plucked from her seat. The look he gave me before he slammed my door shut would have made me snort if I wasn't still reeling.

Wren set Lou on her feet, and while they stood in their drive arguing, I threw my Jeep into drive before backing out and head-ing home.

The second I reached home, I went in search of Four and wasn't surprised to find her in the garage. I was surprised, however, to find her crying.

I swallowed hard, wondering what the hell Ever had done now, and then I felt like a selfish asshole when I wondered if it had anything to do with Bee.

Hearing my footsteps, she looked up and then hurriedly dashed at her tears.

"Too late, kitten." I crossed the garage until I stood next to her, where she was straddling her bike. "What's the matter?"

Her trembling lips prevented her from speaking, so she handed me her phone instead. On the screen was an open email, and the subject read "Your AMA Pro Licensing Application." Scrolling, I swallowed hard when I read the first line.

We are sorry to inform you that your application for a Pro Motocross License has been denied.

Shit.

The email went on to say that Four would be welcome to apply again after obtaining the required points in a qualifying class.

Whatever the hell that meant.

"Fuck, Four. Fuck. I'm so sorry."

Four was no longer crying, but her face could have been carved from stone as she stared at the wall. I'd only seen her race once, but it was enough to know that she could dust the fools that called themselves professionals. What right did they have to deny her?

"Maybe it's just not meant to be."

"What the fuck do you mean by that?" I barked.

Her startled gaze met mine, and her eyebrows rose at my scowl.

"You can't just give up because they told you no. You make them eat shit until they say yes."

"Well, they won't," she grumbled. "Not until I get the sixty points I need. I'd have to compete as an amateur, and I'd have a year and a half to do it."

"So what's the problem? We both know you'll get those god-damn points."

Four tried to hide the worry in her gaze and failed. "What if it takes me the entire eighteen months to qualify?"

I frowned. As amazing as Four was, I highly doubted it. Sure, the competition would be stiffer than she was used to, but if any-one had a chance, it was Four fucking Archer.

"I'd be on the road the entire time," she added. "I can't leave Rosalyn."

"Your mom will be in good hands, Four. She's going to be treated by the best doctors my uncle's guilt-ridden money can buy."

To his credit, Uncle Thomas had tried to care for Four's mom himself until recently when he finally accepted that he was in over his head. Since he wasn't Rosalyn's legal spouse, my uncle was in the process of getting her recommended for involuntary hospitalization.

Four had taken the news with an extra dose of guilt. She'd been taking care of her mom since she was a child, shouldering her schizophrenia and nursing her back to health. Now that the burden had been taken away, she didn't know where to begin liv-ing or even if she should.

"And Ever?" she asked, voicing the other plague on her heart. "He didn't sign up to have a girlfriend who's never around."

"Ever is goddamned pussy-whipped, kitten. He'll be right here waiting for you."

"No," she growled. "He'll be at Cornell with all those *avail-able* co-eds."

"Do you trust him?"

"It's not about—"

"Yes, it is," I said before she could finish that ludicrous state-ment. "You either trust him or you don't. If you don't, then this conversation is irrelevant, and you should be having a different one entirely."

"I'm not breaking up with him," she sassed, catching my meaning.

"*I figured as much.*"

"Can you ever give advice without being such a dick?"

"Nope," I said with a pop of my lips. "My methods are one-hundred percent effective."

"Whatever." I watched as she looked at the email one last time before pocketing her phone.

"So when do you leave?" I asked. I already knew she'd do what needed to be done. And even if my cousin was dick enough to have an issue with her absence, Four would never let it stop her. Girls like Four and Bee are what sad love songs were made of. My baby done left me and all that jazz.

"If I want to have my license in time to compete next season? As soon as possible." After a few seconds, she sighed. "After graduation."

Graduation was in less than a week, which meant she didn't have a lot of time. Pulling out my phone, I searched for the kind of bike she'd need and whistled at the cost. "You don't by any chance have ten grand lying around, do you? If not, Ever's got the cash." I pocketed my phone before saying, "You might need to think harder about giving him that blow job, though."

The indignant look she gave me nearly folded me in half. "I've got it covered, thanks. I didn't risk my freedom racing street for nothing."

She swung her leg over the bike and headed inside and upstairs. When she stepped through her bedroom door, she looked over her shoulder and frowned once she realized I'd followed her.

"Uhhh... Jamie?"

"We need to talk." Reaching behind me, I slammed her door closed. "Tell me what you know about Ever's father." It wasn't a question that she knew more than she should have.

Her deep frown would have been adorable if I weren't on a mission. "Who? Thomas?"

"No," I snapped, giving her an indignant look. The women in my life made a habit of playing coy. "His *real* father."

She blinked, took a step, and then another until she reached me. "Sean?"

Four's bedroom door flew open before I could answer. I swung around, and my heart dropped to my stomach when I found Ever leaning against the jamb.

Shit.

CHAPTER NINETEEN

The Plaything

I T WAS THE NIGHT BEFORE GRADUATION, BUT THE CEREMONY, ONE OF the most important milestones I'd have in my lifetime, was the furthest thing from my mind. Six days had passed since the country club. Six days of agony. Six days of wondering. I couldn't erase the devastation from my mind that I saw in Jamie's eyes. Even when he was angry, I couldn't recall him staying away this long. There were no late-night break-ins or random pop-ups at my school. He'd even deprived me of the mocking texts he always sent in the morning and sometimes throughout the day.

Deciding I'd had enough, I tossed back the bedsheets, shoved on my flip-flops, and snuck from my bedroom and the house. Ready or not, Jameson John Buchanan would just have to face me. Tiptoeing through the backyard, I made my way to the tool shed, hoping it was still there. As I slipped inside, relief and nostalgia flooded my heart when I spotted my old, red Huffy. My bike, the harmonica, and my journal were the last that remained of Bee.

Quietly, I pulled the bike from the shed, hoping the chain hadn't rusted too much. After a quick inspection, I swung my leg over the seat, feeling giddy. I had to pedal a little harder than necessary since there was a little rust, but in no time, I was flying down the dark, empty road.

It was dangerous.

Completely reckless.

244 | B.B. REID

I'd never felt freer.

I was out of breath by the time I reached the huge mansion. It wasn't until I stopped in front of the closed gates that I realized just how rashly I'd acted. It was after midnight. Of course, I wasn't getting through. Not unless I called Jamie.

But it was also the night before graduation, which meant there was likely a party happening and even more likely that Jamie wouldn't even be home.

So much for carpe diem.

Or however that saying went when it was the middle of the fucking night.

Giving up, I started to turn around when the sound of creaking metal filled the night. The gates slowly opened, and I realized someone was coming. I quickly ducked inside the bushes and hid as best I could with a bike for a beacon.

The sound of an engine roaring made me hold my breath. Moments later, I saw a flash of red as Jamie's Jeep flew through the gates. "Gold Digger" by Kanye West was blasting from the speakers.

Where the hell was he going in such a hurry?

I stared at his taillights until they disappeared. The gates began creaking as they slowly shut, and I realized this was my chance. Without a second thought, I slipped through them. There wasn't enough time to talk myself out of it. I left my bike behind in the bushes and decided it would be safer there hidden from sight.

Jogging up the long drive, I bypassed the front door, knowing it wouldn't be unlocked, and slipped around the side of the house. I wondered if Mr. McNamara ever had the lock fixed on the window in the butler's pantry.

It was a long shot, but it was my only one.

This place was huge, which meant there were a thousand places to hide a key. Jamie could return before then. I'd come here to confront him, but now I was more interested in satisfying my curiosity.

Reaching the window, I nearly clapped and jumped for joy when I pushed up on the glass, and it slid open. I wasted no time swinging my leg over the sill and climbing inside. The pantry was dark, but I could still make out the fully stocked shelves and the door a few feet away. Pushing it open, I peeked to confirm the kitchen was empty before stepping inside.

Memories from my time spent here as a kid helped me navigate the dark home. I climbed one of the winding stairs to the second floor and wondered if Jamie still slept in the same room he had as a kid. He and Ever had to share a bathroom then.

There was one memory in particular that still mortified me to this day. I'd come over and shown myself up and somehow walked in on them, measuring their dicks to see who was bigger. Luckily, I hadn't seen much before slapping my hands over my eyes. I ran from the room and all the way home.

I didn't talk to either of them for an entire week after that.

Reaching Jamie's room, I pushed inside. I didn't doubt that it would be unlocked. Jamie didn't hide, and when people told him what they thought of him, he'd laugh in their face.

"No fucks to give" should have been tattooed on his forehead.

Every day, I wished that could be me.

The faint smell of cigarette smoke and potpourri filled my nose as I stepped inside. On one of the black nightstands was a small guitar-shaped tray filled with ashes and several butts. There were several other things cluttered on the surface, including his iPod and speakers.

Black rumpled bedding covered the headboard-less bed. Above it hung the American, Scottish, and Irish flags. I smiled. It was so like Jamie to embrace every part of himself.

Seeing his father's guitars—two Stratocasters, a Firebird, and a Fender Jaguar—I rushed across the room, stepping over piles of dirty clothes, video games, and magazines. Slowly, I reached out, rubbing my fingers gently across the surface of each one.

I'd only met Jamie's father a few times, but I could instantly tell that he'd been a soulful, spirited man.

Like father, like son.

I was bent over, busy admiring the vinyl records that weren't hanging on the wall when I heard the snick of the door shutting behind me. I barely had time to stand up straight before Jamie was across the room, gripping my arms and pulling them behind my back.

"There you are," he said, sounding mostly amused but a little pissed off too.

I swallowed hard. He must have been looking for me. I was the reason he sped out of here fifteen, maybe twenty minutes ago, like a bat out of hell.

"Here I am," I replied. I only hoped I sounded braver than I felt.

"What the fuck are you doing here, and how did you even get in?"

"What? You think you're the only one with skills?"

His only response was to trap me against the wall. My head was resting between the Firebird and the Jaguar, my breasts mashed against the wall. His breath tickled my ear when he leaned in close. "Well, now that you're here, let's discuss some things, shall we?"

"Let me go!"

"In a minute."

I started to scream, to wake his uncle if I had to, but he spoke again, turning my world upside down once more. "How long has your father been broke?" Before I could answer or even ask him how he knew, he said "How long have you been plotting to marry my cousin for his money?"

I gritted my teeth as I struggled to break free, but his hands simply tightened on my arms, keeping me imprisoned. With a huff, I decided to answer him, hoping he'd free me.

"I was never going to marry Ever."

Jamie chuckled, but there was nothing humorous in the sound. "Hard for me to believe, kitten, since you're *still* wearing his ring. Even Jennifer knew when to let Brad go."

Suddenly, the band felt too tight around my finger, the weight too heavy, the implications scalding. I knew what he thought, but typical of us, nothing was ever as it seemed.

"I'm still wearing the ring because my father still thinks we're engaged."

And when I was finally free of him, I had every intention of pawning it and starting a new life with the money. Ever must have known it too, which was why he hadn't asked for it back. Even after he'd bowed out, he was still searching for ways to be there.

My eyes stung with fresh tears.

Friends like that came along once in a lifetime. It only made me sadder that I had to leave them behind.

I felt Jamie's grip on me loosen in surprise before tightening again. "Why haven't you told him? Surely, you'll be eager to search for your next mark?"

I knew then that neither Four nor Ever were the ones to tell Jamie about my father being broke. *If not them, then who?* Whoever the culprit, they clearly hadn't told Jamie everything. Suddenly weary of the secrets weighing heavy on our souls, I finally decided to free us both.

"It was my father's idea to marry me off for money, and it was Ever's idea to make him think that he would. I have no intention of marrying anyone, Jameson. I never did."

I could hear the wheels turning in his head, but it wasn't long before they came to a screeching halt. "*Explain.*"

I knew he must have worked most of it out for himself, but his broken heart wouldn't allow him to trust again so easily.

"My father is willing to do whatever it takes not to just survive but thrive. Your family is worth *billions,* and Ever is going to control it all. If it weren't for the promise of your family's

money, my father would have forced me to marry anyone willing to bid high enough the moment I'd turned sixteen."

Jamie was silent for so long that I would have thought he'd
gone if it weren't for his hands still holding me and the calm rise
and fall of his chest. I expected an explosion, but when he finally
spoke, his reaction was as if I'd told him it was going to rain today.

"Is that right?"

His vapid tone made me think he didn't believe me. And why
should he? I'd been lying to him for five years.

"It's true, Jamie."

"I'm sure it is." He spun me around to face him, and the
gentle kiss he placed on my lips mocked me more than his tone.
"Would you like to know a secret? Just between you and me?"
Jamie's grip on me tightened, keeping me from getting away. His
hard dick warned me of his intentions. "You preyed on the wrong
McNamara, kitten. My trust fund has more zeroes. Dick's bigger,
too." His lips brushed back and forth against mine before saying,
"If you wanted a knight in shining armor, you should have looked
right in front of you." Snorting, he toyed with the drawstring on
my satin sleep shorts. I was vaguely aware of him pulling it free.
"At least now you know there are limits to what *Ever* is willing to
do for you."

"Your point?"

Gently, he tucked my hair behind my ear before placing his
hand on my nape and pulling me to him. Jamie's grip was tight
enough to keep me from getting away but not harsh enough to
hurt. Somehow, tears still stung my eyes. "I had no limits, none
whatsoever, when it came to you, Bette."

"James…"

He was kissing me before I could tell him that I'd been afraid
of that.

Jamie would have torn down mountains for me and not have
blinked once at the destruction he caused. Even to himself. If he'd
known about what my father planned, known about the abuse I

suffered at his hands to make me compliant… I couldn't risk it. Every lie I'd told in the five years since I pushed him away was to protect him as much as myself.

"There's nothing innocent about you, Barbette." Slipping his hand inside my shorts, Jamie cupped my pussy, making me gasp. "Well…except for this." My hand flew to his wrist when his finger began to press inside me. "You haven't been fucked here yet, have you?"

I whimpered as he withdrew to circle my clit instead. My eyes fluttered, wanting to close, but I couldn't look away from the lust in his eyes. Jamie had every intention of fucking me tonight.

And I was going to let him.

Pressed against the wall with nowhere to run, I let him toy with me, bringing my most secret desires to light. Jamie's long fingers so gentle yet brutally relentless had my legs trembling in no time. He freed his hand the second I came, and then he yanked me away from the wall. When he tossed me on the bed is when I began to panic. *Maybe we're going too fast.*

"Jamie," I whined. Grabbing my shorts, I tried to keep them up when he began pulling them down. "Maybe we should talk about this first?"

"You've had a year to talk to me and four before that. The time for talking is over."

He gave up trying to remove my shorts and snatched the engagement ring from my finger instead. Carelessly, he tossed it over his shoulder, and it landed… somewhere. At that moment, it didn't matter where. "I'm not about to fuck you while you're wearing his ring." He wrestled my shorts from my grip and dropped them on the floor. He then nodded toward my camisole. "Get rid of it."

My hesitation lasted a second before I was pulling the thin top that had been hell on my hard nipples over my head. It quickly joined my shorts on his messy floor. Kneeling on his bed, I had to arch my neck to meet his gaze. "Will you promise to go slow?"

"Nope."

He headed for the door, making sure it was locked before pulling his plain white T-shirt over his head. I tried not to drool over his chest and abs and his nipple rings, especially when he was being a colossal dick.

And speaking of colossal dicks…

He stood directly in front of me as he unbuckled his belt and undid his jeans. And when he lowered them along with his boxers, I nearly swallowed my tongue. Fumbling with his dick in the darkness of his limo was nothing compared to seeing it under the bright glow of the moonlight.

I started to back away on the huge bed.

I knew Jamie wouldn't intentionally hurt me, but with a cock that size, I wasn't so sure good intentions mattered.

Wrapping his hands around my waist, he brought me back to him, and then kissed the unease from my lips and my shoulders before gently pushing me onto my back. My mouth quickly fell open when he gripped the back of my thighs and folded me in half until my knees were touching my shoulders. Holding my gaze, he bent his head. I watched transfixed as he pressed a sensual kiss to my lower lips. And then another. *Oh, my God.*

The rueful grin he wore as he lowered my legs immediately put me on high alert.

"Jamie? What was that for?"

"I'm just apologizing to your pussy in advance for what I'm about to do it."

He kissed me, not giving me a chance to respond as he settled between my thighs. The feel of his weight on top of me was driving me wild. I've never loved anything more.

Still, I wasn't about to let him hurt me. Or put me in a wheelchair.

"Jamie, either you go slow," I warned between sensual kisses, "or this is over." I tried to sound stern, but it was hard when I could feel him teasing my entrance with his cock.

"How slow?" he whispered as he held my gaze. Flexing his hips, he pushed inside, stretching me impossibly wide until he'd buried the head of his cock. "This slow?" With teasing thrusts, he began fucking me with just the tip. My eyes fluttered closed at the sensation. "So you like that?" he asked, kissing my lips. "You don't want all of me?"

"Maybe just a little more," I whined.

He gave me another inch while kissing my neck. "Is this enough for you, Barbette?"

"More, please."

My eyes flew open when he pulled out of me completely.

"What? No! Please, don't stop." *I need it.* I went to reach for him, but the no-nonsense look he wore stopped me.

"It's all of me or nothing."

Staring up at him, I knew that Jamie would not yield. He'd given me a taste of how good it could be. How could I possibly turn back now? I could always get my revenge when my head wasn't so clouded.

"I want all of you."

When he leaned in to kiss me, I eagerly met him halfway. Our tongues were still dueling for dominance when I felt him poking my entrance. This time, there was no teasing, and he did not stop. The flexing of his hips was my only warning before he pushed every single inch of himself inside of me. He swallowed my startled cry, took the punches that landed on his chest, and kissed my tears away when they fell.

"Fuck, Bette."

I couldn't respond.

He'd stolen my breath and taken all my words. I saw stars, and he hadn't even fucked me yet. I wondered if sex could feel like this with just anyone or if it was because I'd given myself to Jamie that made it so special. And at the same time hot and dirty.

"You're squeezing my cock, baby. Are you coming already?" He muffled my whimper when he kissed my lips. "Greedy pussy."

Grabbing the back of my thigh, he opened me up. The sound of our heavy breathing and him pushing inside of me over and over quickly filled the room.

He'd gotten me so fucking wet for him.

The bed rocked underneath us, and when he sped up, I was grateful that he didn't have a headboard. My breasts swayed as he pounded me, and the moment he wrapped his lips around my nipple, I was coming a second time.

He hurriedly covered my mouth with my hand before whispering in my ear. "Quiet, baby. My mom is sleeping down the hall."

My eyes bugged out of my head. Mrs. Buchanan was here? I started to ask why, but then I remembered... we were graduating tomorrow.

Jamie's moans became more desperate as he took what he wanted and gave twice in return. He'd made me come three times when he hadn't even come once yet. And then that was when I remembered... *Oh, God.*

"Jamie?"

"Hmm?"

"A-a-are you wearing a condom?" I was pretty certain I hadn't seen him put one on. Maybe that was why this felt so damn good? Because it was raw and unbound?

He stilled, giving me my answer, but then a beat later, he was riding me again. With a groan, he buried himself even deeper than he had before. "It's fine, baby. I'll pull out."

Alarm bells were ringing in my head, telling me not to fall for it. "No, Jamie." I pressed a hand to his chest. "You have to put a condom on now."

"You feel so fucking good." He groaned as he pressed his lips to my neck. "Just one more minute." He hit a spot deep inside of me, and I knew I'd die if he stopped.

"You promise?"

"Mm."

I had no idea what that meant, but then he was kissing me deeply, and I wrapped the thigh he wasn't holding around his waist. My heel dug into his ass, feeling it flex as he pushed and shoved inside of me. Foolishly, I began to wonder what it would be like to feel his hot cum filling me up... just once.

Knowing it was beyond stupid to risk, I counted to sixty.

"Jamie, it's been a minute now."

He didn't respond at first. A moment later, he was rising to his knees, his hands gripping my ass as he lifted me into his defiant thrusts. "Did you count it Mississippi?" He pinned me with his gaze as he fucked me harder. "Did you, Bette?"

Oh, fuck.

"You promised."

It was the only response I could give, knowing he had no intention of pulling out. He felt too good for me to stop him.

"Actually, I didn't." Biting his delectable lip, he closed his eyes as he threw his head back. Seeing the sweat glistening on his muscled chest, and watching his sculpted abs bunch as he worked his cock in and out of me made it impossible to look away. And even though I hated him at that moment, my pussy tightened around him as I came a fourth time.

I told myself it would be fine—that I'd make him wear a condom next time.

God, how stupid was I?

Not even a full minute later, Jamie was coming, and with a hoarse cry, he'd spilled it all inside of me.

Stupid! Stupid! Stupid!

I was lying in the curve of Jamie's body, feeling his cum seeping out of me and coating my thigh. As if I didn't have enough problems, I now had to add "skipping town with Jamie's baby inside of me" to my list of worries.

Maybe he thought I was on birth control.

Or maybe he knew that you weren't.

But that would be ludicrous, right? Jamie would be turning nineteen next month. What nineteen-year-old wanted babies?

The moment I heard his light snores, I carefully freed myself from his arms, wincing at the soreness between my thighs. I found my phone lying among his dirty laundry, so I picked it up and headed to the bathroom.

A few minutes later, I was on the toilet, googling the effectiveness of Plan B when Jamie barged in. Startled, I dropped my phone, and when I went to pick it up, he somehow beat me to it. I watched him read the health article I had pulled up and had trouble meeting his gaze after he tossed my phone on the bathroom sink.

Wordlessly, he turned away to put on the shower, leaving me to wonder if he was upset. I wouldn't give a shit if he was or not, just as he didn't care when I asked him to pull out.

It was a lesson I'd only need to learn once.

No glove, no love.

After cleaning up, I tried to leave to give him privacy, but he pulled me into the glass enclosure with him. For a long while, we stared into each other's eyes as we stood under the spray, letting the warm water rain down over us. *I need to get home.*

I told him so, and his response was to push me against the tile and kiss me deeply. I guess that meant I wasn't going anywhere anytime soon. He confirmed it when he spoke.

"Tell me everything, Barbette. Tell me right fucking now because I'm not letting you marry someone else."

"It's not exactly up to me," I reminded him. Well, that wasn't true. It should have been up to me, but my father was a terrible man with ancient beliefs.

"I'll talk to your father," Jamie absently announced. He must have forgotten that they hated each other's guts. His gaze became unfocused, and I could tell his mind was running a million miles an hour.

"And say what?"

Finally, his focus cleared. "I'll make him an offer he can't refuse." Grabbing his loofah, he poured his body wash on it, but instead of cleaning himself, he ran the soapy sponge down my neck, across my shoulders, and then my breasts. Taking a deep breath, I let him clean me. My mind was still reeling from that revelation to offer much argument.

"Please, don't say you're going to offer to marry me," I said when he was done cleaning me and started washing himself.

The cold stare he gave me made me shiver despite the hot water and the steam clouding the bathroom. "Because you'd rather marry someone else. Anyone else but me?"

I want no one else but you.

Slowly, my hand reached up, and my fingers brushed his cheek. "Because somewhere out there is a girl who deserves you. I won't let you throw that away for a girl you hate." My voice was barely a whisper when I added, "Even if that girl is me."

"What do you want from me?" he pushed through gritted teeth. His frustration was palpable, spurring my own as the truth I hadn't intended to tell recklessly spilled from my lips.

"I want to be friends again."

I didn't expect him to scoff at that, and it was hard pretending that my feelings weren't hurt.

"We were *never* friends. Right from the moment I first saw you, you were mine, and I was yours. You were just too blind and stubborn to see it."

I had a hard time swallowing the accusation he'd just shoved down my throat. The flickering flame I once held for Ever was *nothing* compared to the roaring torch I still carried for Jamie. He claimed I'd been the one blind, yet he couldn't see that my heart had been just as open. I wanted to tell him so, but I knew it wouldn't do any good.

"Can you ever forgive me?"

Jamie stared at me for a long time, the need in his eyes tripling my own until I foolishly believed that he'd give in to my plea. "You can have anything I own, baby, including my last name, but you can't"—his eyes squeezed shut, and I could feel every ounce of the pain I'd caused—"you can't have that."

I didn't stop him when he stepped from the shower and fled. Instead, I stood there, letting the water pour over me and wishing he'd come back.

Even knowing the truth, he still wasn't able to forgive me. I didn't want to understand his reasons, but I couldn't help it if I tried.

The damage I'd done to him was irrevocable. The pain too great to risk ever reliving it. He'd given me his heart, and I'd stomped all over it. Even if I could somehow repair that vital part, I knew Jamie's heart would never beat the same again.

CHAPTER
TWENTY

The Plaything

Summer... Six Years Ago

T HE CHAIN POWERING MY HUFFY THREATENED TO BREAK AS I pushed my bike past its limit. Today was the day Jamie left for home. Last night, I'd cried myself to sleep, and so I stupidly overslept.

Nothing else mattered except getting to him before it was too late.

We'd spent the summer riding bikes, climbing trees, swimming in the ocean, and writing under our favorite tree while Jamie struggled to remember the scales and chords his father had taught him. He was so adorable whenever he'd grow frustrated. I'd mentioned how I would like to write a song one day. He had practiced every day since when he'd barely shown interest before.

I was thankful the gates were already open when I flew through them and up the long drive. There was a silver SUV with the back hatch wide open. I could see Jamie's duffel and guitar already loaded inside.

A few more minutes, and I would have missed him.

My heart squeezed tightly at the thought, and I forced myself to take a deep breath. *Everything's fine. You didn't miss your chance.*

Rounding the SUV, I stopped when I saw Jamie standing

by the front door, arguing with his parents. Throwing my bike down, I shouted his name.

Jamie's head swung in my direction, and his eyes bucked the moment he saw me standing there, breathing hard and dripping sweat all over the place. I could see the relief in his brown eyes even from here. I had the feeling he'd been refusing to leave until he got to see me. My heart swelled even as my knees trembled at the thought of not seeing him for an entire year.

But what if he didn't keep his promise to come back? What if I never saw him again?

Jamie left the porch, and his father said something to him, which Jamie ignored. Pulling me behind one of the trees lining the drive for privacy, Jamie pressed something in my hand.

When I opened my palm, I frowned in confusion. "Stamps? What are these for?"

"For your letters when you write to me," he demanded.

I carefully thumbed the stack. There had to be hundreds. Enough for each day until he returned...

"I'll write every day," I vowed.

Gripping my chin—I loved it when he did that—he lifted my head, making me meet his serious gaze. "You swear?"

"Cross my heart and hope to die." I grinned, but he didn't smile back. In fact, I'd never seen him look quite so serious before.

Glancing at his parents and confirming they weren't paying us any mind as they loaded the SUV, he kissed my lips. It was over far too quickly. Nothing like the lingering, experimental kisses we'd shared all summer long. "Tell me you'll miss me."

I choked back a sob. "You know I will."

"I want to hear the words, Bee."

I didn't hesitate to tell him what was in my heart. "I'll miss you."

For a moment, I wondered if we were getting too intense too fast, but then he kissed me, and all those worries melted away. As he pulled away, I felt him press something else in my hand.

Looking down, I saw his harmonica lying in my palm. He'd been teaching me how to play, but I didn't understand why he was giving it to me when he loved it so much.

"Keep this safe for me."

Mrs. Buchanan began calling Jamie's name, so he reluctantly pulled away. Fresh tears started falling from my eyes. Summer had never seemed so far away.

"Barbette..." Hearing my name, I was instantly alert. He never called me Barbette unless he was upset, serious, or mocking me. "I want you to do something else for me."

I was too busy looking around anxiously to see the storm brewing in his gaze. His parents were only a few feet away. Any moment now, we'd be caught. "What? Anything."

If I'd known he'd ask the impossible, I never would have spoken so confidently.

"Stay away from Ever."

CHAPTER TWENTY-ONE

The Punk

Present

FORGIVE HER? BARBETTE REALLY EXPECTED ME TO *FORGIVE* HER? I wanted to punch the air and then the wall and maybe someone's flesh until they bled. My teeth threatened to break as I replayed her words.

Fuck, no. I couldn't forgive her.

I wasn't sure who I was more upset with—her for asking or me for that split fucking second when I'd actually considered it. I seemed to be a glutton for punishment, and that wasn't her fault. I should have never stuck my dick in her. I already knew I was going to do it again.

I was in the kitchen looking for something to grub on when I heard a sound coming from the pantry. It was a butler's pantry, so it was pretty large and even had a window. Thinking it might be a burglar, I found a weapon seconds before the door opened.

"What the hell, man?" Ever said when he saw me wielding an iron skillet.

I frowned as I lowered the pan. "What the fuck were you doing in the closet?"

"I climbed through the window. The lock is still broken."

So that's how Bee got in.

I would never admit that it turned me on knowing she went through the trouble. She'd snuck into my room in tiny shorts with her ass hanging out and a thin top that could barely contain her nipples. I was starting to wonder if talking was really all that she'd come for.

Ever looked me up and down. "What are you still doing up?"

Turning my back on him, I tossed the pan on the counter. Since that day Ever found me questioning Four in her room, I had a hard time looking him in the eye. The fear that he knew everything wouldn't allow me to. Ever had simply kicked me out of his girlfriend's room, leaving me to wonder what he might have heard.

"Same reason you are. Chasing after pussy."

"I find that hard to believe since you haven't touched anyone in a while."

As if on cue, Bee stepped into the kitchen, and I smirked at the surprise on Ever's face.

His startled gaze traveled back and forth between us before settling on Bee. "Hey, Bee...what are you doing here?"

"I..."

While she struggled for words, I took the time to look her over. It pissed me off that she'd dressed. Did she think she was leaving?

"I came to talk to Jamie," she finally answered.

Ever's frown only deepened. "At two in the morning?"

I stiffened, not liking the third degree he was giving her as if she still belonged to him. According to Bee, their relationship hadn't been real, but I wasn't sure what to believe.

Barbette shifted, looked to me, and then shifted again. I didn't say shit as I crossed my arms and leaned against the counter. She was on her own.

"It couldn't wait," she explained without explaining at all. I waggled my brows at her when she glanced at me. I was here whenever she needed me—morning, noon, or night.

When she started for the pantry, my gaze narrowed. "Where do you think you're going?"

"Home," was all she said without looking back.

She barely got her hand on the doorknob before I was pulling her back. "It's two in the morning," I reminded her. "How did you even get here?"

She lifted her chin, and I braced for more of her bullshit. "My bike."

My fickle heart skipped a beat, hearing that she still had it. She was hardly without it when we were kids, and it made me wonder how much of her was still in there—trapped inside this cold, gorgeous shell.

"So your plan is to ride in the open, down a dark and empty road at two in the morning? I think you're smarter than that."

"Yeah, but you're still an asshole." She tried to pull away, but it got her nowhere except even closer to me. I could smell my shampoo in her damp hair and my body wash seeping from her warm skin. Pleasure rushed through me, knowing she still smelled like me even after washing. "Let me go!"

"I can take you home," Ever offered.

I tossed him a nasty look over my shoulder, and he smiled. He wasn't taking her anywhere. I'd flatten all four of his tires if I had to.

"That would be great, thanks," she graciously accepted.

Her friendly tone baffled me. Ever had just broken their engagement in the most humiliating way. Why wasn't she the one threatening to slit his tires? At that moment, something inside me begged for me to believe her. To believe that there had been nothing between them.

Ignoring them both, I pulled Bee over to one of the stools and pushed her down on it. "Sorry, but that's not an option, either."

Before I could say more, light flooded the kitchen. My head whipped toward the entrance, and instantly, my balls fought to climb back inside my body.

My mother's hair, a little darker than her brother's light-brown locks, was in disarray from sleep. And despite her medium height and curvy frame, my father's robe still managed to swallow her. Her hand remained on the light switch while her cobalt blue eyes, the exact shade as Uncle Thomas's, narrowed to slits.

"Step away from that girl, Jameson. *Right now.*"

I didn't move as I stared down my mom. It was the first time I ever considered openly defying her. The look she gave me in return told me she'd kick my ass all over this kitchen, so I took a step back. Dilwen Buchanan stepped forward, ready to scold, but then Bee turned her head, and the words fell right out of my mother's mouth.

"Barbette?"

With a shy smile, Bee waved. "Hi, Mrs. Buchanan. It's been a long time."

"Oh, my… it certainly has." My mother rushed forward and stole her away from me, wrapping Bee up in her loving arms. For a few seconds, my mother squeezed Bee as if her life depended on it. "You are even more beautiful than I remember."

I was too captivated by the tear that had fallen from Bee's eye to hear her response. My mother held on a little longer than necessary, so Bee slyly wiped it away, the yearning I'd witnessed gone by the time my mother let her go.

How long had it been since Bee felt a mother's touch? Or any touch that was genuine and good and free of expectations?

"What are you doing here at this late hour? Why aren't you home in bed?"

Bee ducked her head, unable to answer. Unfortunately for me, my mother caught on and gave me a withering look. I made a mental note to make myself scarce in the morning. Graduation wasn't until tomorrow evening, so maybe by then, this would all be forgotten.

I knew I couldn't and wouldn't be forgetting that look on Bee's face, which was why, when my mother offered Bee the guest room that she'd been sleeping in herself, I didn't argue. I was as quiet as a mouse even when she informed me that I'd be sleeping in the pool house for the rest of the night. I left without a single word spoken to either of them.

I was sitting on the patio, glowering at the pool water twinkling in the moonlight when my mother appeared an hour later. I didn't sit up when she sat down, but if she noticed, she thankfully didn't speak on it.

"I don't know what's going on between you two, but I don't ever want to see you manhandling that girl or any girl ever again."

"I wasn't—"

"What would you call forcing a girl to stay when she wants to go?"

I pressed my lips together and wisely kept them shut. She wouldn't want to hear my reasons. She'd only call them excuses. And shit, maybe they were.

My mother lifted my chin, the way I'd seen my father do to her so many times, the way I had learned to do to Bee, and my troubled gaze met her understanding one. "That girl's head might wander a thousand different paths, Jameson, but her heart... her heart isn't so fickle. Barbette knows it as well as she knows *you*."

Normally, my mother was a wise woman, but for once, she didn't know what the hell she was talking about. "I guess it's lucky for Bee that hers wasn't the one broken."

"Oh, yes, it was," she argued, making me grit my teeth. "You don't fall apart from a simple hug unless you've been crushed too many times before."

So my mother had noticed Bee's reaction.

My fingers curled, making a fist. It was all I could do not to go to her. I knew my mother wouldn't let me anywhere near Bee, though.

"What do I do?" How do I win her back was the question I really wanted to ask.

"Oh, I don't think so, son. If you're grown enough to play 'hide the missile,' you're grown enough to figure this one out for yourself."

I smiled as my mother stood. She was the one I got my affinity for dirty euphemisms from.

"So, you aren't going to march me over there and make me apologize?" I teased.

The look she gave me made me feel as if I were two feet tall. I was once again a little boy about to be sent to the naughty corner. "I didn't raise you to be forced into doing what's right, Jameson. Be the man your father would be proud of."

As if she hadn't just punched me in the gut, she disappeared inside the pool house, probably to make sure I didn't sneak back up to the main house. I wanted to. God, how I wanted to. I wasn't sure how long I sat there before I crawled into one of the empty beds instead. Closing my eyes, I let sleep pull me under. Tomorrow, I had a choice to make.

Forgive Bee. Or set her free.

Bee was gone the next morning.

Somehow, she'd managed to sneak back home long before the sun had fully risen. And I knew this because just before dawn, *I'd* snuck back inside the main house only to find an empty bed.

As if she knew I would be coming for her, she'd left a note.

The girl you loved is gone, Jameson.
Letting you in had been easy.
To bleed you, I had to cut deep.
She didn't survive.

For a few seconds, I studied the note and the messy chicken scratch I remembered vividly before calmly folding it in half and slipping it inside my pocket.

The rest of the day passed uneventfully. Well, if you could count my little brother and sister bringing a four-foot garden snake inside the house and almost giving our mother a heart attack uneventful. I couldn't believe how beautifully Adara had blossomed or how tall Adan had grown. I swallowed hard, wishing I hadn't missed a year of their life. I no longer felt as close to them as before. I knew it was because the moment I'd returned to Blackwood Keep, all I could think about was Bee and making her pay before making her mine.

If I had to shell out millions to make that happen, then so be it. Elliot would take the money without a second thought, but I had the feeling Bee wouldn't be as grateful.

The girl you loved is gone, Jameson.

Smirking, I shrugged on my navy-blue dress shirt before buttoning and tucking it into my black slacks.

Gone?

I snorted. She'd yet to show me that was the case. If anything, with each day, all she'd done was plant little seeds of doubt in my mind—seeds that sprouted into hope.

My mom and siblings rode with my uncle, who would also be picking up Aunt Evelyn for the ceremony—I had a feeling my mom had something to do with that. Uncle Thomas may have been the older sibling, but my mom was clearly the boss.

Four and Ever rode together, and I'd turned down Ever's offer for a ride, having the feeling I'd need a getaway car when it was all said and done.

The parking lot was already packed, and the school lawn crowded when I arrived. I cursed, bouncing my leg anxiously as I searched for a spot to park. After a few minutes, I spotted Ever's G-Wagon and him standing in an empty spot in front of it, waving me down. I swooped into the space, grabbed my blue cap and gown, and bumped his fist in thanks when I got out.

I looked around, noticing he was alone. "Where's Four?"

"Went to find Gruff." Four's old boss had driven up from Cherry, Virginia, her hometown, to see his young protégé graduate.

We started toward the building, and I tried not to be so obvious as I searched the crowd, but of course, Ever noticed. "Let it go, man. I'm sure that wherever she is, she's with her parents."

I ignored him as I weaved through the crowd. I didn't give a damn about Elliot Montgomery. Bee wasn't his to give. Elliot had lost his claim to her the moment I laid eyes on her six years ago, and I'd be damned if I gave her up. I wasn't so sure I could just forgive her overnight, but for the first time, I was willing to try.

I was ready to give up searching until after the ceremony when I finally spotted her. Dressed in her cap and gown—the guys had been assigned navy-blue caps and gowns and the girl's red—she was indeed standing with her parents. When one of the teachers called for everyone to start lining up, Barbette spoke to them briefly before stepping away. Her father barely spared her a glance while her mother simply smiled. I shook my head, wondering if they'd always been so dismissive of her.

I stalked her with Ever hot on my heels until we rounded the building. Once we were out of her parents' sight, I sped up and grabbed her elbow.

"Jamie?"

Before she could say more, I pulled her through a random door leading into the school. Inside, I tried a few doors before finding the one to the chemistry lab unlocked.

"You snuck off," I growled as soon as the door closed behind us.

"I had to get home before my father figured out I was gone."

"Is that the only reason?"

She shrugged while refusing to meet my gaze. "What other reason would there be?"

Ever's phone going off reminded us that we weren't alone. He grabbed a seat as he texted, and I seriously wondered why he was sticking around. I was sure Tyra and Vaughn were around here somewhere. Wren and Lou had also been given tickets and promised to attend. And then there were his parents and my mom to keep him occupied.

Whatever.

Ignoring him, I refocused on Bee. "You were running from me."

"I didn't run," she argued. "I *walked* away after you fucked me and made it clear you weren't interested in more." Out of the corner of my eye, I noticed Ever's head shoot up from his phone, but he wisely remained silent. "I can't exactly force you to be with me, so what else should I have done?" Bee challenged.

I couldn't help but explode. "Fight for me!"

"What is there to fight for if you won't forgive me?" she screamed back.

"How can I forgive you when you're *still lying to me?*"

"I'm not—" She suddenly paused, making my eyes narrow. "I told you everything."

"How could you trust Ever more than me? You failed to mention that." I knew it sounded like a question born of jealousy, but it truly didn't make any sense. Back then, anticipating Bee's every want and need had been my sole focus and only pleasure. Nothing else mattered. So imagine how crushing it was to find that, when she was actually in need, she'd turned to someone else instead. It mattered less now in the face of the truth, but it still hurt like hell.

"It wasn't like that," Ever responded when Bee went mute. "After her parents came to our place and told you to stay away from her, I went over there to check on her. They'd said she got hurt and that *you* were responsible. I wasn't sure they'd let me see her, so I snuck inside. I overheard her parents talking. What they were planning to do…"

Bee suddenly swayed on her feet, her face ashen. Reacting on instinct, I helped her to the chair behind the teacher's desk, where she collapsed. She still wouldn't meet my gaze.

"It was so fucked up," Ever went on. "I left, but as soon as

I saw Bee at school… I couldn't just pretend like everything was normal. I confronted her, and she made me swear not to tell anyone. *Especially* you. I was her best friend, man. What was I supposed to do?"

"Convince her not to lie to me? Did that ever occur to you? She might have been your best friend, but I'm your goddamn blood!"

"If you think I could have convinced her of anything, you don't know her as well as you think."

I wanted to bash his face in for that comment. There wasn't a person alive who knew Bee better than me. Reading my thoughts, Ever smirked, knowing he got to me. His phone chimed a moment later, and he read the message before saying, "We should get back. Four says everyone's lined up. The procession will start soon."

"I can't believe we're graduating," Bee whispered. I could see the relief in her eyes. She'd finally be free of the place that had judged her without a second look. I'm not sure when they started calling her Barbie, but I knew the name must have cut each time it was uttered. There was so much more to her, and for some reason, she stopped letting them see.

Ever must have seen it too because he muttered, "You should have been running Brynwood. Not me."

Like true royalty, Bee dismissed Ever's claim with a flick of her fingers—as if the issue was of little consequence. Not to Ever. And not to Vaughn and me.

She'd been our queen, once upon a time, and we'd been ready and willing to fall on our swords for her.

At least that much was still true.

"How can you be so sure when your own cousin was so eager to overthrow me?"

I didn't miss the jab she'd thrown and smiled. Bee wanted to pretend I wasn't in the room, but that blush on her cheeks gave her away. I'd bet my fortune those sensitive nipples of hers would be too if she weren't hiding beneath that gown. I wonder if she knew that I was just as hard for her. Harder, actually.

Pushing away from the dry-erase board, I slowly strolled to where she was sitting in that chair, long legs crossed as if they hadn't been wrapped around me half the night. I'd ridden her hard, and though it took all my concentration not to come quick, I'd ridden her long. It still wasn't enough.

Gripping her chin, I forced her gaze to finally meet mine. "Is that what you call making you fall in love with me?"

"I didn't," she breathlessly lied.

"Right," I countered, smirking, "because you were too busy hiding your crush on my cousin to notice that your heart had been stolen."

From the corner of my eye, I saw Ever pause, and after a moment of tense silence, he barked, "What the *hell* are you talking about?"

Before Bee could deny the claim and lie yet again, someone else spoke. "I'd like to know that, as well."

Three sets of gazes flew to the open door where Four stood wearing her red cap and gown.

I wasn't sure how much time passed with us staring at Four and Four staring at Bee as if she would claw her eyes out. Long agonizing moments later, she looked away, and betrayal flashed in her eyes when they landed on Ever. The hurt in her voice when she spoke twisted my stomach until it ached. "Did you know?"

"What? No!" Ever shot to his feet and rushed for the door when Four turned to walk back through it.

Bee and I watched helplessly as Ever lifted Four back inside and slammed the classroom door shut.

"Let me go!" she screamed when he pressed her against it. "You lied! You lied!" Her voice broke as she sobbed. "You said you'd only ever been friends."

"Baby, stop," Ever pleaded as he struggled with her. "I had no fucking clue. I swear to you, I had no fucking clue!" He glanced over his shoulder at us, and the helpless look in his eyes made me feel like shit.

Bee took a step forward, desperate to fix the shitstorm I had caused, but I grabbed her wrist and ignored her glare. I wanted to help them as much as she did, but I wasn't so sure there was anything we could do. We'd both caused them enough pain.

"Yeah, but I just bet you wish you had," Four spat. Suddenly, she stopped fighting him and stared back at Ever through her tears. "Would it have made a difference?"

"Not one fucking bit, princess. You *know* that." He released her wrists and gripped her hips, yanking them into him. "I've never wanted anyone until you." Gently, he kissed her, and relief flooded me when she slowly began kissing him back.

I glanced down at Bee and found her giving me the same wide-eyed look. We both seemed to be thinking the same thing. *That was close.*

Four and Ever's breathing grew heavier, drawing our attention back to the door in time to see Ever pull Four's ceremonial gown over her head. Thankfully, she wore a simple white dress underneath, but when Ever's hand crept underneath it, the back of my neck warmed.

It was obvious that they'd forgotten we were here.

"What should we do?" Bee whispered. I could hear both alarm and amusement in her tone.

My gaze traveled to the back of the large lab, praying there was a second door. Seeing it, I grabbed Bee's hand, and together, we tiptoed for the other door.

We made it two steps before the sound of Ever's voice stopped us.

"Where the fuck do you two think you're going?"

Bee yelped in surprise and pressed herself into my back. I almost laughed when I felt her tremble and reminded myself that she'd just had sex for the first time last night.

"Giving you guys some priva—Hey, what the fuck, bro?" I

barked when Ever flipped the lock and pulled the shades over the mini window.

He whispered something in Four's ear, and she scowled at whatever he was saying. Still, she listened, and as the seconds passed, her frown slowly disappeared until uncertainty and a little interest took over her expression. A moment later, she glanced at us, and I could see the revenge in her eyes. Nodding, she sauntered over to the front of the classroom, and Bee and I watched her hop on top of the teacher's desk. Meanwhile, Ever had taken advantage of our distraction, locking and drawing the shades over the second door.

"Before any of us leave this room, we're going to get something understood," Ever announced.

"Which is?" Bee asked, genuinely confused.

I, on the other hand, was at a loss for words. I was pretty sure I was already picking up what Ever was putting down. Knowing he couldn't stop us, I wanted to take Bee and run for the other door, but I'd only feel like a coward if I did.

"I'm with Four, and one day, she'll wear my ring and carry my babies, and I'm not letting the two of you jeopardize that a second longer."

"Understood. Can we go now?"

"Every time the two of you hurt each other, you use us as weapons," Four spoke from behind us. "It's time you learn that we're no longer an option."

I whirled around. "So watching the two of you *fuck* is supposed to teach us that lesson?" *Yeah, I don't think so.*

It wasn't like I hadn't caught them in action before, but this was different. This would not only be deliberate, but it would mean Bee would see everything, too. I wasn't any more interested in her watching some guy fuck than I was letting some guy fuck her—*especially* if that guy was her ex-fake-fiancé.

"Oh, you won't just be watching," Ever said.

I gripped Bee a little tighter at his words. Ever was leaning against the door with his arms crossed, looking way too casual about this.

"You've got me fucked up if you think I'm letting you touch her," I warned.

Ever rolled his eyes as he stood up straight. "I promise it won't get that far."

I started to curse them both out when I felt Bee tugging on my arm. She put her lips to my ear once I leaned down.

"I-I think we should," Bee whispered, shocking the shit out of me. "We owe them this."

"We don't owe them shit," I barked.

"Actually, you kind of do," Four chimed as she swung her legs. "Who's to say either of you would have risked what we risked?"

Pretend to be someone's fiancé while Bee rode the bench like some dirty little secret? Not a fucking chance.

"We're only asking for a little humility in return," Ever said. He was already making his way to the front of the class while I eyed the door. Now was our chance to escape.

"You can go if you like," Bee whispered. "But I'm going to stay."

Like hell, I was leaving her alone with them.

In fact, I was never letting Bee in the same room with these two closeted pervs again.

"There are other ways to show your gratitude," I argued. Out of the corner of my eye, I could see Ever stepping between Four's legs and lowering the dress he'd already unzipped from her shoulders. "We can send them a card and a fruit basket in the morning."

Bee's only response was to smile and kiss my lips. I immediately went in for a second. With an eager moan, she swept her tongue between my lips, and even though I knew she was trying to distract me, I sank into the kiss. It wasn't long before I was pulling her gown over her head and lifting her onto the teacher's desk next to Four.

This was so fucked up.

I could hear Ever's belt jingle as Four unbuckled him, and at the same time, Bee's shaking, nervous hands went for the buttons on my shirt.

So, so fucked up.

Before my shirt was even all the way open, Bee was pressing hungry kisses on my chest, getting my cock nice and hard for her. Her white dress was tight and molded to her curves, making it easy to shove up and around her waist. The thong she wore was next to go. The second her bare ass touched the cool wood, she shivered, making her tits jiggle. I lowered the straps of the plunging neckline, and then my lips were around her nipple before either of us could blink.

"Oh, Jameson…" She leaned back on her hands, giving me full access as I feasted on her tender, little nipples.

"Princess?"

The shock and lust in Ever's voice drew my reluctant gaze, and I watched as Four fell to her knees in front of him. She wrapped her hand around his thick cock before shyly licking the tip.

Atta girl.

I watched for a few seconds as she kissed and licked Ever's cock before turning back to Bee. Biting her bottom lip, I soothed the abused flesh with a kiss. "This is Ever's first time getting his cock sucked by Four," I whispered to her. "Watch and learn, kitten. I won't be as patient."

While her avid gaze remained on Four and Ever, my finger found her wet pussy, and I slowly filled her, stimulating her other senses. "Sore?" I asked as I slid a second finger inside her. I'd ridden her harder than I should have last night, but she had no idea how much I held back.

"A little," she whimpered. Still wearing those sexy strappy heels, she lifted her feet onto the desk before letting her legs fall open. *Goddamn.* "But I want you to fuck me anyway."

"I was planning on it."

We kissed as I fucked her with my fingers, and occasionally, we'd both look over and watch Four's lips sink further and further around Ever. His lips were parted in awe as he watched her with his hand gripping her ponytail to guide her. The hungry little moans she made told me she was enjoying it just as much.

"Mark my words," I growled as my thumb ruthlessly circled her clit. "I'll be fucking every single one of your holes this summer."

"Oh, my God!" Bee shouted at my words. "I'm going to come. Please, make me come." She rolled her hips, pushing and shoving, racing to the finish.

I almost came in my pants watching her. Seconds later, I felt her pussy tighten and pulse around my fingers.

As she lay flat on her back panting, my hands were ripping at my belt, and then I was shoving my pants down, freeing my cock. Just as I pulled Bee off the desk and bent her over it, Ever was there laying Four on her back. Due to our positions, Bee's lips were hovering dangerously close to Four's swollen mouth, but neither of them seemed to notice. The heels Bee wore gave her the perfect height for my cock to find her entrance. Remembering that just last night, she was a virgin, I went slow as I filled her up.

Both girls let out a long moan as Ever and I stuffed them full of cock.

Leaning down, I began whispering in Bee's ear. "Such a naughty girl," I teased. "Group sex already when this is only your second time getting fucked." She gasped since I'd punctuated my sentence by slamming my hips into hers. "What will your father think?"

I didn't give her the chance to respond before I gripped her neck and shoved into her over and over. Four's cries were just as desperate as Bee's as Ever drove into her from the other end of the desk. He pushed, and I'd shoved, sending the desk scraping back and forth across the floor.

Pulling on Bee's hair, I lifted her head until she had no choice but to watch Four and Ever. "Do you see how good he's giving it to her?" I whispered in her ear. "Do you see how much she loves it?"

"Yes." She gasped, pushing back onto my cock.

"He's lost control, baby. He needs her to know that she's the only one… and he wants *you* to see."

"God… yes," she cried out as I pounded her harder. "I see! I see!"

Tugging harder on her hair, I removed her gaze from them and bared her neck to me. "Then tell me who you belong to?"

"You," she whimpered.

I rewarded her with a kiss on the lips. "Good girl. Now tell him. Tell *them*."

When she hesitated, I started to withdraw. I was playing for keeps or nothing at all.

"I'm Jamie's, and I only want Jamie!" she rushed to say.

With a smirk, I smoothly slid back inside, even though pride made me want to beat my chest and howl at the moon.

Ever didn't miss a beat as he kissed Four. "And I'm yours," he whispered against her lips. They kissed hungrily for a few seconds before he pulled away. Unfortunately, Four started to come just as I heard footsteps down the hall. We were seconds away from getting caught, and Ever seemed oblivious as he closed his eyes and enjoyed her pussy tightening around him. I was ready to slap my hand over her mouth to shut her up when Bee intervened.

I was in danger of spilling inside her unprotected body for a second time when she leaned down and covered Four's lips with her own. Four's cries were muffled just as the person stopped outside the door. Ever's eyes were open now, his shocked gaze flying from Four and Bee kissing hungrily to me. He looked ready to say something, to stop them when one of the door handles jiggled.

I was just grateful he'd taken the time to lock the doors and draw the shade. I could only imagine the eyeful the intruder would have gotten if they'd walked in.

After a few seconds, Ever and I listened as the person walked away. I just prayed that it wasn't to find keys.

"They're gone," I whispered and then groaned when Four and Bee continued to kiss. They didn't seem to notice anything around them as they enjoyed each other's lips. As hot it was, I couldn't help the jealousy streaking through me. Bee was mine, and I wasn't about to share her with anyone. Male or female. "Baby, stop."

I pulled her way from Four, and the greedy little sound Bee made in protest almost made me cave. Turning her around, I sat her on the desk and gripped her neck. "We'll discuss this later," I said as I slid back inside her. The rest of the world faded away as I drowned myself in her. When she came, I immediately pulled out of her, grunting as I spilled myself on her thigh. Last night, I hadn't realized how much was at stake when I selfishly went against her wishes. I couldn't do that to her again.

The last to come, the rocking desk came to a halt as Ever spilled himself inside of Four. I just hoped she was on birth control.

The only sound in the room moments later was our heavy breathing. Catching my breath, I walked over to the small sink in the corner and wet a few paper towels, handing some to Ever when I returned to the desk.

"Thanks," he said before he began cleaning between Four's legs. I quickly averted my gaze when I got a glimpse of her pussy. That was a memory that wouldn't be leaving me any time soon.

Sighing, I began cleaning my cum from Bee's thighs while she laid on her back next to Four with her eyes closed. Once finished, I righted her dress before fixing my own clothes and then helped Bee from the desk while Ever did the same for Four.

"Well, this was fun," I drawled, sarcasm dripping from each word. "Why don't we make it a weekly thing? I'm good for Tuesdays and Thursdays."

While Four had trouble meeting anyone's gaze, Ever sighed.

He already seemed resigned to living with the huge fuck up we'd just made. I would never be able to look at Four again without seeing the way her tits bounced while my cousin was driving into her. I didn't even want to know how much he'd seen of Bee. I'd probably carve his eyes from his skull.

Needless to say, we wouldn't be getting together for Naked Twister anytime soon.

"We should get back," Ever mumbled. "What time does the ceremony start?"

Glancing at my watch, I winced. "An hour ago."

We quickly rushed for the door. As soon as we stepped into the quiet hall, however, we each froze, seeing who awaited us. None of us had time to react, least of all me, before Elliot stepped forward, his expression filled with rage, and backhanded his daughter.

CHAPTER
TWENTY-TWO

The Punk

Summer... Five Years Ago

I STEPPED OFF THE TRAIN AND TOOK A DEEP BREATH. IT HAD BEEN terrifying riding alone from Boston, but I'd had no choice. Clutched in my fist was the last letter Bee had sent me. Like always, I'd responded immediately, but almost a month had gone by and... nothing.

What was going on?

I'd kept the promise I made her a year ago and came back to Blackwood Keep. Our second summer together was even more amazing than the first because this time, there'd been no pretending to hate each other. Leaving her for a second time, however, was even harder. I'd even gone so far as to try to convince my parents to leave Boston. Whenever I brought it up, my dad would simply chuckle around his eighth or eighteenth smoke for the day while my mom would offer me a gentle smile. They both knew my reason for wanting to move.

I was in love at fourteen, and I didn't care who knew it.

Or maybe I did?

I still hadn't asked Bee to be my girlfriend, not officially or anything. Maybe that's why she stopped writing me? Was she tired of waiting for me to ask?

My hands shook at the thought of finally asking her. What if she said no? What if she still secretly liked Ever?

The wind blew, so I zipped my hoodie up. It was the first day of fall—the official end of summer. Sadness whipped through me, chilling my bones like that gust of wind. Recalling the words in the poem Bee had given me before I left, I realized why. Bee had changed the meaning of summer for me, too, and whenever it ended, she somehow felt farther away.

Since I'd hopped a train to find Bee without my parents' knowledge or permission, there was no one waiting for me when I arrived in Blackwood Keep. School would be over in a couple of hours, so I didn't think twice before starting the trek to Bee.

Underestimating how long it would take to walk five miles, I reached her school with less than five minutes to spare. I walked through the doors as if I belonged and beelined to the nearest water fountain and drank my fill. I was sweating everywhere, and my feet ached, but I still wandered the halls in search of Mrs. Newman's class. In Bee's last letter, she'd written to me about her teachers and how her writing teacher was her favorite and last class of the day.

I was still searching when the bell rang. Moments later, several doors opened, and kids spilled out of them. None of them paid me any mind as they rushed past me. Eager to start the weekend, it didn't take long for the hall to empty.

Still no Bee.

Giving up, I pressed my back against the wall and stared at the white tiled floor. I wasn't sure how long I stood there before the door right in front of me opened, and a girl stepped into the hall. The first thing I noticed was the mint-colored ankle boots with a dark-brown heel. Her long, slim legs were covered in white floral tights, and I almost laughed knowing how much Bee would hate them. Whenever her mom forced her into them, she'd say they itched liked hell.

Dismissing the girl without checking out the rest of her, I straightened only to find that it was Bee all along. My heart started to pound as surprise, confusion, and joy rushed through me. I barely noticed the blank stare she gave me in return. Suddenly, I realized there was only a couple of feet separating us now rather than a couple of *hundred* miles. I rushed across the hall and swooped her up in my arms.

"You're okay," I said more to myself than to her. I'd begun to fear the worst. "Why didn't you write me back?" When she said nothing, I set her down, worried that I held her too tight. I couldn't help myself. I thought I might never get the chance again.

The second her feet touched the ground, I stumbled back. I stared at Bee in shock as her worried gaze searched the hall. We were completely alone.

And she'd shoved me.

"Bee?"

"My name is Barbette." She started to walk away, but then she paused. "I hope you find who you're looking for." Was that regret in her tone? What the hell was going on?

I watched her walk—no, *strut*—away in those heels. When the hell had she learned to walk in those? And what the hell did she mean?

She was the one I wanted. She was the reason I'd come all this way and risked being grounded for the rest of my life. After this stunt, my parents probably wouldn't even let me come back next summer. I had told myself it would all be worth it. Of course, I'd called Ever first. All he would ever tell me was that she was fine, so the moment he hesitated to tell me more, I knew something was up.

Finally getting my feet to move, I followed after her. She obviously hadn't been paying attention if she thought I'd let her go that easily. I burst through the front doors of the school, ignoring the curious glances I got and searched the parking lot. A few feet away, I could see Barbette heading straight for a black Escalade. Why hadn't she ridden her bike to school? An expressionless man dressed in a black suit stood at the open back door. I reached her before she could reach him.

"Bee, stop. Wait," I pleaded as I grabbed her hand.

Turning her around, I shoved my fingers through the strawberry locks that had grown out, messing up her perfect curls. It wasn't my first time seeing her hair like this, but she never lasted more than an hour out of her mother's sight before shoving her hair underneath her favorite red baseball cap. At a loss, I pressed my forehead to hers. I'd grown a little faster than her in the year since I met Bee, but in those heels she had on, we were the same height.

"Please, talk to me. Tell me what I did wrong."

I inhaled her scent, fearing it was the last time I'd hold her this close, but she no longer smelled the same—like the sun and the grass and the rain. I nearly choked on the heavy perfume soaking her skin.

"Please, let me go." Her voice trembled, making me hold her tighter instead.

"I'm sorry I didn't ask you to be my girlfriend before. I was afraid you'd say no. I was afraid, but I'm not anymore." Lifting my head, I met her tearful gaze.

"Jamie," she gasped.

Relief flooded my chest at hearing my name on her lips. For a second, I thought she'd forgotten me. Just as quickly, she ruined my hope.

"Please don't ask me."

I couldn't help my frown. "Why?" I growled.

"Because I can't," she said, taking a step away from me. Seeing me follow, she gave up retreating. Glancing over her shoulder at the man waiting, I could see the agony in her eyes when she turned back to me. "I don't *want* to be yours."

She didn't give me the chance to call her on her shit before turning away. The hem of the light-brown dress she wore twirled in a perfect circle before settling around her long legs once more. Every step she took seemed designed to entice. To captivate.

My lips curled. I hated everything about her at that moment.

Trapped inside that plastic shell was the girl I'd fallen in love with, and one way or another, I was getting her back.

Charging forward, my hands shoved into her back, sending her forward.

I heard her startled cry just before she fell onto the concrete, landing on her hands and knees. Instantly regretting it, I rushed forward to help her up, not waiting to see if it had worked—if she would get back up and fight me.

A thousand apologies waited to spill from my heart onto my lips, but the man who'd been waiting for her got to her first. I watched as he helped a crying Bee to her feet and then ushered her into the SUV. The man didn't bother looking my way when he shut the door and rounded the hood. Moments later, I was plagued with a foreign sensation—the feel of a tear slipping from my eye as I watched them go.

I wiped it away, but if I had known the worst was yet to come, I wouldn't have bothered.

Our fight was witnessed by a teacher who, when realizing I wasn't a student, called the police. The police called my parents, and my parents called my aunt and uncle. By the time my uncle picked me up to bring me to his home, the Montgomery's were there waiting. Not only had Bee told her father that I had pushed her, but her hands and knees were scraped in the fall, too. He threatened to press charges if I didn't stay away from his precious daughter.

He hadn't needed to.

Even if I could get past my anger, I could never get past the pain.

Bee and I were *done*.

CHAPTER TWENTY-THREE

The Plaything

Present

THE RAGE ON MY FATHER'S FACE WHEN I STEPPED OUT OF THE science lab with Jamie was one I was familiar with. I'd seen it many times when I wouldn't comply or give up my childish hopes and dreams. I could still remember the words he spewed and the threat behind them the last time he'd beat me.

"You have a duty to this family, and you'll do what must be done. Won't you?"

The backhanded blow my father dealt, the first in almost two years, knocked me off my feet and sent me skidding across the floor. "Whore," I heard him hiss.

He didn't get the chance to say more. As Four helped me to my feet, Jamie pounced, wrapping his hands around my father's neck. He drove him into the cluttered bulletin board hanging on the wall before squeezing his hands tighter.

"You seem to have lost your fucking mind."

Jamie's voice was calm. Too calm. The quiet before the storm.

"She's my daughter!" my father choked out. "I'll deal with her as I damn well please."

"See, that's where you're wrong. You won't be touching her, seeing her, or speaking to her ever again."

"Unhand me!" my father screamed. "You think you can take care of her? You're nothing but a fucking punk!"

"Actually, I can." Jamie leaned forward and began whispering in my father's ear. I knew the moment my father's eyes bulged with fear and regret that it was the same thing Jamie had told me last night. He'd been the key to my father's treasure chest all along. "Because you're my future father-in-law, I was willing to throw you a bone. That's dead now, so mark my words. Your daughter was mine the moment I set eyes on her six years ago. Unfortunately for you and your pet cougar, I won't have to pay a dime to prove it."

I was grateful when Jamie let him go—not for my father's sake but for his own. I stood perfectly still as Jamie rushed to my side. Inspecting my face, his jaw clenched at what I was sure was my father's handprint. Kissing my lips, he pulled me close. "I'm so fucking sorry," he whispered as if he'd been the one to strike me.

"It's not your fault." I was about to mention how I was used to it when I stopped myself. It was a disgusting thing to admit. No one should be used to being abused.

"When we get out of here, I'm going to feed you and fuck you slowly—in that order." His nostrils flared as he pinned me with his gaze. "And then you're going to tell me how many times he's done that to you."

I gulped.

Jamie had refrained from killing my father, making me think I'd underestimated his ability to think rationally, but I wondered if that would remain the case after I told him everything.

"Don't even think about lying to me, Barbette."

His nostrils flared, so I cupped his cheek, feeling his warmth and drawing his strength. At that moment, I knew I trusted Jamie more than anyone. I was just sorry it took me this long to realize it. "Never again."

He looked skeptical for a moment before nodding and turning to Four and Ever. "Make sure this piece of shit doesn't follow us."

"She's not eighteen yet," my father argued. "The law is still on my side. I'll have her back by the end of the night!"

Jamie smirked at his threat. "First, you'd have to find us."

Taking my hand, he pulled us down the hall while my father shouted obscenities. I was still baffled by his taunt. My birthday was still a week away. Surely, Jamie didn't intend for us to hide that long? Where would we even go?

"Jameson John Buchanan, I did not fly three thousand miles to watch everyone else's children cross that stage!" Mrs. Buchanan yelled.

Jamie's plan to feed me and fuck me had come to a dead halt when his mother caught us making a break for his Jeep. I simply held his hand while she ripped him a new one in front of the entire school. Everyone was staring, but neither of them seemed to notice.

Losing his patience, Jamie's head fell back on his shoulder. "Moooom," he groaned aggravatedly.

"Don't 'mom' me. Tell me where you were right now." When her gaze slid to the side and landed on me, I quickly ducked behind Jamie. "Oh, God... it's like we never left. The two of you are going to turn my hair gray, aren't you? Well, you listen to me now. I've still got a few miles left myself. I am too young and too fly to be someone's grandmother."

I pressed my face into Jamie's strong back to muffle my laughter. She was completely serious, which only made it funnier. I could feel Jamie squeezing my hand, telling me to quit it, but I couldn't. Clearly, Jamie had gotten all his looks from his father and a heaping dose of his personality from his mother.

"I'll be sure to wrap it up," he lied as he stepped around his mother. We'd had sex twice now, and both times were unprotected. The smile I wore died.

I glanced back to see if his mother was following and saw that her attention was stolen by Four and Ever, who had just emerged from the building hand in hand. I frowned, wondering where my father had gone. Mrs. Buchanan didn't waste time laying into them, and I realized how lucky we'd been when Ever's parents, along with Four's mentor, closed in on them, too.

"She has a point, you know."

"Oh?" he said, sounding disinterested in anything his mother said.

"We've been taking way too many risks. You need condoms."

"I have condoms."

"Then why don't you use them, and how many girls have you not used them with?"

Opening the passenger door, he lifted me inside his Jeep. "One."

"I hope that's including me."

He leaned down to kiss me before smiling against my lips. "It is."

"As warm and fuzzy as it makes me inside to know I'm special…" I pushed him away before saying, "No more love unless you wear a glove."

Sighing, he slammed my door closed before rounding the hood and climbing inside. As he drove away from the school, I studied his profile, trying to gauge if he was upset. It would really suck if he was because I wasn't backing down. I was rather enjoying sex with Jamie, and it would be a shame to stop. We were barely a mile from the school when he slid his fingers between mine and kissed the back of my hand.

My heart began fluttering like crazy in my chest.

A few minutes later, he was pulling into a pharmacy. "Come on," he ordered before stepping out.

I got out and felt silly in my cap and gown, so I took them both off and tossed them in the back. Luckily, I was still considered a graduate, even though I hadn't crossed the stage or accepted my diploma. It would be a while before I could look Four or Ever in the eye again, but I had zero regrets.

Inside, I let Jamie pull me down an aisle until he found what he was looking for. I waited for him to pick up a box of condoms, but instead, he nodded toward the boxes of emergency contraceptives.

I suddenly had a bad taste in my mouth.

"Pick one," he directed when I just stood there.

Slowly, I reached out, my hand falling on the box that read Plan B One-Step. As I read the back for information, Jamie stepped behind me and wrapped his arms around my waist. I barely noticed him kissing my neck until his hand found my thigh before sliding under my dress.

"Jamie—"

"Shhh," he whispered. "Did you pick one yet?"

"How can I when you're distracting me?" I whined. His long fingers found my entrance, and I gasped when he slid one and then another inside.

"Pick one."

I could feel his hard cock pressing into my butt, and I frantically looked around the empty pharmacy. What if someone noticed what we were up to? "Jamie," I whimpered. "Can we please wait until we get somewhere private?"

He didn't answer me as he slowly slid his fingers in and out of me. My eyes nearly rolled to the back of my head while the Plan B fell to the floor. Pretty soon, I was riding his hand, breathing hard and grinding my ass against his cock. Suddenly, he shoved his fingers up my cunt until the heel of his hand was pressed into my clit, providing the perfect friction. He teased me relentlessly, whispering sweet nothings in my ear until I came apart in his arms.

Jamie didn't cover my mouth when I cried out, and he didn't bother hiding what we were doing when the pharmacy's manager rushed into the aisle.

"Is everything okay?" the short man with a receding hairline asked. When his gaze fell to Jamie's hand up my dress, his entire face turned red. "I'm sorry, but I'm going to have to ask you two to leave."

"No problem," Jamie said. He fixed my dress and took my hand, whistling as we left the store.

Without the Plan B.

"I know you did that on purpose," I said once we were buckled inside his Jeep. I felt like such a fool for falling for his shit again. Why take me if he wasn't going to go through with it?

"Look"—he sighed, shoving his hand through his hair with one hand while driving with the other—"I promise I'm not trying to knock you up, and I promise I'll wear a condom from now on, but you didn't want to take that pill any more than I wanted you to. Admit it."

"That's beside the point, and it really doesn't matter now because I'm getting on birth control." And sooner rather than later.

Jamie shrugged, but I didn't believe his nonchalance for a second. "Make the appointment," he coaxed. "I'll even take you."

"Like you took me to get the Plan B? What will you do next? Fuck me on the receptionist's desk?"

A naughty grin spread his lips, and I rolled my eyes.

Jamie swooped into a burger joint, and I was salivating at the thought of having my first cheeseburger in years.

"Shouldn't you be out with your family celebrating?" I questioned once we were shown to a booth.

He slid in next to me instead of across from me, then threw his arm along the back of the seat and caged me in. The restaurant faded away until all I could see was him.

"They said something about dinner in the city, but you're the only person I want to be with right now."

I tried not to melt, but he made it impossible, especially when he pinned me with that hot gaze of his. "What about your mom, brother, and sister? You haven't seen them in a year. How long are they staying?"

"Not long," he answered with a sigh. "My grandparents are old, and my mom insists on taking care of them herself." His gaze fell, but I could still sense his sadness. "I think she feels guilty about my dad."

"Why would she feel guilty?"

"Because she never once asked him to quit smoking."

"Oh, Jamie…" I could do nothing but try to kiss the pain away. I wasn't sure how long we sat there, lips locked before we heard a throat clear. Giggling from embarrassment, I pulled away immediately only for Jamie to chase me, stealing one last kiss. Only then did he give the waiter his attention.

I sat and listened in awe as he ordered for us both. He still remembered what I liked, requesting French fries on my burger as well as on the side, and hold the mustard and onions. *Yuck, onions.*

The second the waiter left, Jamie turned to me. "It's time to come clean, Barbette. Tell me about your father."

"I've told you everything."

"You haven't told me how long he's been hitting you." I shifted in my seat, suddenly nervous. "How long, Barbette?"

"Since the day you left."

He took a deep breath, and when he spoke, his voice broke. "For Scotland?"

I shook my head, feeling tears cloud my vision. For the first time in five years, Jamie and I had a chance, which meant the last thing I wanted to talk about was my father.

"When summer was over, and you went back home." I closed my eyes, remembering that first time as if it happened yesterday. That was the day Elliot Montgomery stopped being my father. He was supposed to be the one to chase the monsters from under my bed, not be the reason I was afraid of the dark. "My parents had always wanted me to be more delicate and polished, something easily bent, but I always refused. Eventually, they'd grow tired and leave me alone, but not that time." Back then, I never really understood what had changed them, but it was the first time my parents ever refused to take no for an answer. "I fought them, Jamie, from the very first. You have to believe me."

"I do, baby. Go on."

"H-he slapped me that day, and I cried myself to sleep, but in the morning, I still loved him." I just didn't know that he never loved me back.

"What happened?"

"I tried not to give in, but his punishments got worse. Sometimes he'd beat me until I was bruised, and sometimes he'd make me go without food. He said no man would buy me if I were fat, so it was better that way." My father had laughed as if he'd told a joke, and that was the moment I realized how truly evil he was. "The beatings didn't stop until a nurse questioned me about a bruise. I told them I'd gotten it from volleyball. I know I shouldn't have protected him, but I was afraid. What if no one believed me?"

I looked to Jamie for an answer, but by now, his eyes had glazed over. He seemed to be in some sort of haze, and I panicked, wondering what he'd do next.

"Jamie?" I sniffled as I touched his fist, balled on the tabletop. "Please come back to me."

Hearing my words, he blinked, and then his gaze darted to mine. "I'm here," he said before releasing a long sigh. "And I swear to fuck I'm never going anywhere again."

"Don't make promises you can't keep. What happens when the fall comes? You'll be away at college, and I'll be here. I have to learn to stand on my own."

"Pennsylvania isn't that far away," he mumbled. His lips tightened, and I could tell he wasn't happy about having to leave.

"Pennsylvania?" I couldn't keep the surprise from my voice. "Which school? State? Pittsburgh?"

"Penn," he answered with a blush.

"Oh, my gosh! Jamie!" Forgetting my woes, I slapped his chest, making him chuckle. "Congratulations!" A different kind of tears welled up in my eyes before I could stop them. "I'm so proud of you."

"Don't be. It was my uncle's doing. I don't belong there."

"So what? I know you won't make them regret it. Besides, you can fit in anywhere. I hate that about you, you know."

He shrugged, and I could see the uncertainty in his gaze before he looked away. "Maybe."

I kissed his neck, and when he groaned, I did it again. "I believe in you," I told him between kisses. "You're going to kick some serious Ivy League ass."

"Fuck." He groaned when I began sucking on his neck. "I know what you're doing."

"What am I doing?" I licked his neck, making him shudder.

"You're trying to mark me." I didn't respond as I continued to molest his neck. He finally pulled away, forcing me to stop. "There's no need, Bette. I'm yours."

Smirking, I sat back and rested my head against his arm. "I know that already. You could never be anyone else's."

Growling, he hungrily kissed my lips until the waiter returned with our food and made a hasty retreat. "Thanks for the vote of confidence," Jamie said as he poured a mountain of ketchup onto his fries. I cringed, hating when he did that. I'd always tried to get him to dip his fries instead when we were kids. "But I'm not going anywhere until I take care of your father."

Taking his chin as he had done to me so many times before, I forced his focus from his food. "I'm no damsel, and you're no white knight. I'll save my own ass."

He chewed slowly as he seemed to consider it. "How about we save that amazing ass of yours together?"

"I can handle my father."

"I know you can," he patiently admitted. "But I wasn't there for you when you needed me the most. I can't just stand by now."

"It wasn't your fault that you had to move away, Jamie."

"But it was my fault the way I treated you before that."

"You didn't know, and that just means we both could have handled things a lot better."

He looked ready to argue some more before he reluctantly nodded. I knew he'd probably never be able to stop blaming himself for not seeing just like I'd never stop wishing I had just told him everything from the first. Shame had played a role in that, and I realized now that Jamie would have wanted all of me—the beautiful and the ugly. I sighed, reminding myself that I couldn't undo past decisions. I could only course-correct.

The conversation turned much lighter as we ate. I didn't realize how much Jamie and I no longer knew about each other. While it was promising, it was disconcerting at the same time. What if we discovered that we were no longer people we could love?

CHAPTER
TWENTY-FOUR

The Plaything

F OR THE SEVENTH MORNING IN A ROW, I WOKE UP IN A BED THAT wasn't mine. This morning, however, was different than the others—it was the first time I'd woken up alone.

Jamie hadn't taken me to his uncle's home after graduation. Instead, he'd driven us to a hotel twenty minutes outside of Blackwood Keep in case my father made good on his threat. And to stay off his mom and uncle's radar, as well, we'd steered clear of NaMara.

It was really beginning to feel like we were on the lam.

It wasn't until after Jamie made good on his other promise and my fourth orgasm of the day had faded that I began to feel the weight of what I had done.

"Jamie?" Sleep eluded me as I rested my head on his chest, tracing the thin, haunted letters spelling Broken and shaped like a heart. He told me it had been his first tattoo. I couldn't help but notice the date etched into his skin underneath—10-31-2011. His second tattoo had been a guitar with Douglas Buchanan's hand wrapped around the neck.

"Yes, kitten?" The lazy purr in his voice told me he'd almost been asleep.

"I-I need to go home."

"You are home. You're right here with me."

I wanted to melt at his words, but I had to remain rational. "My father will be angry if I stay."

His hands were suddenly around my waist, dragging me up his chest until our eyes met. He no longer seemed sleepy. "And I won't be the same if you go."

I'd stayed, and we hadn't left this room once. Jamie worked overtime to make sure I didn't regret it. Or maybe he'd just been making sure I didn't have time to think. Either way, it worked, but now I was alone, and my mind was running rampant.

What had I done?

This wasn't my plan. I hadn't intended to walk away from my parents without so much as a dime or a shirt to put on my back. And now I couldn't go home. My father knew everything, which meant he wouldn't take chances if I landed in his clutches again. It seems Jamie got what he wanted, after all, which was me at his mercy, even if it wasn't in the way he intended. I covered my eyes with my balled fists, but the frustrated scream bubbling in my throat didn't get the chance to escape.

A familiar beeping sound coming from the door alerted me to Jamie's return. Pulling myself together, I stood from the bed, keeping the damask silk wrapped around me. I wasn't sure how serious Jamie would take me when I told him I was leaving if I was naked.

I had no doubt he'd be upset, but I couldn't let that stop me. I had to salvage what was left of my escape plan before it was too late.

The door opened, and because this room could fit a house inside it, I couldn't see him step through. I waited, frowning when it sounded like more than one set of footsteps traveling the short hall.

"Barbette?"

The gentle voice calling out definitely did not belong to Jamie. A few seconds later, Four and Lou stepped around the corner.

"Shit, sorry!" Four shouted when she saw me standing there wearing nothing but a sheet.

Her gaze darted to the wall behind me, and my eyebrow rose

at her embarrassment. It was as if she hadn't seen more of me and shared what was most definitely not just a friendly peck on the cheek. Remembering our kiss and how much I enjoyed it, suddenly it was me who had trouble meeting her gaze. I hadn't intended to kiss Four, and while it had never crossed my mind before, in the heat of the moment, I reacted on instinct, and I couldn't say that I regretted it. In fact, I wouldn't have minded doing it again. I've always known that I liked Four, but it wasn't until what happened in that chemistry lab that I realized how much. The adrenaline junkie wasn't just someone I wanted as a friend. She was someone I wished I could be again—strong, selfless, and, most importantly, certain of who I am.

A nervous laugh bubbled out of me.

If I hadn't already found my soulmate, I'd wonder if I was in love with her or something.

"Jamie sent us," Lou explained, dark ponytail swinging as she shamelessly checked out every inch of the suite. The taupe walls, gold décor, and plush furniture sprinkled around the suite all screamed luxury. There was even a crystal chandelier dangling from the high ceiling. "Fancy digs you have here."

"What are you guys doing here? Where's Jamie?"

"He sent us to give you this," Four answered while holding out a large paper shopping bag. Taking it from her, I cautiously peeked inside the bag, half expecting a poisonous snake to jump out at me. Instead, I found a pair of distressed denim shorts and a white T-shirt with bold black lettering that read "I'm with him" and an arrow pointing left.

I didn't even want to know.

Seeing that there was more, I pulled out a handful of lace thongs, a bra, socks, and a shoebox. I whimpered with joy at the plain white sneakers inside.

I'd been complaining about only having a robe to wear all week, but Jamie hadn't once been moved to do something about it. Why now, and where was he?

"So we'll just wait out here for you to get dressed," Lou announced.

I looked up from the clothes now spread out on the rumpled bed. *Huh?*

"We thought we could hang out today," Four explained at my questioning look.

I couldn't help pursing my lips at the pair. Something was up, and they'd been ordered to keep me in the dark. "In other words, Jamie's up to no good and sent you to keep me distracted."

"Yes," Lou admitted without hesitation. One could almost appreciate her inability to beat around the bush. "But you should know we only agreed because Jamie might be on to something, so we want to get to know you better."

Gee, thanks?

Plopping down on the edge of the bed, Lou leaned back on her hands and crossed her legs with a smile. "So, what do you say?"

"About graduation," Four whispered while Lou was preoccupied with a phone call. It had been Lou's idea to come to this skating rink, and despite not knowing how to skate, I was enjoying myself. "If that was weird for you, I'm sorry. I don't know what came over me. Ever and I don't do stuff like that. It was a first for us too," she admitted with a blush.

I didn't think it was something I'd ever do either but seeing them together and knowing that I hadn't ruined everything made it all worth it. Jamie and Ever had both staked their claim openly and thoroughly. Hopefully, there'd be no more room for jealousy or doubt.

"I think it was weird for all of us," I mumbled as I gripped Four's hands tightly. She wasn't having much luck at skating either, so we were holding each other up as we slowly made our way around, sticking to the edge where the rails were. "I guess it's only a big deal if we make it one. We didn't do anything damaging. It's not like I couldn't have seen you naked in the locker room at school, right?"

"Right…" She twisted her lips, trying to hide a smile. "Except you probably wouldn't have kissed me if we'd been in the locker room."

"Yeah, probably not." I suddenly found interest in the scuffed purple skates I wore.

"I'm not mad," she rushed to say. "It was nice. Besides, you aren't the first girl I've kissed."

My eyes widened while she wore a goofy grin. "I'm not?" When she shook her head, I couldn't help prying for more information. "Who was it, and does Ever know?" It was hard keeping in my laughter, but I didn't want to make any sudden movements and risk falling.

"Tyra laid one on me once after Jamie dared her to, and yes, Ever was there." My eyebrows rose at that while hers furrowed. Of course, Jamie would be behind them kissing. "That reminds me," Four announced. "Jamie promised us a dare, but he didn't hold up his end of the deal."

"Which was?"

"He was supposed to write a letter from the heart and pick an audience to read it to before graduation." Panicking, I tried to stop only to stumble instead. Luckily, Four saved me from falling by tightening her grip. "Are you okay?" she inquired. Her brown eyes that were more cinnamon while Jamie's were chocolate widened as she waited for my answer.

No, I wasn't okay.

It now made sense why Jamie had been after my journal. Almost every line, lyric, and rhyme had been written for him, and he had planned to read it in front of the entire senior class. Making a deal with Jamie was as dangerous as making one with the devil. There was always a loophole. No one could deny his feelings for me, and knowing him better than the back of my hand, I could just hear him gloating now:

"It was a letter from my heart. She obviously wrote it for me."

"I'm sure that would have been fun, but a word of advice? Don't bet against Jamie. You'll lose every time."

Four wore an evil grin. "Well, I guess there's a first time for everything because graduation is over, which means we get to see him make out with Vaughn. I suppose Ever's off the hook, though, since they're related." As soon as the words left her lips, her smile faded, and she wore a troubled frown.

"Everything okay?"

"Huh?" She seemed to snap out of whatever was plaguing her thoughts. "Oh, yeah. Fine."

I couldn't claim to know Four all that well, but apparently, I knew enough to know when she was lying. She began chewing on her lip, and I wondered how many times she'd worried like this while I pretended to date her boyfriend. Shame bubbled up in my throat, forcing me to take a deep breath before I vomited all over my new friend.

"I don't think I ever actually thanked you," I whispered. She met my gaze but remained silent. "I also think you were right. I'm not sure I could have done what you did, so… thank you."

Four simply nodded, but then that worried look was back in her eyes. "Ever says you're leaving town. Is that true?"

I swallowed past the lump in my throat. "Yes."

"Why? Your father can't actually make you marry anyone. There are laws against that now, you know?"

I shook my head. My father would find a way to get me to consent. He'd already hinted before at hurting my mother. She foolishly believed she'd been my father's equal, helping him plot against me when all along, she'd been nothing but a pawn.

I'd tried to summon hatred for the woman who'd given me life, but I couldn't. How could I blame her for being weak when I'd allowed my father to weaken me, too?

We do the best we can with the information we have. No one person gets to decide what makes an individual weak or strong, even if their decisions aren't what we would have done ourselves. It takes more courage to be selfless than it does to be selfish.

Channeling my inner Four, I realized I couldn't leave my mother at the mercy of that monster. Convincing her to leave my father wouldn't be easy, but I had to try. Knowing what I know, I couldn't live with myself if I left without her.

"He'll find a way."

"What if you went to the police?"

I was surprised at her eagerness to get me to stay. I would have thought she'd be happier if she never saw me again. "It would be pretty hard to prove that my father intends to marry me off against my will. I'd need concrete evidence."

Four squeezed my hands, determination filling her big brown eyes. "Then get some."

I suddenly felt like I'd been hit with a thunderbolt and brought back to life stronger than ever. I never realized how much I'd given up by giving up. I'd alienated good people while allowing bad ones to push me around. *No more.*

"You've got to be fucking kidding me!" Lou shouted before I could respond to Four. She'd suddenly appeared next to us, her gaze moving back and forth between us. I hadn't realized until now that Four and I had stopped skating. We now stood off to the side, still standing close and still holding hands. "I spent two hours on the phone convincing Jamie that you two weren't going to run off together after you kissed, and here I find you looking like you're about to do it again!"

Shock and guilt had Four and me pulling away from each other and carefully swiveling on our skates to face Lou.

"Jamie told you?" Four questioned, looking peeved.

"About your little foursome in the science lab? Yeah, he told me. I'm his bestie, duh." She rolled her eyes and crossed her arms.

What a brat.

"It wasn't a foursome," I argued. "We didn't have sex with each other."

Lou waved me off. "Potatoes, po-tah-toes." The look she gave us was stern. "What did I just walk in on?"

"Nothing," Four answered sighing. "We were just talking."

"Great," Lou chirped. "Then fill me in."

"We were talking about why you told Jamie about Sean," Four snapped.

I blinked in confusion because that definitely wasn't what we were discussing—far from it—and Lou was right... I did want to kiss Four if only to thank her for helping me see. Besides, who the hell was Sean, and what did he have to do with Jamie?

"I didn't," Lou denied. "Jamie already knew. I just told him that you knew, too. Oh!" She snapped her fingers. "And that Wren and Ever might be brothers."

"Whoa!" I interrupted before Four could lay into Lou. It was a good thing too because that would be the fight of the century. "What are you guys talking about?" My gaze darted back and forth between them.

"Long story," Four and Lou said at the same time. They immediately returned to glaring at one another. I almost laughed because one would think they were sisters the way they constantly fought.

"Well, then, I guess you better start from the beginning."

It was dark and pretty late when we stumbled onto the beach a few hours later. The things Lou and Four divulged when we'd gone back to the hotel had me reaching for the whiskey Four had snuck out of the manor. I couldn't stop giggling at the name she'd given the McNamara's mansion.

Apparently, Ever wasn't a McNamara at all.

He was a Kelly.

And he didn't know that his biological father was still alive.

He'd also been a very bad boy joining Exiled to find his mom. I'd glimpsed the tattoo on his back once or twice but didn't know and hadn't cared what it meant. I thought his mom leaving was his only demon and was too wrapped up in my own to ask.

Some friend I was.

Unlike Jamie… he'd risked his life for his friends. And all the while, I'd been hating him without ever knowing how close I'd come to losing him. I wasn't the only one with secrets, after all.

At least now I knew where the hell Wren and Lou had come from. From the outside, it seemed like they'd just popped up one day and fit themselves right into our lives. And oh, how well they fit. As often as Lou made me want to pull out my hair, I couldn't imagine life without her challenging me every step of the way. Wren was too much like a steel vault. I couldn't get a detailed reading, but I had the feeling he was a good guy. He had to be after caring for Lou for years while believing they could never be. If Wren and Lou could beat the insurmountable odds they once had stacked against them, then maybe Jamie and I could have too if I hadn't planned to leave Blackwood Keep forever.

As we approached the familiar blue beach house on stilts where Vaughn held all his parties throughout high school, I tried not to think about how I hadn't heard from Jamie all day. It was thoughtful of him to send Four and Lou to keep me company, but a "thank you, ma'am" after he wham-bammed me all night would have been nice.

I glanced over my shoulder as we climbed the wooden stairs and saw Four texting furiously on her phone. She was the only one who'd opted out of drinking since she was driving Ever's G-Wagon.

"Hey, Bee, open the door, will ya? I think I'm wasted," Lou announced.

I frowned because I'd had more to drink than she had, and I was nowhere near as wasted. Tipsy maybe. Glancing at the door, I wondered if I'd been led into some kind of trap. Lou watched me expectantly while Four fought a grin. If they had been anyone else, I would have got the hell out of there, but I trusted them. I may have been in social exile for the last five years, but I still recognized good people when I saw them. Taking a deep breath, I decided I could handle whatever was waiting for me on the other side of that door.

Pushing it open, I stepped into the dark house and looked around. I could make out the outline of a couch and maybe a lamp or two. Moving farther inside, I jumped when the door behind me slammed shut. Whirling around, I saw the shadow of a man looming over me. Panic speared my chest a second before there was a click, and then a flashlight illuminated his grinning face.

"Hello, Clarice," my stalker greeted in a raspy voice.

"Jamie! Ugh! I'm going to kill you!" My fist balled as I flew toward him. I was very much looking forward to seeing blood pour from his pierced nose onto his lush upper lip. Before I could land the first punch, however, light flooded the entire room.

"Surprise!"

I paused mid-swing and looked around in shock. Ever, Vaughn, Wren, and Tyra stood at the helm of the room filled with people, half of whom I didn't recognize. I had no doubt they were all friends of Jamie's.

I stood there, not knowing what to do or say. No one had ever done anything like this for me. It was more than I could have hoped for, more than I deserved.

"I hope we didn't scare you too much," Tyra apologized as she walked up to me with a gentle smile and a tiara in her hand. She was so tiny that I had to bend down a little for her to place it on my head. "I told Jamie not to scare you like that."

"It's fine," I whispered with a grin.

"I'm sorry I couldn't be there to hang out," she said when she was done positioning the tiara. "Someone had to make sure the guys didn't screw up your party or invite strippers."

I didn't get the chance to respond before I felt Jamie locking his arm around my waist and pulling me back until my ass rested against his groin. At five foot ten, I used to hate being taller than most girls, but being in Jamie's arms always made me feel like my height was just right—especially when we played together.

"Happy birthday, baby."

"But my birthday isn't until tomorrow." It was all I could think to say. Jamie was destroying me in the best possible way.

Wordlessly, he lifted his phone and showed me the time.

12:01.

I sucked more air than I needed into my lungs.

I was eighteen today.

I was free. Or at least… I would soon be.

Jamie pulled me deeper into the house, where he introduced me to his friends. I was in awe at how many he'd made in the year he'd been here. Most of the kids here attended some of the public schools nearby, which meant Jamie had been busy.

I pursed my lips, wondering just how popular he'd become. I looked around, searching for the jealous gazes of scorned lovers and was surprised to see that there were only three other girls besides Four, Lou, and Tyra in attendance. The girls didn't keep me in suspense as to who they were either as they flanked some short Latino, who introduced himself as Matty before introducing me to his extra limbs. By the time he'd finished speaking their names, I'd already forgotten them as I watched the trio and their fuck-me smiles drink in the sight of Jamie.

"Well, aren't you a peach," Matty gushed, "and I do mean a peach. Your ass is amazing, girl."

"Uhhh, thanks?"

He batted his long lashes, making me giggle. "You're welcome."

"Back off," Jamie warned. "I don't give a shit if you are gay. Stop staring at my girlfriend's ass."

My eyes nearly bulged out of my head. *Girlfriend?*

I ignored the butterflies taking flight in my stomach and wondered when Jamie and I had discussed that? We'd spent the last week alone together and talking wasn't even in the top three of the things we'd done with that time.

I could never allow myself to become Jamie's girlfriend, knowing I was still planning to leave town.

"Cute," Matty complimented as he gestured to our shirts.

Already knowing what mine said, I glanced at Jamie's. I was just now noticing that he wore the same white T-shirt with bold black lettering except his read "I'm with her," and there was an arrow pointing right at me.

Oh, no.

Oh, no, no, no, no, no.

The last thing I ever wanted to do was to break Jamie's heart again. What choice did I have? I had to tell him.

Jamie glanced down at me, and whatever he saw in my eyes made him lower his head and kiss me with every ounce of passion he possessed. He'd taken the fateful words from the tip of my tongue and devoured them.

I could hear Ever's voice in my head pleading with me not to run and Four telling me to find a way to stay. And Jamie... all I could feel was his heart pounding inside his chest. I recognized that long-lost rhythm because it matched my own.

When Jamie finally came up for air, he searched my gaze. He seemed satisfied with whatever he saw and pecked my lips. "And that's a promise," he whispered.

"A promise?"

Skimming his lips across my cheeks, I enjoyed each caress of his breath across my flushed skin until he gently nipped the shell of my ear. "That whenever you're hurting, I'll kiss it better."

I had just barely caught my breath when Jamie stole it away again. How could I possibly walk away from him now?

I knew right then that I wasn't going anywhere.

This town was no longer big enough for my father and me, but one way or another, he'd be the one to go—not me.

I didn't get the chance to respond before I was pulled away by Tyra for birthday cake, which Vaughn carried from the kitchen, and I snickered at all the little bumblebees and their crowns before everyone began to sing.

I knew what I wanted long before I was told to make a wish, so closing my eyes, I blew out the eighteen candles.

"Did you enjoy your party?"

My eyes were closed, my head tipped back, and my lips, which Jamie had kissed until swollen, were parted as he moved in and out of me slowly from below. Dawn was creeping in outside the open window. I could hear the waves crashing in the ocean and feel the cool breeze whispering over my skin as I rode him.

"Yes."

"Did you feel like a princess?"

Tonight wasn't the first party I'd been to, but it was the only one I'd ever enjoyed. Before, I was too afraid of damaging my reputation and embarrassing my father, but tonight, I'd sung, danced, drank, and laughed. It all felt new to me. As if I were learning how to walk for the first time. I now had friends who felt more like family, and they were people who gave me no choice but to fight because I could never let them go.

"Yes."

"Look at me, Barbette."

The willpower it took to open my eyes when he was making me feel this good was great. The adoration in his eyes when my gaze found his, however, made it worth it.

"Do you know that I never stopped loving you?"

I gasped, and it had nothing to do with the orgasm rippling through me. It was the first time I'd heard those words from him, and I never realized how much I craved them until now. If I were honest, I always knew. Jamie hadn't given me a little of himself at a time. He'd been all in from the very first.

"I…" The words were right there on the tip of my tongue, but I couldn't bring myself to utter them. Not until I knew for sure that I wouldn't break his heart again. I just couldn't relive the pain I saw in his eyes the first time I cut him deep. Cradling his face in my hands, I kissed his lips through the tears soaking my face. "I know."

CHAPTER
TWENTY-FIVE

The Punk

Halloween… Five Years Ago

"**M**AKE SURE YOU HOLD YOUR BROTHER'S AND SISTER'S hands whenever you cross the street," my mother scolded. It was Halloween, and we were in Blackwood Keep, visiting my uncle and aunt before we left Boston for good.

As if having my heart broken the first time wasn't bad enough, my father informed us shortly after that he was moving back home and taking us with him—*to fucking Scotland.*

Anger whipped through me at the thought of leaving everything I cared about behind.

"I've got it, Mom. Can we go now?"

I was still grounded for sneaking away a month ago. The only reason my parents were letting me loose was so that I could take my two-year-old siblings trick or treating. They were reluctant to trust me again, and my anger management issues these last few weeks hadn't exactly helped my case.

She nodded, so I took Adan's and Adara's hands. I hated to admit it, but they looked fucking adorable in their Peter Pan and Tinkerbell costumes. My mother had made me wear the Captain Hook costume and took about a thousand pictures of us together as she cried and gushed.

Dad had driven us to the next neighborhood over where the

houses were closer together. I couldn't help but think about how easy it would be to sneak over to Bee's place.

She was so close that I felt like I could reach out my hand and touch her. Against my will, I kept scanning the street, hoping to spot her. She loved Halloween and horror movies. Every year, she dressed up. Last year, she'd gone as Freddy Krueger and sent me pictures. They were still decorating my bedroom wall, even though I hated her guts.

"Candy! Candy!" Dara demanded. She was tugging against my hand, no longer content to walk. Screams and laughter filled the night as kids of all ages ran up and down the street. I led the twins down the sidewalk of the first house with their porch light on and rang the bell.

"Trick or treat!" Adan and Adara sang when a woman answered.

"Well, aren't you three simply the cutest!"

"Thanks," I mumbled. I felt stupid as hell wearing this costume, but at least I was out from under my parents' scrutiny. My brother and sister, not yet masters of small talk, simply held up their buckets, waiting for her to fill them with candy.

We were walking away from our fourth house—Adan and Adara, struggling to carry their haul—when I heard my name called. I turned to see Jason dressed as a werewolf and jogging toward me.

"Hey, man! I thought that was you," he greeted excitedly. "When did you get in?"

"A couple of hours ago." I was about to ask him if he'd seen Ever since he hadn't been home when we arrived, but Jason beat me to it.

"Sweet. Someone from Brynwood is throwing a costume party tonight, and Ever wants to crash it. You should come with us."

"I don't know," I hedged, even though every molecule in me wanted to go. "I'm still sort of grounded."

"Oh, right. I heard you ran away from Boston, and your parents freaked out or something? What was that about?"

"Nothing." I couldn't tell if it was the truth or a lie. I just knew I had no interest in setting the record straight. In fact, I preferred that Jason thought I ran away than to know the truth. I'd fallen for a thieving bitch who stole my heart and refused to give it back. My eyes drifted closed as embarrassment coursed through me. I'd actually *begged* her to be with me.

"Well, if you change your mind, the party is at 678 Fitch Lane."

678 Fitch Lane.

Shit. Why was I trying to remember that?

"I've got to get back." It was the only goodbye I offered him before grabbing my brother and sister and walking away. I wasn't going to that damn party. I was still upset with Ever for lying to me. He had to have known Bee had lost interest. They were best fucking friends. Why hadn't he warned me? Neither of them knew me very well if they thought I'd just take being ignored lying down. I was used to having the upper hand and would fight tooth and nail to keep it. Shaking my head, I accepted the fact that it wasn't just my heart that was broken but my ego. I still wasn't sure which I hated Bee for crushing more.

Hours later, my parents had gone to bed. Rather than spend the night tossing and turning, I snuck out of my uncle's house to get those answers.

If Ever was at that party, it was a good chance Bee would be too.

As much as I wanted to hate her, I couldn't stand the thought of leaving without holding her one last time or saying goodbye. Maybe we didn't have to at all. I seriously doubted that an ocean could keep me away from her. Up until a couple of months ago, we'd been writing each other nonstop. There was no reason that it had to end.

The party was in full swing when I walked through the door.

Getting in had been easy enough. Since I was a freshman in my high school back home, and this wasn't my first party, I knew how to look like I belonged. I could also beat the shit out of anyone who said I didn't.

I didn't make it three feet inside before I was grabbed. I inhaled sharply when I looked down and noticed the red, furry devil horns resting on strawberry locks. My hands went around her small waist when she swayed into me.

"Bee?"

Disappointment weaved through me when she looked up and smiled. Although pretty, it wasn't the face that haunted my dreams. I couldn't tell if this girl had lost her balance or was just that eager. Either way, the amount of alcohol seeping from her pores told me she was certified jailbait.

"Nice costume," she slurred with a hiccup. "Are you Jack Sparrow? You're even hotter than Johnny Depp."

I didn't give her an answer before I pushed her aside. The small house was packed wall to wall, making it harder to navigate through. Eventually, I ended up at the sliding glass door leading to the pool out back.

There was a shitload of people out here, too, so I stood in place, letting my gaze scan the crowd. I was ready to head back inside and check upstairs next when I spotted Ever standing by the hedges. He was speaking to someone I couldn't see, deeply engrossed in whatever they were saying. The crowd parted a little, and I could see that it was a tall girl with platinum blonde hair, wearing a white, blood-splatted wedding dress, a black leather jacket, and combat boots to match. Thanks to Bee making me watch Bride of Chucky with her, I didn't have to wonder who the girl was supposed to be. I snorted knowing Ever must have been trying to win the bet we'd made over the summer to see who could lose their virginity first. It was one bet I wouldn't care if I lost. I wanted my first time with Bee to be special and not rushed because of some dare.

312 | B.B. REID

As I made my way across the backyard, I wondered why he suddenly looked so worried. My cousin had rarely cared about anything lately other than giving his parents, teachers, and the Blackwood Police Force a hard time.

I started to call out to him, but then he leaned forward, and the girl rose onto her toes to meet him halfway. Pride swelled in my chest because I knew I was about to witness Ever's first kiss. I almost wish I had a camera so that I could capture it and tease him about it later. My first kiss with Bee had been my first ever, and even though we'd fumbled through it, it hadn't taken either of us long to get the hang of it. My heart sped up, and my blood rushed south in anticipation of kissing her senseless once I found her. After I left for Scotland, it would be a long time before I had the chance again.

"Jamie, you made it!" Jason called out as he suddenly appeared by my side.

The pair broke apart before their lips could meet, and when their heads swung my way, the first thing I noticed was the alarm in his gold and her bright blue gaze.

No.

I blinked and then blinked again.

I didn't trust what my eyes were telling me.

The two people I trusted most in the world wouldn't betray me like this. Looking away, I took a deep breath that shuddered out of me when I exhaled. I only hoped that when I faced them again, it wouldn't be Barbette that Ever had just been ready to kiss.

Please, don't be her.

"Jamie..."

The moment I heard Bee softly gasp my name, I knew my prayer wouldn't be answered. I stepped back, refusing to look at either of them. My hands shook, and it was all I could do not to ball them into fists. Only God knew what I'd do then. When I turned to go, I felt gentle fingers circle my arm, begging me to stay. The way I felt, those fingers might as well have been claws, ripping at me.

"Jamie, please wait! I can explain!" Barbette broke down sobbing before I could even tell her to go to hell. She was a far cry from the girl who'd turned me away so coldly a month ago. For a moment, I had hope that I hadn't lost her after all until I realized that no longer mattered. She'd betrayed me in the fucking worst way. "Please, *please* let me."

"There's no need to explain." Snarling, I snatched my arm away from her. "You wanted him. You got him. Congratu-fucking-lations."

"Jamie," Ever called out, seeming to finally free himself from the shock that had kept him frozen. He moved away from the fence, and I toyed with the idea of tackling him to the ground before discarding it. Bros before hoes, right? "It's not what you think. I—"

He reached out to touch me, and I flipped the fuck out. "Stay away from me! Just stay the fuck away!" My fist connected with his eye and then again with his lip. I guess Bee meant more to me than I was willing to admit at the moment. I turned and pushed through the crowd that was now watching before either of them could see the tears that had fallen.

I was tempted to turn back and burn that house down with them in it so that they could truly be together forever.

Barbette hadn't just been the first girl I'd fallen for. She'd been the only one I ever wanted to know the real me. With her, I never had to hide or pretend to be someone I wasn't. I *believed* her when she showed me that it was okay to care. To love. To feel.

And with one almost-kiss, she'd taken it all away.

There was nothing she could tell me to replace what she'd stolen from me, so with God as my fucking witness, I swore I'd come back one day and make her pay.

CHAPTER
TWENTY-SIX

The Punk

Present

"Who's got the beers?" Vaughn asked for the fifteenth time. We'd just finished loading Four's recently acquired dirt bike onto the utility trailer attached to my Jeep. Her first race was in the morning, and I wasn't going to miss it. Four had told me so after claiming that I'd practically twisted her arm. The only ones who couldn't be there were Tyra because she couldn't get the weekend off, and Wren and Lou, though neither had provided an explanation. Wren was up to something, and Lou was growing impatient. I just hoped for his sake that he came clean soon.

Even though we had plenty of water and sand in Blackwood Keep, we were driving down to Atlantic City for some fun and sun since the town Four's race was being held would be less than an hour away. It also helped that we had a NaMara in A.C. The only thing filthy rich assholes such as myself loved more than acquiring money was never having to spend it.

"I told you already," Bee snapped. "The cooler's in the hatch, where you'll be riding duck taped if you ask again." She'd styled her hair in two French braids that swept her breasts and made her look hot as fuck. The white cutoffs that molded to her ass and thighs looked even shorter on her because of those legs that just went on and on...

Damn. Today's T-shirt, selected by yours truly, was a black number with a single slice of pizza printed in white on the front. Mine was also black with the entire pie minus her slice.

Crossing her arms, she stared Vaughn down, oblivious to me lusting over her. Vaughn grinned and draped his arm around her shoulders. "Missed you," he flirted.

Bee playfully rolled her eyes before shrugging him off. Thank God. It was too early in the fucking morning to be rumbling with my best friend. I was pretty sure I was still hungover from last night, too. I tried not to dwell on the fact that I also hadn't slept much after telling Bee I loved her and getting zip in return.

She'll say it when she's ready.

I clenched my teeth, wondering when the hell that would be. She already had my heart and soul in her back pocket. The only things I had left to give were my balls and my ego. I'd needed the former to tell her that I loved her, but after she hadn't said it back, the latter was now in serious need of repair.

I lost my train of thought, staring at Bee's ass as she climbed into the front passenger seat. *I can wait a little longer.* Ever started to follow Four and Vaughn into the back seat when I stopped him.

"What's up?" he asked after following me out of hearing distance of the Jeep.

"I wanted to thank you for being there for Bee when I was... being an idiot."

I wouldn't make the excuse that I couldn't have known. Bee had just been betrayed by the two people she trusted above all to protect her. Of course, she was afraid to tell me what was happening. She'd felt ashamed and utterly alone, and I'd selfishly piled all of my feelings on top of hers as if they'd mattered more. If I had been more patient and less a puppet to my emotions, she would have come to me—eventually. Instead of waiting, I pushed her away and shut her out. The way I'd handled things made me think Bee was on to something.

If you knew the match you were holding wouldn't just flame

but would start a fire so wild nothing on earth could tame it, would you light it?

Too often, I'd given in to my emotions. If I had known Bee's fate back then, I might have taken her and ran. How far would a thirteen- and fourteen-year-old have gotten? It couldn't have been very far. Or maybe I would have stayed and started a war with her father that I couldn't win. They were two possibilities with the same tragic ending.

Bee could try to shoulder the blame all she wanted, but for the rest of our lives together, the burden of those five years we lost would be mine and mine alone to carry.

"I'm not going to say you're welcome because I didn't do it for you," Ever replied. "I did it for Bee, and I didn't give a shit how you felt about it."

I simply stared at him for a few seconds. Four had turned him into such a sap that sometimes I forget how huge a prick my cousin could be.

"If you say so." I knew Ever well enough to know he'd been torn. However, my feelings for Bee wouldn't allow me to be upset over the fact that Ever had been willing to sacrifice our relationship to protect her. She'd always come first. "Just tell me one thing," I demanded.

"What?" he growled irritably.

"Whose idea was it for the two of you to kiss that night?" I asked, referring to the Halloween I'd caught them about to kiss.

"Mine."

I pinned him with my stare for the longest time but never once did his golden gaze waver. Bee had given me the exact same answer when I asked her. Knowing they were protecting each other from losing me forever, I accepted the fact that I'd never know, and maybe it was for the best. The only truth that mattered now was knowing neither of them harbored secret feelings.

"Gee, thanks, man. I hope I can do the same for you someday."

Ever's sour expression almost folded me in half.

Thanks to those two and their "bright ideas," I now knew how Four looked naked, how she liked to be fucked, and the sounds she made when she came. Of course, that meant Ever now knew the same about Bee.

I started to knock his teeth down his throat on general principle when the sound of a car approaching stole our attention. I sighed when a silver BMW came into view. The windows were tinted, but I already knew who was inside.

"Before we go, there's one more thing I need you to do for me."

Ever didn't respond as he watched the car door open, and the driver stepped out. "What the hell is Portland doing here?" Ever snapped.

Jason was watching us warily as he slowly made his way over. He had every right to be cautious, especially with the way Ever was tracking his every move.

"He's here to talk."

"Talk? Talk about what? You do know he's the one who told Elliot where Bee was on graduation day?"

I clapped his shoulder. "Then I won't have to explain the split lip."

Jason stood in front of us now with his shoulders hunched forward and his hands shoved in his jeans.

"'Sup, Jason? How's the lip?"

His gaze flickered my way before resettling on Ever. "Can we talk?"

"What. The fuck. For?"

"For my sister," Jason responded, nostrils flaring. "The one you slept with and then ignored."

Any second now, this thing was going to go south. I could already hear the Jeep's doors opening behind me and footsteps closing in.

"He's also the reason she's still alive," I pointed out. Four came to stand at Ever's side, and I could feel Bee standing at mine. Warmth flooded my chest when she slipped her soft fingers through mine.

"If he hadn't—"

"Jason," Ever interrupted. He stepped forward, and I braced myself to play the referee until I realized the anger was gone from his eyes. My friends and I, as well as Jason, seemed to be experiencing the same amount of shock. Ever could be cold, callous, and cruel even when he was dead wrong. "You're right. I shouldn't have slept with her. You were my friend, and I didn't think about who she was. I was too selfish and messed up to care that she was your sister. I know it won't change a damn thing, but I'm truly sorry."

"*Sorry?*" Jason spat. "How can I believe that when you won't even say her name!"

Jason's hands slammed into Ever's chest, shoving him back. Four hugged herself as her worried gaze bounced between Jason and Ever. Any other time, Vaughn and I would have wasted no time pouncing on him but not today. Ever didn't seem inclined to defend himself either as he stared at the ground in shame. Never had I seen my cousin so humbled before. I realized then that this was the first time they actually talked about Olivia and probably the first time Ever bothered to apologize. The few interactions they've had since Jason blew back into town usually ended in blows.

"Olivia," Ever croaked when he finally found what was left of his voice. His gaze glazed over, and I knew he was probably picturing the face that haunted him every day since she slit her wrists in front him. "Her name is Olivia, and I am sorry. So fucking sorry."

Jason dropped his head, but not before we saw the tear that fell. He seemed defeated, and I was sure not one of us felt triumphant about that. "Was."

Ever's head shot up, his face a mix of confusion and disbelief while my entire body went cold.

No.

That's not what he told me. He'd said—

Suddenly, I remembered the grief in his eyes when he told me she was better now, and I realized what he'd meant.

I was distantly aware of Bee's hand slipping from mine in shock. "What?"

"Her name *was* Olivia." Sniffling, Jason finally lifted his head. "You weren't there to save her the second time. No one was." Before anyone could find the words to say, Jason continued. "I'll *never* forget what you did," he said as he backed away from us, "and I'm not sure I have it in me to forgive you, but my sister wouldn't want me to waste another second on you. You're not even worth it."

He turned, and no one stopped him when he got in his car and sped away.

Four's first pro-am race hadn't gone quite as expected. Out of eighteen riders, fifth place wasn't bad, but for Four, who for years had been undefeated, it was a massive disappointment. She now had thirteen of the sixty points she needed for her license, but her small victory did nothing to erase the scowl from her lips.

After that bomb Jason had dropped, I could understand why Four's heart hadn't been in the race. A cloud had followed us all the way from Blackwood Keep, and Ever had barely spoken two words since.

Olivia had killed herself.

And even though my gut told me Ever wasn't the reason, nothing would stop him from feeling guilty. I almost wished I hadn't forced him into talking to Jason, but the truth would have come out eventually. At least they both were able to speak their piece. I knew Ever had wanted to apologize, but his ego wouldn't allow him after Jason made it a point to be a massive pain in the ass. He'd even gone so far as to target Four last Halloween, which had temporarily pushed aside all Ever's guilt.

"So should we head home?" Vaughn asked, breaking the silence as I drove us back to NaMara. We'd left our stuff at the hotel after we decided to celebrate Four's win tonight. Who knew?

"We should celebrate," Bee announced. She then turned in her seat next to me, briefly stealing my attention from the road. "I know it might not seem like much," she told Four, "but I think you kicked ass out there and took thirteen riders' names today. I hope I can call you my friend because nothing would give me more pride."

I looked in the rearview mirror in time to see Four, after only a moment of hesitation, smile and nod.

Bee then turned her attention to Ever. "I know you're determined to blame yourself for Olivia, but you didn't break her. Maybe her family will never know what did, but until they stop wallowing in hatred, they'll never get the closure they need."

Ever's only response was to lean his head back as he closed his eyes tight. Bee was right, even if my cousin wasn't ready to admit it. Ever shouldn't have slept with his friend's sister—a girl he never bothered to look at twice—but that didn't make him a murderer. The Portlands were too busy pointing in one direction to see the many reasons Olivia couldn't bear this world anymore, and until they opened their eyes, they'd never see.

"And you," Bee said, addressing Vaughn. "You need to find a way to get us some more beers since you drank them all."

Vaughn responded with a lazy grin. Yesterday and this morning, he'd chosen to drown his sorrows in an entire case of beer.

When Bee's gaze fell on me, I flashed her my most flirtatious smile. "I love it when you take charge, kitten. If we were alone, I'd pull over right now."

"Don't let me stop you," Vaughn drunkenly slurred. "I already know Four and Ever got to see you do it."

Unintentionally, my foot slammed on the brakes. *How the hell did he know?*

"Who told you?" Bee screeched.

"Tyra."

Everyone's gaze fell on Four.

"Well, I didn't tell her!" Four screamed. "I didn't even know she knew."

"Lou told Tyra, and Tyra told me," Vaughn explained. It was amazing we had as many secrets as we did since none of us seemed able to keep them for long—most especially me.

The back of my neck grew hot when I felt Bee's gaze. I made sure to keep mine firmly fixed on the road as I picked up speed again.

"Don't even try it," Bee snapped. "I already know you told Lou."

"What's the big fucking deal?" Vaughn said while chortling. "We're teenagers. Banging while other people are in the room is like a rite of passage. I've done it at least four times."

"Please tell me Tyra wasn't one of those times," Four fussed. One glance in the rearview showed her glaring at the six-foot-plus, broad-shouldered quarterback as if she could actually take him. Hell, she probably could.

"It wasn't Tyra," I answered for Vaughn. "She's definitely still a virgin."

"And how do you know that?" Bee questioned.

My jeans tightened a little at her jealous scowl. "Because she acts like she needs dick in her life."

We all looked to Vaughn for confirmation and realized he'd passed out. Heavy snores could already be heard coming from him. Five minutes later, we were pulling into the hotel's garage.

"Should we wake him up?" Bee questioned as we climbed out of my Jeep.

"Hell, no," Ever groused. "I'm not carrying his drunk ass up-stairs. We're all the way up in the penthouse. Let him sleep it off here."

"We can't just leave him in the car," Four argued.

"Yes, we can," I said, siding with my cousin. "I'll crack the windows."

Bee and Four stood back with their arms crossed as I did just that. It was easy for them to expect us to help him since they weren't the ones who'd have to carry his heavy ass. Vaughn had trained every muscle in his body, putting both Ever's and mine to shame.

"He drank an awful lot," Four remarked. "Was he close to Olivia?"

"He barely fucking knew her," I answered before sighing. "This is something else." My guess was his prick of a father was the culprit. Franklin Rees was a bad fucking man, who would stop at nothing to corrupt his only son.

"Have you talked to him lately?" Four asked Ever.

Ever rubbed the back of his neck. "Whenever I try, he just shrugs me off and says that nothing is wrong. He's so closed off now that I feel like I barely know him anymore."

When you had a father willing to exploit any weakness, no matter how cruel or contemptible, it was no wonder Vaughn remained a blank canvas to everyone except himself. And maybe Tyra. The tiny slip of a girl had gotten through to him more than any of us could, and we'd known him longer. I just wondered if it would be enough when it was all said and done.

Sighing, I stared at my sleeping friend. I guess we'll all just have to wait and see.

Vaughn was dead to the world with his head back and mouth wide open. Unable to resist, I stole the pen I knew I'd find in Bee's purse and drew a picture of my dick and balls on his cheek. Maybe that will cheer him up.

Glancing over my shoulder, I met Bee's blue gaze. "Look familiar?"

She pursed her lips.

Shutting the door, I locked it before kissing her deeply and leading her by the hand to the private elevator. NaMara had an oceanfront location with five-star-quality amenities for a hefty price. Of course, our stay here was complementary since my family owned the joint. The penthouse suite had three bedrooms, a living room, dining room, wet bar, kitchen, and an outdoor terrace with a panoramic view of the Atlantic. We even had a private beach cabana, which I made a mental note to make use of before we left tomorrow.

As we stepped inside the suite, I snickered when Four and Bee looked around in awe as if they were seeing it for the first time.

Ever immediately grabbed Four before she could do whatever it was she was about to do. "Come take a shower with me."

The look Four gave him told me she was on to him, and I watched Ever enthrall her with his hooded gaze as he pulled her toward their room and shut the door.

Alone at last.

Bee was sitting cross-legged on the couch, staring at the blank TV screen. It was obvious something was on her mind, and I'd been patiently waiting all day for her to tell me what was eating her. Lifting the charcuterie that room service had set out, I carried it over and placed it on the coffee table in front of her.

"Hungry?"

She smiled before picking up one of the meats.

I watched her bite and chew for a few seconds before saying, "Tell me what's wrong."

She swallowed and licked her lips, refusing to meet my gaze. "I tried to run away once. I packed a bag, stole my father's car, and I just drove away. Actually, it was more like I sped away. I could actually smell the burning rubber from the tires." She chuckled as a tear slipped from her eye, and she wiped it away before I could. "I didn't know what I was doing. I was five miles outside of town when I ran a stop sign. A cop pulled me over and called my parents. My dad was *furious*. It was the first time he'd used something to beat me with other than his hand."

Jesus Christ.

Bee didn't know how hard it was for me to sit there and listen to her when all I wanted was to drive back to Blackwood Keep. If I ever got Elliot's throat in my hands again, I wouldn't stop squeezing. It had been all I could do to keep from killing him the first time. The only thing that stopped me was the realization that I wouldn't be able to protect Bee from jail.

Not able to stand the distance between us anymore, I pulled her into my lap.

"It was right after I found out your father had died," she continued with a whisper.

My ravaged heart twisted in my chest at the thought of my father. At the time, nothing else had mattered except every last precious moment I had left with him, but a part of me still wished I could have been there for Bee.

"Where were you going to go?" I was sure if Bee got away, no one would have ever found her, and even though I couldn't stand the thought of never seeing her, I couldn't help but wish she had. At least she would have been safe.

Bee hid her face in my neck, and I held her close as her silent sobs shook her body. "Scotland. I know it was stupid to try, but I just couldn't stand the thought of you needing me as much as I needed you and not being there."

My head fell back onto the couch, and I closed my eyes.

Fuck.

All this time, I'd been the one place she felt safe, and while she'd been fighting her way back to me, I had already written her off. And my first act in discarding her had been losing the virginity that I had promised to her.

When Ever had made that bet to see who could lose theirs first, I'd been tempted but reluctant. I didn't want my first time with Barbette to be because of a stupid bet. Even after discovering that Bee had betrayed me for Ever, I hesitated. I didn't realize it was because I was still hoping for us until Bee stayed with Ever after he cheated with Olivia. I knew then that there was nothing left of us to hold on to. I thought she'd wanted Ever no matter what—even if he was unfaithful to her.

Angry at Bee for being so goddamn weak, I'd given myself to the first pretty girl who batted her lashes at me. I thought I would finally move on after. Instead, I'd found my revenge.

Every single girl I'd screwed after Lindsey Muir was my way of punishing Bee and breaking my promise to her as thoroughly as she'd broken me. I might have slept with half a dozen girls before I realized I was only punishing myself. After a while, not wanting to give them more of me than was necessary, I stopped looking for pleasure when there was none to be found, and I'd simply get them off before walking away.

The mountain of mistakes Bee and I made in the last five years kept rising higher and higher.

"Jamie?"

I slowly opened my eyes to find Bee watching me, her blue eyes rimmed with red. "I don't want you to feel guilty."

Ah, it's much too late for that, kitten.

"Then how should I be feeling knowing that I wasn't there to protect you?"

She leaned in, and I met her halfway, kissing her lips. "That's not your fault," she whispered against mine. "You're here now. We can protect each other."

Shoving aside the past because there was nothing we could do to change it, I smiled against her lips. "I stand when I piss," I said with a growl rising in my chest. "That means protecting is my job. Means I get to make the decisions, too."

I almost snickered when she glowered.

"Oh, is that the only requirement? Well, we both sit when we shit, and I'd say you're full of it right about now."

I was ready to retort when the sound of moaning stopped me. The blush suddenly warming Bee's cheeks told me she heard it, too. Standing up, I set her on her feet and kissed her as I removed her shorts and the black T-shirt with the words 'nothing,' 'sense,' and 'we're.' Each word was stacked on top of each other. Mine was white with 'makes,' 'when,' and 'apart' in the same style.

Once she was naked, I removed a rubber from my wallet before shedding my clothes. After I rolled the condom on, I lifted her up and wrapped her long legs around my waist.

"Where are you going?" she questioned when I headed in the opposite direction of our room. "Our room is that way." She pointed behind me as I opened one of the bedroom doors. I could hear the shower running and the sound of wet skin slapping. "Oh, my God!" Bee squealed. "Jamie, what are you doing?"

"Payback."

I slowly lowered her onto my cock, making her gasp as her wet pussy wrapped around me like a glove. Steam filled every inch of the bathroom when I carried her inside and headed for the occupied shower. It was a glass enclosure with a rainforest showerhead and more than enough room for four people.

Revenge was most definitely sweet.

Bee could barely keep her eyes open as I toweled her hair dry in our room. We had to take a second shower after the hottest sex I'd ever had. I lost count of how many times I'd almost blown my load prematurely.

"What?" Bee asked when she noticed me watching her curiously.

"I'm starting to think you and Four bat for more than one team." My gaze narrowed as I replayed the way their hands and lips had wandered and explored each other more than once.

Batting her lashes, she pursed her lips that had been wrapped around my dick an hour ago. "Jealous?"

"Insanely." I dropped the towel and tossed her onto the bed before climbing between her legs. "I won't share you."

"I'm not asking you to." Sliding her hand between us, she began stroking me. "I only want you."

Feeling my toes curl, I quickly reached for the box of condoms resting on the nightstand. For some reason, I believed her and didn't stop to question my sanity. I'd wanted to hear those words for so long that I wasn't about to look a gift horse in the mouth.

"One more time?" I pleaded, figuring she might be too sore or tired. Bee's only response was to spread her legs as she watched me roll the condom on through lowered lids. "Just a warning…" I teased her slick entrance with the head of my cock before sliding right inside. "This will be quick. I'm talking five or six pumps, tops." I tried and failed not to moan like a bitch when I felt her hot pussy gripping me.

Wrapping her arms around my neck and her legs around my waist, she smiled, and for a moment, I was starstruck. "It wouldn't be the first time."

Goddamn, I love this girl.

Sinking my teeth into her shoulder to hide my grin, I made her eat those fucking words.

CHAPTER TWENTY-SEVEN

The Plaything

I SAT CROSS-LEGGED ON JAMIE'S BED, WEARING NOTHING BUT HIS T-shirt and mismatched socks as I watched him frantically search for a clean tie. We'd just arrived in from Atlantic City a couple of hours ago, and Jamie just *had* to get that quickie, knowing he'd be late for work. I wasn't sure what he did around the office, considering he had no business experience, but his uncle was adamant that he show up, especially today, after missing all last week.

As Jamie searched through another pile, I made a mental note to clean up this mess once he left. The first thing to go would be the poster of Nicki Minaj crouched in nothing but a thong, bra, and sneakers. No offense to the rapper, but my ass was the only one I wanted Jamie staring at. Also, I could barely see the floor. When I'd searched his dresser earlier for something to wear, I found it mostly empty. All his clothes, clean *and* dirty, were in piles on the floor.

"What about that one?" When he turned his irritated frown on me, I pointed to the dark-green tie with white stripes hanging from the closet doorknob.

To think it had almost made it inside where it should have been.

Rushing across the room, he slipped it over his neck without checking to make sure it was clean.

Guess he's given up caring. Climbing from his bed, I made my way to him and took over tying it when he fumbled one too many times.

"Is today important or something?"

"No." He blew air from his nose before mumbling, "My uncle texted and said if I'm not on time, he's sending you home."

My hands paused from knotting his tie. "Oh."

"Don't worry about it," he said as he took over, wrestling the knot I'd made up to his neck.

"Maybe he's right. I probably should go home." *And never ever be seen again.* I stepped away from Jamie while avoiding his gaze. "There's some stuff that I need, and I have to talk to my mom." I couldn't put off facing my parents forever, and Jamie, no matter how hard he tried, couldn't shield me from that unpleasantness. I had to learn to stand on my own again. I had to be the girl that Jamie and I had both fallen in love with.

"You're not going back there."

"I wasn't asking your permission." I had my back turned to him as I scanned the messy room for my clothes.

"If your legs still work enough to carry you through that door, then maybe I didn't fuck you hard enough." Jamie's chest was suddenly pressed against my back as he toyed with the hem of my tee. "Is that it, Barbette?" Slowly, he lifted the T-shirt, letting the soft cotton brush against my thighs until my bare ass was exposed to the cold air blowing through the vents. "Do you need more?"

His hand pressed into my back and bent me over his bed before I could respond. I was lying flat on my stomach, my ass and pussy completely at his mercy. "Stop trying to distract me with your dick, Jameson. It's not going to work." I could hear the sound of his belt being undone and then his zipper lowering.

"Let's be honest..."

I looked over my shoulder in time to see him tear open a condom wrapper and sheath himself.

"It usually works," he boasted.

I moaned as he slowly sank himself deeply. I still wasn't used to his monster cock, but my pussy couldn't seem to get enough as it welcomed him with a tight grip and a sloppy wet kiss. "You're going to be late," I tried to reason as best as I could. It felt like the air had been stolen from my lungs.

"Then we'll find somewhere else to stay," he answered as he fucked me with short, hard thrusts. "I really don't give a fuck."

"This can't be healthy," I whined. "We need to talk about our issues."

"So talk," he encouraged.

Unfortunately, he chose that moment to hit a spot deep inside of me, and the only thing I could say was "Harder."

Fuck it.

There was nothing either of us could say that would change the way we felt. We'd loved each other through the good and the bad—even when we didn't want to.

Jamie suddenly leaned over, one hand planted on the bed above my head while the other lovingly moved my hair from my face. "I'm listening," he insisted as he stroked me.

It was much too late, however. I was no longer capable of cognizant thinking. The only thing that mattered was getting more of his cock as deep inside of me as possible and maybe keeping him there. Sensing my thoughts, Jamie ruthlessly pounded me into the mattress until I came, all the while insisting that I had his full attention.

"Oh, my God! I love you!" I blurted just as my orgasm rippled through me. Even as the pleasure nearly blinded me, I realized what I'd done. I pounded the mattress with my fist and wasn't sure if the scream that ripped from my throat was from pleasure or frustration. Maybe both. I'd meant it when I'd said I loved him, but I wasn't supposed to say it yet. Not until I was certain I could stay.

God, I can't do this to him again.

Jamie pressed gentle kisses to my shoulder soothingly as I

rode the wave, and when I finally settled, he pulled out of me. Out of breath, I could do nothing but listen to the water run after he disappeared inside the bathroom. When he returned, he gently turned me over, then cleaned me up with a warm washcloth. I stared at his cock, now tucked inside his pants but still very much hard.

"You didn't come."

"Perceptive." His tone was clipped, making me wince.

"Did I do something wrong?"

Jamie had told me he loved me two days ago. Surely, he'd be happy to hear it back finally? The truth was, I'd loved Jamie from the very first, and I never stopped. It no longer mattered that I hadn't been ready to tell him. He deserved to know.

Jamie leaned over me, and I closed my eyes as he pressed a kiss to my lips. "I'll see you later."

Was that sadness I heard in his voice? I went to grab him, but he was already gone. My eyes flew open in time to see the door shutting behind him. My mind raced to replay everything that occurred after I'd uttered those fateful words, and then I gasped.

Did he know I hadn't wanted to tell him?

Feeling my aching heart reaching out for Jamie, I grabbed his pillow, pushed my face into it, and screamed.

When it came to Jamie's heart, it seemed I was fated to always do the wrong fucking thing.

"Are you sure about this?" Four asked as I dismounted from her bike. The ride over had been both exciting and harrowing. I was already eager to do it again.

"No." I looked at the house where my childhood and the most precious parts of me were stolen. "But I have to."

Especially now more than ever.

Once I get the evidence I needed, I could make Jamie see

why I hesitated to tell him. Maybe he thought I hadn't meant it or that I did mean it but didn't want to be with him. Whatever was going through his mind right now, I was determined to nip it in the bud as soon as possible.

I wasn't going anywhere, and Jamie was mine.

Four peered at the house behind me, probably hoping to reassure herself that no one was home. "Maybe I should come inside with you."

I immediately shook my head. If I put Four in danger, Ever would never forgive me. He'd be pissed enough if he knew that I was here. I was sure he'd side with Jamie about me not coming back. I knew it was a huge risk, but for Jamie, I'd do whatever it took to keep him.

"You should go," I said as I handed her the open-face helmet she called number six. I liked that it was red, shiny, and had *Hellfire* written on the side in white. She wore number thirteen. Another open-face that Ever had gifted to her this past Christmas. He'd designed the skull on the back with high, purple pigtails and in black grunge underneath the words *Ever's Wild Thang*, giving it a Harley Quinn vibe. "If my father comes home early and he sees you, he'll know I'm here. I can just ride my bike back."

"But—"

I quickly shut her up by pressing my lips against hers and laughed when her eyes widened before blinking rapidly. When I pulled away from our awkward kiss, she watched me in that same curious way Jamie had when we were in Atlantic City.

"I don't know why I was ever worried about you and Ever… you seem more attracted to me than him."

Winking, I turned and walked away. It was true I had a bit of a girl crush on Four, but who wouldn't? She was strong, badass, and reminded me so much of the girl I used to be. After eighteen years, I'd finally found a female I could call my friend.

I also realized that perhaps I was being a tad overzealous about that and should chill the fuck out.

Girl or not, Ever wouldn't hesitate to kick my ass if he thought I was poaching on his territory, and I didn't need his emotionally fragile cousin getting the wrong idea either. Jamie was who I wanted. He was more than just the person I'd fallen for. He was my soulmate.

I was surprised to find that my key still worked. The moment I stepped through the door, I heard the roar of Four's motorcycle as she raced away and let out the breath I'd been holding.

The last thing I wanted to do was put my newfound friends in danger. I didn't know how far my father would be willing to go to keep me here if I was caught.

So I guess I better not get caught.

Deciding not to leave anything up to chance, I checked all the rooms before retracing my steps back to my father's office. Every Monday, my mother had her grooming appointment, and for as long as I could remember, she never missed it.

I pushed into my father's office, knowing it wouldn't be locked. It wasn't that Elliot Montgomery had nothing to hide. He simply had no fear of his wife and daughter ever stepping out of bounds.

Well, today's the day, asshole.

I took in the dark oak of his large desk, the matching wood-paneled walls, the plush furniture, and the remaining antiques he hadn't sold off yet. This was the place where he'd spent so much of his time discussing selling me like I was his prized cow. All so he could keep his pretty things.

Sauntering over to the statue that was probably worth a hefty penny, I lovingly ran my fingers over the marble before sending it crashing to the wooden floor.

Whoops.

I lifted the Japanese vase my father could never resist showing off to his guests. I could remember him mentioning that he'd won it at an auction for over seventy-five big ones. So beautiful. Such a shame that it didn't go with the décor.

Clumsily, I let it slip from fingers.

There were a few first edition classics, each worth over ten grand, but I couldn't bring myself to destroy those, so I grabbed the crystal decanter of red wine and one of the glasses on the shelf underneath. Sadly, when I went to pour, I missed the cup entirely, spilling red wine all over the rug that set my father back forty grand.

By the time I was done, my father's office had looked like a tornado was let loose inside. There wasn't a single thing of value left to sell.

Satisfied, I sank into the desk chair and typed in his computer password. I bet he had no clue that I knew. Or maybe he did and figured I'd never put it to use—such arrogance.

The first thing I pulled up was his email. My stomach turned when I saw the many recent emails he'd sent bragging about me to his friends, golf buddies, and even some of his business associates—most of whom had sons and... some who didn't. *Gross*.

In all of them, he'd attached various photos of me while boasting of my docility and subservience. I was relieved to see that some of the men hadn't taken the bait and steered the conversation away to safer waters while others...

I took a deep breath, fighting the rising bile.

The men without sons had asked if I was pure. The ones with sons expressed interest in the hopes of forcing them to settle down. Countless had wanted to know if I was fertile.

And my father had answered them all with gusto.

Tears ran down my face when I came across the email from Mr. Portland:

I have it on good authority that your daughter is no longer spoken for. I'm hoping it's not too late to make an offer. This family has suffered enough shame thanks to my daughter. I will not allow my faggot son to embarrass me further.

I quickly closed out the email, unable to stand anymore.

Oh, Jason.

I waited for shock over the news that he was gay to come, but now that I had confirmation, I realized I'd always known. I used to think he'd been a sore loser whenever he'd storm away after losing a wrestling match with Ever or Vaughn, but one person hiding a crush definitely recognized another.

And just as he was going through a confusing time in life, his sister—his twin—had killed herself, and he believed one of his best friends to be responsible.

Two wrongs never made a right, but I understood now more than ever why he was being a giant asshole and hoped that it wasn't too late for forgiveness. We might not ever be able to trust each other again, but maybe we could all come to more than just a reluctant truce.

None of us are innocent.

A ping drew my attention back to the computer screen. In the right-hand corner was a notification for an incoming email to my father's business account. Without a second thought, I opened it and saw that the head of Human Resources at MontGlobal had sent it. Apparently, an analyst was suing the company for wrongful termination after reporting "questionable accounting practices" to both my father and the CFO.

I searched the analyst's name in my father's inbox and saw ten different message threads dating back six months. The analyst had been trying to understand the reasons behind all the unapproved bonuses, loans, and extravagant company spending. For example, why had MontGlobal footed the bill for my father's summer home in the Hamptons? The same one my father had recently sold.

There was also mention of angry investors requesting a detailed account of how exactly their money for all my father's "groundbreaking" ventures was spent. My father had blown off every one of the analyst's concerns and had even mentioned providing him a hefty bonus to reward him for his thorough attention to detail.

I couldn't claim to be well-versed in corporate lingo, but that sounded an awful lot like a bribe.

One that the fired analyst obviously hadn't taken.

Charles Dennis, MontGlobal's Chief Financial Officer, had been cc'd in every email, so I searched his name in the inbox. Surely, he noticed.

I frowned as I opened email after email.

Not one of their conversations mentioned the analyst's concerns.

I stared at the screen for a few seconds before my disbelief turned to suspicion. Switching back to my father's personal email account, I searched for Charles Dennis but found nothing in the inbox. Maybe he'd deleted them?

Checking the archived folder, my eyes bulged with disbelief. *Jackpot!*

The two men had been arguing back and forth for *weeks*. I couldn't read each thread fast enough.

For years, my father had been stealing money from his own company, namely investors, and he and Charles were in on it together. It seemed as if my father selling off everything had been his attempt to put the cookies back in the jar before anyone noticed. Charles, dear that he was, had been trying to get my father to understand why the idea was ludicrous. Especially when there was a trail of crumbs my father had left leading right to them. Apparently, my father got greedy and gone rogue, and now both men were fucked.

Doing a happy dance in my father's chair, I printed off the emails, including the ones my father had been sending to his friends in an attempt to sell my wares. I had no idea whose hands I needed to put this evidence in, but I figured it couldn't hurt to start with the SEC.

Just in case, I forwarded every one of the private emails

exchanged between my father and Charles to every member of MontGlobal's board, along with the investors who'd been swindled. I'm sure they'd know exactly what to do. After logging off, I rifled through his desk drawers, hoping to find more evidence. In the very last drawer, I found something better.

A loaded Smith & Wesson.

Grabbing the emails, the gun, and a couple of the first editions—I was a fool but not a damn fool—I headed upstairs.

There was no tinge of regret as I stepped inside my bedroom and looked around. The luxurious room with it's white, pink, and gold décor had been designed for someone of value, but for years, my parents had made me feel anything but precious to them.

If I had one wish, it would be never to see this room again.

Grabbing the designer tote I'd used for school, I dumped my findings inside and shoved aside my nightstand. Lifting the plank, I smiled when I saw my journal, the gold bangle with its cheeky inscription Jamie didn't think I'd notice, and the harmonica resting safely inside. There was nothing else here that I gave a damn about.

My finger had just wrapped around the items when a familiar voice sent an eerie chill down my spine.

"I knew you'd come home."

Scrambling to my feet, I found my father standing behind me.

Blocking the door.

His expensive cuff links gleamed in the light as he reached behind him to close my bedroom door. "I hope this means you're ready to do what must be done."

Fear stabbed my skin, wanting to creep inside my veins, but without a second thought, I shoved it aside. It took a long time for me to find my voice, but when I did, I was proud to hear how strong it had gotten.

"That will *never* happen."

"Oh, yes, it will. Do you really think I'll let you leave?"

Whatever his intentions, he was certainly doing a great job of upping the creep factor. To the world, my father was a stunningly handsome man, but to me, he'd always been the ugliest monster.

"Let me pass."

"Or what?" he challenged as he pressed in closer. "You're all alone. That tattooed punk isn't here to save you. What are you going to do? It's just you and me, Barbette."

My breaths came harder and faster with each step he took. My father was stronger than me and probably faster. What could I do if he grabbed me? I wouldn't be able to fight him off or out-run him.

"I've got a buyer lined up. He wasn't my first choice or even my third, but he's willing to pay. You're even friends with his son, so I suppose you should be thanking me." He actually smiled as if he'd done something kind.

"You suppose wrong. I'm not marrying Jason."

He paused, his eyes flashing with surprise. "Who said anything about Jason?"

It was my turn to be confused, though I didn't let it show. If not Jason, then who? Just as quickly, I decided it didn't matter. Perhaps my father was just surprised that I knew more than I should. "Well, then whoever," I snapped. "I don't care because I'm done taking orders."

"Ah, but think of your mother and the consequences if you don't do what I say."

"You can't hurt my mother if you're behind bars. Can't spend all that money, either."

It occurred to me that this was the longest conversation I'd had with my father in years. Probably since the day he told me that he'd be marrying me off.

"And what makes you think I'm going to prison?" There was no anger or worry in his tone as he continued to toy with me. Well, he wouldn't be having his fun with me much longer.

"Because I found the emails between you and your CFO. I

also took the liberty of sharing them with the board and the investors you robbed."

This time, when he paused, rage filled those blue eyes that I'd inherited. "I don't believe you."

I shrugged. "So what if you don't? I'm sure the SEC and the Feds will when I tell them about all the money you stole." I smirked, making his face turn reddish-purple.

"Oh, I assure you that won't happen. Even if I have to keep you bound and gagged until it's time to say 'I do.'" He charged toward me, and I knew that this was it, the last stand I'd ever have against my father.

I dove for my bag.

My hand was still blindly searching inside when I felt my father's harsh grip in my hair. Ripping the bag from my hand, he tossed me to the floor, and I scrambled away when he charged for me.

"The first thing I'll do," he spoke harshly as he removed his leather belt, "is give you a sound beating, and this time, I won't stop until you *bleed*."

After folding the belt in half, he raised it over his opposite shoulder, preparing to deliver a punishing blow. Before he could, I raised my arm, pointing the gun he hadn't noticed me holding.

"One more step and I'll shoot."

Slowly, he lowered his arm, but his gaze turned from shock at seeing me holding his gun to mocking. "You won't kill me."

I almost scoffed at the notion that my dad thought I still loved him enough to care if he lived or died. Or maybe he just thought I didn't have the guts? Maybe I didn't but killing him wasn't the only way I could finally be free.

"I never said I would." Removing the safety, I turned the gun on myself, pressing the muzzle against my right temple. The last thing I wanted to see was my father's face. I wanted to close my eyes and picture Jamie's smile one last time, to see the look in his eyes when he'd said he loved me for the first time. But what if I did, and I couldn't go through with it? The alternative was just too horrible to consider.

"You expect me to believe you'll shoot yourself?" His gaze narrowed, seeing the truth in my own. "Why?"

Lifting my chin, I curled my finger around the trigger. He needed to know that I was completely fucking serious. "Because if I can't have me, no one will."

The silence that fell over the room as my father and I continued to face off was so heavy that I could swear I heard his heart skip a beat. I'd left him with no choice. We both knew it. If I died, he'd get nothing. If he let me walk, there was always the chance he could come after me later.

Wanting to get as far away from him as possible, I stood before cautiously collecting my bag. My grip on the gun remained firm. Our identical blue gazes never once parted.

"This isn't over," he spat. "I'll be seeing you real soon, Barbette. Make no mistake about that."

I almost choked on the sheer hate I glimpsed in his eyes. *It doesn't matter now, Barbette. You're free.*

"Well, Father, if you happen to escape the hard time you're looking at, I'll be waiting."

I could barely see where I was going as tears clouded my vision and soaked my cheeks. I pedaled my old red Huffy as fast as it would go as I raced down the drive for the open gates. For freedom.

My father had let me go.

It didn't matter that it was because his back had been against the wall. I stopped pining for his affection long ago. I'd been searching for love in all the wrong places when I had it all along. And Jamie had given it to me freely.

I reached the end of the drive, prepared to fly through

the open gates when several vehicles turned in, blocking the entrance.

Panic speared my chest, thinking it had all been a lie. I hadn't won. My father only made me think I had to play some sick game.

I heard car doors opening and footsteps running my way as I quickly dashed at my tears. I rushed to climb from my bike so that I could fight, but strong hands were already circling my waist and lifting me.

I pounded my fists against the hard chest, locking me in like a wall, and struggled against the harsh grip holding me hostage.

"Jesus, kitten. Calm the fuck down!" a familiar voice barked.

Blinking, I finally cleared my vision enough to notice the green tie I'd picked out this morning. Now that I wasn't panicking, I even recognized the smell of the aftershave soothing my senses.

It was Jamie standing in front of me.

"Jamie?" I gasped as I looked around. It was his car, along with Ever's and Wren's car and Four's bike blocking the entrance. I could see the apology and worry in her eyes as she watched us. Had she called them? I looked to Jamie for answers. "What are you doing here?"

"Funny," he bit out, "I was about to ask you the same." He looked furious, afraid, and relieved all at once. I could understand why. The very thing that he'd been afraid of had almost happened. The outcome, however, was worth the risk. *Jamie* was worth the risk.

"I was going to run away," I admitted and felt his grip tighten on me. "I thought it was the only way I could be free of my father, but…" I swallowed the words, unsure if I should go on.

"But?" he prodded almost desperately.

"But you gave me something to fight for. That's why I came back here. To fight for you." Although I knew this wasn't what he'd meant when he said as much on graduation day, his emotional outburst had never once stopped ringing in my head.

His throat bobbed as he pressed his forehead against mine. "You didn't have to do it alone. God, Bee. I thought I'd lost you forever."

"Yes, I did. It was me who let him turn me into a coward. I had to face him alone." I dug my fingers into his chest, wanting to get as close as possible. "And you don't ever have to worry about losing me again. I'd never let you. I love you." I felt a fresh bout of tears, remembering his sorrow from this morning. "I always did. I didn't want to tell you until I was sure my father couldn't come between us anymore. I couldn't break your heart again, Jamie. Please believe me."

Jamie took a deep, shuddering breath before standing up straight and looking toward the house. "Where is he?"

"Inside."

Meeting my gaze, the muscle in his jaw began ticking as he looked me over. "Did he hurt you?"

Out of the corner of my eye, I felt Ever and Wren press in closer, eager to hear the answer as well. I knew what it would mean for my father if he had. Lucky for him, he never got the chance.

I quickly shook my head. When his gaze narrowed, I knew he was looking for a sign that I was lying. "He's not going to be a problem anymore."

The steel in my tone made his mouth purse with reluctant amusement. "What did you do?"

"I beat him at his own game," I boasted as I fiddled with the tie I'd helped him put on this morning. It felt like such a lifetime ago. "I also found evidence that he's been stealing from his investors and ratted him out."

"I'm sure it's a lovely story," Wren snapped. "Can we go now?" He was looking around as if expecting men with guns to jump out at any moment. Given his background, I suppose it was a very rational fear.

Jamie nodded at him. He then stared in my eyes for a few seconds as if trying to convince himself that I was real before kissing me deeply. When he pulled away, he pointed to his Jeep, his voice was sharp when he spoke. "Get in."

CHAPTER
TWENTY-EIGHT

The Punk

I T WAS AMAZING THE THINGS BARBETTE COULD DO TO MY HEART.

Like how she could make it come to a complete fucking stop without ever lifting a finger.

It had been five days since her little standoff with her father, and I was still pouring and obsessing over the printed emails she'd given me. Even after seeing the proof with my own eyes, it was still impossible for me to believe that Elliot could be so vulgar and dismissive of his daughter. Her well-being had been the least of his concerns, and to think I'd left her alone with that monster for five fucking years.

I wasn't sure what kept me from going over there and wringing his neck, but I figured if Barbette wanted him dead, she would have used that pistol I'd glimpsed in her purse. The only explanation she'd given was that it was his, and I hadn't bothered questioning her more. I was still tempted to wring *her* neck, too.

She'd told me she loved me.

The most coveted words I'd ever wanted to hear spill from her lips, and I... I choked. I didn't expect that. I'd been holding my breath, waiting for her to say it back, and when she did, I fucking choked. I knew Barbette meant it, but I also knew she loved me then, too. Yet she still broke my heart. I guess the why doesn't matter when all you can remember is the fucking pain. She said she'd waited to tell me until she was sure she wouldn't break it again, but I was scared as hell to believe her.

A shadow suddenly darkened the wrinkled pages I'd read so many times. Looking up, I found Uncle Thomas standing over me. The circles darkening his puffy eyes were even more pronounced than the day before. Covering up so many lies must be hard work.

"You can go home," he announced before pushing away from my cubicle to leave.

I stood from my chair and called his name.

He faced me with a complete lack of interest. "Yes?"

"When you told me I'd be the one running the company because your blood runs through my veins, you also told me I'd have to start making decisions that were best for more than just myself. Do you remember that?"

He sighed. "Of course."

"Well, I think I'm ready to start now." I smiled at the wary look he was giving me now. "For my first decision as head of the family, I've decided not to take the job."

"Excuse me?"

"Actually, that's not true. I will take the job, but only if your son knows exactly why he was passed up."

"That's none of your business, Jameson."

"It is when you force me to look my best friend in the eye every day and lie to him. I won't do it a second longer. Tell him the truth, or I walk."

"Everson doesn't even want the job. He wants to be an architect."

"Of course, he doesn't want the job." I fumed. "Who'd want to sit at a table where they're not welcome?"

"So…" My uncle frowned, suddenly looking very disturbed. "He knows?"

"You've been showing me off as the future face of the company for months. He'd have to be an idiot not to. Besides, I think he's known for a long time."

"Does he know—" He seemed unable to speak the words.

"That his sperm donor is alive?" I finished for him. "I doubt it, but you should tell him. Sean isn't behaving like a man content to stay in the shadows."

My uncle was a foolish man, but he wasn't an idiot. He knew he couldn't keep Sean at bay for much longer. After eighteen years, he suddenly wanted to play daddy, and nothing on earth was going to stop it.

Unless we somehow found something that Sean wanted more.

"It was my fault his mother left," my uncle announced, which sent me reeling, even though it wasn't much of a surprise. "Ever thinks it was because of him, but it was me all along. She wanted to tell Ever the truth about his father. I didn't. I raised Ever. I was there for his first words and his first steps. I was the one who taught him to catch." In an explosion of anger, he slammed his fist on top of the cubicle wall. "He's my goddamn son!" I silently watched my uncle's chest heave as he tried to regain control of his emotions. Taking a deep breath, he shook his head. His voice, though still laced with anger, was much calmer when he spoke. "We argued about it for months, and when she found out that Sean was still alive, she sought him out. I'm still not sure if it was because she thought he'd be a better father or because she still loved him."

I decided not to point out the obvious fact that they all seemed to be making decisions that were best for themselves and not for Ever.

"What about you?" I asked, instead. "Do you still love him?"

By now, I'd lost count of how many times I'd managed to shock my uncle in a single conversation.

"What are you talking about?"

"I'm talking about this weird little sex triangle you're in." I waited for him to admit it, but he simply stood there... blinking at me. I sighed. "I'm going to take an educated guess and say that you and Sean found each other early in life. You were best friends until one of you realized you wanted more. Since I already know Sean is Crow, I'm also going to guess that you hit a fork in the road. Only his path was much darker than yours. Years pass before you see each other again. By now, you've met a nice, wholesome girl. You think you're in love. And because fate is cruel, here comes your old flame. With your heart in one hand, he steals hers with the other. Knocks her up too before he disappears again, leaving *you* to pick up the pieces."

My uncle looked like a fish out of water, probably wondering how I possibly pieced everything together. Sticking my nose where it didn't belong was a favorite pastime of mine. The sound of clapping had me spinning around. Sean was making his way toward us, looking like a thief in the night dressed in all black. The feeling that he was fucking bad news just wouldn't dissipate. I couldn't say if he was an evil man or simply mischievous. Good morals and bad intentions aren't always mutually exclusive. I should know.

"I'm impressed, Jameson."

"And what a waste of your time since I don't give a fuck." I started past him toward the bank of elevators when I stopped and spun around. They were both watching me. "Either you two tell Ever everything and let him hate you for a little while, or I tell him, and he hates you forever."

I didn't stop this time when I turned to leave. The moment I stepped onto the busy New York street, I reached inside my vest and removed the carton that had been burning a hole in my pocket all day.

When was my last smoke?

I couldn't recall. I just knew I couldn't go another minute without one.

I could always quit again tomorrow.

When I flipped open the top, my brows dipped at the slip of paper I found inside. Every single of my little sticks of heaven were gone. Plucking the paper from the pack, I unfolded it and found a note. Or rather…

My heart skipped a beat.

All I ever wanted was to pick wildflowers with you
To swim in the ocean, to run in the sun
To write fumbling poetry while you strung your clumsy notes
Being bad was the only thing we were good at
All I ever wanted…

I frowned even harder.

What? What was it that she wanted?

I practically snatched my car keys from the valet before racing home to find out. My heart pounded as my mind raced. There was nothing I wasn't willing to do for her, but what if what she wanted most was for me to let her go?

Damn you, Bee.

"Jameson, a word?"

I sighed, staring at the stairs longingly. Bee was up there, and I knew she was waiting for me. However, I also knew my mother wasn't about to let me blow her off. For the last two weeks, I'd been either missing in action or blowing off my family. My mom would be heading back to Ireland soon, and we'd hardly spent any time together after not seeing each other for a year.

"What's up?"

"I'd like to know what you and Barbette think you're doing? She's been staying here for almost a week."

I frowned, not expecting that. "Is that a problem? I didn't know you had an issue with her."

"Did I say that?" my mother snapped as she propped her hands on her hips. "I love Barbette—you know that—and she's more than welcome here, but that doesn't mean you're allowed to move her in without an explanation."

I scrubbed a hand down my face. My mother was right, but I didn't know how much I should reveal to her. "Barbette isn't… safe… at home. Her father was abusing her," I said, telling only part of the truth. "I saw him slap her with my own eyes at graduation. That's why we missed the ceremony."

I realized only part of the truth worked fine when I watched my mother's hand cover her trembling lips. Or maybe the reality Barbette had been forced to live in was so horrid it could only be handled in small doses. It was a testament to how strong Bee was even if she couldn't see it yet.

"Is she okay?"

I nodded, even though I wasn't entirely sure. Barbette had risked everything so that we could be together when it would have been easier just to run. And how did I thank her? By ignoring her for three days.

God, I'm such an asshole.

"What is she going to do?"

I shrugged, feeling like a deer caught in the headlights. I hadn't bothered to talk to her about that, either. Barbette was once again in control of her life, and I'd been too angry to ask her what she planned to do with it.

My mother gave me a reproachful look. "It sounds to me like the two of you need to spend a little less time in each other's pants and a little more time talking. I hope you're using condoms."

After I assured her that I was, she ordered me upstairs but not before demanding to be kept up to date. My mother just loved reminding me that while I may be legally an adult, I was still her child.

The first thing I noticed when I stepped inside my bedroom was the clean floor. My clothes no longer covered the plush carpet, and I looked around, wondering where they could have gone. My desk had also been cleaned off and organized, the ashes in the tray on my nightstand dumped, and my bed made. I could already tell by the crisp lines in the sheet that they had been cleaned. I frowned, wondering if my mom had cleaned up. Mrs. Greene stopped bothering a long time ago. I checked the bathroom for Bee, but when I didn't find her, I headed back downstairs.

Where could she be?

I checked every room downstairs before heading out back. My heart was beating a mile a minute, wondering if she'd left me. Could I blame her if she had? Could she blame me when I tracked her down and dragged her back?

The sigh of relief I breathed was loud when I finally spotted her standing by the line of trees I'd chased her through the day we met. Her hands were covering her eyes, and she was shouting something.

As if on autopilot, I drifted toward her. I was halfway across the yard when I realized she was shouting numbers, counting down. Curious, I held my breath when she got to one.

"Ready or not, here I come!"

She moved into the trees, and I frowned as I followed, keeping my steps silent and Barbette oblivious.

"Come out, come out, wherever you are!"

Giggling had our heads swiveling in the direction of the noise. I could see the sneaky grin on Bee's face as she tiptoed toward the hollow tree the sound had come from. She was two steps away when two small figures darted out, squealing as they ran farther into the trees to escape capture.

"Oh, come on, guys!" Barbette shouted after my brother and sister. "No fair!" She started to chase after them when she suddenly spun around. Her lips parted when she spotted me standing there. "Jamie," she gasped. "You scared me."

"You scared me, too," I admitted as I closed the distance between us. Of course, it wasn't what she meant, but I didn't care. I needed her to understand why I'd been an asshole to her after she risked her life for me. It didn't excuse my behavior, but at least she'd know the truth. "I read somewhere once that fear is temporary. It's regret that lasts forever." Before she knew what was happening, her back was against the tree. "I don't want to let you go because I was too chickenshit to love you."

Her small hands fluttered against my chest as her blue eyes filled with hope. "Then don't let me go, James."

The tips of our noses nuzzled as I brushed her lips with mine. "I'm sorry I've been such a dick. Do you still love me?"

"You've been a dick since the day we met, and I still fell for you." She frowned before giving me that same look my mother gave me. Yeah, I was an idiot.

Kissing her because I didn't know what else to do, I wrapped my arms around her. "Please don't stop."

"Never."

I didn't even try to hide my relief, which made her giggle. "I have to leave for school in a couple of months."

"Philly isn't that far away," she assured me, even though she looked sad to see me go. "Promise to visit every weekend?"

"Now that's an idea… or you could just come with me."

"Go… Go with you?" She was so shocked I could tell the thought had never occurred to her. "Jamie, I can't do that."

"Why? What's keeping you here?" I challenged.

"Nothing, but you don't actually expect me to live with you in your dorm, do you? Is that even allowed?"

"I've got an apartment. You can decorate." She punched me in the chest, making me laugh, and then I kissed her senseless.

"Don't you think it's too soon?"

"We lost five years, Bette. I'm not losing another day." My hand started creeping up the red tank she wore. I was pleased to find she'd skipped a bra today. Her nipples had been beckoning me from the moment she caught me stalking her. "Besides, there's no one who knows you better." I swept my thumb back and forth over her hard right bud as I waited for her answer.

"I know what you're doing."

I bit my bottom lip to keep from smiling. "Is it working?"

"Yes," she whined. "You're not playing fair."

Deciding on mercy, I let my hand slide to her waist. I wanted her as clearheaded as possible when she made this forever decision because that's what Bee and I were. Forever.

"I want to fight with you over leaving the toilet seat up and forgetting to take out the trash. I want to see your smile when I tell you the new curtains are nice even if they're ugly as fuck. I want to hold you when you fall asleep every night and kiss you awake in the morning. I won't be able to concentrate when I'm away, knowing you're home waiting for me, but I wouldn't have it any other way." My grip tightened on her before I said, "I also want to know that in the next place you call home, you're safe. I can't promise that we'll always get it right, but I want nothing less than my world revolving around you." I took her hands in mine and kissed each palm. "Tell me what you want." I stood there pretending my heart didn't drop to my stomach when she pulled her hands from mine.

She dug her hand inside my vest before pulling out my lighter. The moment I saw writing on the side, I plucked it from her fingers.

…was to be bad with you.

The confused frown I wore disappeared when I remembered the poem.

All I ever wanted…

All I ever wanted was to be bad with you.

The kiss I pressed to her lips was hard enough to make her cry out. "You've fucking got it, kitten." I softened the kiss before pulling away and getting lost in her blue eyes. "You know what today is, don't you?"

"No," she answered as she tried to catch her breath. "What?"

"It's the day we met. First time I saw your boobs, too." Slowly, I started pushing up the hem of her tank top. "It was in these very woods where you flashed me, so in celebration of our sixth anniversary, I'm down if you want to repeat history."

"It didn't happen then, and it's not going to happen now." She stood on her tiptoes, and her top fell back into place as she kissed me. "But if you take me inside, I'll give you all the second-base action you can handle."

I started to deepen the kiss when I heard the snap of a twig. Turning my head, I spotted Adan and Adara's nosy asses peeking at us from behind a tree fifteen feet away.

"You call that hiding?" I yelled at them.

They glanced at each other before turning back and singing, "Jamie and Bee, sitting in a tree, K-I-S-S-I-N-G!"

Chuckling, I stepped back as I met Bee's amused gaze. "You go left, and I go right?"

Her evil grin was her only response before we took off after the squealing twins.

EPILOGUE

The Plaything

Six Months Later

"Elliot Montgomery, the former Chief Executive Officer of MontGlobal, and Chief Financial Officer, Charles Dennis, have been indicted on charges of fraud and the embezzlement of over two hundred million dollars…"

I stared at the haggard appearance of my father as he was led from a building in handcuffs. It was an old clip but one I never got tired of seeing. The first time I saw it, I reached out to my mother immediately after, but she'd made it clear that she wanted nothing to do with me. I could remember her parting words just before she hung up on me.

"You ruined us, Barbette. I have no daughter."

Shutting off the TV, I got busy putting up, or rather hiding, my camera and makeup. Jamie would be home soon, and I wasn't quite ready for him to know what I'd been up to the last couple of months. There was a chance it could go nowhere, and I just… I wasn't sure if I could handle that. Or what I would do if it did. I got the idea from Tyra when I did hers and Four's Halloween makeup. Jamie had insisted on driving the six hours to check on Tyra after a few weeks of her not answering our calls.

Our summer had certainly been one for the drama books, starting with my father getting arrested, which was actually a cause for celebration, and ending with Vaughn cheating on Tyra.

Needless to say, they'd broken up. Or whatever it's called when your relationship goes from 'it's complicated' to 'no longer exists.'

Tyra had gotten into Harvard, *freaking Harvard*, and was now living in Cambridge, which was only ten minutes from Jamie's old stomping grounds. Ever was halfway to Canada and was the furthest away from home. He tried to take Four with him like Jamie had done me, but she wasn't ready to be so far away from her mom, who was now in psychiatric care. Vaughn, who'd had several offers from colleges to play football, had rejected them all to work for his father instead. Worry roiled in my gut. Even though no one knows what his father does, everyone back home keeps a wide berth of Franklin Rees. Whatever it was, it wasn't legal.

Tyra was determined to push us away, but for every shove, we pulled twice as hard. She wasn't getting away from us that easy.

Vaughn... he hasn't been so easy to convince.

No one had laid eyes on him in months. Our only option was to storm that castle he was forced to call home, but it was pretty hard to go against the armed men with guns who'd mysteriously appeared, making sure no one came in or out.

I'd just finished putting everything back in its hiding spot when I heard the front door open. Jamie and I lived in a three-bedroom townhome not far from Penn's campus. So far, every one of Jamie's wishes had come true. I was constantly getting an ass full of toilet water and hauling the trash to the road when he forgot, which was often. He was also constantly drinking straight from the milk and juice cartons and leaving toothpaste smudges all over our bathroom sink. And he never ever *ever* took the time to put a new roll of toilet paper on the damn handle.

He made it all worth it every night and each morning, though. During the day, Jamie would find the time—even if just a few minutes—to assure himself that I wanted for nothing. In the early days, while he was busy with orientation and preparing for his first week of school, I kept busy making our apartment comfortable for us. After countless runs and too much money spent at Target, I was pretty proud of what I'd done with the place. There was one thing Jamie got wrong, though. I hadn't bothered to ask his opinion on any of the decoration choices I'd made, but he never once complained. In fact, the only reaction he'd given was to our dining room table. We'd christened it thoroughly less than an hour after it was delivered.

I rushed downstairs in time to see Jamie closing the door. Snowflakes sprinkled his gray hooded parka, but he seemed oblivious to all the snow he was tracking on my freshly swept floor as he stared at his phone. Sensing me, he looked up, and I wondered at his curious gaze.

"Hey, baby," I greeted nervously since he was still eyeing me. "How did it go?"

He took his time kissing me while I pushed his coat from his muscular shoulders before answering. "Statistics was kicking my ass for a little bit, but I'm Jamie fucking Buchanan. Of course, I aced it."

"Uh-huh… and it wouldn't have anything to do with me agreeing to make a home video with you if you aced all of your final exams?"

"Does it matter?" he retorted, grinning. "A deal's a deal."

I grabbed his hand when he reached for the hem of my oversized Christmas sweater. It was the only thing I wore besides the white thick slouchy socks. "Hold your horses, mister. You don't have those scores back yet."

With a cocky smile, he ignored me as he gripped my ass and yanked me into him. "Where are your panties?" he asked the moment he felt my bare skin.

"I don't know," I flirted, playing coy. "I guess I lost them."

"Where?" he growled.

I peeked up at him. "Under your pillow."

Rather than go for them as I'd expected, he pulled me into

the living room. After sitting down on our large black sectional, he sat me on his lap.

"Care to explain this?" Showing me his phone screen, the back of my neck grew hot when I saw the video I'd posted on YouTube a couple of weeks ago. The caption read "Holiday Glam," and it had over ten thousand views. That was nothing compared to the more established beauty gurus, but it was more than I could hope for. Even though my mother had forced me to master the art, I chose not to run from my demons and embraced them instead. If I could somehow turn my negative experience into a positive experience for girls and women everywhere, then that was something, right?

"It's... it's a makeup tutorial."

"I see that," he said as he caressed my back. I wondered if he could sense my nervousness. "What I don't understand is why you didn't you tell me you were doing this?"

I shrugged, keeping my gaze pinned to the floor.

Gripping my chin, he turned my head until our eyes met. "Talk to me, Bette. There's no one here but me and you."

"I... I just wanted to make sure I could do this before I told anyone."

He frowned, clearly not liking my answer. "Since when am I just anyone?"

"You're not, but you're also the only person I'm afraid of disappointing."

"You could never disappoint me."

"Jamie, I—" Tears suddenly pricked my eyes, but as soon as they fell, Jamie wiped them away. "I don't know what I'm going to do. I see you leave every day for school and apprentice for your uncle. You have such a bright future while I... I never had the chance to dream. What if it's too late?"

He pulled me down until our foreheads touched. "It's never too late. Don't you see where we are? This is the endgame, Bette. Even if it takes forever, I'll make damn sure all your dreams come true."

"Good, because I really want to do this," I admitted.

"Then *we* will."

I sat up in surprise. "We?"

"You've stayed up with me every night for two weeks, helping me study for exams. I want to be there for you like you are there for me."

"How?"

He grinned. "Well...to start, I've got some ideas for your channel."

I stared down at him warily. "Like what?"

"You'll see."

He flashed me a devious grin, and my stomach flipped not only because he was gorgeous as hell but because I had a very valid reason for being nervous. Wisely, I had the urge to say no. Jamie was mischievous when he was good and downright wicked when he was bad, which was often.

But...

How could I resist this boy who brazenly wore his heart on his sleeve so that everyone could see it beat only for me?

He pressed his lips against mine, stealing away the last of my doubt. "I've got some ideas for us, too," he said after he finished kissing me senseless.

"Oh?"

"You're a Montgomery, but Barbette Elizabeth Buchanan has a better ring to it, don't you think?"

My heart skipped a beat.

Was Jamie proposing? Was I ready for that? I'd spent the last five years thinking that being someone's wife was all I could hope for, and now I knew better. I knew in my heart that I'd marry no one else but Jameson Buchanan, but for now, I wanted to spend some time rediscovering myself. There was no one standing over me anymore telling me who to be, and Jamie... he was ready to love me no matter what.

"All you have to do," he added, sensing my hesitation and,

as always, knowing exactly what I needed, "is say yes when I ask someday. Deal?"

He held up his pinky with a challenge in his eyes. I never could back down from one, and Jameson damn well knew it.

Holding his daring gaze, I hooked my pinky with his.

"Deal." Just as he leaned in to kiss me, I shot from his lap, causing his eyebrow to perk as he glared. "Sorry, but we have to start packing if we're going to make our flight in the morning." Jamie and I were heading to Ireland to spend Christmas with his mom and twin siblings. He also said he wanted me to meet his grandparents before they finally kicked the bucket. His words, not mine.

"Fine." Huffing, he unfolded his long body from the couch. "But you're going to make it up to me later."

"How about I make it up to you right now?" With a lascivious smile, he eagerly reached for my sweater, but I quickly dodged his hands. "You know that's not what I meant," I said before turning away. Silently, he stalked me as I rushed for the small laundry room. I quickly removed what I needed from its hiding place and spun to face Jamie who was practically breathing down my neck. He had a hard time concealing his surprise when I held out a small, narrow box wrapped with shiny, red paper and tied with a black bow.

"What is it?" he asked, and I giggled at the wary look in his eyes.

"An early Christmas present."

He flashed me a crooked smile as he accepted the box. "But I thought you'd put that under my pillow already." Biting my lip, I didn't say anything as he pulled the bow free and tore into the wrapping. When he lifted the top, I watched his Adam's apple bob as he stared at what lay inside.

"You came back for me just like you promised," I whispered, feeling unsure since he hadn't spoken.

With nimble fingers, he plucked his father's harmonica from

the box and closed his tatted fist around it. "And you kept this safe just like you promised," he mumbled.

Through all the years, the distance, the hurt, and the hate, we'd kept our promises to each other even when we didn't want to. If I didn't already know that Jamie and I belonged together, there'd be no denying it now. I didn't get the chance to tell him so before he dropped the box and rushed me.

Lifting me onto the washing machine, he stole my lips in a kiss that was both brutal and beautiful. "I can't wait to make more music with you, Bette. I missed your terrible poetry."

Stroking my fingers across his cheek, I lost myself in his brown eyes. "And I love your clumsy notes."

ACKNOWLEDGEMENTS

I think with each book I get even more irrational than the last. Tijuana Turner and Sunny Borek can attest to that so I'd like to thank them first. Deal with it, Mom. If my eyes didn't hurt from staring at my computer screen by this point, I'd count the minutes I spent bombarding you with my rants over voice record. It's a good thing my voice is super lovely, huh? Thank you for listening and keeping me off the cliff. This book wouldn't have been possible without you. Seriously, I'd have run away to some beach and assumed a new identity.

I'd also like to thank my editors, graphic designer, and formatter. So sorry, Stacey, for being an epic fail. I'd promise it won't happen again but that would make me a liar too. Rogena and Colleen, despite the tough time you've both had over these last weeks, as always you were very much reliable and expert in your work. I don't take that lightly. Amanda, I knew you were amazing, but to go through what you have these past months and still find time to be a rock star has left me in awe of you. The cover and marketing are fantastic and so are you. I enjoy our sarcastic talks so don't even think about retiring.

A huge thank you to my beta readers: Sarah, Ratula, Raj, Heather, Janese, Serena, and Tijuana. Thank you for reading this book at its worst and helping me make it the absolute best. It takes courage to be honest, and I'm grateful you didn't shy away.

Reiderville, I couldn't get enough of your excitement while I wrote this book. You kept me laughing, crying, smiling, and encouraged. The most amazing women can be found in this group so if you haven't joined us yet, please do.

Last but not least, my family and friends. You're stuck with me, but I'll thank you anyway. How could I not? The core of my support system starts with you. I constantly ignore your texts and phone calls but you *still* put up with me. That's love.

I'm sure I forgot someone. It's not that I don't love or appreciate you because I do. The reason is actually quite simple. I waited until the last minute to write this.

CONTACT THE AUTHOR

Follow me on Facebook
www.facebook.com/authorbbreid

Join Reiderville on Facebook
www.facebook.com/groups/reiderville

Follow me on Twitter
www.twitter.com/_BBREID

Follow me on Instagram
www.instagram.com/_bbreid

Subscribe to my newsletter
www.bbreid.com/news

Visit my website
www.bbreid.com

Text REIDER to 474747 for new release alerts
(US only)

ABOUT B.B. REID

B.B. Reid is the author of several novels including the hit enemies-to-lovers Fear Me. She grew up the only daughter and middle child in a small town in North Carolina. After graduating with a Bachelors in Finance, she started her career at an investment research firm while continuing to serve in the National Guard. She currently resides in Charlotte with her moody cat and enjoys collecting Chuck Taylors and binge-eating chocolate.

Printed in Great Britain
by Amazon